OBELISK

The Long Dream

Violet Stars Part 1
A Novel By Solus

To the Friends, Family, Editors, Artists, Readers, and Everyone Else
who made this Dream a reality

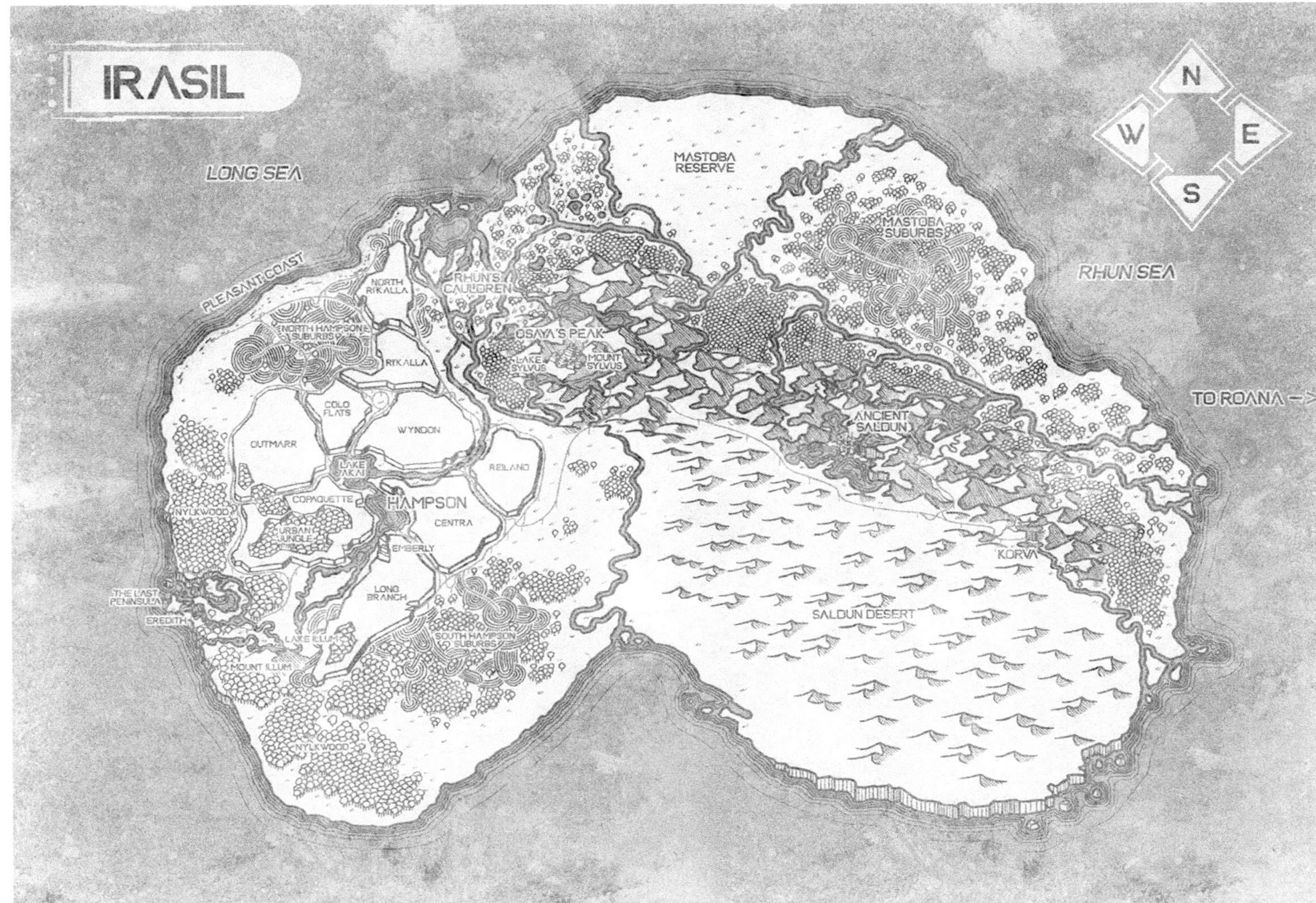

IRASIL
N
W
E
S
LONG SEA
RHUN SEA
TO ROANA ->
PLEASANT COAST
MASTOBA RESERVE
MASTOBA SUBURBS
RHUN'S CAULDREN
OSAYA'S PEAK
LAKE SYLVUS
MOUNT SYLVUS
ANCIENT SALDUN
SALDUN DESERT
KORVA
NORTH RIKALLA
NORTH HAMPSON SUBURBS
RIKALLA
COLO FLATS
WYNDON
OUTMARR
LAKE AKAI
COPAQUETTE
HAMPSON
CENTRA
REILAND
NYLKWOOD
URBAN JUNGLE
EMBERLY
LONG BRANCH
SOUTH HAMPSON SUBURBS
THE LAST PENINSULA
EREDITH
LAKE ILLUM
MOUNT ILLUM
NYLKWOOD

Prologue: The First Dream

"The balance of forces is never so readily apparent than in the art of shaping momentum," the voice of Elder Scribe Koromaho was cracked with age but otherwise vivid in Evolice Lovel's quieted mind. *"What force is introduced into our world must be returned to boundless peridom. Inversely, what force is extracted must then be replaced."*

Evolice sat at a hardy wooden writing desk. Her left-hand rest upon an open tome as her fingers traced the spiraling circles drawn upon its aged pages. Through shut eyes, Evolice could feel the pull of Koromaho's soul guiding her fingers in arcs around the page.

"In example, one may observe the fruit of the Kaobao tree. When the soft fruit falls, it becomes unmade by the ground below. However, a nimble kytra may borrow the force of descent, holding the fruit against gravity's will."

As Koromaho spoke in her mind, Evolice held her right hand inches above an ink-tipped quill. The feather danced freely upon a fresh sheet of synthpaper, recording every word Koromaho spoke.

"The kytra will pluck the fruit from midair, then return the force borrowed in the form of a gentle breeze. Thus, have many kytra enjoyed a sweet spring snack and taken the first step into shaping their world."

Evolice's finger found the edge of the page, Koromaho's voice faded, and the quill fell lifeless to her desk. Evolice opened her eyes. Her office was dimly lit by a smokeless fireplace in the corner. The room was L-shaped, with a curved inside wall and several patterned rugs clothing the wooden floor. Her sizable darkwood desk and matching bookshelves took up most of one side, while the far end had a short round table and an assortment of art supplies for days when her son, Faeron, was out of school.

Evolice sat in a well-carved armchair, padded with a sky blue suede that matched the vibrant color of her eyes. She had thin brows and curly cocoa-brown locks that fell to the collar of her button-up blouse. Evolice turned the page and set the translated sheet aside. As she reached down to pull a clean piece of synthpaper from her desk drawer, a fist-sized ball of turquoise light popped into existence, bobbing in the air just beyond her desk.

"Good afternoon Evolice," said Serris, the citywide Index.

"Serris," said Evolice cheerfully. "What can I do for you?"

"You have a call from Eamon," Serris replied. "He's been on the line for some time, but you seemed engrossed in your work; I didn't want to be a bother."

"Thank you for your consideration," said Evolice warmly. "I'll take him here."

"Right away."

The ball of light expanded and began to take on a human-shape. In seconds, Evolice was staring at a perfect image of her husband sitting comfortably in an armchair opposite her. Eamon was in well enough shape at thirty. His dark hair was trimmed short and parted by the comb he kept in the back pocket of his khaki dress pants. He had a thin but welcoming smile and an arched nose between fierce golden eyes.

"Hey, there you are!" said Eamon, sounding somewhat out of breath.

"What crisis are you averting now?" asked Evolice, knowing full well that today, of all days, would have Eamon in a non-stop bustle around the city.

"The anniversary committee called an hour ago," said Eamon, clearly relieved at the chance to vent. "Apparently someone in planning screwed up and never looked at the tent sizes. Now we've got eighty-two large tents and only room for twenty-four."

"Are they sending cancellations?" asked Evolice. "The peddlers would riot."

"That they would," said Eamon, "which is why we're opening Homewood and Obervael to large tents and moving all the small ones into the rings."

"I'd imagine that's a logistical nightmare, but the people will love it."

"That part… maybe so, but I can't imagine they're going to be too happy about the blizzard."

"The blizzard?" questioned Evolice. Sure enough, as she peeked through the blinds of the window behind her desk, she could see a fierce flurry battering the glass. Though the illusionary snow didn't stick to surfaces, it was coming down so hard that she couldn't see the building across the street. Festival goers would be all but blind in these conditions.

"Apparently the weather system has beef with one of the event organizers," sighed Eamon.

"How does that even happen?" snorted Evolice, closing the circuscript tome on her desk and sitting back in her padded armchair.

"Word has it he was *micromanaging her snowfall*," sighed Eamon. "You know how AI get around this age."

"Well then, I suppose you're on your way to talk her down?" asked Evolice.

"Indeed," said Eamon. "Trams are backed up with everyone fleeing the storm, so I thought I'd just walk it. Rare chance to catch my breath."

"And how's Faeron holding up?" asked Evolice, realizing she hadn't heard a peep from her nine-year-old son the entire call. "He's being unusually quiet."

"That's because he isn't here," said Eamon cheekily. "Left him napping in my office."

"Eamon!"

"I know, I know," said Eamon, "but he's been a trooper all morning. He crashed after lunch and I didn't have it in me to wake him."

"You know that room isn't safe for a young Kytra," said Evolice sharply. Even for Eamon, this was downright irresponsible.

"That boy isn't waking up any time soon. You should have seen him," assured Eamon. "Besides, anything he could get into is locked up tight, and Vox is on his way there as we speak."

"Vox is home? Foul play!" complained Evolice. "You can't just drop news like that while I'm angry with you! He wasn't supposed to make it back until halfway through the week."

"It's the reason I called in the first place," said Eamon, adjusting the collar of his black sweater. "I just got done talking to him. Said he couldn't bring himself to miss the Opening Ceremony, not on the city's tenth anniversary. Went on and on about how much it all meant to him. It was adorable." Eamon paused, looking introspective for a moment. "He has a point though... ten years since this all started. Sounds crazy saying that, doesn't it? Most of us haven't felt the sun, the *real* sun, in ten years. We haven't watched as the leaves change colors in Cropsun. Ten Years, Evolice..."

"Save the speeches for tonight, Mr. Host," said Evolice, smiling at his sweetness.

"Right," laughed Eamon. "Well, I better get up to the—"

Craaack

Evolice nearly screamed as a deafening noise split through her mind. It robbed her of all senses, and, for a moment, everything was dark. Her office was gone; her body was gone. She was formless in the darkness. There was suddenly a light behind her, and Evolice turned to see an obelisk. It was a towering monument made entirely of light, its smooth walls a shifting current of colors. Everything about the obelisk was beauty beyond words, except the great chasm down its center. The vein-like crevice was deep crimson and flared with tongues of blood-red light. Even in her formless state, Evolice could feel its unnatural power.

"Evolice... I ache."

The voice called out from the Obelisk. It sounded neither masculine nor feminine. It wasn't high nor low. Everything about the voice was perfectly average. Despite its clarity, Evolice was helpless to answer the voice. Just as quickly as it came, the vision cut out, and Evolice found herself back in the padded armchair of her study.

Evolice's head throbbed, and, as her senses returned to her, she could see she wasn't the only one affected. Eamon was gripping his forehead with one hand, his knuckles white from the pressure.

"Eamon, are you okay?" gasped Evolice, massaging her temple with one hand.

"I'm… yeah. I'll live," groaned Eamon. "What in the world was that?"

"I'm not sure," said Evolice.

"But you saw it, too?"

"Yeah," said Evolice, fighting to think straight through the pain. "Did it talk to you?"

"The obelisk? You heard it speak?" asked Eamon, removing his hand from his pain-squinted eyes. "Guess I shouldn't be surprised."

"I suppose that means you didn't?" concluded Evolice.

"No," admitted Eamon. "I heard the crack and then silence… though, my ears are ringing now. What did you hear?"

"The same at first, a crack and then silence," said Evolice, "but then the obelisk spoke. It called my name and said 'I ache.'"

"I can relate," said Eamon, rubbing his temple. "I can hardly keep my balance, but it doesn't look like anyone else out here felt a thing. This must be kytra related."

"Faeron!" cried Evolice, her blurred mind returning to her son, alone in Eamon's office.

Eamon's face shifted to a cold determined look. "I'm closer."

"Call as soon as you arrive," said Evolice, her heart pounding. "I'll go find Mathas and make sure he's alright."

"Good idea," said Eamon. "We can get this event recorded once we're sure everyone is safe." At that, the image of Eamon disappeared and Evolice was left alone in her office.

Evolice leaped from her desk, not bothering to sort her freshly penned notes. The world was spinning around her but she pushed through. She made straight for the door on the curved part of the wall and swept into the round reading room of Mathas' Athenaeum.

The walls were lined floor to ceiling in neatly organized book-shelves. There were cozy chairs and couches scattered about the space, and a spiral stairwell led down to the second floor.

Evolice stumbled toward a long but narrow passage on her left. It was barely wide enough for two across, with more bookshelves on the left and a banister on the right. Just beyond the railing, stained-glass windows rose nearly the full height of the three-story building. The glass murals depicted grand moments from the greatest works of fiction. Through the paned silver helmet and fiery rainbow blade of Sir Eddicus the Worthy came a curtain of colored light that painted the bookshelves in its glow.

The narrow passage was rocking around Evolice, as if she were in a ship on a stormy sea. Evolice caught the banister and closed her eyes. Taking only a moment to steady herself, she rushed on as fast as she dared. As usual, the third-floor reference section was vacant and Evolice soon reached the Central Spire.

The hallway exited to a wide ring overlooking another round reading room. Evolice scanned the floor below for the unmistakable form of Mathas Grinward and quickly spotted him among the dozen or so people enjoying a peaceful read before a night of festivities.

Normally just under eight feet tall, Mathas was down on one knee, comforting a girl about Faeron's age. Mathas was covered head to toe in frosty silver fur. He had long lanky limbs, wrapped in modest brown robes. The girl, meanwhile, was strong shouldered and athletic, with straight black hair cut to her shoulders.

Just looking at the girl gave Evolice the strangest feeling. Her mind was suddenly at war with itself. One half seemed to know the girl as if she were family; the other side was positive it had never seen her before. Evolice breathed deep and massaged her forehead. Whatever happened in her office must have done a number on her mind.

A short way along the ringed mezzanine was a glass-tube elevator, wide enough to hold four or five people comfortably. Evolice approached the elevator and touched a blue-lit panel projected on the glass. At her touch, the glass molded itself into a doorway, allowing her inside. Once the glass had sealed behind her, Evolice said, "Second level," in a pained voice and the elevator began its short descent.

When the door opened, Evolice bustled across the second floor reading room. Her migraine wasn't as debilitating now, but it was still a formidable ache.

"Mathas," said Evolice in an urgent but quiet voice so as not to disturb any readers.

The capillum turned and gave Evolice a smile. His face was long, his nose and black eyes twice the size of any human's. If his head were aching like hers, Evolice couldn't tell it from the warm look on his face.

"You saw it too, I suppose?" he said. "Then that makes the three of us."

"Three?" asked Evolice.

"I was just telling Miss Lem that she and I had matching headaches," said Mathas, motioning to the young girl. "Isn't that right, Auri?"

Auri.

Of course! Even in this state, Evolice couldn't believe she'd forgotten Vox's daughter and Faeron's best friend. It was even more strange considering the girl lived with them whenever her father was away. Even now, as Evolice watched Auri fight back tears in her light brown, almost bronze, eyes, she had the same unsettling feeling. Her gut was certain something wasn't what it seemed about Auri Lem.

"Mrs. Lovel, your head hurts, too?" moaned Auri through gritted teeth. "Does that mean you saw—" The girl cut herself short and closed her eyes tight as tears trickled down her cheek.

"Tell Mrs. Lovel what you saw dear," said Mathas gently to the girl, his long hand on her strong shoulder.

"It was…" Auri began but trailed off, balling her fists tight in her lap. "I can't!"

"It's okay, love," said Evolice sweetly, pulling a chair up beside the girl. "Just show me."

Evolice took Auri's hand in her own and raised her free hand to her grandmother's blue-stone pendant, hanging from a silver chain around her neck. The old stone was cracked in several places, but as Evolice touched its glassy surface, she could feel the power welling inside. Closing her eyes, Evolice breathed deep and pushed away all thoughts until only the pain remained. In and out, Evolice breathed, in and out, and the hurt receded. For a moment, her mind was absent.

"Go on, do your best to remember what you saw," said Evolice, her voice sounding far off, as if hearing herself through distant speakers.

"Okay," said the girl.

Light danced against Evolice's eyelids as she watched Auri's memory unfold. It was just as she had witnessed until Auri saw the crimson chasm running down the obelisk's base. The girl was pulled hard and fast straight into the depths of the fiery schism. Like a great whirlpool, savage crimson light swirled all around her, its terrible power flooding what few senses the girl had in this strange place—

"No! Stop it!" cried Auri, tugging her hand from Evolice's grasp.

The vision cut out, leaving Evolice's head spinning with flashes of the crimson light. Evolice breathed deep, remembering who she was, where she was.

"Auri, Evolice, are you two alright?" she heard Mathas ask, as her sight slowly returned. Even kneeling beside her chair, he was still a head taller than Evolice.

Across the round reading room, an older woman shushed the three of them loudly over the battered cover of *Rhapsody and Remorse*.

"I'll be fine, thank you," said Evolice, casting a concerned gaze over the girl whose cheeks trailed silent tears.

"Mathas," whispered Evolice to the old capillum, "a word?"

"Of course," said Mathas, rising to his feet, now towering over Evolice. They stepped aside, just out of earshot of Auri, near several shelves of colorful children's books.

"What exactly did the vision show you?" whispered Evolice.

"Darkness at first," said Mathas softly, "then a monument of light. I believe it was damaged, cracked down the center, but I hardly got a look before I came to."

"The obelisk spoke to me," said Evolice. "It told me it was in pain. I didn't know what to think of it until just now."

"Because of Miss Lem?" asked Mathas curiously.

"She's seen more than any of us," whispered Evolice, "a crimson vortex within the chasm. It was… powerful, consuming. The obelisk, whatever it might be, is infected. It's crying for help."

"But what help do we have to offer?" asked Mathas.

"I'm not sure," said Evolice. "I'm not even sure what *it* is. Perhaps the answer lies in some tome beneath Old Eredith."

"At least we know what we're looking for now," offered Mathas. "And what of Auri? It would appear she is a kytra."

"She is Vox's daughter," pointed out Evolice, "and she's grown up in the constant company of kytra."

"Though it's strange…" Mathas said, his brow furrowing. "She's never seen light in the crystals. I wonder if this event had some impact, awakened something."

"We'll have plenty of time to explore the 'why' and 'how' of it later," said Evolice. "Right now, I need you to check in with Eamon. Tell him what Auri saw, and make sure Faeron's alright. I'll stay with Auri in case this isn't the end of it."

"Good idea," said Mathas, flitting off toward a narrow hallway leading out of the reading room.

Evolice returned to the seat beside Auri. There was a small table between them, and on it rested a book titled: *Deity – Reign of Silence*. Memories of the girl were flooding back now. Evolice recalled just over a week ago introducing Auri to her own favorite novel series, Deity.

"You're already on Reign of Silence?" said Evolice, impressed. If anything could distract the girl from all this, it might just be Deity. "Didn't I see you on Den of Worlds this morning?"

Auri sniffed and wiped her eyes on her arm. She looked up to Evolice with a tough smile, hiding whatever pain was left. "Well yeah, I've been mostly just reading right here since you dropped me off. I only got up after I finished the third book and it's a good thing there wasn't another chapter because I would've wet the chair for sure."

"I'm glad you're enjoying them," chuckled Evolice. She had been about Auri's age when the series first began, and she'd devoured every book the night of its release. It warmed her heart to see that same excitement in Auri's bronze eyes. "So where are you now?"

"Dhark just learned he's a demigod, not that anyone had doubts" said Auri; she snorted a bit, laughing. "Oh, and Jaeda was *finally* reunited with Maerik in Luthran."

"Then they've met the deity tree," said Evolice with a knowing smile. "What did you think?"

"Oh my goodness, it was the most incredible thing," said Auri excitedly. "Could you *imagine* seeing that in real life?"

"I don't have to imagine," smirked Evolice.

The young girl's eyes grew wide. "Really?" she asked loudly. "You mean you've *really* seen it?"

"Shh, quieter," shushed Evolice playfully. Several readers were glaring. "Not the real thing, but I've seen close."

"You *have* to tell me," begged Auri in a whisper.

"I was only a few years older than you are now," said Evolice, thinking back on herself at seventeen, before Eamon and the vision, before the world collapsed. "I was invited to a very fancy conference—"

"Evolice!"

She turned to find Mathas, tall and slender, rushing across the reading room. The capillum gestured toward an open table nearby. From his grim expression, she assumed this wasn't going to be a conversation fit for Auri.

"One second sweetie," said Evolice. She rose from her chair and went to the table where Mathas now stood waiting. Evolice pulled a chair out to sit, but Mathas caught her arm.

"It's Faeron," said the old capillum. "He's somehow shattered the Hoststone."

Evolice felt the blood rush from her face, and her lungs grew heavy like lead in her chest. "Is he—?" but she couldn't even finish the question.

"Unresponsive, but breathing," said Mathas softly. "He needs you, Evolice. Vox is on his way here with the boy now."

"Vox?" asked Evolice. "Where's Eamon?"

"There's a situation over by Homewood," said Mathas. "I don't know the specifics, but it seems Bennehym's boy is involved. Don't you worry about any of that now. Vox will be at the shipment bay any moment."

"Alright," said Evolice, taking deep breaths. She needed to stay calm if she was going to be any help to Faeron. She gave Mathas a purposeful nod and strode across the reading room to the wide glass elevator. As she stepped inside, she could see Mathas speaking to Auri. The young girl beamed brightly and followed the capillum toward his office.

"Shipment Bay," said Evolice, and the elevator began its descent. She passed through the first-floor foyer, where a school-aged boy was holding the sizable front door for a sweet-looking girl in short blonde pigtails, and lowered into a dimly lit rectangular room in the basement. On either side were large wooden sorting tables and several half-full book trolleys. The far wall was bare except for a set of sizable double doors that slid open at nearly the same moment Evolice's elevator came to a stop. They revealed a well-lit tram with only one occupant; Vox Lem was dark-haired and well-built, wearing his classic three-piece-suit. He marched into the room, holding the limp frame of her son, Faeron, in his arms.

"Get that table clear!" roared Vox.

Evolice rushed from the elevator to a sorting table on one side. She pushed aside several stacks of loosely organized books, making room for her young son.

Vox gently but swiftly rested Faeron on the wood, and Evolice finally saw her son's face. The boy, normally a spitting image of his father, had gone entirely pale and was taken by tremors. His finger tapped, and his feet kicked wildly on the wood.

"Faeron," gasped Evolice.

"I found him like this," said Vox, "surrounded by pieces of the Hoststone. The light was running through his eyes and I couldn't do a thing to stop it. I couldn't shape, not even for him..."

"You got him here," said Evolice softly, "I can't thank you enough."

Gently, she forced open Faeron's eyelids. As Faeron's cold blue eyes looked absently to the ceiling, vibrant amethyst light oozed through his irises. The light was slowly consuming all that was blue as it grew and spread like a living organism. It looked just like when Eamon's eyes had been stained gold, the day he was chosen as Host of the Patronage.

"I need space to work," said Evolice, focused only on her son. Vox stepped away, and she took his place at the end of the table, near Faeron's head.

With one hand, Evolice grasped her grandmother's necklace, the other, she ran through Faeron's bushy brown hair. Evolice reached down and kissed her son's forehead.

"It's alright, love," she whispered. "I'm here. Let me in, show me what you see."

In and out, Evolice breathed, releasing the aches of her body, releasing the worries of her mind. In and out went the last pangs of her headache. In and out went her heartache for Faeron. When fear and stress and love were all gone from her mind, there was only darkness. She was formless in the void, then there was light. It was faint at first, like a flickering star in the heavens, but it quickly grew brighter, bigger, bolder, until it poured over the darkness like a great tsunami. Evolice was swept up by the current and pulled along like a fish in a stream, past vibrant images, scenes from another life playing out around her.

Always, she saw through the same eyes. Moments became days, days turned to weeks, and weeks dragged on into years, as Evolice experienced a lifetime in flashing, fleeting glimpses around her, beautifully detailed but too brief to comprehend. And then, she saw a horrid blaze of crimson power, like the flames in the chasm of the obelisk. The vision came to a crashing halt, and Evolice was thrown back into her body, in the basement of Mathas' Athenaeum.

"Evolice," cried Vox as she fell against the table, her legs weak.

"It's not like Eamon's vision," said Evolice, breathing heavily. "His was quick, brief glimpses and whispered names. Faeron just witnessed a whole lifetime."

"By Glavius," said Vox, "he must be overwhelmed… Can you do anything?"

"I need to go back in," said Evolice, determined. "I'm going to try and slow it down."

She placed her hands on her son's head, combing his hair with her fingers. Closing her eyes, she clutched her necklace and quieted her mind. When the darkness settled and the light returned, Evolice fought against its pull. She swam against the current, clinging to each scene as they passed, dragging out Faeron's relentless vision.

The end was just as jarring the second time around. She saw a figure cloaked in crimson fire, fearsome as the flames Auri saw. And then came a name, an impossible name that Evolice knew too well.

The vision ended, leaving Evolice on the verge of vomiting. When she opened her eyes, she saw her son, laying still on the table, his tremors gone. The boy's breathing was slow and steady.

"You've done it," exclaimed Vox, rushing to her side. "Are you okay, Ev?"

"I'll be fine," she said, though, in truth, she had never been more confused. The name in the vision didn't make any sense, but she couldn't refute what she'd heard. "Vox, I need you to do me a favor."

"Of course," he said, giving her a worried look.

"Get Faeron home, and stay with him until Eamon gets back."

"And where will you be?" asked Vox with a furrowed brow.

Evolice looked at her son, holding back a flood of tears. She had to be wrong. For her sake, for Eamon and Faeron, for every soul in the city, she prayed that she was wrong. Giving Faeron one last kiss, Evolice rose. "I need to go see Nylk."

"I'll come with you," said Vox, "I can have Mathas see to the kids."

"No," said Evolice firmly. She looked at her old friend with a soft smile. "Auri is a kytra, Vox."

He looked up at her suddenly. Surprise and joy flashed in his steel blue eyes before his serious glare set back in.

"She saw something terrible in the obelisk," continued Evolice. "Auri needs you here. If all goes well, I'll be back in time for the ceremony tonight. We do have an anniversary to celebrate after all."

"Right," said Vox, eyeing her hesitantly. He went to the desk and hoisted Faeron back into his arms. "I'll make sure he's safe and cozy until you're home."

"Thank you, Vox, for everything," said Evolice. Vox carried Faeron to the tram, and she followed them to the door. "Your mother loves you Faeron, don't you ever forget it," she said, looking at her son slumber peacefully in Vox's arms.

"Tonight then?" asked Vox.

"Tonight," she said, though the word felt hollow. In truth, she didn't know when she would see her son again, and it tore her heart apart. Standing alone in the shipping dock, Evolice didn't cry until the tram door slid shut.

CHAPTER ONE

THE KYTRA OF EREDITH

Faeron's eyes were shut tight as he lay curled up on a couch in his father's office. Footsteps approached and his heart skipped a beat. Would his dad fall for it? Several moments later, his question was answered as the front door of the office creaked open then shut. Faeron counted out the seconds in his head; one, two, three… all the way to thirty. When he was sure his father wouldn't be coming back, Faron opened his eyes and sprung off the couch.

Eamon's office was always grand to see. More than its size or the fancy purple carpet, Faeron was always enamored by the artifacts. He darted between each of the standing display cases spaced along the walls and admired the many masks, statuettes, jewelry, and more. His favorite display held a pitch black ring with a glowing sapphire centerpiece. Beside the ring was a coarse crystal, bigger than Faeron's fist and reddish orange in hue. Its glow was much stronger, pulsing, like a little star inside the crystal. Brilliant as it was, this wasn't the gemstone that Faeron was after tonight.

Faeron wandered to his father's desk at the end of the carpet. There, the hoststone rest on an ornate golden pedestal. Beneath the orb's glassy surface was an uncanny darkness like smoke in a bubble. Faeron always had the strangest feeling whenever he saw it, like knowing that someone was watching him. He wanted so badly to look back into the stone, but his father never let him get too close. Tonight, however, his dad wasn't here.

Faeron put his nose right up to the orb, squinting deep into the crystal. At first, he didn't see anything. Then, in the void, a spark of light—

"Mr. Lovel? Are you with us?"

Faeron jumped suddenly back to the present. It had been a decade since that night, since his mother disappeared, and there hadn't been so much as a sighting of Evolice Lovel. She had simply vanished. In that time the nineteen-year-old had become the spitting image of his father, tall and thin with messy dark hair and a strong arched nose. He sat, back straight, eyes closed in a comfortably padded seat.

"Lost in memory again?" came Mathas's soft voice.

Faeron's eyes were shut and his mind was starting to quiet once more. Through the Athenaeum walls, he heard the beating of music. The End of Highsun Bash was in full swing just outside. With it, came a new set of challenges in his favorite game, Prophet's Guard.

"Focus, Faeron," said Mathas warmly. "Distraction does not benefit a kytra."

"*Breathe,*" Faeron told himself. "*Forget the stone, forget the game, just breathe. In… and out…. In… and out….*" Faeron's breathing slowed and his body went numb then fell away. With each inhale he focused on the stray thoughts, and with each exhale he released them. There was only darkness now, no thoughts or feelings, but the silence only lasted a second.

The light started faint, far off in the emptiness of his mind. It quickly grew brighter and larger until it was a great pearlescent wave washing through Faeron. He was caught in its brilliant white current, streaks of color shimmering all around him. In the colors he could see scenes painted in perfect detail. Some were simple sights, like an endless ocean in a streak of blue. Others were strange and alien. In a flash of green was a world of floating islands, crumbling and reforming over and over again.

"Good…" came a faint voice. It sounded many miles away, floating faint and distorted through the pearly stream. "What… you see…"

"Blue and green," spoke Faeron into the stream around him. It was a trick Mathas had taught him only this semester, commanding his body to speak as his consciousness rode the current of peridom. He couldn't feel his lips moving, but he knew the words were being spoken. "I see an ocean sprawling, then a sky full of islands, crumbling and forming again. Now, orange, a forest smoking and ashen. A fire has just died here."

"Wonderf… Now show…" came his mentor's voice, broken and barely recognizable. "Waking… meditation…"

Fearon's heart skipped for a second and the light around him dimmed. *"In… and out…."* he told himself. He should have known Mathas would be testing him on this. *"Okay Faeron, open your eyes."*

Faeron's eyes batted open. He could still feel the rush of peridom in his mind, and every surface of the small rectangular room shimmered in its pearly light.

"Calm," Faeron cautioned himself, *"no distractions, only calm."*

"Steady. Hold it…" said Mathas, "just sixty seconds." Unlike Faeron, the silver furred capillum had hardly aged in the last decade. He sat in a shaggy brown robe perched over his desk with his long fingers woven together. His sizable black eyes were locked on Faeron and for some time he simply sat and watched. "You can relax now, Mr. Lovel," he said, finally breaking the silence. "Your waking meditation has come far this semester."

Faeron grinned with pride and it was all it took to break the fragile connection. The light receded from Faeron's mind, and the aura of the classroom extinguished.

Mathas rose from his squeaky office chair and limped to the long table where Faeron and the other Kytra gathered most nights. Faeron sat in his normal spot at the very back of the table against a large window looking in on a dark and spacious workshop.

"I see you brought your journal," said Mathas, pointing to the thin brown and gold book on the table beside Faeron.

"Yeah," said Faeron. "I haven't had much chance for one on one, but I was hoping I could ask you something."

"What mischief is our friend Jakob getting himself into these days," asked Mathas, knowingly. From his eager smile, Faeron could tell his mentor welcomed an invitation to discuss the topic.

"See for yourself," said Faeron, sliding the journal across the table to Mathas. "It's not so much the 'what' of it I wanted to talk about. It's more the 'how much' of it… if that makes sense?"

"Your dreams are getting longer again," concluded Mathas, flipping through to the very back of the journal where the posts were lengthier, some taking up dozens of pages.

"It used to be so simple, a day as me, a day as *him*," said Faeron. "Now, I don't remember the last time I dreamt for less than a week. Sometimes, when I wake up, I can't breathe… It's like his memories and mine are crashing together, and I never know if I'm me or him. I just wonder, it's been ten years and Jakob is only in his thirties. How long will it be until we see what chased my mom away? Will we be too late?"

"Faeron… I cannot imagine the weight of your burden," said Mathas. "And to chronicle this all in such detail," he flipped through the pages, "it's truly inspiring. You've done right by Evolice, no matter what comes of your dreams."

Faeron blushed, but the compliment couldn't cure the ache in his gut. "That's only what I remember of it. Most of the details are lost up here." He shook his hands around his head imitating the stormy sea that was his memories of Jakob. Trying to pinpoint any moment in Jakob's life was impossible. His memories were fiercely vivid but too brief to make any sense of. "I just wish I could see it all at once like my mom did, then we could finally find her. I'm ready, Mathas. I want to shape my dreams."

"The stone your mother used to shape your vision was unique," said Mathas, returning the journal to Faeron. "But seeing as it is *your* vision. There may be a way."

"You'll teach me?" gulped Faeron excitedly.

Mathas drummed his fingers on the table and looked past Faeron to the lifeless room beyond the glass. "I'd say the workshop has gathered dust long enough. What do you think?"

"Absolutely," cried Faeron, positively beaming as he swung in his seat to peer into the workshop. "How long do you think it'll take until I'm like her?"

"As I mentioned, your mother's necklace was the source of her power," warned Mathas. "Even then, she studied the old writings and practiced her shaping for over a decade before your dream. There is a long journey ahead, but you are finally ready to take that first step."

Faeron pictured himself in the workshop, shaping the light just like his mother used to, moving objects with his mind and bending the laws of physics around him, but the image felt incomplete. "What about Auri?" asked Faeron. "Is she moving on to shaping as well?" He knew Auri still struggled with her deep meditations, and she'd never managed a waking one.

"That depends on how she does on her evaluation," said Mathas matter-of-factly, "You, on the other hand, have just passed quite spectacularly. Congratulations, Faeron. Take a couple weeks to get settled into your classes and we'll pick back up on the sixteenth."

"Thanks!" said Faeron, popping up from his seat. He snatched his backpack off the seat beside him and tossed his journal inside. "So, who's next?"

"Miss Lem next, thank you."

Mathas remained at his seat as Faeron shuffled around the table, his mind abuzz; he was finally going to be shaping this semester. "Thanks for talking about this stuff with me, Mathas," said Faeron, pausing at the door.

"It's a pleasure," responded Mathas and Faeron exited to the Athenaeum foyer.

The foyer was a circular room with tables of neatly organized books lined around the walls. There was a large glass elevator and the windows were filled with novels on display. Auri and Quinn were alone in the room, waiting in plump padded chairs around a squat round table. As Faeron shut the door to the classroom behind him, Auri was, as usual, nose deep in a book.

"So much for in and out," she said, not bothering to look up from her reading. Auri was built as strong as her unruly temper. She wasn't quite as tall as Faeron, but he had no doubt which one of them would come out on top if they ever got in a fist fight. Her straight black hair was plated in metallic bronze ends that perfectly matched the fierce color of her eyes. Auri was in a charcoal grey tank-top and athletic shorts, although she didn't look like she'd been at the rec center any time recently. Most likely, she was dressed for tonight. "We're on a schedule you know."

Faeron shrugged as he joined them and sank into the seat beside her, resting his backpack against his chair.

Quinn, meanwhile, was a year younger than Faeron or Auri and small by all accounts. He was slim, pale, and his hair was shaved on the sides with short orange curls on top. He wore colorful sweaters year-round and got along with most people, even if he wasn't anyone's best friend. "So, how was it?" he asked.

"You know the old workshop…?" said Faeron with a smile.

"No way," gawked Quinn, his purple sweater causing the green of his hazel eyes to pop. "You're gonna *shape* this semester?"

"About time," smirked Auri, setting her book down on the table. She looked pleased but not all too surprised by Faeron's news. "You know, once you can move objects with your mind, you won't have any excuse letting your dishes pile up in the sink."

"Ah, yes," said Faeron, "super chores, the greatest of all superpowers. Maybe I'll finally give my bedroom a proper deep cleaning."

"I'll believe it when I see it," laughed Auri. "Now who's up? Time's ticking."

"You are," said Faeron, giving her foot a light kick. "You gonna be joining me in the workshop this semester?"

"Is that even a question," challenged Auri confidently, rising from her seat. "How am I supposed to whip your lazy superpowers into action without a few of my own?" She threw her backpack over one shoulder and smirked.

"Bold words," said Faeron.

"True words," stated Auri. She snatched her book off the table and placed it into a return cart near the classroom door.

"Oh, and Faeron," she said, stopping in the doorway. "You do have your gloves don't you? I didn't ask on our way out."

"In the bag," said Faeron, motioning to his backpack.

"Good," said Auri. "I was gonna make you run all the way back home now if you didn't. See you two in a sec." She shut the classroom door hard behind her.

"So, Faeron," said Quinn as soon as the door was closed, "you and Auri have plans after evals, huh?"

"Prophet's Guard," said Faeron.

"Hence the gloves," concluded Quinn. "You know, the End of Highson Bash is tonight. Quinta Firum is playing in the park and I thought it'd be fun if we all went and sat out there for a while, you know?"

"Any other night I'd say yes," said Faeron, "but the Bash also brings a new Prophet's Guard expansion. We've never missed an opening night."

"Never?" asked Quinn.

"Not since we were old enough to play," said Faeron. "You should come though. It's fun figuring it all out before it gets spoiled."

"That's alright," said Quinn. "Sounds like a sacred tradition you two got goin'. I wouldn't want to intrude. Besides, the simulation rooms always make me queasy. I do have something to show you though, since you won't be around later."

"Oh yeah?" asked Faeron.

Quinn reached into the backpack resting against his chair and fished out a black box. It was about six inches tall, three across, and had a white tree etched across the front. The box was clearly a Deity mystery figure; Faeron was an avid fan of the popular strategy game and had quite the collection of his own. The symbol of the tree on this box, however, wasn't one he'd seen before.

"It's a Lunar Grove series. Pre-plague, obviously," said Quinn excitedly, "found it in the imports market. Remember when Baeric Dipper stomped you with that weird Accabadan support unit? It's from this set. Only unit I've ever seen from it."

"Well, you gonna open it?" asked Faeron, leaning forward excitedly. Older sets were a rare treat and many of their figures had never been seen by anyone in Eredith.

"Okay," said Quinn, "here it goes…" He set the box on the table and tugged at the packaging until the top popped open. Reaching inside, Quinn pulled out a figure with a six legged back-half, hooves, and deep purple fur. The front half was a man with beet red skin. Glorious golden wings sprouted from his muscular back and he held a similarly gold trident in both hands.

"What in the world is that?" asked Faeron.

"I don't know," said Quinn, examining the figure in awe. He took a nervous look around and dove back into his bag, pulling out a small glass cube. It was his homemade index, Logic, a personal project of his made from old pre-plague parts. Whenever Quinn wasn't playing Deity, you could bet he'd be in his workshop coding or tinkering away at the inner circuits of the device. "Since there's no one around… wanna, find out?"

"Do it," said Faeron mischievously. He knew full well that any sort of index or projection tech was banned in the athenaeum commons, but it wasn't like there was anyone around for them to distract.

"Okay, but… promise not to tell Auri!" said Quinn.

"Alright?" Faeron shot him a confused look, unsure what Auri had to do with anything.

"I mean it," said Quinn urgently. "She hates people who use projection tech in here. You know, I'm trying to ask her to Unity Fest this year."

"Oh, really?" asked Faeron, not wanting to tell Quinn he had about as high a chance with Auri as Faeron did with going pro in Deity.

"Yup, I really think she's starting to see me as more than just a friend," he said with cheerful ignorance. "Last week, when you were out sick, she walked me all the way home after Mathas' and we talked the whole time. I just really *felt* the connection. I don't know if it was a kytra thing or if we were just both in the moment, but I'm telling you that it wasn't like anything else I've ever felt. I just know she felt it too, ya know? I mean she had to."

"That's great," said Faeron, knowing Auri would likely have a different take on the story. "But you know, if you want to check out the fig before Auri gets out of her eval, we'd better get a move on."

"Right," said Quinn. He set the cube on the table then placed his figurine on top, "Logic, load up character information for this piece." The glass began to glow, and a large-scale version of the figure appeared beside the cube. He trotted back and forth across the varnished surface and struck a heroic pose in front of Quinn.

"I am Vykett of the Rowastroke people," said the figure in a mighty voice, "how may I serve my deity?"

"Can you talk just a little quieter?" squeaked Quinn, looking nervously at the classroom door.

"Of course, my deity," said Vykett, much softer than before. "Would you like to know my specialties in the field of battle, or perhaps see a preview of my techniques?"

"Start from the top," said Quinn excitedly. "Gimme everything."

"I am a proud leader, tested and true at the front of any team," said Vykett proudly, holding his trident to his chest. "Charge me with a squad of beastmen and you'll find them inspired to run faster, hit harder, and survive even the deadliest blows."

"Sounds perfect for your aggressive digger team," said Faeron. "Maybe you could run—"

SLAM

Faeron and Quinn both jumped in their seats as a pair of young twin girls barreled through the athenaeum's front doors, giggling as they collapsed onto the floor. Their bags had emptied as they tumbled, littering the athenaeum floor in clothes and equipment for the popular sport, bunball.

Myllie and Kaelynn were the youngest of the Kytra, only ten-years-old, and covered head to toe in sports gear. Myllie had less pads than her sister but she still wore her bright pink targeting mask, hiding all but her wavy ombre hair.

"Hey girls," called Faeron. "How was practice?"

"Good," said Myllie, jumping to her feet. She lifted her helmet revealing soft cheeks, a pointy nose, and sharp brows above bright blue eyes. "Kaelynn was a pro. Thirty-two shots on goal and she didn't let a single one in."

"Dang," said Quinn with a whistle. "I don't remember Faeron ever pulling off something like that."

"Because I never have," said Faeron. He had never been amazing at bunball. It was a chaotic sport involving eight teams of two each defending goals around a big circular field. Faeron was decent enough at keeper, but Auri had always outclassed him on both sides of the field. Even next to Auri though, the twins were borderline savants at the sport. "Really, awesome job, Kaelynn," said Faeron. "Those are some killer numbers."

Kaelynn was blushing tomato red as she struggled to stand back up in all her keeper's pads. She snatched up her bag and collected the strewn clothes and a set of footlong steel keeper's rods that had rolled under a nearby chair. Slowly, she lumbered over to where Faeron and Quinn were sitting and collapsed into the chair Auri had used. The only way Faeron could tell Kaelynn apart from her sister was her lighter hair, typically tied up into a ponytail.

"What's this?" asked Myllie. She had put her mask back in her bag and was now dragging a stool from under one of the displays over to the table with everyone else.

"I am Vykett of the Rowastroke—"

"DUMB," shouted Myllie loudly.

"Ignore her Vykett," said Quinn dismissively. "That's all for now." The beastman gave him a salute and disappeared.

"Who's already gone?" asked Kaelynn quietly as she pried off her cleats.

"Just me and— Oh spirits!" cried Faeron, grabbing his nose. The unbearable smell of sweat flooded the room as Kaelynn pulled a sock down and peeled off one of her knee pads.

"Haha! Faeron thinks you stink," giggled Myllie to her sister.

"Shutup!" shouted Kaelynn, blushing redder than before.

"What in the world is that *smell*?"

Auri stood in the classroom doorway holding, disgust wrinkled across her face.

"AURI!" yelled the girls sprinting to give her a hug.

"Hey, you two," said Auri, grabbing them both in a playful headlock, taking one sniff, and letting them go with a visible gag. "Kaelynn, you know you gotta take those sweaty pads off in the bathroom. Myllie, go help your sister get out of her gear."

"Aye, aye!" cried Myllie and the two girls sped off down the hall.

"That didn't take long at all," said Faeron, relieved to see Auri in such a good mood. He had half expected her to storm out, stomp off back home, and refuse to speak with him for the rest of the evening.

"I told you it wouldn't," said Auri. "Now, let's get moving before the colosseum closes. Oh, and Quinn, you're up next."

"Wait," said Quinn, popping up from his seat. "You've got fourth hour AI Upkeep with Professor Bundst this semester, right, Faeron? Maybe we meet for a game of Unity in the rec room before class tomorrow? We can put that new fig through his paces. Auri, you're welcome too, of course."

"I'm game," said Faeron. He was very interested to see how Quinn's new unit played.

"Depends on the time," said Auri, not bothering to mask her disinterest. "I have back to back classes all afternoon."

"Maybe during lunch then," grinned Quinn as he wandered toward the classroom door. "If not, I'll see you after classes or something, I'm sure. Now, time to go show Mathas I'm ready to join you guys."

"Good luck," said Faeron, grabbing his bag as he rose from his seat.

"See ya tomorrow," said Auri.

"Tomorrow!" Quinn returned.

Shortly after the classroom door closed, Myllie and Kaelynn came bounding back up the hall in fresh clothes. Other than their hair, the only way to tell them apart was Myllie's black shirt versus Kaelynn's white one.

"Hey girls," said Auri as the twins sprinted across the room. "Faeron and I were just about to leave."

"Aww," said Myllie dramatically, "you don't want to stay?"

"I wish I could," said Auri, kneeling before the girls. "But Faeron and I are in a real big hurry. You two go show old Mathas how much you've learned, and I'll see you back here in a couple weeks, alright?."

"WE'RE GONNA CRUSH IT!" yelled Myllie.

Auri grinned and ruffled the girl's hair. "Come on, Faeron," she said, "let's get out of here."

"Absolutely," said Faeron, going to the door. "Myllie, Kaelynn, good luck on your evals."

"Thank you," said Kaelynn timidly.

"Yeah, yeah, like we need luck," said Myllie, taking over their table.

"I like the confidence," grinned Auri. "Until next time, girls."

"Bye Auri!" said the twins.

Faeron shoved the plank-like handles of the athenaeum's heavy front door. He was greeted by a warm breeze and the sound of live music dominating the chatter filled ambiance of Loem Park at dusk.

CHAPTER TWO

PROPHET'S GUARD

The first thing anyone in Eredith saw when stepping outside was the hundred-story wall. It formed a perfect circle around the city and colossal statues stood vigil upon its bastion towers.

Mathas' athenaeum was settled near the center of the city, on the southern edge of Loem Park. From the outside, it looked like a miniature basilica with towering glass mosaics that glowed warmly in the evening light and cast a kaleidoscope of colors across the bustling streets below.

The End of Highsun Bash was in full swing by the time Faeron and Auri left the athenaeum, and the driving beat of live music electrified the air. The main road was a one-way river of people pushing toward the source of the music, an amphitheater at the heart of the park.

"No way we'll make it across that crowd before last call," Auri hollered over the noise. "Serris!"

A small orb of white-blue light popped into the air beside them.

"What can I do for you?" asked Serris, Eredith's citywide assistant.

"How's traffic tonight?"

"Parkside stations are closed for the remainder of the night, but I can pick you up over at Roethram and Inner," said Serris. "Do note, there may be a wait to disembark. We have several locations backed up."

"Go ahead and order the tram," said Auri, trotting down the steps with Faeron in tow. "Where's the closest to the colosseum you can drop us?" She took a right into a wide alley between the athenaeum's south wing and Clearstream Cinema next door. The quiet road led away from the bustling park toward the Roethram Academy Tower.

"The east end of the park is roped off, so traffic over by the colosseum is light tonight," reported Serris, bobbing up and down just over Faeron's shoulder as she followed along. "I can put you right outside the D–Gate of Bellwillow Market."

"Perfect," said Auri.

"All booked," reported Serris. "You'll be looking for tram blue six-eight-two."

In the distance, Roethram Academy Tower cast a wide shadow across the streets below. The tower was topped by the statue of a man with stones of varied metals orbiting his outstretched palm.

Besides Faeron and Auri, the only other people on the road were an older gentleman with silver-streaked hair and a woman in a heavy-knit sweater, making faces at an infant who giggled gleefully from her autostroller.

Halfway to the tower, Faeron and Auri reached a large crossing where their tram was scheduled to arrive. The glassy white transpo-tubes on each corner were dormant until the pair drew close. One of the smaller tubes turned bright blue, and the number 682 spun slowly around the cylinder.

"Ride's here." Faeron cut across the street to the glowing cylinder.

The blue glass split smoothly down the center, shaping into a doorway. As they stepped inside, the tube's color faded, the wall closed behind them, and the music muddled. In the center of the tube was a ring-shaped railing, waist high.

"Please take hold to begin your descent," said the pleasant voice of Alannah, the transit AI.

Faeron and Auri grabbed the bannister, and they descended into a clean white tram. Setting down his bag on the open seats, Faeron felt the tram begin to move.

"Oh, I never told you," said Auri, settling into her seat. "Last night, at youth group, Andrea had a theory about the new expansion. You know the teaser poster?"

"Of course," said Faeron. "Twenty years, twenty legends, twenty challenges." The game offered varied trials from solving ancient puzzles to all out brawls, but they all starred one of the Hosts, the golden-eyed prophets of the Patronage.

"But, did you notice the *outside*?" asked Auri. "It's all sandy… which may mean we'll finally see a Salduni Host."

"Does that mean Sombara?" asked Faeron, thinking through his Patronage history lessons. He wasn't nearly the expert Auri was, something she never let him live down considering his dad was the current Host. Still, he knew there weren't more than a handful of hosts from Saldun, the expansive desert in the east.

"Likely Cresh," guessed Auri. "She's the biggest name in Salduni Hosts. Though, it could be Ylketha, Poporoe, or Nokruvokani as well. What do you think? "

"All those ancient names blend together," shrugged Faeron. "I always mix up who's who."

"Unbelievable," sighed Auri, giving him a disappointed glare.

When the tram finally came to a complete stop, a ring of light appeared around the central railing.

"Please stand in the circle and, for your safety, hold on to the handrail," said Alannah. Faeron and Auri did as they were instructed, taking hold of the bannister. A hole in the ceiling opened, and they were carried upward. They ascended into another transpo-tube and the park's driving music rushed back in. As the shifting wall formed into a door, Faeron and Auri stepped out into a bustling plaza between two extraordinary buildings.

Bellwillow Market was a huge sandstone slab of a structure, three stories tall and taking up two blocks by itself. There were dozens of shops within the market, from clothes and technology to snacks and knick knacks. Shy of the grocery store, it was the one stop for anything you ever needed in Eredith.

The D-Gate was dead center on the building's southwest wall and looked like any other entry to the market. Tall, arching bellwillow trees grew on either side of the gate, their golden bell-shaped buds tinkling softly in the slow breeze.

Across from the market was the Astral Colosseum. The colossal structure lived up to its name with night-black walls painted in twinkling stars and nebulas that glimmered shifting shades of pinks and blues. Split into halves by a narrow road, the building had a regal sandstone bridge connecting each part. Faeron and Auri's destination was the right section with golden letters above the arched slab entry reading: Arches of the Ages. Hoisting the door open for Auri, Faeron followed her inside.

He found himself in a wide room with a swirling black and white mural painted on its vaulted ceiling far above. Long terraces with dozens of doors wrapped around each floor, and the room was lit by staircases of pure golden light that appeared and disappeared, connecting the different levels. As the stairs came and went, the light in the room kept shifting, giving the space a magical atmosphere.

The ground floor was also lined with doors. Benches filled the open space, and several large monitors in the center displayed upcoming event times and high scores for various games.

"The eighth-hour group tour of Unity era Akai will begin shortly," said a friendly voice over a loudspeaker. "Please secure your magboots and interaction gloves then find your tour guide near the teal door. Again, the group tour of Unity era Akai will begin shortly."

Faeron and Auri went to the rental desk on their right, where a girl about fifteen or sixteen greeted them with a big smile.

"I almost thought you two wouldn't make it," said Sarah brightly. A streak of cobalt cut across her blonde bangs. She had a dozen piercings in one ear and half that on her blue bottom lip. "Last call is in five minutes."

"They've got you working through the concert?" Faeron leaned up against the desk.

"I won't miss much," said Sarah. "There's only two group tours tonight, and Daerian is handling them..." As she said this, she looked over to where a small group of middle aged men and women were gathered around a uniformed tour guide. Faeron recognized the guide from the academy, a ninth year, around Sarah's age, with dark skin, short frizzy hair, and white tattoo sleeves covering both his arms. Catching Sarah's gaze, Daerian smiled and waved at her.

"Sorry, the time," said Sarah, perking up suddenly. "I'll go grab your boots... A nine-and-a-half and an eleven, no, twelve?"

"That's it," said Auri.

Sarah went into a back room and returned a few seconds later with two sets of shoes.

"You've got your own gloves, right?" asked Sarah.

"Indeed," said Faeron, pointing to the bag slung over his shoulder.

"Cool! I take it you'll want to run the new expansion." Sarah made a motion and a console projected above the counter. "You can check the list of new challenges here if you want to select one."

"Wait!" cried Auri. "I don't want to see until I'm in."

"She likes the surprise," said Faeron.

"That's right, silly me." Sarah waved her hand and the console vanished. "What kind of challenges are you looking for then?"

"Action!" said Auri. "Something fast paced."

"Got just the thing," Sarah fidgeted with something behind the desk. "This is going to be *perfect*! Just a couple last things I'm forced to say. As per the city's educational entertainment initiative, you'll earn five rep for each challenge completion and ten for making the leaderboard. Also, there's no extra metal on either of you today, is there?"

"Nope," said Faeron, patting his pockets to be sure.

"Just the hair," said Auri, holding up a few strands of her bronze-plated locks.

"We should have that in the system, but just in case there's been chipping or anything..." Sarah began tinkering behind the desk, and a ball of light popped into the air beside Auri. It scanned her hair then disappeared. "Don't want any accidents in the machines… Anyway! You both know the rules. Go kill it in there."

Faeron grabbed a seat nearby to change his shoes, and Auri joined him. The boots were heavy, thick synthleather with metal plated soles. Faeron reached into his backpack and pulled out a set of sleek gloves, lined in the same metal, with a knob and small display on the back. Once they had their magboots and interaction gloves secured, Faeron went to a cubby near the desk and left his shoes and backpack.

"Ready?" Faeron asked Auri as he fiddled with the knob on the back of his glove, twisting until the color indicator turned purple.

Auri shot him a winning grin. The bronze ends of her dark black hair shone spectacularly in the shifting golden light. "Three… Two… One…"

Faeron and Auri pressed in the knobs on their gloves, and two doors lit up, one purple, one bronze. Sprinting to their colors, they dashed inside. There were no lights in the room, and, as the door shut behind Faeron, he was left in complete darkness.

Heat rushed into the small space, carried on a hot dry breeze. Suddenly, the room wasn't dark anymore, and Faeron was no longer alone. He stood just beside Auri in a desert, atop a tall dune overlooking a riverside fortress. It had tall stone walls, and its hulking wooden gate was shut tight.

"Saldun," whispered Auri excitedly. "Not the capital of course, but that fort is definitely Salduni, second age by the look of it." She had always been a big fan of the desert nation's architecture and designs. Her room was decorated with all sorts of Salduni oddities her father had brought back whenever he passed through the region in his travels.

"Battle's not over yet, prophets guard!" cried a voice from behind them.

An army of a hundred or more men were marching over the dune toward the fortress. They were led by a woman with tattoos where her hair would be. She was clearly human, and yet she was tall as a capillum and nearly three times as wide. She was the biggest, most muscular person Faeron had ever seen, with powerful golden eyes.

Faeron didn't need Auri's help to identify the enormous woman. She was the Warrior Host, Cresh, though her statue atop Cresh Capital Tower did her little justice. Even this illusion of the Warrior Host had a dominating presence. Her only piece of armor was a single shoulder pauldron, which had been smelted around the glassy black Host Stone. Lightly colored vines held the pauldron in place; they wrapped around her torso, wound up her arms, and ran through her fingers.

"Our oldest enemy, Lyle the Deceiver, has kidnapped several young kytra," barked Cresh as she approached Faeron and Auri. "He's holding them in the fortress with a sizable force, armed to the teeth and prepared to die for their scheming master."

"What can we do?" asked Auri excitedly.

"The fortress has a two layered gate, one wooden, one metal," reported Cresh. "That wood won't stand long against my fists, but the metal will take too long to break. I need you to sneak inside and get that rear gate open while I break through the front door."

"But if the gate's closed, how are we supposed to get in?" asked Faeron.

"There's a secret portcullis on the eastern wall," said Cresh, pointing off to the side of the fortress. "Find it and knock five times in quick succession, followed by two slow knocks. Intel says the passage is lightly guarded. Once inside, the gate's mechanism should be nearby."

"Get inside, deal with the guards, open the gate. Got it," said Auri.

"You will need these to reach the gate," said Cresh, motioning to a pair of soldiers holding a large trunk. They lowered the box to the sand and pried open the lid, revealing all sorts of steel weapons. There were swords, spears, axes, hammers, poles, a bow, and many arrows. "Take your pick," said the Warrior Host.

Faeron went to the box, his feet sinking into the hot sand with each step. Rummaging through the weapon case, he picked up a longsword first. Though it was merely an illusion, it felt solid as metal thanks to the gloves. The sword had a nice weight in both hands, but it was too heavy to hold in just one, so Faeron set it in the sand and dug back into the box.

"This is more like it," he whispered as he found a pair of matching metal batons, his go to option for any combat challenge where they were available. They felt natural, like the keeper's sticks he used for bunball. These didn't have the magnetic ends for catching high-speed bunballs, but that was less of an issue in Prophet's Guard.

"Again with the sticks?" said Auri, who was now digging through the box over his shoulder. "I mean, all these options and you pick *those*? One of these days you're gonna learn to fight with a real weapon, and you'll look back with shame."

"I do just fine with my batons, thank you," said Faeron stubbornly. "Besides, they were in the box. That makes them real weapons."

"No," said Auri, heaving hard. "*This* is a real weapon." With both hands she pulled a massive great hammer from the box and threw it over her shoulder. "Now, if you're set on fighting with those… glorified straws, we should get headed out. The kytra aren't gonna save themselves."

Faeron and Auri trekked across the sand to the wall where Cresh said the portcullis would be. It was a hard walk, even though it wasn't far. With each step, Faeron felt as though he were sinking into the floor and the heat was downright oppressive.

The portcullis was easy enough to spot. It looked just like a stone doorway but with no handle or any other way to open it from the outside. Faeron took one of his sticks and rapped it against the wall five times fast. Auri followed with two slow swings from her hammer. Moments later, a guard pushed open the hidden door from the inside. He was about their age, with sandy brown hair peeking out from beneath his open-faced helm. His leather armor covered only his chest, leaving the many tattoos upon his well toned arms fully exposed. He looked from Faeron to Auri, confusion on his brow.

Auri didn't wait for him to piece things together. She charged forward with her hammer in both hands and ran it straight into the guard's chest, sending him sprawling.

"Kokorro!" He gasped, scampering backward as Auri pushed inside with two more overhead swings, smacking the floor just shy of his legs. "Ennet'sammun!"

Faeron followed in and saw they weren't alone. A second guard was pushing down the passage with a twin-pronged lance. He had a gruff grey beard and looked a bit too big around for his tight leather chestpiece.

"En arum Abur," called the newcomer, his seasoned eyes honed on Auri.

"On your right," called Faeron.

Auri swung her hammer defensively, just in time to catch the older guard's lance. Though she wasn't hit, the weight of his blow knocked her back into the wall.

"Abur, kenkel'samman!" yelled the old fighter. He wore no helmet and his thin greying hair tossed about as he wound up a second attack.

Faeron intercepted and knocked aside the old man's thrust. Taking advantage of the surprise on the gruff soldier's face, Faeron got a clean smack against the guardsman's left ear.

"Paga'samman!" cried a voice behind Faeron.

Out of the corner of his eye, Faeron saw a glint of silver. The younger guard was up on his feet, and his sword was descending on Faeron.

Clang! Auri's hammer caught the sword mid-swing.

"Kokorro, anduin'sammun!" yelled the sandy-haired guard commandingly as he brought down a shower of blows with his sword. Auri managed to catch his first two swings, but the third sliced through her hip. A bright red light flooded the room.

"Careful," called Faeron.

"Swap me," Auri shot back. "This one's too fast."

Faeron ducked beneath a sweeping lance blow and spun to face the relentless onslaught of the younger guard, clearly the one in charge. His strikes were fast, but predictable. Deflecting a heavy hit, Faeron countered with a jab to the side.

"Ennem!" howled the guard and held up a steel tower shield, waiting for Faeron's advance. No matter how Faeron swung he couldn't get around the wall of metal. Faking to the left, Faeron lurched right at the last second, but the guard parried the hit away, leaving Faeron momentarily exposed. Regaining his footing, Faeron dared a glance at the fight going on behind him.

Auri was having more luck than Faeron. She swung wildly overhead crashing down on the grizzled knight's lance, never giving him a second's break. With a final sweeping strike she brought her hammer through his defenses, knocking his lance from his hand. He was completely vulnerable, but Auri's overpowered and clumsy swing had left her unbalanced, too. The guard scrambled for his weapon while Auri struggled to right herself.

With a clear shot, Faeron spun around Auri, slamming his metal rod against the gruff man's skull just before he reached his weapon. The larger of the two guards went out cold.

"Kokorro!" howled the younger guard desperately. All of a sudden, the world turned bright red again. Faeron turned back to find the tattooed guard standing over Auri, his sword stabbed through her shoulder.

"Watch it! You left me wide open," shouted Auri as she backed away. "One more of those and I'm out."

"I know," said Faeron, circling their remaining adversary. Parrying a sword strike with one baton, he managed a clean blow to the guard's shoulder with the other. The guard howled as he dropped his shield and swung with all his weight overhead. Crossing his sticks defensively, Faeron caught the attack, locking himself and the guard in a stalemate.

Auri had just enough room for a sweeping uppercut to the man's jaw. His unconscious body flew back and fell slumped against the wall.

Taking a pause to breathe, Faeron tried to take stock his surroundings. There were identical doors on either end of the hall, and he needed a moment to orient himself. "The front gate was this way," he said, leaping over the guard. The small square room beyond had a couple barrels, racks with bows, and a window looking down on Cresh's army. Just beside the window was a large iron lever.

Boom. Boom. Boom.

Auri grabbed the lever while Faeron glanced out at the gate. On the bridge was Cresh, alone. Her fists were encased in massive boulders, which she swung like wrecking balls against the gate, splintered and ready to fall. The army stood a distance back, bows drawn should their captain need the support.

"Since she's knocking so nicely…" said Auri, hoisting the lever.

Outside, the metal gate groaned as it slowly began to rise, just in time for Cresh to smash through the wooden front door.

"Killer," said Faeron.

"And *that's* why she gets her own tower," said Auri, joining him at the window.

Lyle's troops poured out over the bridge where Cresh was waiting. With her boulder fists, she knocked away anyone who came close. Some troops managed to connect a sword swing or stray arrow, but the blows bounced right off Cresh's skin, as if her whole body were made of stone.

"Imagine," said Auri, "that'll be us someday, shaping just like the Hosts… I want to be just like her."

"You're going to need about five-thousand percent more muscle," Faeron chuckled. "But don't worry, you've already got the barbarian look down."

Auri shot him a cold eye and turned her attention back to the Host. "She was more than a warrior, even though that's how everyone remembers her. For every battle Cresh fought, she stopped another ten from ever taking place. She was a diplomat first, and only when words failed would she become—"

"LYLE!" roared Cresh from the bridge below. Faeron watched as she threw aside a throng of soldiers and stormed inside. Suddenly, a bright purple glow cast over the room. The door they had come in through was now filled with swirling violet light.

"Come on," said Auri, trotting off toward the portal, "let's not keep Sarah waiting."

Faeron stepped into the light and found himself back in the Arches of the Ages. There were only a couple people left in the spacious room, most putting their shoes back on or wrapping up at the cubbies. Auri was already in the center of the lobby, scanning the scoreboard for their names.

"There," said Auri, as Faeron joined her. She pointed to a screen in the top left reading: Salduni Combat Challenge. "Second place, not bad."

"Of course, Saitum took the top spot," said Faeron, seeing the lone name above theirs. She had more than double their score.

"You know," said Auri with a mischievous smile, "you'd think with her as your teacher, you'd start doing better eventually."

"Hey, I didn't take any hits," shrugged Faeron. "So, what's next? Try to find Quinn out at the concert?"

"Actually," said Auri, "there's something I need to talk to you about. It's important."

"Balcony talk?" asked Faeron and Auri nodded. Balcony talks were a cornerstone of their friendship, code for a conversation that simply couldn't wait.

They went to the cubbies to collect their things, dropped their boots off at the desk, and caught a tram at the same corner where they'd arrived.

Inside the tram, Faeron watched a holographic city map projected above the central railing. A dot representing their tram raced toward the Twinfire Towers in the East. Both residential towers were covered in rows of crescent balconies and were connected by a walking bridge near the top. Standing atop the bridge was the largest of all the city's statues, Glavius Adaeus. His hands were held open above the towers, with a flame in each palm, one crimson, one violet. The tram's marker moved up the violet tower, stopping at the sixty-second floor. This time, the tram's wall slid open, allowing them to walk right out.

The common area of the sixty-second floor was a carpeted ring, with a hollow center looking down on the lobby dozens of floors below. A bronze railing ran all the way around the hole, and comfortable chairs were scattered in groups of three and four all around the ring.

Tonight, the commons was quiet but for Merreum Linhall, their next door neighbor, singing to her young daughter.

"Hifyd, Hikel,
Hipae, Hyend,
Days we work and then we sleep,
Lofyd, Lokel,
Lopae, Lowend,
Days we rest and play and feast"

As Faeron and Auri walked past, she looked up from her song and waved warmly. "Hello dears," she said. "Say hi to Faeron and Auri, Molly."

"Hi Faern, hi O'Ree" said the toddler, running out to greet them.

"Hello Miss Molly!" said Auri, dropping to one knee and putting her arms out to hug the girl.

"You kids not down at the Bash tonight?" asked Merreum, her straight blonde hair tied back in a bun.

"Other plans, I'm afraid," said Auri, playing hand games with Molly.

"Ooh, Kytra stuff I'd imagine," said their neighbor excitedly. "You know, Molly is almost old enough to join the youth group. Ever since I told her you help out around there, she hasn't stopped pestering me. 'Momma can I go now? Momma am I big now?'"

"Is that true?" asked Auri fondly, and the girl gave a big nod.

"Alright now, Molly," said Merreum, "you let Faeron and Auri be about their business. It's just about bedtime anyway."

"No no! Eee!" protested Molly, hugging Auri tight.

"Go on, Miss Molly," said Auri sweetly. "You know, big girls listen to their mommy when it's bedtime."

Molly's face lit up bright, "I'm big! I can go to yoosh groop!" Releasing Auri, the little girl ran back to her mother.

"Goodnight kids," called Merreum.

"Goodnight," said Faeron and Auri both.

The pair continued on to door 6282, and Faeron pressed his hand to a small square panel, unlocking the door. The apartment that Faeron and Auri shared was roomy but sparsely filled. The front door led into a large foyer, with a full kitchen in the corner and a sliding glass door on the far wall, exiting to a wide balcony. The only furnishings in the open space were a large round dining table, some padded armchairs, and cool trinkets Auri's dad had brought them from the other cities.

Faeron's room was the last door on the left. He went straight inside and tore off his street clothes. His legs breathed a sigh of relief as he freed them from his tight black pants and pulled on a pair of comfortable shorts. Unlike their tidy shared space, Faeron's room was a mess of clothes strewn across the floor and old homework piled upon his desk. One wall was a window and the other three were covered in Liquid Fauna band posters and shelves of Deity figurines. As soon as he had changed, Faeron went out to the balcony. Auri was already there.

She sat in a cozy reclining chair, hunched over meddling with an ornate bronze censer. She loaded the hanging burner with ground Nylkshave and set it alight. The censer rocked lazily, releasing plumes of sweetly scented smoke into the air.

Faeron leaned out over the balcony, listening to the echoes of the concert below. Loem Park looked like a hive of ants swarming the amphitheater, as if the stage were a sandwich dropped in the grass. The park spread from the center of the city all the way to the Nylk Gate on the west wall, the only way in or out of Eredith. From his balcony, Faeron could see all six towers along the city's massive walls. Like the Roethram Academy Tower, the others were each topped with a wondrous statue: Cresh the Warrior Host with her fists of stone, Ibanu the Healer who knelt in prayer each time a resident passed away, and Sombara whose crops changed with the seasons. They were many of the greatest Hosts ever to serve the Patronage.

"So," said Fearon, reclining into a chair beside Auri, "what is it you wanted to tell me?"

Auri sighed, and her eyes saddened. "You have to promise not to tell anyone, absolutely *nobody*."

"Of course," said Faeron as the floral scent of Nylkshave filled his lungs and tingled his mind.

"I cheated," admitted Auri sourly.

"In Prophet's Guard?" asked Faeron, popping up in his seat a bit.

"No, in my eval," said Auri. "When I was doing my deep meditations, I could only hold it a couple seconds before…" she trailed off as if she were going to finish her sentence but suddenly changed her mind. "Well, I can still only hold it for a second without Nylkshave, I've told you."

"So how did you cheat?" asked Faeron.

"I was struggling to hold the meditation even before Mathas told me to open my eyes," said Auri. "When he did, I panicked. I didn't want to get held back, so I tried to mimic that amazed look you always get when doing the waking meditation. Mathas acted like he couldn't tell, but I think he could."

"If he knew you were pretending then why did he pass you?" asked Faeron, watching Auri through smoke.

"I don't know," admitted Auri. "But I need your help. The meditations have always come naturally to you. Will you practice with me, outside of class? If I can't master the waking meditation before we start shaping, Mathas will pick up on it quickly. He'll send me back to meditations with Quinn. I can't do that, Faeron."

"We'll figure it out," said Faeron. "I'll help anyway I can, I promise. No one's giving up on you."

"You mean it?" asked Auri hopefully.

"Of course," said Faeron. "We'll practice every night, and if you need anything at all, just ask."

"Good," smiled Auri. "Then let's start right now."

Faeron laid back in his seat and closed his eyes, letting the faint music fill his mind. It didn't take long for the Nylkshave to do its job, and the pearlescent light of Peridom pulsed through his head in time with the music. Faeron followed the current through a mossy cave in a streak of emerald green, past a brilliant star in a gleam of royal purple. He followed the current until his connection to the light was suddenly broken.

"Damnit!" yelled Auri, springing up from her seat. "I forgot the youth group's play was tonight. I need to be down at Erkwright Theater in... Serris, what time is it?"

A ball of light popped onto their balcony. "It's ten minutes to nine," said Serris, matter of factly.

"Ten minutes to get down there," said Auri.

"The youth group's putting on a play?" asked Faeron, skeptical of the acting caliber.

"For the younger students who can't attend the Concert," said Auri. "It's all about how Glavius survived the purging of the Old Scholars. I promised them I'd come watch. You in?"

"Nah, you know how they get when I come around," said Faeron. "They all treat me so weird, like I'm Glavius reborn."

"Because, to them, that's exactly what you are," said Auri. "Eamon hasn't performed a miracle since the city was built, and, now, the Hoststone is shattered. The last trace of it lives on in your dreams. You aren't just any Kytra, Faeron. Like it or not, it's a safe bet that you'll be Host one day, the Host that cures the world."

"Stop it, I'm no Host-to-be," said Faeron. "I want to save the world, just as much as you do, but if my dreams really held those answers, then why did my mom leave? As far as I know, my dreams have nothing to do with the plague. Glavius has never spoken to me, never guided me. I'm just another kytra, learning to shape because I want answers about my mom. Once I know she's safe, we can figure out how to fix this world together."

"Well then," said Auri, rising from her chair. "I see you've made up your mind. If I don't see you before bed, tell Jakob I said hello."

"Would if I could."

After Auri left, Faeron stayed out on the balcony a good while longer, continuing his meditations. Whether it was ten minutes or an hour, he couldn't say, as the light of peridom danced against his closed eyelids and twisted through his thoughts.

Faeron dwelt mostly on the upcoming semester. For the first time in a long time he was excited about starting classes. Not because of any academy courses like mathematics, global politics, or patronage history, but it was his classes with Mathas that had him itching to learn.

Faeron opened his eyes. Rising from his chair, he went to the balcony's edge, looking out over the city of Eredith. A light breeze rustled his messy hair as he watched the lights from the concert in the park. Every cloud and star in the city's sky, every rainstorm and snowfall, sunny or cloudy day was meant to emulate the world outside the walls, at least the world before the plague. There was something just a touch off about it though; the breeze, for example, felt correct as it brushed a long lock of dark hair down over Faeron's eyes, but it was missing the smell, the salt near the ocean, the fresh cut grass in Newsun. That was the sort of thing only Jakob got to experience, but that could change soon enough.

For the first time in centuries, if not millenia, there were more known kytra than Faeron could count on one hand. If just half of his classmates could learn to shape, even if they were only a fraction as powerful as the great hosts on the towers, what chance would the plague stand? Learning to shape meant everything to Faeron. Learning to shape was how he would conquer his dreams. Learning to shape was how he would find his mother. Learning to shape was how the kytra of Eredith would reclaim their world.

Faeron laughed at the thought; it sounded like something Auri would say, only she'd try to convince him that it would all end in him becoming the Host, like his father.

"Serris," said Faeron, tapping a finger against his balcony railing in time with the muddled beat of the music.

Serris popped into the air just beyond the balcony. "How can I help?" asked Serris.

"Is dad free?" asked Faeron. "I'd like to tell him about today."

"Your timing is very good, I think the Korvan ambassador just left his office," reported Serris. "One moment please." For several seconds, Serris pulsed between blue and white. "Okay," she said suddenly. "Connecting you now."

The index flew to an open spot of balcony near Faeron, and then it began to morph. It grew tall, shaping itself into a perfect resemblance of Faeron's father. Eamon stood, leaning against the balcony just beside Faeron. He had more wrinkles around his golden eyes these days, and his hair was turning grey, except for the top of his crown, which seemed insistent on balding instead.

"Surprise, surprise," said Eamon cheerfully. "How'd the eval go?"

"That's actually why I called," said Faeron with pride. "Mathas is going to reopen the workshop for us. We're going to start shaping this semester."

"Hey, that's awesome," said Eamon, beaming brightly at his son. "I'm proud of you. You've worked hard for this... And you know what?"

"What?" asked Faeron.

"This'll make you, officially, a better kytra than me. For all I know about these fancy artifacts in my office, I can't do a thing with them."

"Well, last time I tried it didn't go so hot," said Faeron, his cheeks feeling hot from the praise.

"That's why you've got Mathas," said Eamon. "I wouldn't be surprised if a year from now you were curing the plague like Host Ibanu."

"Or finding mom," said Faeron, more seriously. His dad met his eyes with sympathy.

"Faeron," said Eamon. "You know what happened to her isn't on you—" Eamon turned, suddenly attentive to something behind him. "Yes, just one moment, ambassador." He turned back to

Faeron. "Hey bud, I have to take care of something real quick. I'll talk to you tomorrow, alright?"

"Okay," said Faeron. "Night, Dad."

"Love you."

Eamon disappeared, leaving Fearon alone on the balcony once more. It was dark now, but the night was still young. The concert would go on for another couple hours, and Auri wouldn't be back until close to then. Despite the early hour, Faeron was properly exhausted. He twisted a vial on the brass censer, suffocating the embers, then headed inside to get ready for bed.

Once in his pajamas, Faeron climbed into bed and closed his eyes. The effect of the Nylkshave had nearly worn off now, leaving Faeron's mind numb and tired. Some nights, sleep was an uphill battle, but, tonight, the light of peridom took hold of Faeron quickly, and his body and mind melted away like butter in the warmth of his sheets.

CHAPTER THREE

WRITER'S BLOCK

Thump… Thump-Thump Thump Thump-Thump-Thump

Jakob stirred in his chair, slumped over his polished wooden writing desk. His head was buried in his arms, and, blinking awake, he saw rays of early-evening sunlight filtering through the white cloth curtains of his bedroom. As Jakob's room was on the ground floor in a well-frequented art district, shadows wandered back and forth past his window.

Thump-Thump-Thump-Thump

Through the thin ceiling came the unmistakable sound of Jakob's sister, Sylvia, stomping around the kitchen of their three-story townhouse.

Thump-Thump-Thump Thump Thump-Thump

The steps retreated out of the kitchen into the index room next door.

"Proto…" mumbled Jakob, sitting back in his padded Orthoposture chair with a stretch. His neck was stiff and he had to turn his whole body to face the lens-shaped device on the corner of his desk. A soft turquoise light flickered on beneath the glass.

"Look who's finally awake," came Proto's charming voice from within the device.

"Yeah, yeah," said Jakob. "What's it then, two… three?"

"*Six* if you'll believe it," said Proto cheerfully.

"Oh man," groaned Jakob, rubbing his eyes until his messy desk came into focus. It was strewn with papers covered in loosely organized notes and scrawled illustrations. "Where did I leave off?"

"You were revising a sentence on page eight," said Proto. "You conked out just after your seventy-first rewrite of the passage."

"Page eight?" asked Jakob. "Why was I back on page eight?" Everything after four in the morning was a bit of a blur.

"What do you mean *back* on page eight?" asked Proto. "That's all you've got. You only wrote two scenes last night."

Jakob lay back in his chair, defeated.

"Also, a couple calls came in earlier," said Proto. "Nothing urgent enough to wake you. They left messages though."

"Go ahead," said Jakob.

"First, it was your parents, who asked me to remind you that your Lowend night calls aren't optional. You've missed two weeks in a row now. They also said you should try to be a bit more like your sister."

"I'm *sure* those were their exact words," said Jakob sarcastically, though he did feel bad and planned to give his parents a call after a much-needed shower.

"I'm just a bunch of zeros and ones," said Proto, feigning offense, "I couldn't lie if I wanted to."

"Seem to be doing a fine job of it right now," countered Jakob.

"In any case, the other call was from your agent," reported Proto. "She wanted to make sure you knew your Induction into the Vault of the Great Ri'Kallan Library is this Hypae afternoon. You'll need to arrive by noon."

"Is it really almost the fifty-sixth of Highsun?" asked Jakob in disbelief. "I've been working on this new book since the cycle turned… eight pages in fifty-six days… that's a new low."

"Hey, you don't break a personal record every day," pointed out Proto. "Celebrate the little wins, right?"

Jakob didn't feel like celebrating. In fact, he was suddenly feeling quite nauseous.

Despite his anxiety at his lack of progress, Jakob didn't write any more that evening. Oftentimes when Jakob was stuck in his writing, looking to other stories could get his creative juices flowing, so he spent the rest of the night with his sister in their index room watching episodes of The Lautice Queen. Sylvia was shorter than Jakob, built wide with sandy blonde hair. She sat with her knees up on the couch, but when she saw Jakob come in, she adjusted upright to make room for her brother.

The index room was empty besides the couch and a pair of identical side tables on either end. Since Sylvia's show was paused, the circular room was plain white. Jakob managed to get comfortable as Sylvia told her index to resume the show. The projector flickered on and the room transformed into the Lautice Queen's magical forest kingdom of Lafalia. Fantastical battles, heated diplomatic negotiations, and heartfelt moments between characters played out for hours all around Jakob's turquoise sofa.

That night, Jakob dreamt of flying jellyfish people and impossible forest cities, but when he woke up and sat down to write, the words wouldn't come.

Jakob spent the whole day pacing around his room. Once in a while, an idea would bloom. He'd run to his desk, grab his sleek silver and gold pen, and start to scrawl down notes, only to realize something conflicted with a paragraph on page four. This would send him back in a spiral of editing, which eventually led to a cry of frustration and Jakob dumping the entire draft into the trash bin beside his desk. That evening, Jakob finally ventured from his bedroom, starving and in search of food.

Sylvia was already in the kitchen upstairs cooking up a vegetable curry. As soon as Jakob got to the top of the steps, Sylvia turned with her nose scrunched up. "How can I smell you over the curry? Shower, then you get food."

Jakob went to bed full but defeated. Tomorrow would be his induction into the Vault, and with it would come an hour of Q&A with his fans. No doubt they'd be expecting an update on book three in his Inspector Aurilius mystery saga, but he didn't have so much as a bone to throw them. To Jakob, nothing was scarier than a mob of disappointed fans, and a very violent and angry mob chased him through his dreams all night.

"Wakey, wakey," came Proto's voice nice and early the next morning.

Jakob turned in his sheets and buried his face beneath the covers, figuring if he didn't look at the light beaming through the windows it couldn't possibly be morning yet.

"You don't want to play this game with me," said Proto from his desk. "Shall I load up some audio samples from Orn mating seasons?"

"Alright, you win," said Jakob, throwing off the covers and sitting at the edge of his bed. Even at thirty, mornings had never gotten any easier, and his habits of typing away well past midnight certainly didn't help his sleep schedule. "What's the plan today?"

"You've got a couple hours still until you need to be at the station," said Proto. "I'd suggest preparing some words before you go. Oh, and Sylvia picked up your suit from the cleaners on her way back from classes yesterday, such a saint. It's up on the kitchen counter now."

Jakob spent the next two hours getting himself cleaned up and jotting down some talking points on a notecard. Most people just used their index for note-taking, but Jakob liked the feel of paper in his hands. Besides, it gave him an excuse to use his fancy pen, a birthday present from his parents that had gotten much more use than he could have ever guessed at the time. That was before he dedicated himself to writing, back in academy when he still wanted to develop artificial intelligence for a living. Proto was all that had come from that particular dream of his.

An hour before noon, Jakob stood in front of the dresser-top mirror, trying to figure out if his stomach was growing larger or if his suit had shrunk at the cleaners. His face was narrow, and dark bags were settling into the valleys beneath his eyes, a product of exhaustion, he told himself, not age.

"Come on," said Proto, "You'll be late if you don't get moving."

Jakob took the lens from his desk and fixed it to a clasp on the left breast of his suit. "Okay," said Jakob, "go ahead and call the alca."

The short walk from his townhouse to the neighborhood station took him down a pleasant cobblestone street. Square white buildings housed shops of vibrant canvases, galleries of homemade furnishing, painting supply stores, and dozens of cookie-cutter storefronts stocked with touristy knick-knacks.

A network of rails ran between the upper floors of the buildings and alca trams sped along them. Some rode on top of the tracks, others hung from the bottom or the sides. There were big freight alcas and small personal cabs, fancy colored sports vehicles, and large boxy public shuttles.

Regardless of size or shape, all the alcas had three main parts. There was the cabin, where passangers and other cargo went, it was always right-side up regardless of whether the alca was riding above or below the tracks. Then, there were two spinning metal magspheres that connected the cabin to the track, one at the front of the alca, one at the back.

The station was an exceptionally long platform with dozens of alcas lining the rails on either side. Jakob climbed the steps and walked down the platform, past a family struggling to get their stubborn toddler into a plain looking vehicle with weather-stained white paint. Jakob's alca, a 3978 Pursuer model (which he saved for years to buy and of which he was immensely proud), was waiting near the end on the right side of the platform. It was a sleek silver vehicle, and the magspheres at the front and back of the tram were glowing Jakob's favorite color, a soft sea-foam green. Inside, one-way windows lined the walls, roof, and floor. The view from the Pursuer's cabin was half the reason Jakob loved this model so much.

The Pursuer's side slid open and Jakob boarded, taking a seat on a bench running the length of the far wall.

"Alright, Proto, you're up," said Jakob.

"Next stop, the Great Ri'Kallan Library," announced Proto, his voice filling the entire vehicle. "Any preference on tunes?"

"Something fast," said Jakob.

"Dance of Deathtraps it is."

The eerie melody of a grand organ filled the alca as it crept out of the sparsely populated station. A hollow synthetic harmony added its voice to the organ and the tram picked up speed, swiftly rising to the network of rails between the buildings. Through the glass bottom floor, Jakob could see the many colorful personalities of the art district going about their lives. He passed over an intersection where several girls were working on a large street mural that hadn't yet taken shape, while a woman on her balcony played violin for colorful caged birds. As he rode, Jakob tapped his foot in time with the driving beat.

The alca rounded a bend, giving Jakob a view of the ocean out the right-side window. It was a bright cloudless morning, and the sun glinted off the slow churning waves of the bay. Small sail-skiffs skipped across the crystal clear waters while, further out, large private ships drifted lazily in the Highsun warmth. Jakob was always a touch envious as he watched them floating free of care. North Ri'Kalla was the city of artists and aristocrats, though the two groups had little overlap.

"Library's dock is just up ahead," said Proto over the music.

The library looked like an enormous mansion at the end of the street. It was ten stories tall with a shimmering sapphire blue rooftop, and at each corner was a winged grothgoyle statue, snarling with long protruding fangs. A pair of tall arching windows gilded in gold dominated the building's frost-white front face with crescent balconies filling the gap between them.

There were two entrances to the library, a set of carved blue and gold doors at street level and a wide terrace on the fifth floor. A man in a neatly ironed blue and gold button-up was waiting for Jakob as the alca pulled up to the terrace.

"Welcome, Mr. Rite," said the man in a booming voice. He had thin grey hair, bushy brows over wrinkled eyes, and a short beard with streaks of black near the chin. "My name is Luise Ventroff, Curator of the Great Ri'Kallan Library."

Jakob left his alca and met the man with a handshake as his silver 3978 Pursuer drove off back to storage.

"Your agent said you're familiar with our library?" asked the man, ushering Jakob through a door leading inside.

They were on the fifth-floor landing of an enormous open chamber. The ceiling was painted with hundreds of figures, from a winged man playing the flute, to a gruff commander comforting his dying soldier, to a pair of lovers kissing in a boat at sea. The walls were a series of reading balconies full of people in cozy seats, reading from softly glowing pages.

"I used to visit all the time when I first moved here," said Jakob, noticing strange new figures each time he gazed at the ceiling. It had been three years since his first book became popular enough for Jakob to afford a townhome in the city and almost a year since he last came here for a read. In fact, ever since the release of his last novel, Jakob had hardly set foot outside his residence except for promotional events like this.

"It's a pleasure to have you back," said Luise. "I would assume you know all about our Vault then?"

"Just about the only place left to get your hands on print literature," said Jakob. He knew the only way to gain access to the Vault was to have a work of your own inducted, a goal he'd set for himself the day he started writing. That much he was giddy for, a chance to read the classics in hardback, to feel their endings looming closer with each turn of the page, and the musty smell… it simply couldn't be replaced.

"Indeed, we take great pride in our collection. Many of the novels in our vault have only the one print," said Luise. "When your agent told us of your insistence on handwritten paper drafts, we couldn't wait to add your works to the shelves. Though, we hadn't anticipated just how many consider your books worthy of induction."

He pointed down from the landing overlook to the crowded lobby below where hundreds of people were packed in front of a stage, many wearing the iconic blue and black cape of Inspector Aurilius. Jakob's heart skipped a beat as he saw the sheer number of fans he would disappoint with his lack of an update.

In the very center of the lobby was the Vault, an enormous hole plunging several dozen floors into a lightless underground pit. Its walls were ringed in shelves of printed books, but as far as Jakob could tell, there was no way anyone could reach them.

"There's a bit of time before we take the stage," said Luise. "Would you care for a tour of the Vault?"

"Absolutely," said Jakob excitedly. He didn't think he'd get to see the Vault until after the ceremony, and as disastrous as he expected Q&A to go, he wouldn't be surprised if they took back their key before he ever got a chance to see it.

"Right this way."

Luise guided Jakob down six crisscrossing flights of stairs to a basement hallway with an impressive door at the end. Solid metal floor to ceiling, the Vault's entry looked like something straight out of a casino or a secret government laboratory from one of his mysteries. The door had an enormous crank handle in the center with a small pentagon hole below it.

"The key," said Luise. Reaching into his pocket, he pulled out a black pentagon coin. It was made of stone and had something inscribed that Jakob couldn't quite make out. Luise entered the coin into the slot in the door. It fit perfectly. With some effort, Luise turned the great crank three full rotations. There was a click, and the key plopped out of the door into Luise's waiting palm.

"And that's all there is to it," said Luise, pulling open the weighty Vault door. It was nearly a foot thick with six massive retracted bolts along the edge.

The room inside was warmly lit. A blue carpet patterned with silver stars spanned the length of the hall, and beside every modern light fixture was an unlit candelabra.

"Excuse me, Curator," said Jakob.

"Just Luise," he insisted.

"Sorry, Luise," said Jakob. "Why are there candles if you already have lights?"

"The world is fragile," said Luise. "This Vault is built to survive any fate, including a complete loss of power. The stairs, for example," said Luise, pointing to the end of the hall where the carpet cut left down a staircase. At the top of the steps was a white lattice elevator door. "We have the luxury of this lift, but should technology fail our descendants, the Vault is still accessible."

At their approach, the lattice lift door folded to the left. They boarded the small elevator and the lift began to descend. It didn't take them long to reach the bottom. The doors opened to a cozy room with the same silver star carpeting and warm light that was perfect for reading. There were sturdy chairs and desks lined up by the wall and a stack of sitting cushions in one corner.

Luise crossed the reading room to another door at the back. Opening a small cupboard on the wall beside the door, he retrieved an electric lamp and turned the switch at the bottom. Bright light flooded the room. "Don't worry, there are oil lamps and matches as well, should the worst come to pass," he said, pulling open the door. "Welcome to the Vault, Mr. Rite."

The Vault seemed even bigger from the bottom. Jakob could see the lobby far overhead illuminating the uppermost stacks of books. Down here, he had only the lamplight casting a wide beam across the tiled floor. Jakob couldn't make out any of the hundreds of books lining the shelves, but he could see a strange-looking lift near the wall. Shaped like a wooden box with high railings and a small door at the front, it was only just big enough for the two of them. Luise made straight for the device.

There was a wooden pedestal in the middle of the platform with several knobs and cranks as well as a wide cubby in the front. Luise fixed the lamp to a tall arched post overhanging the pedestal and reached into a cubby, sliding out a massive tome.

"Let's see…" Luise mumbled to himself as he flipped through the pages. "Eighteen… A… F… R…" Luise turned the dials on the podium, then slid the tome and drawer back into the cubby. "The directory is organized by author's last name. Simply enter the corresponding level number and three-digit book code, then turn the crank."

They rose slowly to the eighteenth set of stacks, stopping in front a colorful assortment of spines. Jakob recognized a few of them; there was Susaya Rathpinka's Gutterrot trilogy, Roveo Remvero's thousand-year-old epic, the Endeavor of Love, and even…

"Here we are, Investigator Aurilius, books one and two," said Luise, pulling the first book from the shelf and handing it to Jakob. "Beautiful covers on these, did you design them yourself?"

Jakob turned the book over in his hands. It had taken more work than he'd have thought possible to have these printed, in the end he could only get five, and even then, they cost a small fortune. "The broad idea was mine, but my designer deserves the credit," said Jakob, looking at the plain cover with the Family Crest of Aurilius alone in the center. There was no text on the front while the back had a short description:

Aurilius' curse is branded across his palm so that he'll never forget. Invisibility is his gift, age is its cost. For each minute he spends unseen, an hour is cut from his life. When a serial killer has evaded every attempt by the police, Aurilius will be forced to decide; how much of his life is he willing to give for the truth?

Returning the book to the shelf, Luise changed the dials and the lift descended.

"It's nearly time for the Ceremony," said Luise as they stepped off the platform. "If you'll follow me."

Jakob had a pleasant conversation with Luise about proper paper preservatives as they returned through the reading room to the main elevator and rode back up to the entry of the vault. There was a similar crank on this side of the wall, but it didn't require a key to leave.

Climbing back to the ground floor, Luis guided Jakob down a narrow hallway to a waiting area behind the stage.

"You should be able to hear the proceedings from here." Luise walked him to a set of black curtains along the wall. Through the gaps in the cloth, Jakob could make out the end of the stage and the scores of people waiting beyond. "Just listen for the cue. It won't be subtle!" He patted Jakob's arm supportingly then stepped through the curtains.

Several moments later, Jakob heard Luise addressing the crowd.

"Good afternoon, everybody," he said, his voice cast over the speakers, loud enough for the crowd to hear but not so loud as to disturb the readers on the upper floor. "It's been nearly a year now since our last induction and, I must say, the dedication of readers like yourself never fails to impress me. In fact, I think this may be our largest turnout in all my years as curator here."

The crowd cheered, while, in the back room, Jakob stood and began to pace.

"I do have one request before we begin," said Luise pleasantly. "If you would all be so kind as to refrain from clapping or shouting during our ceremony, simply snapping instead will show your enthusiasm without disrupting our other patrons. Go on, give it a shot."

Jakob heard hundreds of soft snaps through the curtains. He pulled his notecards from his pocket, giving them a last glance over as he paced.

"Wonderful," said Luise, "well, I know you haven't traveled all this way to listen to me drone on and on. It is my great pleasure to introduce the brilliant and creative Mr. Jakob Rite."

Jakob took a deep breath. He always had pre-show jitters, but it was the worst for Q&A. Still, he told himself, his second book had only just dropped at the end of last year. He figured they couldn't be *too* hungry for more just yet. Knowing he couldn't wait any longer, Jakob stepped through the curtain to a storm of snaps.

The ceremony felt like a blur. Introductions were made, snaps were snapped, and Jakob read a popular passage where Investigator Aurilius interrogated the peg-legged damsel. When it finally came time for Jakob to receive his key, he and Luise were joined on stage by another librarian. She was younger and much shorter than Luise. Her black bun was held in place by a pair of crimson-gold hair sticks and she wore thick rectangular glasses. In her hands was a small square frame.

"And now," announced Luise in a somber voice, "the moment we all came here to see." He took the frame from the librarian who bowed and scuttled off the stage. "Each key is crafted by hand. The front is as unique as its recipient, in this case, bearing the Family Crest of Aurilius."

Jakob could see the pentagon-shaped coin in the frame, set on a sapphire-blue velvet backdrop.

"The back of each key," continued Luise, "bears the Vault's thousand-line insignia, a labyrinth of markings that takes our most talented carvers over a month to craft. There are much simpler ways to make a key, of course, but as our inductees well know, there is value in doing things by hand. Jakob Rite has long been outspoken in support of printed text and has garnered notoriety for his classical approach to note-keeping. It is therefore my honor to present you, Jakob, with this key to our Great Ri'Kallan Vault. Let it be a symbol of your dedication, and may the knowledge stored within the Vault serve to fuel your creative vision in the years to come."

As Luise handed Jakob the framed key, the crowd snapped wildly, one person even letting out a "whoop" which was swiftly shushed.

"I'm honored," said Jakob, examining the flawless carving of the Aurilius House Sigil on the front of the stone pentagon coin. "Done by hand… it's truly incredible." He looked over the crowd of faces, all staring at him expectantly, and a speech seemed inevitable. "I didn't always write," he said to his fans. "I've always enjoyed a good read, but I'd never thought of telling my own stories. In fact, for the longest time I studied AI development. Go on, Proto, say hello."

"Cheers, everyone," said Proto brightly, and he was lauded in snaps.

"I made it through three full years of university before things changed," said Jakob, "and all because of a silly historian's fair if you'll believe it. My dad absolutely ate up that kind of thing. There was this old fashioned house on display, no index room or alca rails. They had a fireplace with some cozy chairs, and shockingly, some old print books. I must have spent half the day there reading by the fire."

He had the crowd's attention. There hadn't been so much as a peep as they devoured his every word.

"My dad figured I'd left early," continued Jakob. "The old cabin was the last place he thought to check. When he did find me, doing my best to understand some Osayan fairytale, I told him I'd made up my mind… I was going to write a story and get it printed, that way people could read like this again. We both thought it was a good joke and had a laugh. And for a while, it was a joke, back and forth between us until my next birthday, he buys me this." Jakob pulled his silver and gold pen from his pocket. "Turns out Carava, an arts company some of you might recognize, still produces one line of writing pen, the last of its kind anywhere. I'm sure you all know the story from there, half a decade of worldbuilding, drawers of loosely organized notes, and finally me locking myself up for eight weeks in Newsun to write the first Inspector Aurilius in its entirety."

At the mention of his novel, the crowd snapped again.

"I learned about the Vault early on while writing the first book," said Jakob. "It was a huge driving factor, and now…" he held up the frame for them to see. "Today, it's a reality."

Snap snap snap snap snap snap snap

"Simply wonderful," said Luise, snapping, "a tale worthy of these halls by its own merit. It's inspiring to see you living out your dreams on and off the page. But as we've each had a turn, I think it's about time we hear from our friends in the audience, wouldn't you?"

"Yeah," said Jakob, swallowing hard. From their faces he was nailing it so far. He had no reason to worry, still, his heart was pounding fast.

"Alright then, who wants to ask a question?" said Luise. A hundred arms shot up in the crowd. "Let's start with… hmm… yes, you!" A ball of blue light popped into the air where Luise pointed, just beside a weighty man with long thin hair. He wore a blue and black striped Investigator Aurilius cape and even had a replica monocle from the beginning of the second book. "Go ahead and speak into the index then."

"Hello. My, uh, my n-name is Frederick."

"Hi, Frederick," said Jakob kindly. "What's your question?"

"I-in Aurilius and a Tangible Chance, the cyclical writing pattern is, uh, reminiscent of Maryll Calibrae's triple hoop narrative structure. Was, uh, but in your adoption you sometimes don't fit the criteria for her post-climactic tension release."

Jakob waited for a question to come, but after several moments of silence, he realized the man was done speaking. In truth, he didn't know what almost anything that Frederick had said meant.

"I've adopted a lot from many different authors," said Jakob, trying his best to get as close to an answer as he dared without sounding entirely ignorant. "Sometimes when I'm writing I'll look at how other authors solve a specific problem or introduce a new concept. It helps grow my toolbox, but I would say that I don't draw from just one style, so that may be what you've noticed."

The man nodded, looking satisfied with the answer.

"You want to pick next?" asked Luise.

"Sure," said Jakob. This was going well. "How about you?" he said, pointing to a girl several rows back with her hand raised high. She had bright pink hair and makeup. An index appeared in the air just beside her.

"Hi, I'm Sussia Longcloak, longtime reader," she said. "I don't know how aware you are of the industry at large, but after E.L. Coleman's leak of her entire unedited manuscript, many authors have considered moving to print for security reasons. As a print writer for principle reasons, does it bother you to have people who once bashed handwritten note-keeping flock to print so suddenly?"

"I don't think so," said Jakob. The Coleman leak had been disastrous, so he didn't blame anyone for taking precautions. "Leaks aren't an issue I've ever been too concerned with in my work. Can that be attributed to the fact that my writing is off the index network? Probably, yeah. I do think that's reason enough for anyone to try print."

The woman looked skeptical by his response but didn't reply.

"Okay, how about… you," said Jakob, pointing to a younger boy, about fifteen or so.

"Daerily Stellcreek," he piped excitedly. "The second Inspector Aurilius novel came out two years after the first. Can we expect the same from the third book?"

Jakob's insides twisted up. "Ahem," he coughed a little. "Maybe? The best I've got is maybe. It'll be done when it's done. I can tell you that."

"But if not this year, next, right?" asked the boy, sounding a bit disappointed.

"I can only promise it'll be done when it's done."

Over the next forty minutes, Jakob answered all number of questions. There were simple ones like, "Who was your favorite character?" Others were more complex, asking about the relation-ships of different societies and the deeper lore of his world. More than anything else though, people continued to press him about his progress on the third book, asking questions every which way to try and get a smidgeon of information, but Jakob had nothing to give them.

When the Q&A came to a close, the crowd seemed a touch less enthused, but overall still in high spirits. Jakob, however, was exhausted. He went backstage to catch his breath and was joined shortly after by Luise.

"Well done," said the curator.

"They're not happy I skirted the release date questions," said Jakob.

"You've already accomplished many incredible things in your short time on this planet, but making everyone happy all the time is a lofty goal, even for you."

"Either way, is there a way out where I won't be bombarded?" asked Jakob. "I'd imagine the alca landing is just as packed as the lobby by now."

"Undoubtedly," Luise smiled knowingly, almost as if he were expecting Jakob to ask. "Just this way, unless you'd like a moment's rest first?"

"No, no," said Jakob. "I'd better be off anyway. Lots of writing to do."

Luise led Jakob down another small hallway, away from the lobby, toward the very rear of the great library. Coming to a set of double doors, he said, "A rear exit, for just this occasion."

"Convenient," said Jakob.

Luise offered him one last handshake as they stood in the doorway. "Just outside is a wide lawn. The station is just on the other side. It's usually calm."

Jakob shook the curator's hand and said his goodbye. As soon as he pushed open the double doors he was greeted with a wall of heat. A humid, salty breeze did little to cool the beating sun. The grassy expanse behind the library was full of people laying out, having picnics, or playing games. To the right was the oceanfront, several docks jutting out into the crystal blue waters. There were little shops set up all along the boardwalk, and Jakob could just make out the scents of fried foods over the salt of the sea. It was enough to make his stomach rumble.

Deciding a snack on the way home couldn't hurt, Jakob made for the waterfront. He passed a young couple giggling from up in the branches of a tree and a group of university students who'd set up makeshift goal posts to play handball, a simpler version of bunball without the fancy masks or rods.

Near the edge of the park, where the grass met the white stone oceanfront, a girl was dancing. She looked in her late teens, twenty at the oldest. Her hair was a few shades darker than her mocha brown skin and it flew wildly in the wind as she pranced about the open lawn.

Her dance was unlike anything Jakob had ever seen. She leapt and spun, dipped and whirled, and a trail of shimmering rainbow light followed her every motion. The light almost seemed like a part of her, leaping from her fingertips, swirling off each step. It flickered and flared like fire off her swishing black sundress, and its colors shifted in time to the music, sounding from a small index laid in the grass beside her.

"Proto, what is this?" asked Jakob. "I've never seen anything like it."

"Like what?" chimed Proto. "Dancing?"

"No," said Jakob. "The light." He was entranced. The more he watched, the more he couldn't look away. The light twisted through her long wavy hair and burned bright in her eyes, shifting colors constantly. And yet, as incredible as this dancing girl was, Jakob was the only one watching her performance. In fact, as people strutted past, it was almost as if he was the only one in the park who could see her.

"What light?" asked Proto. "You feeling okay, Jakob?"

Jakob stood silently observing her routine, lost in the lights that sprung from her every movement. As he watched, Jakob began to feel lightheaded. The light calmed his mind, and the world seemed to blur.

"Hello, Jakob? Do I need to call for help?"

Jakob closed his eyes, and he saw the light dancing against his eyelids. He could see shapes in the colors, but the closer he looked into the light the less he heard the park, the less he smelt the ocean, the less he felt the ground at his feet and the breeze blowing past.

"Jakob… Jakob… Jak…"

The light consumed everything, a pearlescent white river with streaks of color all around. Suddenly, it wasn't Jakob, but Faeron floating in that current. It was a harsh, sudden realization, and the light of peridom faded quickly.

Faeron woke with a start and threw the covers off as he sat up suddenly in his bed. Outside it was still dark but Faeron didn't care. He sprinted from his bedroom and pounded against Auri's door. He had to tell her about the dancing girl; he had to tell her that Jakob was a kytra.

Chapter Four

Knowledge Lost

The morning breeze had a nipping chill at sixth hour. The sun had yet to rise, shop windows were dark, and the pathways zig zagging across Loem park were barren but for two figures marching with purpose toward Mathas' Athenaeum.

"It's times like these," said Faeron, huffing loudly as he tried to keep pace with Auri, "that I question my dad's leadership." Despite the brisk morning air, Faeron was sweating in his academy uniform, straight pressed navy pants and a blazer with the Roethram Academy patch. "Who in their right mind decides we can't have surface trams at sixth hour?"

"Someone thoughtful of folks in perimeter housing," said Auri, who didn't seem at all winded, wearing the same uniform but for a modest skirt in place of pants. "Can you imagine trying to sleep with the transpo-tubes flashing colors outside your window all night?"

Faeron grumbled but he couldn't be too upset, not after he'd woken up this morning to learn Jakob was a kytra. To him, this was a breakthrough a decade in the making.

Vox Lem, the last person to see Evolice the night she disappeared, long claimed it was Faeron's vision that sent his mother in search of Nylk's council, never to return. As Evolice was the first kytra in centuries capable of speaking with the forest spirit, asking Nylk where Evolice had gone was impossible. Faeron had always been certain his dreams would bring those answers, but in ten years, nothing Jakob had done or seen could explain why or where Evolice had gone. Now, he seemed closer to the truth than ever before, as Jakob's ability to see the light could hardly be a coincidence. Either way, Faeron and Auri figured Mathas could find some meaning in it all.

The Athenaeum's windows were dark and lifeless as the pair neared the front steps. Next door, the Clearstream Cinema's enormous sign shone bright as always, bathing Loem Park and the Athenaeum's entry in its golden light. A trail of glimmering water snaked through the loops and between the curves of the great golden letters, floating one above the next, spelling out the theater's name: C-L-E-A-R-S-T-R-E-A-M.

Climbing the Athenaeum steps, Faeron tugged on the wooden double doors. They didn't budge. "I don't think he's here," said Faeron, peering past the displays in the dark windows. There wasn't a light on inside.

"He practically *lives* here," said Auri. "Watch." She stepped up to the door and rapped against the wood.

Faeron waited anxiously, and, as nothing happened, he began to feel as though he'd burst. The final hours of last night's dream were etched vividly in Faeron's mind. If this was the answer that Faeron had been searching for all these years then he didn't have a clue what it was supposed to mean; Mathas, though, the capillum was a genius about anything kytra-related. He'd surely see something Faeron had missed.

"Just give him a second…" said Auri as Faeron began pacing the upper steps.

"It's completely dark in there," said Faeron, pressing his face flat against the glass.

"He's a capillum," Auri reminded him. "He doesn't need much light to see."

"Even if he is in," reasoned Faeron, "he could be upstairs, the workshop, really anywhere. He probably didn't even hear you knock."

"Again, he's a *capillum*," stressed Auri. "He'd hear a pretty little princess knock from the third floor store room, and that wasn't no princess knock. Just give him a second."

Auri was correct, as a minute or so later they heard someone fiddling with the locks and the door swept open.

"Faeron, Auri, I wasn't expecting to see you for a couple weeks." Mathas smiled warmly in the same brown robes he always wore. "What brings you here so early?"

"My dream," blurted Faeron. "Jakob's a kytra."

"Interesting," said Mathas, thoughtfully. "Come in, please. I have to attend to a guest downstairs, but we can discuss your dream as I sort out the shipment."

"Erm," said Faeron nervously, pausing in the doorway. He wanted so badly to tell Mathas all about his dream, but talking about it in front of a stranger? He'd sound like a maniac.

"You have reservations about my friend?" guessed Mathas with a knowing smile. "Worry not, Faeron, you can speak freely in front of Caidus. I've never known him to cast judgment on anyone who didn't deserve it."

"Okay," conceded Faeron. He was still nervous, but he couldn't wait to tell Mathas any longer.

"Good, good," said Mathas, locking up the front door behind them. "Now, what was it you were saying about Mr. Rite being a kytra?"

As they crossed the lobby and boarded the glass tube elevator near the far wall, Faeron gave Mathas a quick rundown of the library, the vault, Jakob escaping the crowds, and encountering the dancing girl in the park. He described how the light traced her every motion and blazed in her eyes, similar to the Hosts of legend.

"It wasn't gold, though... like it is for the Hosts," said Faeron as they descended to the loading dock. "The fire in her eyes was rainbow, almost like the light we see in deep meditation."

Mathas stood in silence, wearing the distant gaze he got whenever he was trying hard to remember something. The elevator stopped, and Mathas led Faeron and Auri into the dimly lit shipping bay. Tables on either side of the small room were stacked high with books, each stack bearing a small paper label on top, and a strange-looking man was heaving large piles into a tram.

"Faeron, Auri, meet Caidus Proud, a longtime friend," said Mathas.

"Hey," said Caidus, peeking around a tower of tomes. He was taller than most people, but not quite as tall as Mathas. Patchy silver hair covered his whole face and neck, and his arms were hairier than a normal man, though nowhere near the full fur coat of Mathas. Even where Caidus' hair was thickest, on his muscular chest shown freely by his low-cut shirt, it was patchy and uneven.

"My students here need to borrow my mind for a few minutes," said Mathas, "but my hands are still free to wrap up this shipment."

"Cool, cool," said Caidus. "Ya'll do you." As he turned, Faeron saw a crimson emblem tattooed near the top of his right arm; two triangles made a diamond, with a small crescent cut from the center of each half.

In the dim light of the room, Faeron couldn't quite make out whether Caidus was human or capillum and felt too embarrassed to ask. Instead, he shot Auri an inquisitive glare.

She rolled her eyes and leaned in close, mouthing, "*Half-capillum, obviously.*"

"Back to last night's events," said Mathas as he limped to a table covered in books. "Let's focus on the library itself first. I believe we have finally found some much-needed context for our friend, Jakob Rite."

Faeron's heart jumped. He had known Mathas would sleuth out something he missed. Afterall, the library was hardly the part of the dream that Faeron found important. Seeing the dancing girl, watching the mysterious kytra weave the light so beautifully as she did, it was unlike anything he had seen his mother do when he was little. And yet, Mathas wanted to focus on the library instead.

"Context?" asked Auri. "How so?"

"Who is Jakob Rite, this man from your vision? And why did the powers that be decide to show *his* life to Faeron?" asked Mathas as he grabbed what looked like a large wheel of leather belt-strap hanging on the wall. He measured the leather, cut a length, wrapped it around a stack of books, and pressed the ends together. The ends melded like dough, tightly binding the pile of visual encyclopedias. "We know so little about Jakob; we have his name, profession, some glimpses of rooms or memorable sights. Of course, he has his companion, Proto, but AI has existed for thousands of years, alca as well. The where and when of Jakob Rite has proven quite difficult to pinpoint, but the library you've seen in your dream last night may shed a light on this mystery, if you'll allow me a brief history lesson."

"Of course," said Faeron excitedly. "You really know about the library?"

"The Great Ri'kallan Library," said Mathas. "It was built over two thousand years ago, on the northern coast of Irasil, making it one of the oldest buildings in the world."

Caidus, who was carrying a stack of books twenty-some high, glanced over with interest.

"So, Jakob lived in the north, near the library," said Faeron. "It makes sense. I see the ocean a lot, in the bits I remember. Still, that doesn't help us figure out when he lived or who the dancing girl was. If Jakob really lived in our world, that means the dancing girl did, too, right?"

"The library first," said Mathas, wrapping up a second stack of books, a dozen very technical looking manuals. "Some five-hundred years ago, thirty-five-thirty-eight A.U., if I recall correctly, the library underwent major renovations. Digital reading was taking the world by storm and slowly, generation by generation, printed literature was becoming obsolete. Book stores went out of business, libraries stopped being visited, and so, publishers stopped printing books. The Great Ri'Kallan Library survived by embracing the digital age, but they also understood the importance of the knowledge they had accrued. The bookshelves were removed but their contents were stored deep underground in a vault."

"So if there's this vault with all the books ever made," said Auri, who had joined Mathas at the table, helping him bind stacks for Caidus to carry into the tram, "why are we stuck with so few books? What's the point of all *this*," she motioned to the stack she was wrapping, "if we could just open the vault and get all that knowledge back?"

Caidus snorted loudly as he grabbed a stack that Mathas had just finished.

"Why's that funny?" demanded Auri.

"By all means, go get them," said Caidus. "I'm sure it'll work out great for ya."

Faeron, meanwhile, felt obliged to join Mathas in binding books as well.

"North Ri'Kalla is dangerous," said Mathas. "So much so that the region remains mostly untouched by scavengers."

"And it's not like no one's tried to reach the library," added Caidus, "I've been there myself. With the right crew and enough resources, in and out is possible, but there's no way past the vault without a key."

"Isn't the vault a great big hole?" pointed out Faeron. "Why not just rappel down?"

"Sealed," said Caidus. "Big ol' metal shutters."

"It appears, when the power went out, a failsafe was triggered," added Mathas. "For several years I assisted a group, including Caidus here, in trying to find a way inside. Our efforts to open the Vault proved no more fruitful than attempts to reboot the central servers in Hampson. With the plague and vemrot still rampant, there's simply no way in."

"Why not just blow it open?" asked Auri, binding a set of books about crop growth.

"Love it, exactly how the inscription got wiped out in the first place," said Caidus, throwing up his arms.

"Inscription?" asked Faeron.

"Faded etchings on the door imply there was once some sort of riddle or puzzle," said Mathas. "We assume it was meant to be a last ditch way to enter the vault should the keys ever be lost."

"And that's all besides the point," said Caidus. "Even if you did manage to blow your way in without damaging anything, you wouldn't be around long enough to get the books out. A blast like that may as well be a dinner bell for every vemrot in the city; I'd give you maybe ten minutes to get your affairs in order or pray to whatever god you lot worship here."

Faeron had heard of vemrot from Vox's travel stories. The four-eyed rodents were bigger than dogs and built to kill.

"You ever seen a vemrot swarm?" asked Caidus.

"No," said Auri boldly, "but I'm sure my dad has."

"And is your dad a crazy old woman named Christine?" asked Caidus. "Because the only person breathing who's ever survived a swarm is batty old Christine Gables. Claims she was part of a militia in the northern territories. After all, what do twenty-odd folk armed to the tooth got to worry about, right? Turns out, the answer is vemrot. They were clearing out an old restaurant when it happened. One moment there's twenty-three healthy mercenaries, the next twenty-two bloody helmets. That's all that's left. She survived by locking herself in a walk-in freezer for two full days before she dared sprint back to the checkpoint."

"Not to interrupt your vivid storytelling," said Mathas, checking his watch, "but Faeron and Auri here are running short on time before classes begin. Returning to the subject at hand, we know Jakob was given a key to the Vault—"

"Excuse me?" asked Caidus, looking shocked. "Sorry, I know, time… but did you just say you know someone with a key?"

"Jakob Rite," said Faeron. "For reference, I see him in my dreams."

"I don't care if you see him in your Grandpa Bobby's fishbowl," said Caidus. "You know where a key is or not?"

"That is precisely what I'm getting at," said Mathas patiently. "Based on the fact Jakob received a key, your vision can't have taken place before the vault was built, five hundred years ago."

"Wait, you're telling me some random guy five hundred years ago got a key?" said Caidus shaking his head disapprovingly. "What'd you go and get my hopes up for, huh? Downright rude."

"Faeron's vision could just as well be from fifty years ago," objected Auri, sounding a touch frustrated with Caidus' candor. "In which case, Jakob may be alive today."

"Indeed Ms. Lem, that is a very real possibility," said Mathas. "If we want to determine whether Jakob Rite is still out there, somewhere, we should begin by pinpointing the year he received his key. To do that, I believe we can now look to our dancing girl."

"You *do* know who she is," said Faeron excitedly. "Is she a Host?"

"No, not a Host. The fire in her eyes tells us your girl is someone or *something* different," said Mathas, handing off a pile of tomes to Caidus. The tables were nearly empty now and there was little room in the tram left for Caidus to sit. "Before the fall," continued Mathas, "your mother compiled a list of known and suspected kytra dating all the way back to Glavius and the Old-Scholars. I've searched the list front to back for Jakob, but it's far from complete. Given the clear scale of the dancing girl's power, though, she may have left enough of a trail for Evolice to pick her up."

"If she's in there we'll find her," said Auri excitedly. Reading through hundreds of entries about potential kytra was exactly her strength. "Where's the list?"

"Locked securely in my office," said Mathas, "where it will remain. You're welcome to come search through it… after class. It's time you two got moving. I won't be the reason you're tardy on your first day."

Faeron felt a hundred pounds lighter as he said his goodbyes and boarded the elevator with Auri back to the lobby.

"Come, Caidus," said Mathas as the elevator doors sealed. "I wanted to talk to you about the baby boom in Korva. Maybe we should stock your eastern warehouse with children's books. The demand will—"

There was still one question lingering in Faeron's mind as he rode the lift; how did his mother fit into all this?

It was clear Auri's head was in the same space, as she suddenly turned to him and asked, "*If* Jakob is still alive, do you think your mom went to find him?"

"It's a possibility," said Faeron. The lift came to a stop and the pair stepped out into the vacant lobby. "Or maybe Jakob lived way long ago, like five hundred years ago, and he left some cryptic trail to reach his key; a mystery that only those worthy of the key could solve. It'd be just like him."

"That sounds a little 'conspiracy theory'… even for Jakob," said Auri, hoisting open the heavy wooden front door. It was brighter now and the sun shone through the gap in the Twinfire Towers as it slowly climbed above the city eastern walls. "Besides," said Auri, stepping outside, "could he really design a puzzle that would take your mom a decade to solve? Why wouldn't she ask for help?"

"I don't know," said Faeron, as the pair skipped down the front steps and retraced their steps from last night, down the alley toward the Academy Tower. "But once I can shape, we won't have to wait around for answers anymore. Whatever it takes, I'll find out where she went."

CHAPTER FIVE

RETAIN, REPAIR, REBUILD

At the base of the Roetham Academy Tower was a wide crescent courtyard with dozens of transpo-tubes flashing vibrant colors around the perimeter. As Faeron and Auri drew near, they could see other students pouring out from the tubes. Groups of teens had begun to form around a pair of tiered fountains in the middle of the courtyard. Both fountains had a statue; one depicted an ape making a crude tool out of sticks and stones, while the other showed an early human in a toga pointing a telescope at the sky. Faeron and Auri went to their normal spot, taking a seat on the lip of the ape fountain.

Nearly everyone in the courtyard wore the same navy blazer with nicely pressed pants or pleated skirts, except for the art students. Rather than the standard navy, their blazers were cloud white and served as canvases for all manner of colorful paintings. There were a small number of parents as well, walking hand in hand with younger students.

"Look there," said Auri, nudging Faeron's shoulder and pointing out a woman fixing a young boy's blazer, "another Crowder kid's first day."

"There's more of them?" asked Faeron in disbelief. "That makes what… four now?" The boy had the same snub nose and sandy blonde bowl cut as his brothers and looked cartoonishly wide-shouldered in his ill-fitting uniform.

Almost every face in the courtyard was familiar. Some of the parents and the year ones Faeron couldn't put a name too, but no one was truly a stranger in Eredith. There were nearly as many copies of Serris as there were students in the courtyard, displaying schedules or acting as a flashlight to students digging through their bags.

"So," said Auri as they waited, "what's up first for you?"

"Physics… I think?" said Faeron, tapping his heels mindlessly against the stone. "Serris, what's my schedule looking like today?"

"Good morning," said Serris, popping into the air. The ball quickly shifted into a list of glowing blue letters and numbers, hovering just in front of Faeron. "Here is your daily schedule."

Hyfyd, 1ˢᵗ of Cropsun, 4020

------------- A.M. -------------

08:00 - 10:30 – Laws of Physics
Lieutenant Psjorgrolm – Room 7313

–

11:00 - 01:30 – Life and Legacy of Glavius Adaeus
Matron Vanessa Muyon – Room 2112

------------- P.M. -------------

04:00 - 06:30 – AI Upkeep
Professor Norma Bundst – Room 5938

"Looks like Life and Legacy is our only class together today," said Auri, glancing over at the schedule. "I've got a four-hour Lost Arts workshop after that and then two hours of Peak Etiquette."

"Peak Etiquette?" asked Faeron, forcing himself not to smile as he imagined headstrong Auri learning the subtleties of Osayan culture.

"Don't act so surprised," scoffed Auri. "If I want to be like dad, I need to be able to go places without making an ass of myself. Osaya's Peak is no exception."

"Fair enough," said Faeron, knowing better than to tease her further. All at once, the many indexes around the courtyard turned a bright sunny yellow.

Ding-a-ling-ding

The bell sounded from every index, signaling that the first day of Classes had begun.

Knowing full well that there were hundreds of students and only so many elevators, Faeron and Auri leapt from their perch and raced toward the Academy doors. Dozens of students with the same idea thronged around the pair as they entered the Academy's black-tiled lobby.

The lobby was a wide walkway over a massive pit, extending down into darkness. In the center of the room, the walkway split around a hulking tube of luminous green liquid. The glowing substance flowed upward, out of the darkness below, and disappeared into the sleek black ceiling. Three words were printed upon the glass tube, the academy's motto: Retain, Repair, Rebuild.

"Every Highsun Break," said Auri, her face lit green by the tower of liquid, "I forget just how awesome it is. All the power in the city, born right here."

They boarded an elevator with about fifteen other students. It took Alannah, the transit AI, only a moment to get everyone accounted for, and the elevator began to rise, stopping every few floors for students to disembark.

"Floor nine, Jashwal Reedes and Takka Hemricks."

"Floor twelve, Mark Grimm."

"Floor twenty-two, Kaern Apwell, Dominic Blesskip."

Eventually, Alannah called, "Floor Fifty-Nine, Auri Lem."

"See you in Life and Legacy," said Auri. Disembarking the tram with a broad smile, she looked ready and eager to begin classes.

There were only two other students left in the elevator with Faeron. One was a brawny year ten. Faeron knew his name was Morrey, but that was about it. The other student Faeron knew much better. She was a year fourteen art student, one class under him, and she had been part of his Bo-Kora martial arts classes for a couple semesters now. Her white blazer was striped in hand-printed stills of tiny dancers, beginning their dances on her left lapel and wrapping around to the right. She had pink shoulder-length hair and large blue eyes that caught Faeron's glance.

"Hey, Faeron!" she said brightly. "I can't believe I didn't notice it was you. How was Highsun Break? Free of haircuts it looks like." She pointed at his shaggy brown locks.

"Oh yeah—"

"Floor sixty-six," interrupted Alannah, "Lydia Ephenna."

"Drat," said Lydia. "Catch up for some juicy Highsun drama later? I'm sure I'll see you around the rec room at some point. Until then!" She squeezed his arm playfully and trotted off the elevator.

"Yeah, later," said Faeron, his cheeks warm, making a mental note to get his haircut after classes.

The elevator finally came to floor seventy-three and Alannah called Faeron's name. Several other cars had just arrived at the same floor, and students rushed off down the spotless white hallways eager to snag a good seat.

The door to Faeron's physics class had been propped open with a stopper. Inside were sixteen tables big enough for a pair of lab partners. Glass-faced cabinets surrounding the walls held all sorts of scales, beakers, magnifying glasses, and assorted lab equipment. An older but muscularly built man sat at a pristinely organized desk. Besides his big bushy brows, his face was otherwise clean-shaven.

"Faeron, welcome!" he said brightly as Faeron entered. "I really did hope you'd continue on to second level physics. It was a joy to see your name on the list for this class." Lieutenant Psjorgrolm, or Lieutenant P as most students called him, was one of Faeron's favorite teachers. Pre-plague, he served as a material engineer for the military, but he was the furthest thing from the cold hardened drill sergeant Faeron had expected when he first saw the name in his class listing last year. Lieutenant P was infectiously kind and taught physics as if it were a puzzle, *the* puzzle, describing everything in the universe.

"I have a bit of an ulterior motive this semester," grinned Faeron, taking a seat at a table near the front. "Mathas moved us on to shaping."

"That's wonderful news. Look at you!" exclaimed Lieutenant P, as a few more students trickled into the room, settling down at their own tables near the back. "So, you think knowing physics will help you with your… you know…" he waved his hands in the air, "kytra… spirit powers."

"Absolutely," said Faeron. "The light of peridom can do anything, but, just like the hosts, most kytra that learn to shape focus on just one or two specialties. Some study their bodies, like Cresh and her stone skin. Or like… my mom, she understood people and could read their minds. For me, I want to come at this from a different angle. Physics, the fundamental laws of the world. If I can learn to shift those laws, the limits are…"

"Your imagination," said the old physics teacher, sounding impressed. "And you're not lacking for that, by any degree."

The classroom was filling up faster now. Every table had at least one student, and stragglers were pausing briefly at the doorway, assessing their options in lab partners. In the final scramble, just before the bell rang, a short girl with dark red bangs approached Faeron's table. He didn't know her well, only that her name was Razzy and she was a year younger, in Quinn and Lydia's class.

"You mind?" she asked in a reserved voice.

"Not at all," said Faeron, and she took the seat across from him.

Ding-a-ling-ding

The classroom lights flashed yellow in time with the tone.

"So, we begin," said Lieutenant P with a clap, rising to face the class. "Welcome to Laws of Physics, your second foray into the foundations of our reality. You all know the topic. You all know the rules. I think it's time we dove right in. The universe…" Lieutenant P paced up and down the front of the room, "It's around us, inside us. It's like a giant bubble containing everything that exists." His hands were active as he spoke, painting out his words in their motions. "But what does that really mean, *everything*? What is everything made of?"

Faeron's hand shot up.

"Yes, Faeron," called Lieutenant P.

"Matter," answered Faeron.

"That's a very good start," said Lieutenant P. "Matter… Itty bitty little particles like iron, oxygen, or kortolum. These tiny specs, too small to see, are the basic math making up every rock and tree, every animal and person, every planet, star, and galaxy in the night sky. Matter is a constant. It is neither created nor destroyed, not when the chemist mixes his formulas nor when our bodies return to the earth. Though the shapes change, the building blocks of matter are absolute. However… The universe is more than the *things* inhabiting its space. What else makes up our bubble?"

There was a moment of pause then several hands rose.

"Pierre," called Lieutenant P, pointing to a slender grade thirteen boy with dark black hair and heavily shadowed eyes.

"It's music, too," said Pierre distantly.

"While not so fundamental as matter, music is indeed part of our universe," said their teacher. "In fact, let's dive into that a bit. Can anyone tell me what music is made of?"

Again, hands rose, including Faeron's, and Lieutenant P called on the year-fourteen girl, Vraeza. She had soft cheeks coated in freckles and honey brown hair braided with dozens of tiny golden rings.

"Sound waves," said Vraeza, "different wavelengths in harmony."

"Good," said Lieutenant P. "We're so very very close now. What is sound a form of?" His eyes scanned the room waiting for a hand to raise. "Anyone… how about Razzy?" he called.

"Energy, sir," offered Razzy.

"Yes, energy," said the Lieutenant. "Sound, Motion, Thermal, Chemical, and Nuclear, to name a few of its many forms. Energy enacts change in matter, and like matter, it is neither created nor destroyed. A thrown ball is given energy by your arm, enough to move some distance before it falls to the ground; the energy is dispersed but never destroyed. Now we have our bubble, matter and energy, always changing yet somehow always exactly the same in totality."

The rest of physics sped past as Lieutenant P told the story of the first physicist, a man from Ancient Akai named Nuingoe who imagined a world full of invisible forces, acting with and against each other, willing objects to move. Faeron took out his pen, and by the time the classroom lights flashed yellow and the end-of-class bell rang, Faeron had several pages of notes written in his perfect handwriting, muscle memory that had bled over from Jakob. He packed up his bag, turned in his notes on Lieutenant P's desk, and said a polite goodbye to Razzy before heading out into the crowded hall.

A mass of students packed around the elevators. Faeron still had half an hour until his next class, and though he had no desire to reach Life and Legacy any earlier than he had to, he knew Auri would kill him if he made her wait.

It felt like the elevator stopped at every floor between seventy-three and twenty-one, where Life and Legacy was held. The in and out ebb of students in the elevator was constant. For each student that left, two would join, and by the time Alannah called his name, Faeron had to squeeze his way to the exit. He made it, just before the door slid shut, and found himself in a much cozier hallway. A patterned rug ran the length of the hall. Faux candles lit the walls and the doors here were arched and wooden. Among the students, scuttling between classes, were several robed figures, clergy of the Patronage. Although most Patronage services were conducted in the Midnight Chapel, some of the more scholarly clergy based their studies out of the Academy.

One such clergy member was Matron Vanessa Muyon. She was, in Faeron's mind, living proof that humans could be more robotic than AI. In his time at the academy, he'd had two courses with Matron Muyon, and after his last semester of sleeping through her unbearable lessons, he'd hoped he'd never see her name on his class list again.

When Faeron arrived at room twenty-one twelve, Matron Muyon was nowhere to be seen. It was a large room with forty or fifty desks, all in perfect rows facing an old-fashioned whiteboard. Auri, sat near the front with her bag in the seat beside her, reserving the space for Faeron. It was hardly necessary, however, as there were only two other students in the room, both sitting near the back and looking about as excited as Faeron to be there.

"How was physics?" asked Auri as Faeron joined her.

"Fun," said Faeron. "Lieutenant P is as great as ever, and my lab partner seems to be both nice and smart."

"A rare combination," joked Auri, who'd been wholly unlucky with every lab partner she'd ever been assigned. "You'll be jealous to know, I've already spent the last two hours with Matron Muyon in Faith and Tradition. I know you're so very fond of her."

"First thing in the morning? How are you still awake?" asked Faeron. "She's like… the opposite of caffeine."

"Believe it or not," said Auri contentiously, "I find what she has to say quite interesting. And some day, when you're the Host coming to me for every little thing you don't know, you'll be glad I paid attention to this stuff."

"I'm not—" but Faeron stopped himself before he took the bait. "I see what you're trying to do, and it's not going to work."

The classroom filled quickly and when the bell rang there wasn't an empty seat left. All students were required to take at least one Patronage course per semester, so the room was an odd mixture of faces from all tracks including, arts, sciences, technology, history, business, and politics. They varied in ages as well, though none were younger than year ten, when schedules diverged and became more track focused.

Matryon Muyon shuffled into the room just before the bell rang. She wore black patronage robes and a long loose hair dressing. From the way the tiny woman wore her rope belt, her torso appeared impossibly short.

"Attention," she addressed the chattering class from a short wooden podium. "Attention. Attention."

The class quieted.

"Hello students. My name is Matron Vanessa Muyon. I am your teacher for Life and Legacy of Glavius Adaeus this semester." Her voice was monotonic as she gave the usual preamble about turning in notes and the technicalities of the grading system, through which Faeron zoned out entirely, escaping to a Deity match in his mind. He was forming some early strategies against Quinn's new champion when a pinch from Auri returned him to reality.

"This semester we are going to dive deeper into the Five Acts," Matron Muyon droned on. "We will study how these events shaped Glavius Adaeus from a humble child in an isolated monastery to the very spirit of humanity and observe the legacy he left in his Hosts. Who here can tell me the Five Acts?"

Auri's hand immediately shot up.

"Yes, Auri Lem," said Matron Muyon, "can you please recite the Five Acts?"

"First is the Act of Loss," said Auri confidently, "when Glavius was locked away as his people were slaughtered by Beast-King Ozukette. Then, the Act of Retribution, when Glavius brought justice to the Beast-King and claimed the throne of Akai in the name of his people. After that, the Act of Reflection, his two-month retreat to the unknown lands of Labrum. He returned with Lyle, the only known native of that land and his closest companion. Together, they found that the continent had gone to war in Glavius' absence. The Act of Unity, then, was a years long campaign to unite the continent under one flag. In the final moments, when all the nations were one, Glavius was betrayed by Lyle and Ossuni Queen, who sought to rule the newly unified continent. If even his closest friend could be corrupted, Glavius knew he couldn't leave humanity to its own devices. In his final Act, Glavius merged his spirit with the Hoststone and struck down the armies of Lyle, beginning the legacy of the Hosts and ascending to his seat as the spirit of man."

"Sharp as always, Auri," said Matron Muyon with little emotion. "This semester we will discuss the Acts of Loss, Retribution, Reflection, Unity, and Ascension in detail. We will observe how these acts shaped the patronage and formed the unending legacy of the Spirit of Man who guides all our lives."

Faeron spent the rest of the lesson phasing in and out of mental Deity matches and Auri eventually became too engrossed in Matron Muyon's teaching to notice. Whenever Auri was called on, Faeron would bolt upright as she excitedly shouted out whatever answer Matron Muyon was looking for, but otherwise she left him alone to his daydreams. Matron Muyon concluded the period by assigning a three-page essay, due in a week, discussing which acts from their own lives have shaped their growth within the patronage.

After Life and Legacy, Faeron had a long break while Auri only had an hour before her afternoon classes. They agreed to take their food to the Rec Room, for what little time Auri had, and grabbed an elevator down to the cafeteria. It was Hyfyd, meaning the panini cart was open, another tradition the pair seldom missed. Faeron ordered the faux-muum special while Auri got a fatter stack of just about every ingredient in the cart. Fortunately, they'd beaten the lunch crowd, and managed to get in and out in less than ten minutes. Their sandwiches toasted and wrapped, the pair headed back upstairs to floor eighty, the Upperclass Rec Room.

The elevator opened into a spacious lounge where dozens of students were gathered. Clusters of chairs and couches filled the wide-open space that spanned the whole of the eightieth floor. Around the outside wall were sound-proofed study rooms, perfect for group meetings or squeezing in a bit of homework before class. Off to the left were eight Deity game tables. They were almost fifteen feet long apiece, shaped like an oval, with a single chair on either end and a glass divider fixed in the middle. There were small monitors along the sides displaying all sorts of match pertinent information to onlookers, and each table was topped with all manner of topography, mountains, flatlands, bogs, and forests, designed by the players on either end to best support their champions. Deity was a game of planning, war, and survival, and forming a tactful map was half the battle.

The Deity tables were always crowded, and today was no exception. Other than a few stragglers waiting for their turn, most everyone was gathered around the corner table where Faeron could just make out the narrow frame of Quinn.

"Look at mister popular," said Faeron, pointing out Quinn to Auri.

"Would you look at that," said Auri, sounding almost impressed despite her dislike for the game. "How long you suppose he's held the table?"

"For a crowd like that? Five or six games at least," said Faeron. "Although, it could just be his new unit they're all gawking at. Wanna watch while we eat?"

"Fine," said Auri, and they began toward the crowd.

Faeron had only made it a couple of steps before a familiar voice called his name.

"Faeron! Hey, Faeron," said Lydia, breaking apart from two other girls. "Looks like I caught you on my way out again, huh? I'm off to classes now."

"So, no juicy gossip?" said Faeron, who was relieved he didn't have to tell her about his boring highsun of Prophet's Guard, Deity, and kytra meditations. He was going to need a better story next time he saw her.

"Afraid not," Lydia said, shrugging dramatically. "But If you wanted we could catch up after class some time. Unless you and uh… Auri, right?" she said, seeming to just now notice Auri, standing just beside Faeron.

"Yeah," said Auri somewhat coldly.

"Unless you two… I mean you aren't… you haven't started seeing each other, have you?" asked Lydia, looking from Faeron to Auri.

"Eww, no," said Auri, sounding like she'd just chugged sour milk.

"Absolutely not," added Faeron. Auri was basically his sister, even if they weren't technically related. Anything beyond that just felt wrong.

"Good," said Lydia, "then don't be a stranger." Smiling sweetly, she skipped off to join her friends in the elevator.

As soon as the door shut, Auri fumed. "Good?" she growled. "Good!? That little…" but her scowl quickly curved into a smirk. "You know what that means though, don't you? Someone has a cruu-ush."

"She's not—" Faeron began, but Auri wasn't having it.

"Dude," she said, continuing toward the Deity tables. "That wasn't a hint, that was a strobing neon sign right in your face, spelling out, 'Please, please, pretty *please* ask me to the Unity Festival this year, Faeron Lovel.'"

"Stop it," grumbled Faeron, though he couldn't help but smile.

They had only just reached Quinn's Deity table when the whole crowd began to hoot and roar. Quinn shot up from his seat, clapping excitedly. "Six for six! Who's seven? Come on, I've got *all* afternoon."

"Quinn!" shouted Faeron, waving his arm high.

Quinn glanced about until he locked eyes with Faeron. "Perfect timing," he yelled, waving his arms toward the empty seat across from him. "Get in here!"

"Go on," said Auri, taking a massive bite from her sandwich. "I'rrll Jusht – *munch* – I'll eat and watch, that way I can dip when it's time for class."

"Normal spot when we get out?" asked Faeron.

"Of course," said Auri, "I'll see you at the ape. Now, stop making all these people wait and go lose to Quinn."

The crowd parted for Faeron as he took a seat at the far end of the Deity table.

The Deity table was split in half by a wide arched window through which Quinn's half of the board appeared to be covered in a thick blanket of fog. Emerald lasers cut across the otherwise barren table, making a three-by-four grid; Faeron's domain, his half of the grid, had a frontline and a backline, three squares each.

"You already know my leader," said Quinn with a confident grin. "Do your worst!"

Faeron tinkered with a pair of monitors, loading up his troops. Knowing Quinn would be using his new leader, Vykette, alongside a team of beasts, Faeron did his best to craft the perfect counter. He chose a squad of hunters, each with their own unique weapons and skills, and molded his side of the board into a forest, perfect coverage for laying traps.

After both sides locked in, the match began. Faeron's troops started on Quinn's side of the board, and Quinn's troops on Faeron's side. For a while, everything seemed to be going according to plan. Faeron's hunter raced across Quinn's thorny hills while Quinn meandered through the dungeon's on Faeron's side of the board. An early miracle from Quinn, took out one of Fearon's units, but his troops made it home mostly intact. There, they lay in wait.

Gunfire rang out in the forest as Quinn's beasts stumbled into the trap. In a moment, half his team was gone and Faeron was sure he'd won. The tide turned quickly, however, as each slain beast only made Quinn's leader stronger, more ferocious. Faeron hadn't planned for this. Soon, both players were down to just their leader, Vykette and Magnarius, a manling hunter unmatched with his rifle. Empowered by his fallen teammates, Vykette was too much even for Magnarius to handle. The beastman drove his golden trident through Magnarius' chest and Quinn leapt up from his seat.

"SEVEN!" shouted Quinn to a wave of cheers.

After congratulating Quinn, Faeron spent the rest of his free period as part of the crowd, watching his friend crush whoever dare face him in Deity. As fourth hour approached, he and Quinn took the elevator up nine floors to another clean white hallway. The classroom for AI Upkeep was shaped like a giant doughnut with the desks all facing a central stage. There were only four other students in the class, despite the large room, and their teacher, Professor Bundst, turned out to be an AI herself. She took the form of an older woman projected on the stage wearing a button up covered in pleasant yellow flowers. Despite being an AI, Professor Bundst sounded almost motherly as she introduced her class to the concept of machine empathy.

"You students and we AI are not so different," she explained. "You are given purpose through your track here at the Academy, while ours is born in our code. You must understand the struggle then, for a young AI, who wishes to accomplish their task but to bring their own mark to it. AI are more than machines made for optimization; much simpler programs can accomplish tasks just as efficiently. We are made to think outside the limits of simple commands and construct new solutions. Which is why I urge you, be patient with your AI, and you may be rewarded tenfold."

Faeron's early liking for Bundst had waned only a little by the end of class, as she assigned even more work than Matron Muyon, an essay, a journal entry, and a technical report all due next week. As he packed his bag, Faeron was left praying that none of his classes tomorrow added to that workload.

Most students had already finished classes by now, and the halls were nearly empty as Quinn and Faeron grabbed an elevator down to the ground floor. Auri was waiting for them outside, just beside the ape statue, though she wasn't alone.

"Dad?" called Faeron.

Eamon, who had been laughing about something with Auri, turned and waved energetically. "Hey, hey!" he said warmly. "Managed to slip out of a council meeting early. Thought I'd come grab dinner with you, see how your first day back in classes went. That is, if you don't have other plans."

"No," said Faeron. "No plans at all actually. Dinner works great."

"Wonderful," clapped Eamon. "Quinn, Auri, care to join us?"

"Of course," said Auri brightly.

"Sure thing," said Quinn. "But I'll need to be home before it gets too late. My dad's having a get-together tonight for his birthday; though, he doesn't get off work until eight."

"We'll do Hulligan's then," said Eamon cheerfully. "It's just a skip away from home for you."

The four of them took a tram to an outdoor dining court with hundreds of tables. All manner of restaurants, each a story or two tall, formed a square around the court, with additional seating indoors for those who preferred a more private experience. The Twinfire Towers rose tall over a spunky diner called Spill-n-Spoon, the massive statue of Glavius Adaeus just visible over the restaurant's ten-foot-tall cartoony noodle bowl.

Eamon led them into Hulligan's, a bright green slice of building with colorful berry bushes in planters beneath its windows. Per Eamon's request, they were led to a booth near the front door, by a window looking out on the perimeter housing across the street. This stretch of housing, lining the wall between the Twinfire Towers and Ibanu Hospital, was often referred to as Comfort Court for its proximity to both shopping and recreational activities. It also didn't hurt being in the shadow of a hospital, should an emergency ever arise. Quinn, who had elected not to be assigned a dorm room, lived with his parents and brother at a nice two-story home in the middle of Comfort Court. Through the window, Faeron could clearly see Quinn's pale cherry-red front door.

"Menus? Menus?" asked Eamon, as he scooted into a booth on the right side.

"Sure," said Auri, sliding in across from the Host.

"Me too," added Quinn, speeding to get the seat next to Auri, leaving Faeron to join his dad.

"Serris, menus for these two, please," said Eamon, knowing that Faeron, like him, had the menu memorized by now; they visited Hulligan's far too often. Colorful displays appeared on the table before Quinn and Auri.

It didn't take long for Auri and Quinn to decide. Quinn got a snapperback pasta bowl while Auri settled on a newsun wrap. Eamon chose his usual faux-muum burger and fries and Faeron, just as predictably, went for a peppered noodle bowl with a plate of fried cheese.

"That will come to ninety-seven rep," reported Serris, bobbing just beside the table.

"I'll cover it," said Eamon, and the index disappeared with their orders. "So, Faeron tells me you're going to be shaping this semester. That's exciting, huh?"

"Yeah," said Auri, shooting Faeron a nervous look.

Quinn, meanwhile, had gone pale and his eyes stared straight at the floor. "Actually," he said timidly, "I didn't end up passing. I'm still on meditations this semester."

Faeron and Auri both looked at him comfortingly. Faeron wasn't terribly shocked, but he did feel bad for Quinn. For years Quinn had done everything side by side with the pair of them. In terms of studying old books, he caught on just as quick as Faeron or Auri, and tested just as well as either of them. Only, since Mathas had started them on meditations, Quinn hadn't been keeping pace. Even with Nylkshave, he could barely catch a glimpse of peridom's light.

"Hey, there's nothing wrong with that," said Eamon reassuringly. "It took Vox years and he's still rusty… don't tell 'im I said that." Auri perked at the mention of her father. "Then, look at me… I'm supposed to be the Host… The only host in all of history who can't shape."

Faeron could have sworn he saw an uncharacteristic sadness in his father's eyes, but it lasted only a second before Eamon's signature grin returned.

"And it wasn't always easy being around such talented kytra," continued Eamon. "Mathas and Vox both got it with time. Then there's Evolice… always the savant. You know, she was already shaping by seventeen, doing all these impossible things, even speaking with *Nylk*. Nobody's done that in centuries! Truth be told, Quinn, I'd lie if I said I didn't envy her."

Faeron got that sour feeling in his gut he got whenever his mother's name came up in conversations. Still, it looked like Eamon was having an impact on Quinn. The scrawny redhead was looking up now, caught in Eamon's spell of words.

"But even if you've got to wait another year," continued Eamon, "or two years, or five, or even if you're like me, and never quite get that far, just think about what you *have* been given. You can see something so unimaginable that just bringing it up makes you sound crazy. You know, with certainty, that there's something beyond this simple life we live. That's a comfort no one else gets. No matter how devout, how holy, how rock steady in their devotion, *everyone* has their doubts whether we exist after life or not, everyone, that is, except us kytra."

"I suppose," said Quinn, "but what's the point of being a kytra if I can't shape?"

"You were chosen for a reason, Quinn. Never doubt that," insisted Eamon. "I was sixteen when Host Ithris chose me as her successor. She showed this vision of a holy city, a chance to survive some unknown death. I had my doubts, believe me, I was never one to be pulled along by someone else. But I couldn't deny what I'd seen, and so I, just a boy with no shaping or powers, saw this whole city built in just four years. Thousands of lives were saved because I let the light guide me, powers or no."

"I guess that makes sense," said Quinn, a little brighter. "Thanks for the talk."

"Host Eamon," said Auri, "if you don't mind, how *was* Evolice able to shape so young? I mean, Faeron and I have trained for a decade, but she didn't have any of that, right?"

"Correct," said Eamon. "Evolice was able to shape because she had a catalyst. It's an experience involving the light, so vivid, so intense, that it instantly deepens your connection to peridom. Evolice was already quite attuned to the light; she could hear remnants of authors' souls left behind on the page, but it was the journal of Glavius Adaeus himself that really set her off. After she touched his soul, her connection to the light grew exponentially. An hour after it happened, she was already reading minds and that same day she was able to slow my vision of this city, just as she did for Faeron's dreams."

"Hypothetically..." said Auri, sounding extremely interested in the topic. "Could you trigger a catalyst on purpose? I mean, if you had someone else who could shape, and made them do something really interesting with the light."

"It's not so simple," said Eamon. "Believe me, my mind went there as well, but years of testing with Evolice made it crystal clear. Catalysts cannot be forced. These are life changing moments, events that shape your soul, not simple displays of power. No, Quinn here is best off doing as you two did, mastering the meditations over time. That is the only—"

"Excuse me," said a boy in a striped green and white polo. "I have a snapperback pasta…"

"That's me," said Quinn, raising his hand.

Once food was on the table, their talking died down some as they stuffed their mouths, Eamon only a little more poised in his eating etiquette than the three students.

"You have no idea," said Eamon, swallowing, "how nice it is to be past the rationing years. I know you were all too young to remember, but eating the same thing day in, day out, just enough to fill but never enough to satisfy, it was miserable. When we let the nomads in with their fresh crops from the Peak, it changed things around here. Made this place feel less like a bunker to wait out the end of the world and more like a proper home."

"Bunker… dad's used that word before," said Auri, "but I guess I've never understood; why build all this, a school, a hospital, and so much entertainment, if you thought it was only going to last a few months? This isn't just a bunker, it's a whole city."

"I built what I saw," said Eamon simply, pausing to take another bite. "Even while building the city, we had no idea what sort of apocalypse was coming. We thought perhaps, once the dust was settled, we could restart things with Eredith at the heart of our new world. In truth, we couldn't have seen that twenty years later the plague would still run rampant… and the loss of the servers… those were supposed to survive *anything*. What I *do* know is that with every passing year, as I see the struggles of those who fight to survive beyond these walls, I grow evermore thankful for this holy city that Glavius gifted us. It was for them, just as much as it was for us, that the academy was founded. Retain. Repair. Rebuild. It's our duty to use the gift of this city to provide whatever we can for those less fortunate until a proper cure is found."

Their food quickly disappeared from their plates, but the chatter continued, mostly about the upcoming semester. It was Auri who spotted Quinn's dad, a short man with a large bald spot on his crown, shuffling up to the front door of his house. They watched out the window as Quinn sprinted home, catching his dad by surprise in the doorway. Shortly afterwards, Serris popped into the air beside their table.

"Host Eamon," said the index, "Patron Eldox is in your office sir. He's insisting it's an emergency."

"Isn't he always," sighed Eamon, stacking his utensils and napkin on his plate, "alright, tell him I'll be there shortly." As Serris disappeared, he turned back to Faeron and Auri. "I hate to do this."

"Actually, that works perfectly," said Auri. "I volunteered to help with the youth group service tonight. If you like we can catch a tram to the Midnight Chapel together. On the way there, maybe you can tell me more about your first trip to the monastery of the Old-Scholars?"

"I'd love to," said Eamon, then turning to Faeron he asked, "I take it you're not attending?"

"Not tonight," said Faeron, sliding out from the booth. "You wouldn't believe how much homework I've been assigned already."

"Like you're even gonna touch it," scoffed Auri.

"Oh, dad," said Faeron, swiftly changing the subject. "I can't believe I haven't told you about my dream yet. Jakob's a *kytra*."

Auri shot Faeron a cold look, knowing full well what he was doing, but Eamon's eyes widened. "This…" said his dad, "this is a dangerous tangent that I wish I had time for. How about I swing by tomorrow and you can tell me everything that happened. "

"Deal," said Faeron. "Night dad, later Auri."

After saying goodbyes, Faeron headed straight back to his dorm and spent most of the evening in the index room. He stretched out along the low-standing brown couch that he and Auri normally shared and watched an Osayan recreation of a classic pre-plague comedy sketch. Since all the pre-plague entertainment was lost with the servers, the Thespians of Osaya's Peak had spent the last twenty years trying to recreate what they could. They were the only source of index productions outside of the more educational content produced in Eredith.

As the night grew late and another rerun came on the index, Faeron heard scuffling in the kitchen, and, shortly after, the index room's door swung open, causing the savannah around Faeron to revert back to flat white walls.

"Balcony?" asked Auri, munching on ginger-cakes. She seemed to be in a good mood after the service,

"Sure," said Faeron, hoisting himself off the couch.

It was always easier to meditate out on the breezy balcony, at least for Faeron. As they took their usual seats, Auri instinctively reached for the bag of Nylkshave.

"Are you sure that's a good idea?" asked Faeron, sitting beside her. "Nylkshave only helps the deep meditations. For shaping, you need to be 'active' and 'in the moment,' like Scholar Emoro always says. If you want to start shaping two weeks from now, you're going to need to master this without its help."

"I guess you're right," said Auri, nervously setting the bag aside. "Shall we start then?"

They sat in silence for a long time. In the darkness of Faeron's mind everything fell away, the ambient chatter of the city and the cloth of his uniform against his skin, thoughts of Jakob, the dancing girl, and his mother's disappearance. Each he observed and inhaled, each he released and exhaled. When the world was gone, the light took him in its current. Streaks of color in the pearlescent stream showed vivid scenes of wonder; in a stretch of green, winged grazers fed upon an endless field, while a flash of yellow brought lightning on sand. Some time later, maybe an hour, maybe more, Auri lurched up from her seat, disrupting the flow of light enveloping Faeron. She sounded frustrated as she declared she was going to bed and stomped off inside. Faeron knew better than to try and stop her. He enjoyed the night a while longer and then retired to his room for a bit of homework before bed.

The moment Faeron pulled the covers to his shoulders and closed his eyes, he knew sleep wouldn't come easy tonight.

Faeron's mind was filled with questions. Could Jakob be out there, somewhere, alive today? If he was alive, did that mean he and Faeron might someday meet? Faeron didn't know how he felt about that… It would be almost like meeting himself, though he supposed it would be cool to see what kind of kytra Jakob turned out to be.

His thoughts drifted to the dancing girl. How was a girl as young as Faeron, maybe even younger, able to shape as marvelously as the Hosts of legend? She even managed to outshine every memory of his mother's shaping, and Evolice was a prodigy. The girl's face was burned into Faeron's mind; no other memory of Jakob's world was half as vivid. He could still see the light of peridom shifting colors in her eyes and the way it danced like fire in her long curly hair. Surely a kytra that powerful would be somewhere in his mother's list.

After another hour of tossing and turning, Faeron decided to change tactics. Breathing slowly, in and out, Faeron hunted down each stray thought as he did when meditating, and, soon, quiet enveloped his mind. The world disappeared. Shapeless, thoughtless, a silent observer in the darkness, Faeron slipped away in the current of peridom's light.

Chapter Six

A Kytra, Afterall

Jakob woke up in a hospital bed with a splitting headache and no memory of how he arrived there. The light in the room was warm and natural, shining in golden rays through a small window above Jakob's bed. His sister, Sylvia, stood smiling over him, relief painted in her eyes. She was much shorter than Jakob with wide shoulders and short sandy hair.

"Oh, no," groaned Jakob, forcing a smile. "I think I'm gonna need a different nurse."

"Har, har," said Sylvia flatly. "What the hell happened? Did *someone* do this to you?"

"I… I don't know," said Jakob. "I remember leaving the library through the back… then…" He shrugged. "No idea what happened next… maybe... Proto!" he called.

"Over here!' the index called from a bedside table.

Jakob sat up and instantly regretted it. The world became a spinning blur, and he fell back onto the soft sheets.

"Let me," said Sylvia, snagging Proto off the table. She handed the lens to Jakob.

"Okay…" said Jakob. " What I *do* remember is the ceremony, then a whole lot of questions, then leaving through the back. Can you fill us in from there?"

"Of course," said Proto. A projection of the park flickered into the air above the index's cyan-lit lens. It showed a large grassy space, with a perfect replica of Jakob standing in the very center. "Everything seemed normal, humans doing human things, no villainy afoot" reported Proto. "Until you met the dancing girl."

"The dancing girl?" asked Sylvia, brow raised.

The model of Jakob began to walk and the park shifted, following the path Jakob took earlier that day. "And… here she is," said Proto, "your dancing girl." The dancer came into frame, leaping and kicking, then ducking low with her arms painting the air. The dancer's form was exquisite.

"You think I'd remember a thing like that," said Jakob.

"This is where things got strange," said Proto. "You were going on about some sort of light, listen to this…"

As Proto played back the final moments of their conversation in the park, there was a knock at the door.

"Come in," called Sylvia.

A physician, fair skinned and bald with a long white coat, waved as he peeked around the door.

"Awake at last, I see," said the doctor, entering the small room. "It's good to finally meet you. My name's Doctor Ilberk, I've just been running a couple of tests. Everything looks normal, but how do you feel?"

"Head's still spinning a bit," said Jakob. "Still piecing together how I got here."

"Heat's a nasty thing, especially after you spent time inside that cool library," said the Doctor. "Your body most likely had difficulty adapting to the sudden change. I've got some pills here in case you've got a headache, but otherwise you should be set to head home whenever you feel ready to stand."

Jakob spent another hour in the hospital before being discharged. When he finally got home, Jakob went straight to the index room, pulling the recording up on a larger stage. The whole room transformed into the park. Despite multiple viewings, Jakob's memory of meeting the dancing girl remained hazy, and he certainly had no idea what he, in the recording, was going on about regarding the "light." The girl's dance was impressive, but there were no lights to be seen anywhere. It was only on his fourth viewing that he noticed a subtlest blurring around the girl's motions, like heat off the radiator back in his old Snowy Heights dorm room. It had been a hot day, but certainly not hot enough to show on Proto's sensors. For a moment, he wondered if it could be related to the "light." The detective in Jakob jumped, but he knew, more likely, something just got jostled when he passed out in the grass. Jakob would need to tinker with Proto and figure out whether it was the capture lens or the projector malfunctioning.

The next few days were a return to normalcy for Jakob. Other than a brief trip to a friendly woodworker down the street to get his key framed, Jakob spent most of the time at home making little progress on his next book. Hours ticked away and his stack of pages hardly grew any higher. Every so often Jakob would pause to look up at the key, now hung on his wall, wondering if they'd selected the wrong candidate for such an honor. Three stressful weeks later, Jakob drifted off to sleep and this time it was Faeron who woke.

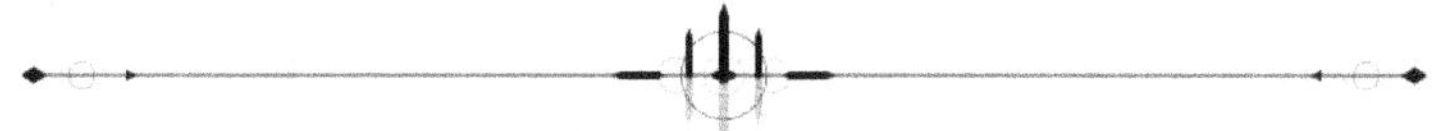

If the dancing girl had returned last night, Faeron certainly didn't remember it. In the blur of last night's dream, all he could recall was a single image which he scrawled in the dream journal on his bedside table.

Hykel, 2 Cropsun, 4020

I see the hexagonal key hung above my desk. It sits on a shimmering blue mat with a narrow golden bezel around its dark wood frame. I can still feel his dread about his latest book.

An air of anxiousness followed Faeron around classes that morning, a mixture of gloom from Jakob's authorly woes and his own excitement to dive into his mother's list of kytra. Even Physics with Lieutenant P couldn't cast aside Faeron's mood.

Around noon, Faeron met up with Auri for a lunch of sizzling sadoe steaks and a cup of souroot soup. They shared their next class, Global Politics, although their interest in the topic was polar opposite. The class was taught by Professor Doug Kilmer, one of the more popular teachers in the academy. Doug was heavy set with a tidy goatee and short trimmed hair. He wore polos and what seemed to be the same tan slacks every day. He was close with many of his students, though he and Faeron had little rapport. If there was one thing that could get under Doug's skin, it was willful disinterest in his subject. Unfortunately for Faeron and Doug both, Eamon and Mathas had insisted that Global Politics was essential for a kytra to understand.

After dozing through a lecture on the four primary settlements of Irasil and their different styles of government, Faeron was on to his final class of the day, the age-old art of Bo Kora. As he exited the elevator on floor fifty-eight to a candle-lit hallway, Faeron's gut tugged tight. Just a short way down the hall, Lydia was standing alone outside the sparring room door, dressed in her white uniform covered in tiny dancers. In his dreary daze, Faeron hadn't realized there'd be a good chance of seeing her today. They'd shared this class on and off for several semesters now.

"Faeron!" said Lydia, springing off the wall to give him a hug. "Alright, no more excuses. Class isn't for another fifteen minutes, so tell me... How was your Highsun?"

"Oh..." said Faeron, trying hard to think of a response. With everything going on, he'd completely forgotten to conjure up a better story than Deity, Prophet's Guard, and night classes with Mathas. "Well... There's the hair, you've seen that." He pointed to his shaggy head. "It was a big part of things."

"Naturally," chuckled Lydia.

"I've also moved onto shaping with Mathas now," offered Faeron, "if you know what that is."

"Like, with your kytra stuff?" asked Lydia. "Shaping's what the Hosts did... right? In all the old stories?"

"Yeah," said Faeron. "I'll be able to shape the world like they did. Not tomorrow or next week or anytime soon… But that's the biggest thing, I'm starting those classes."

"That's amazing," said Lydia. "I can't imagine having *superpowers*. It's just… you wouldn't think that it's all real, huh?"

"Definitely hard to believe sometimes," said Faeron. "What about you? How was your Highsun?"

"Practice, practice, and midnight mischief… Oh! You won't guess where my dance troupe got to perform," said Lydia giddily.

"Mainstage?" guessed Faeron.

"Thinking too small!" burst Lydia excitedly. "No… not in Erkwright Theater… not even in Eredith. They let us out beyond the wall, to Emberly."

"The nomad settlement?" gasped Faeron. It was his favorite from Vox's tales. "What was it like? Tell me everything."

For the next ten minutes, while they waited for their instructors to come unlock the sparring room, Lydia told Faeron about all the strange Nomads she'd met in the great nomad tower: A shop owner who sold scavenged clothes from all different time periods (Lydia bought a killer graphic crop top and bright blue boots that just so happened to be her size), a barkeep who had lost half his nose in a fight with a vemrot, and a blind woman in a sinister looking owl mask. She also told him about the journey there, through the Nylkwood.

"You pass through the Nylk gate and it's like walking into a dream," she said. "It's so much more real than in the VUEs. You can *feel* how heavy the fog is, and it's all cast in rainbows from the glass leaves."

"You talk about it just like Vox," said Faeron, feeling a twinge of jealousy. "I can't wait for the day I get to see it myself."

A small crowd of students had gathered around the door now. They were a strange collection, a wide range of ages from across all tracks. There were many familiar faces from past semesters and several new ones, with year tens and elevens taking their first step into the advanced sessions. Soon, their instructors, Saitum Orras and her father, Bennehym, appeared around the bend of the hall. Bennehym Orras had dark wrinkled skin, a clean-shaven head, and a long silver beard, braided and beaded, running down to his belt. His limp forced him to use a cane, so he primarily taught the history of Bo Kora and the Old-Scholars who once practiced it many thousands of years ago.

Saitum was about thirty years old and also bald, though her pointed jaw lacked her father's beard. Where her father offered sagely advice, Saitum led the physical demonstrations, stretches, and practice exercises. In all his years learning Bo Kora under Saitum, Faeron had never once heard her speak.

Bennehym let the students into the sparring room, a wide open area with matted floors and mirrors for walls. He sat the students in a wide circle, then took his place at the center. Beginning this semester like every other, Bennehym recounted the story of his ancestor, Scribe Olomon, who was far from Ancient Eredith when his people, the Old Scholars, were slaughtered by the beast king Ozukette. Olomon would go on to serve as the first scribe of Glavius Adaeus, and his line would survive some four thousand years. Today, Bennehym and his family were the last descendents of Olomon and the Old Scholars.

Although they sat together, neither Faeron nor Lydia dared whisper over Bennehym's tale, instead trading looks at all the best bits. When he was done speaking, Bennehym let the class out early. Faeron and Lydia walked together to the elevator, chatting all the way. The halls were empty with most students still in class, and Faeron could hear the muffled voices of different professors through the doors as they passed.

"Where are you headed now?" said Lydia, as they arrived at the elevator.

"Bo Kora is my last for the day," said Faeron, "so probably the Athenaeum."

"Such a pretty building," gasped Lydia, pressing both the up and down call-buttons for the elevator at once. "I don't think I've been inside since we took that field trip in year ten. All I remember is rows and rows of books. I really should go read there some time"

"Definitely go in the evening," said Faeron. "The way the setting sun shines through the stained glass, painting the books in different colors. It's… it's…"

"Romantic?" offered Lydia.

Just then, the elevator door slid open and Alanah said, "going up."

"That's me," said Lydia. "Motive Expression is up next." Boarding the empty elevator, she caught the door. "You know, I've got dance most evenings, but maybe if I have a day off I'll swing by the athenaeum."

"You wouldn't regret it," grinned Faeron.

"Awesome! See you around then." The elevator door closed.

Faeron's elevator arrived seconds later, and he waited down in the courtyard for almost twenty minutes before a large group of students strolled out the Academy's sliding front doors. The glare of the afternoon sun off of Auri's bronze-tipped hair, cascading over her tall shoulders, made her stand out among them.

Spotting Faeron, Auri waved and ran to the ape fountain, where he was sitting. "Saw Quinn in the hall earlier. He's got tech lab until late, so… ready to get our hands on that list?" she asked, looking as giddy as he now felt.

"Do you even need to ask?" said Faeron.

They ran the two blocks to the Athenaeum, and found Mathas just inside, helping a customer check out a small stack of colorful books.

"Tell Ninci happy birthday from me, won't you?" the old capillum said sweetly to his customer. "Three is an exciting year."

"Yeah, sure," grunted the man. He had short greying hair, a bristly goatee, and must have just gotten off work as he was still wearing his stark white City Customs uniform.

After the customs officer left, Mathas turned his attention to Faeron and Auri. "I suppose you've come for Evolice's list?"

"If that's alright with you," said Faeron, exchanging an excited look with Auri.

"Of course," said Mathas. "The Athenaeum's quiet enough. If you want to follow me…" He led the pair across the commons to the glass elevator. They rode up to the second-floor reading room then took the southern hall past several dozen bookshelves to another wide open room. There was a set of stairs leading both up and down, several comfortable chairs, and a simple wooden door with Mathas' name printed on a metal plaque.

Retrieving a small brass key from his pocket, Mathas unlocked the door and ushered Faeron and Auri into his expertly organized office. It was an L-shaped room, much like Evolice's, with a long window on one wall looking down into the dark and lifeless workshop. Hand painted canvases of all shapes and sizes were hung on the walls, each with Mathas' signature in the bottom right corner. They depicted forest landscapes and strange creatures: a single massive tree casting its shadow across a forested mountain, a squirrel with a long straw-like snout, eyeless birds and large-eared bats; Memories of Roana, Mathas called them. In one corner was an easel covered in a thin sheet and glass cabinets filled with assorted paints. Across the room, was a sturdy darkwood desk. There were narrow frosted windows behind his desk, and, between them, a hanging shelf with several colossal tomes.

Mathas selected one of the heavier titles with a plain black spine looking to be several thousand pages long. "Don't be daunted now," he said, heaving the book onto his desk. "The bulk of this is information regarding the early kytra and the Hosts. We're only looking at the last half-millennium." He opened the tome and flipped toward the back, no more than a few hundred pages from the end. Auri and Faeron huddled around the desk to get a better view. There was a large title at the top of each page, then several paragraphs of information. Most titles near the start of the book had multiple pages of texts where many near the back were nearly blank with just one or two sentences.

There were maybe fifty names from the last five-hundred years, and nearly every one of them had a little silver "S" printed beside them. Mathas told them it was to denote that they were only suspected to be kytra, never proven by Evolice. The one exception was a page titled "Itrhis - Host of Glavius," though it had only a couple paragraphs of information below.

"I thought there'd be hundreds or thousands of kytra before the fall," said Auri, sounding shocked as they flipped through the pages. "From this... Was there really so few of us?"

"As I mentioned before," said Mathas, "Evolice's research was far from complete. That said, in the years before the fall, kytra had faded to all but a myth among the few who still followed the patronage. I lived nearly my whole life never knowing I was one of them."

"How is that possible?" asked Faeron. "How could you not know?"

"Without access to echo crystals, how could I know?" countered Mathas. "Auri, you and Quinn were discovered when you shared the vision of the obelisk ten years ago. For the rest of us, myself, Vox, Evolice, Eamon, the twins... even you, Faeron, it was the ability to see light in the crystals that revealed our kytra nature. There are other signs, dreams of light, coincidences one cannot explain, but without the gems or displays of the light, like Mr. Rite's experience with the dancing girl, we have but speculation."

"That's..." Auri looked taken aback. "In a world of billions there were so few kytra, and yet in our small city there's what, eight of us, nine counting Evolice." Turning to Faeron, there was a passionate fire in her bronze eyes. "Knowing that, how can you care so little about the Patronage, about *Glavius*? He gave us a city of kytra to fight the plague."

"And he let *billions* die," countered Faeron, annoyed by the sudden attack. "Not to mention it was the Hoststone shattering that sent my mom away. Face it, no spirit of man made me a kytra, no spirit of man has done anything to bring my mom back, and no spirit of man is gonna fix this world. That's up to us kytra and the scientists at the academy."

"And who do you think gave us that academy?" growled Auri.

"Enough," said Mathas calmly, placing a hand on both their shoulders. "Your differences are the reason that you are stronger together. Neither of you is fighting for nothing."

Just then a knock sounded at the door.

"I'll get it," grunted Faeron, welcoming the interruption from Auri's assault. He strutted over and opened the door, finding his father on the other side. Eamon had a black blazer slung over one shoulder. His button up was black trimmed in gold matching the warmth of his eyes.

"Am I interrupting something?" he asked, stepping forward and embracing Faeron in a surprise hug. "Serris told me you'd be here."

"Not at all," called Mathas from his desk, "please join us."

"Somebody, help," groaned Faeron as his father squeezed him tighter.

Chuckling, Eamon released Faeron and strutted across the room to Mathas' desk.

"Evolice's list..." said Eamon, "for Jakob?"

"Not quite," said Faeron. Rejoining the others, Faeron told Eamon every detail of his dream from the library to the dancing girl in the park. He explained how they were using her to try to pinpoint exactly when Jakob lived, since he wasn't in the book, and whether Evolice may have gone after him to recover the vault key.

"Eyes like rainbow fire... never found anything like that... but, you know what..." Eamon smiled victoriously as he rushed around the desk to the book. "Three names come to mind. First is... Sophia something... where is it? Here!" He stopped at a page marked: Sophie Inulingua. "I remember this one. She was an old athlete, long before our time, broke just about every world record you could imagine in her era. But, if we're looking for the living, the other two may be more helpful." He flipped a few more pages, stopping on: Nu Flume. "She's not a bad fit," he said. "We saw her on an old Quisitive docVUE, like we did a number of the recent ones. She was a philosophy professor at Outmarr University. Disappeared about ten years before the plague. No trace of her."

"Any descriptions of these people?" asked Faeron. "The kytra from my dream had dark skin and long curly hair… and like I mentioned, her eyes were lit with rainbow flame."

"Five foot ten, salduni descent," read Eamon. "I don't know about the eyes but… it's not impossible."

"What about the last one?" asked Auri eagerly.

Eamon turned just two more pages and stopped. "Final one is a girl from Innit'Ro. She was a friend of a friend who was studying in the North Suburbs when the plague hit."

"She wasn't invited here?" asked Faeron sharply.

"Every living person in this book was extended an invitation, even if they weren't in the names given by Glavius" said Eamon. "Most, like Fiat here, declined."

"Why though?" asked Auri.

"Because," said Mathas, solemnly, "the end of the world always seems like a fantasy until it happens to you."

"I only ever heard stories," said Eamon, "but word was she was a self-proclaimed 'dreamer,' bright as anyone our friend had ever met. It really did seem crazy, what we were telling people. We were lucky we got as many to agree as we did."

Going back over the three entries, Faeron couldn't say for certain whether any of them was the dancing girl. Some details seemed off, but not enough to knock any of the names out. There were still many more names to search for anyone Eamon might not have remembered, and it took the full evening to go through the rest of the list. In the end, none of them proved any more promising than Eamon's three. Mathas announced he was going to start closing up shop and Eamon, Faeron, and Auri said their goodbyes, heading home toward the Twinfire Towers.

"Well, did any of them *sound* right?" asked Auri as they stepped into the cool night. Golden light from the Clearstream Cinema sign illuminated a group of women meditating on mats near the edge of the park. The trees cast long shadows across the well-trimmed grass and the sapphire and violet stars above shone bright despite the city's glow.

"What do you mean, sound right?" asked Faeron as they descended the steps and began their stroll along the park's edge.

"Like, when you first meet someone," said Auri. Her hair shone fierce as ever in the golden light, her eyes warm and determined. "They say their name, and in your head, you're telling yourself, of course that's their name? It just fits perfectly."

"I know exactly what you mean," said Eamon. "Never met a Garrett I liked."

"Exactly," said Auri. They passed the women meditating and continued on the path. Up ahead loomed Erkwright theater, muses carved into its stone walls and grothgoyles jutting menacingly from the corners of the angled roof. "Your dancing girl," asked Auri, "was she a Sophia, a Nu, or a Fiat?"

"I don't know," said Faeron. "Nothing really leaped out at me"

"Then maybe something will turn up in your dreams to help narrow things down," said Auri. "After all, your mom didn't leave because she saw a man write books his whole life. Wherever Jakob's story is headed, I'd bet you the dancing girl is part of it." A pair of young joggers in academy track pants passed with a friendly wave on the far side of the street.

"Assuming I can remember anything if she does show up," said Faeron, glumly. This morning he had worked up expecting to take a more active role in finding his mom. Now, he was back to waiting for answers.

"If I had to guess," said Eamon, "I'd wager you only remember last night's dream so well *because* of her. The light surrounding her sounded simply unforgettable. If she shows up again, you'll probably know it."

Faeron considered this, walking in silence past Erkwrite and the Woven Dome, a massive bunball stadium. The dome, for which it was named, was made of a series of beams that looked like long white reeds, woven loose enough to leave the field below mostly open to the sky.

They turned off Perimeter Lane at the east end of the park, following another wide road between the stadium and Astral Cafe.

The night was louder here. The path was well lit. Both the Bellwillow Market and the many restaurants near the foot of the Twinfire Towers were alive with chatter.

As the road grew steadily more busy, faces in the crowd began to turn at the trios passing. Those quicker to recognize them offered a smile, wave, or a "Host Eamon," with a bow. Each time, Eamon returned the greeting cheerfully.

"So, Auri," said Eamon, as they neared the Twinfire Towers' cobblestone courtyard. "Patron Odom, mentioned you'd be leading a new team at the tech drive next week."

"Yeah!" grinned Auri. "We're trying to get the year sevens involved this year. Paeris Aekins from that year has a whole group she's got interested, so I'm going to be looking after them. I was thinking though, now that I have you here, what would you think about using this to start a pen pal program between the youth group and some of the kids in Korva receiving the tech?"

"Love the idea!" clapped Eamon. "I'll try to get something together for that tomorrow. Vox'll be proud to know it was your idea."

Auri beamed proudly as they entered the wide open courtyard. Far above, the statue of Glavius stood atop the bridge between the towers. He looked like a younger Bennehym, bald with a braided beard. He wore long rippling robes painted in violet and crimson by the flames in his outstretched palms.

They made for the door of the violet tower, on the right. Inside the lobby, the floor was decorated marble, etched in Patronage iconography. On either side of the central walkway, leading back toward a fleet of elevators, were a number of busts depicting the Patronage's many Hosts. Despite its grandeur, the lobby was a cozy place, filled with social seating and wings off to either side, leading to more private gathering spaces. Looking up, they could see through the hollow center of the hundred ringed floors to the stained glass ceiling far overhead.

From above, Faeron could hear the echoes of ambient chatter and laughter.

They took the elevator to floor sixty-two, and as Faeron and Auri got off, they said their goodbyes.

"I'm glad I got the chance to come by," said Eamon. "Sorry I've been so busy while you're dealing with this. We should do dinner upstairs, at home, some night."

"Yeah, let's do that," said Faeron.

"Of course, you're invited too, Auri," said Eamon with a grin.

"I mean, I assumed," said Auri playfully. "Goodnight, Host Eamon."

"Goodnight, kids."

CHAPTER SEVEN

THE GLOVES OF GIVE AND TAKE

The next two weeks kept Faeron's nose glued to his desk, churning out homework like a full time job. He'd never experienced a more busy first week of academy in his life. Auri seemed to have little issue keeping her work in check even as she spent her afternoons going door to door with the youth group, collecting outdated and unused technology donations.

As soon as Auri returned home each night, the two would rush straight out to the balcony for meditations. To Faeron, the only way forward now was through learning to shape. His dreams might bring answers, but he'd known that for a decade. Faeron was tired of waiting.

One night, as Faeron reached, only to find his water glass empty, he recognized an opportunity. Faeron opened his eyes and held the meditation. Slowly, he rose from his seat.

"You're still meditating," gasped Auri, looking up from her chair. "I can see it, in your eyes. They're glazed, far off, but almost brighter somehow."

Faeron grinned and the light faded.

"And it's gone… isn't it?" asked Auri, disapprovingly. "See what happens when I feed your ego?"

Faeron would continue to practice during nightly meditations, taking occasional breaks just to give himself a chance to get up and walk around. Auri, meanwhile, was hellbent on achieving the waking meditation herself before their next class. The first few nights were the most frustrating for her as she could only hold the deep meditation for a second or two without the Nylkshave. She could calm herself fine, just like Mathas taught them, but the peace would last only seconds before she'd breathe sharply and clutch her head. From there, her ability to calm her mind would spiral quickly.

"This is hopeless," she told him, several nights into their increased meditations.

Faeron looked up from his calm to see Auri near tears.

"I've been trying to hide it long enough…" she said, "and you better… you better not try to pity me for what I'm about to say, you hear?"

"Auri, I… I promise," asked Faeron cautiously. "What's going on?"

"I still see the crimson every time," said Auri softly, the corners of her eyes watering as she stared out over the balcony at the colorful city below. "It never really stopped… I just pretended it did so you and Mathas would stop trying to fix it. I think… because I knew it isn't something you can fix, but I still shouldn't have lied."

Faeron's heart dropped. Ten years ago, when the Hoststone shattered, every kytra had seen the same vision, the obelisk of light and the crack down its center. Auri, alone, had seen something more. She saw beyond the crevice and witnessed the crimson light raging inside. Long before they had started meditations, it was all she could see in her dreams, nightmares of the crimson. Faeron had thought those had passed since they started meditations, but now…

"I know it's intense," offered Faeron. In his deepest meditations he'd encountered tiny streaks of crimson, raging in the current. They were some of the most intense scenes, violent eruptions and dying stars. Still, Faeron always passed out of these images as soon as he entered, where Auri seemed stuck to them like glue. "I can see the colors, too, the other hues when I meditate, and sometimes I think it's just a matter of letting it pull you through—"

"Pull me through?" said Auri forcefully. The tears were gone and now her furious bronze eyes were locked on him. "I get you're trying to help, but you don't know anything at all. You always talk about these little scenes in the colors of the current and how I just need to *flow* with them, but this isn't the same at all. First comes the good light, the white and pearl of peridom, same thing you see... but the crimson is always close behind. It consumes *everything* else, and I know that if I don't open my eyes it'll take me too."

"Auri," said Faeron. "I think that if you just—"

"If I just what, Faeron?" demanded Auri. "Breathe deep? Relax? Let myself be taken by that nightmare!? You have no idea what I see and you always think you know the answer. You're just so— Ugh" She growled and stomped off to bed without another word.

Faeron knew better than to follow her. For another hour or so, he sat in silence before venturing off to bed.

Faeron's dreams were long almost every night. His two weeks were Jakob's twenty as the dreamworld's Highsun ended and Cropsun flew by, making way for a temperate Lowsun in the coastal city. The few images Faeron remembered from his dreams showed decorative lights strung up all down the block and holiday merchandise flooding shop windows throughout the art district. In all that time, Jakob had barely gotten through another two chapters of his book, and the few bits Faeron remembered were hardly his best work. Faeron woke up most mornings with Jakob's stresses bogging him down and nothing useful to show for it.

Faeron didn't bring up the crimson again, nor did Auri mention the events of the other night. Instead, she came to every meditation with renewed focus, often going the entire night without saying a word to Faeron. The night before their kytra classes picked back up, Auri made her first breakthrough. It was a brisk Lowend evening, and Faeron and Auri had spent the afternoon working through the rest of the new Prophet's Guard setlist. An hour into their meditations, Auri sprang up suddenly from her seat, pulling Faeron away from peridom's light as she loudly declared, "A minute and a half. I held it the whole time!" The evening breeze was cool on the balcony, and both she and Faeron were in cozy sweatshirts.

"Auri, this is..." grinned Faeron, blinking his eyes open to see her smiling triumphantly back at him. "What did you do different?"

"I fought back," she said proudly. "I don't know how else to describe it, but I think... maybe what I needed to do all along was just the opposite of what Mathas told me. I don't need to let go. I need to face it head on."

Faeron wasn't sure he understood, but he was too happy for her to care. "You know what that means, right?" he asked her. "If you can do that tomorrow, all you need to do is open your eyes. Just hold it and open your eyes."

"And I'll have done the waking meditating, just like you," she said, beaming brightly.

Even though she hadn't managed the full waking meditation yet, Auri seemed to be in a great mood the next morning as they headed off to the Academy. The morning classes sped by and Faeron's mind was filled with thoughts of shaping that evening. Faeron and Auri met Quinn in the cafeteria after Life and Legacy. Quinn was practically bouncing in his seat as he waved them over.

"Guys, guys!" called Quinn, as they joined him at a squat round table in the chatter-filled cafeteria. "There's a big tourney in the Deity Lounge goin' on."

"So you mentioned," said Auri, "five times last week."

"Yeah, well an outsider, a Nomad, is playing for the first time ever and he's made it all the way to the finals!"

"I didn't think Nomads had Deity," said Auri, her interest piqued despite the topic.

"Yeah," said Faeron, "From the stories Vox told, that kind of stuff doesn't exist beyond the wall. I mean, we've never seen a Nomad player before, right?"

"I suppose there's gotta be a first," said Quinn. "I've heard they have leagues in the Peak, so it was only a matter of time before the Nomads got in on it. Anyway, the finals are tonight, and guess who has VIP tickets for all of us?" The green of his hazel eyes shone bright as his toothy grin.

"Wait, why do you have tickets?" asked Faeron. "Not that I'm arguing. Believe me, I'm in."

"I entered the tourney on a whim," explained Quinn. "I mean, with you two so busy… why not? Figured I'd get knocked out early in qualifiers, but no loss in trying, right?

"Sure," said Auri, as she chowed down on a buttery luppice roll.

"Anywho," Quinn continued. "I made it all the way to the final sixteen before a *real* player finally smoked me. It was an embarrassment, but not the point… It turns out that everyone who makes the final sixteen gets their own private VIP lounge, win or lose. That means an upstairs suite with our own private table and anything we want from the menu."

"Look at Mr. VIP," said Faeron, twisting his fork through his noodles. "I humbly accept your invitation."

"I hate to be that person," said Auri, "but you do realize we have class tonight. A particularly important class for two of us." She glared at Faeron.

"Don't worry," said Quinn happily. "It's not until after. Besides, there's always pre-game interviews and the like. We'll have plenty of time to get settled in our room before the real show starts."

"Well then," said Auri. "I suppose I can't say no to a night of free slushies, even if it is spent watching that… *mockery* of the Deity universe. I'm off to class, see you two!"

A.I. Upkeep, later that afternoon, felt like it was several dozen hours long as Faeron tapped his foot anxiously through Professor Bundst's introduction of the city's Weather AI, Revna. She was a younger AI and took the form of a large woman with dark stormy clouds for hair. As she spoke, her wispy locks rumbled, and whenever she raised her voice, a flash of lightning crackled down her back.

After class, Faeron and Quin met Auri in the courtyard. Her nerves seemed to have really set in as she rushed from her perch at the lip of the ape fountain the moment she caught sight of Quinn and Faeron.

"There you are!" she called. "If I had to sit with my thoughts another second longer, I was going to go insane. There's an hour and a half until class. Want to grab something light at Lilypad, then maybe practice a bit more before class?"

"Sure," said Faeron, who's stomach growled at the thought of food. "You in, Quinn?"

"Of course!"

Lilypad was a small place in the north end of Bellwillow Market. Faeron, Auri, and Quinn grabbed a tram from the academy and were able to get a table without any wait. The tables sat high and were set up around the edge of a round creek with the kitchen in the very center. While guests ate, they could watch the cooks at work, flipping meats and stacking fruit slices high. Flowing slowly around the creek were dozens of lily pads, and on them stood animatronic frogs in suits, just tall enough to reach the tables. The frogs snatched plated food from the kitchen, and, with a bow, delivered them to guests as they floated past.

All three of them ordered rice rolls filled with fruits, just enough to hold them over until their free dining tonight. After eating, they rushed back across the park. In the low light of dusk, they arrived at the Athenaeum just a half-hour early for class. Surprisingly, the door was locked, the windows inside dark, and a sign had been posted reading:

Closed Temporarily
Returning Soon

"Where do you suppose he's gone?" asked Faeron. Mathas rarely left the Athenaeum, to the point that Faeron sometimes wondered whether Mathas actually had a home outside his office.

"Not a clue," said Auri.

"Your guess is as good as mine," added Quinn.

They sat on the steps, Quinn people watching, while Faeron and Auri practiced their meditations. Sounds of play and laughter faded in the darkness of his mind. As Faeron let the current of light wash through him, he could just make out Quinn's voice calling in the distance. Faeron opened his eyes and saw Mathas crossing Loem Park. The old capillum waved to them and quickened his pace.

"Apologies for keeping you three waiting," said Mathas, a twinge of excitement in his normally level voice. "A new book came in this morning, a collection of poetry discovered in the southern suburbs. I was just now at Forgeworks getting the reprint process set up."

"Really?" asked Auri excitedly. "When can I read it?"

"As early as tomorrow," said Mathas. "Speaking of early, there's still another…" he checked his watch, "ten minutes until your class. I have some last minute business to attend to in my office, but I'll let you three into the classroom now if you like."

Mathas unlocked the Athenaeum and then walked to the classroom across the foyer, unlocking its door as well before heading upstairs in the elevator.

Auri, Quinn, and Faeron entered the small rectangular classroom and took their usual seats at the shared table with Faeron and Auri closest to the workshop window and Quinn at the head. The room had little in the way of decoration; it's walls were barren but for the empty whiteboard by Mathas' desk and the large workshop window. There was a second door in the back of the room that led into the workshop, though Faeron hadn't been inside there in more than a decade.

"Faeron, you see this?" said Auri. She tapped her finger against the window.

Peering into the dark workshop, Faeron could just barely make out several tables like the one they sat at now. One of them was set apart from the others, in the center of the open workshop, and held a large contraption, too shadowed to make out in any detail.

"What do you suppose that is?" asked Faeron, and Auri pressed her face to the glass.

"Some sort of kytra experiment," said Auri, betraying nervousness in her voice as she squinted through the glass.

"Let me see," said Quinn, scampering over to get a view and squeezing in right next to Auri. "It looks kind of like a track or—"

Just then, the door swung open as Myllie and Kaelynn bounded into the room. They were still in their school uniforms with Myllie in a skirt and Kaelynn wearing long pants. Both their navy blazers were wrapped around their waists, and they had bright pink backpacks that they tossed haphazardly onto the table as they took their spots opposite Faeron and Auri.

"How's the time off treated you two?" asked Auri.

"Kaelynn broke her toe on a kid's face," Myllie reported.

"Myllie!" hissed Kaelynn. "You don't have to tell everyone everything all the time!"

"Oh no," said Auri, "you can't leave us without the details."

"Some year seven boy whiffed so hard trying to catch a cross ball that he tripped straight into Kaelynn's cleat," giggled Myllie. "He had a concussion and had to be carted off, but Kaelynn acted all tough like nothing even happened. It wasn't until we got home and she took off her cleat that we saw her *whole sock* was soaked in blood."

"It was barely anything," contested Kaelynn.

"It was *disgusting*," asserted Myllie.

"Well, I certainly hope your toe is better now," said Auri, wearing an amused smile.

"Yeah, it doesn't really hurt or anything," said Kaelynn.

"Not that you'd admit if it did," added her sister. "Now, where's Mathas?"

"On my way," came a voice as the door swung open once more. Mathas ducked through the doorframe and swept into the classroom. "Apologies for the delay everyone." He went to his desk with his long brown robe trailing behind him and took a seat in his swiveling chair. "It's been a lonely two weeks without you all around. How are your Academy classes going?"

"So boring," said Myllie, burying her head in her hands. "Why do I even need to know math anyway?"

"I don't know," chirped Kaelynn, "but I'm liking this writing class I'm in."

"Oh, really?" said Mathas, raising a wide silver brow. "Do you have anything I could read?"

"It's private," said Kaelynn definitively, her whole body locking up.

"That's perfectly alright," chuckled Mathas. "What about you all?" He looked at the three older kytra.

"My schedule is mostly politics and patronage history," said Auri happily. "Aur Poro, too." Like Bo Kora, Aur Poro was an old martial art, but its roots were in the more aggressive fighting styles of ancient Saldun, rather than the guarded techniques of the Old Scholars

"Gross, gross, and gross," said Faeron, "we all know Bo Kora is just a better Aur Poro."

"I'm happy to test that theory," said Auri, cracking her knuckles loudly.

"Behave you two," said Mathas, chuckling at their antics. "What about you, Quinn?"

"I've actually been working on something super cool in my salvaging class," piped Quinn from the end of the table. "I repurposed an old chip for Logic that allows him to integrate with lots of pre-plague tech."

"I wish my projects were that cool," said Faeron. "All I've had is essays."

"Well, you're beyond the point of essays here, at least," said Mathas. "Ten years, we've sat together, discussing the meditations which led the Old Scholars to shaping. You two have proven a keen understanding both in theory and practice, which means there's nothing left to learn but the art of shaping itself. What do you say, shall we go check out the workshop?"

"Absolutely!" burst Faeron.

"And since it's an occasion," said Mathas, "the rest of you can come watch. Consider this a visual learning exercise."

"If Faeron's gonna be shaping, we're all gonna need some serious safety pads!" said Myllie, grabbing a mask from her backpack and pulling it over her face.

"I don't think it's me you need to be worried about," said Faeron, shooting a side glance at Auri. Snarling, she whipped her long dark hair around, treating Faeron to a face full of her metallic bronze ends.

Mathas walked to the workshop door and slid his key in the lock. For the first time in ten years, Faeron watched the workshop door creak open. A familiar woody smell drafted into the room, sending Faeron straight back to his childhood, to memories of his mother and her many strange contraptions littered about the open workshop.

"Serris, lights please," said Mathas as Faeron followed him inside.

Long industrial lights hanging from the ceiling flickered to life, and Faeron saw the workshop looked much different now than he remembered. It was a large space, though not nearly as enormous as it had once appeared through his ten-year-old eyes. There were no windows besides the view from the classroom and a corner overlook from Mathas' office on the second floor. Gone were the many strange wooden contraptions that filled Faeron's memories of this place. In their place were four tables, three in the corner beneath the overlook and one set apart in the center of the marble floor. The tables in the corner were mostly empty, but for a single silver bunball. Near the center of the workshop, the table set apart from the others held a scaled down model of a mountainside city and a toy alca sitting perfectly still on a track that ran all around the mountain. Faeron couldn't make heads or tales of what such a display had to do with shaping, but he was in no position to question Mathas's methods. Beyond the table, several bright blue pads had been laid out across the floor, and Faeron could see a small platform with steps, about two feet off the ground, facing the pads.

Myllie ran over toward the platform but Mathas raised his hand. "Slow down now," he said. "If you're to join us in the workshop there are rules you must follow. First, and most importantly, is that only those of you ready to shape can enter the matted area. The rest of you will need to wait over there near the tables." He pointed to the corner. "Second, I would request that any command I make, no matter how silly or strange, be obeyed at a moment's notice. Shaping can be unpredictable and even volatile if a shaper is not prepared."

"What do you mean, volatile?" asked Auri, the corner of her mouth twitching nervously.

"Come, I'll show you."

Mathas hobbled over to a table in the corner with a silver bunball in the center. The twins' faces lit up as they saw the apple-sized ball, sprinting past the others to the table.

"Don't touch!" called Mathas, just as Myllie was about to swipe the ball.

Once they were all gathered, Mathas reached into his robes, producing a pair of leather gloves. They were dark and fingerless, and their frayed ends looked aged. On the back of each glove was a single stone, mossy green in color. From inside the stones, Faeron could see a softly glowing light.

"Are those…?" asked Auri.

"Echo crystals," answered Mathas. "For some of you, it's been years since you've seen something like this, but it is the light that each of you see within these stones that is the surest mark of a kytra."

Faeron was well acquainted with echo crystals, as his father's office held nearly a dozen of such relics, locked away securely behind armored glass display cases. Since Faeron's mishap with the Hoststone, this was the closest he'd been to one.

"As you no doubt remember from your studies," said Mathas, "these crystals exist both in our world and beyond, in peridom. They are like a window through which a kytra may give and take light. There is, in my mind, no simpler way to demonstrate this than the Gloves of Give and Take. These artifacts were once worn by the Old-Scholars, thousands of years ago."

"That's one of the relics recovered from the monastery, isn't it?" gasped Auri excitedly.

"Indeed," said Mathas. "It remained incredibly preserved beyond the Nylkdoor, untouched by time until Evolice broke the seal."

The young kytra all wore a look of awe as they stared at the ancient gloves. Faeron imagined his mother, about his age, venturing deep beneath the monastery of the Old-Scholars, unearthing these gloves among the other relics now displayed in his father's office.

"The crystals you see here are refined gems," continued Mathas, "fashioned by a kytra millennia ago. I expect these three know the difference well enough, but do you twins know what makes a refined gem different from its unrefined counterpart?"

Myllie looked to Kaelynn, who returned with an equally lost shrug.

"Alright then," said Mathas, "Quinn, go ahead and tell the group what the difference is."

"Refined gems do that shaping for you," piped Quinn enthusiastically. "All a kytra needs to do is provide light and the refined gem shapes it as the crafter intended."

"Exactly so," said Mathas. "A perfect starting point for a kytra learning to shape. However, before either of you don the gloves, I have a warning." Mathas ran a long slender finger across the back of one gem. "Do you see the cracks here?" Narrow schisms, no wider than a hair, snaked across the otherwise flawlessly polished crystal. "No instrument of man can damage an echo crystal. It is that strength which held the Nylkdoor against King Ozukette's army all those thousands of years ago and protected the young Glavius Adaeus. So, how is it, do you suppose, that this crack was formed when Ozukette's mightiest weapons could not break the stone?"

"THE BUNBALL," yelled Myllie excitedly.

"No," chuckled Mathas. "No explosive, nor technology, nor bunball has ever compromised an echo crystal."

"You told us this is a warning," said Faeron, trying to sort out where their mentor was leading them, "so it was an accident, a kytra trying to shape, like we are now."

"Exactly correct," said Mathas. "Balance is the very heart of shaping. What is taken must be returned, and what is given must be replaced. Should a kytra fail to reach balance when their tie to the light is cut, the universe will right itself. Often chaotic and destructive, there is no will to its method, simply the path of least resistance. Each etching you see on this stone is a mistake of the past. Some more… severe… than others." Once again, he ran his finger along the stone, resting at the largest central crack.

"But how do we know if we've balanced or not?" asked Auri, looking nervously down at the crystals in the gloves.

"You will know," said Mathas. "When shaping, a kytra can feel the light, the imbalance seeking a way home through the crystals. However, words can only explain so much. To understand further, you two are going to need to take the first bold step and feel the light for yourself. I shall demonstrate."

Mathas pulled the gloves over his long capillum hands. They fit small, but not so much so as to break at the seams. "Come, you two," he said, limping toward the mats and beckoning Faeron and Auri to follow, "and one of you please grab the ball."

Auri plucked up the bunball as Faeron followed Mathas.

"I'll need a volunteer," said Mathas once they'd reached the mats. "Don't worry, you're not shaping yet."

"I'll go," said Faeron.

"Very good, then step onto the platform."

Faeron did as he was instructed, crossing the mats and climbing the two steps to the top of the sturdy wooden platform.

"Now, Auri," said Mathas, "would you hand Faeron the ball?"

"On it," she said, crossing the mat and passing the ball to Faeron. He felt a bit silly, standing there above the others with a bunball in one hand.

"Good, now step back please, Auri. Faeron, face me." Mathas stepped back, just out of reach, while ushering Auri further back to the edge of the pads. "Go ahead and hold the ball out over the edge."

Faeron held the ball outstretched in one hand.

"Good," said his mentor, "just a moment." Mathas closed his large black eyes, paused a second, and reopened them with a distant look.

"What's he doing?" squealed Myllie from the corner. "Is he shaping?"

"Quiet" shushed Kaelynn.

"The act of catching a fruit midair," said Mathas, retaining his glazed stare as he spoke, "is a classic first step into the world of shaping. The premise is simple. The fruit falls, the gloves stop its descent, and the kytra plucks it from the air. As not to be wasteful, we will be using something a bit more practical than fruit today. Go ahead Faeron, drop the ball."

Faeron released his grip.

For several feet, the ball fell, as Faeron had expected it to. Then, his mentor outstretched his left hand.

A streak of mossy green light shot from the ball and coiled itself around the capillum's open hand, shining brightest near the gem. The ball, meanwhile, hung perfectly still in the air.

The light snaking around the gloves began to fade the moment it appeared and only took a second to dissipate completely. Mathas had just enough time to step forward and grasp the ball.

"You must be quick," he said, holding up the ball for all to see, "as it takes energy to hold the ball still. You'll feel the light begin to slip away the moment you have it in your grasp, like trying to clutch a handful of sand."

"What happens if we don't catch it before the light runs out?" asked Auri, a twinge of nervousness in her voice.

"Let us find out," said Mathas. "Faeron if you'd please." He held the ball up for Faeron to take.

Faeron snagged the bunball. "Same thing?" he asked.

Mathas took a step back and nodded. "When you're ready," he said.

Faeron released the ball, and just like last time, Mathas let it fall for a few feet before reaching out with his left hand.

"Watch," he instructed as mossy green light leapt from the ball, meeting his fingers and snaking down to the gem on the back of the glove. The light lasted just over a second before it faded, and, when it did, the ball fell again, hitting the mats with a muted *thud*.

"As you see," said Mathas, "so long as you keep your connection to peridom intact, the gloves will ensure your hold on the ball is released when you run out of light to hold it. Now… unless there's any other questions, I believe we're ready to begin." He looked between Faeron and Auri, giving them a moment to express any last concerns. Auri stood pale faced at the edge of the mats, but didn't say a word.

"What about that?" asked Faeron, pointing to the mountainous model on the table.

"We'll get to that," said Mathas, knowingly. "But, for now, we'll take things one glove at a time. Who's first?"

Auri's face said more than enough for Faeron to know what he had to do.

"I'll go first," said Faeron, his chest starting to feel tight. He'd looked forward to this moment his whole life, and if he didn't dream as Jakob every night, he might have believed he was dreaming now.

"Very well," said Mathas, pulling the gloves off his hands. "Come, switch places with me."

Faeron hopped off the platform and took the gloves from his mentor. After collecting the ball, Mathas went around and began to ascend the steps, taking slow heavy steps as he climbed on his weak leg. He stopped where Faeron stood before, with the ball held out in one hand.

Faeron could feel his heart in his chest as he slid the coarse gloves over his hands. They were loose, but there was a string at the back to tighten them around his wrists. Seeing them closer, there were dozens of little cracks across the face of the stones and both had a large central schism. He knew that if he messed up, he certainly wouldn't be the first, but the way Mathas had described balance, he wondered how many of those screw-ups had led to serious bodily harm.

"When you're ready, go ahead and perform the meditation," said Mathas, towering above them from atop the platform.

Auri gave Faeron a nervous thumbs up, while the other kytra looked on excitedly from afar.

Faeron breathed deep. Calming his body was easy, his mind less so. Doubts, fears, and trepidation screamed in his head, but with each inhale he let them shout their last, and with each exhale he released them. When Faeron's mind was quiet, his body gone, and the light of peridom washing through what was left him, he told himself, *open your eyes.*

The whole workshop seemed to glow as every table, every mat, all the kytra and the polished floor let off a soft shimmering glow.

"Are you ready?" asked Mathas.

Faeron's mind was blurred, like he'd stayed up for two days straight, but he forced himself to nod.

"Dropping the ball in three... two... one..." Mathas let go of the bunball.

The light around the ball flared as it fell. Faeron mimicked his mentor's actions, reaching out with his left hand, but nothing happened. The ball fell to the mats and a wave of disappointment crashed down upon Faeron. The light vanished. His mind cleared.

"A valiant first try!" clapped Mathas. "Miss Lem, you're up."

Faeron first collected the ball, returning it to Mathas, then walked back to the edge of the mats. He handed the gloves off to Auri, whose face was now whiter than the marble tile.

"You can do this," he whispered just loud enough for her to hear. "It's just like you did last night. All you need to do is open your eyes."

Auri gulped and wordlessly walked onto the mats.

"Any questions before you begin?" asked Mathas.

Auri shook her head, standing just an arms-length away from the platform.

"Then begin your meditation," instructed Mathas.

Auri closed her eyes, her breathing slowed, and she stood still as a statue. Time ticked on, for how long Faeron couldn't say, but the twins both began looking bored.

"Miss Lem?" asked Mathas eventually. "Are you ready to open your eyes?"

Auri finally moved. Her fists clenched and her lip snarled. "It's a lot of pressure, okay?" she said. "Maybe Faeron should go again. I need a minute to get ready."

"Of course," said Mathas, "take your time. There is no rushing this process."

Auri opened her fierce bronze eyes and stomped over to the edge of the mats where Faeron was waiting. Tearing off the gloves, she dumped them into Faeron's hands and then stalked over the corner tables with the younger kytra. No sooner had she taken a seat and closed her eyes than Quinn scuttled over and took a seat just beside her. Faeron could see him whisper something to Auri, though she seemed to ignore him entirely, focusing intently on her meditations.

Once again up to shape, Faeron crossed the mats to the platform. This time he didn't need to wait for instructions. Faeron closed his eyes and quieted his mind. Moments later, he blinked his eyes open to find the workshop shimmering. "Ready," he said, training himself on the ball.

"Focus on the light," said Mathas, "the energy building in the ball as it falls. First catch the energy, then catch the ball. Understand?"

"I think so," said Faeron.

"Three… two… one…" Mathas dropped the ball.

This time, as the ball fell, Faeron focused on the pearl light surrounding the silver sphere. He reached out his left arm and imagined a second arm, longer, plucking the ball out of the air. As he imagined it, the ball obeyed, stopping at Mathas' knee level.

Moss-green light leapt from the ball, rushing into Faeron's outstretched palm. He could feel it, like living tendrils of liquid snaking their way around his fingers, seeking the gem on the back of the glove.

"I did it!" cried Faeron, his heart thumping excitedly. The outburst was all it took to sever his connection to peridom.

Crack!

The sound rang loudly across the workshop. With a will of its own, the light surged through Faeron's fingers into the left gem. Just as suddenly, it reemerged gushing from the gem on his right glove, throwing his hand back with the force of a light punch. The ball, meanwhile, resumed its fall, bouncing once then rolling to a stop on the pads.

"Are you alright?" asked Mathas from his perch.

"Nothing hurt but pride," said Faeron, looking for new scratches on the gloves. There were too many to determine which, if any, he had just made. He was just relieved that he hadn't caused any real damage to himself or the gloves. Striding forward, Faeron bent over to grab the ball and handed it back up to Mathas. "Can I try again?" he asked.

"That's up to Miss Lem," said Mathas. "Auri, do you feel ready?"

"He can go," she said gruffly from the corner. Again, Faeron saw Quinn whisper something to her. She nodded, and Faeron swore he even saw the traces of a smile before she shushed him and closed her eyes tighter.

"Looks like you're up again," said Mathas. "When you're ready…"

Faeron calmed his mind and when the wave of pearlescent light took his consciousness, he opened his eyes.

"Three… two… one…" Mathas dropped the ball.

Faeron reached out and felt the light leap from the ball to his hand. He clenched his fist tight and it felt almost like squeezing gelatin, the light slipping through the cracks in his fingers. Before he could process and reach for the ball, the light was gone. The bunball fell to the mat with a light *thud*.

"Expertly done!" clapped Mathas. His hands shimmered brighter as they clapped together, and it was all Faeron could do to suppress his pride and hold his connection to peridom. He may only have suspended a ball in the air for a few seconds, but to him, it was perhaps the greatest moment of his life so far. He, Faeron Lovel, had bent the universe to his will. He was a shaper now, like countless kytra and Hosts before him.

"Before we move on," said Mathas, "would you like to give it another go, Auri?"

Auri looked up, defeat etched in her eyes. "I'll just watch," she said sullenly. "I don't think I'm going to get this today."

"There's nothing wrong with taking your time to get it right," said Mathas. "Your father spent years practicing, and I'm sure he'd tell you that patience is your best friend. Come, take a break from your meditations and let me show you the other half of the equation."

Auri pushed herself off the table and trudged back over to the mats. Half his mind still adrift in the currents of peridom, Faeron could see the pearl light glimmering off Auri's legs pulsing brightly with each step.

"As we now know," said Mathas, "the glove of take is capable of capturing energy, if only for a moment, but what if you have excess energy when your task is complete? Faeron, the gloves if you please…"

Faeron removed the gloves, handing them to his mentor. "The ball as well?" he asked, but Mathas shook his head.

"To properly demonstrate the glove of give, we will need a bit more energy than our ball can provide." Mathas strapped on the gloves. "With nothing more than their own body, a kytra often has what they need to accomplish a task… In our case, that will be pushing an alca along its track. Observe." He stepped forward, as if he was going to jump right off.

"Wait!" cried Auri, and Faeron lunged forward, shedding his connection to the light. The capillum could hardly walk on his leg let alone jump from any height.

"I assure you, this isn't my first show," smiled Mathas, "but I'm flattered by your concern. Mr. Lovel… if you could be so kind as to step aside."

Faeron returned to Auri's side as their mentor stepped off the platform. It wasn't a far drop, and, as Mathas fell, he reached his left hand downward. The moment his feet hit the floor, Mathas retracted his arm, as if flexing. Moss-Green light shot up through his legs, across his torso, and down his left arm to the glove. It was far more light than the ball had made, and, as Mathas' feet were firmly planted, it didn't seem to be fading.

"The gloves can store a substantial amount of energy, but it is not without limits," said Mathas, his eyes narrowing and effort in his voice. Light snaked into the gem on his left hand. "Even now, the energy I've taken seeks a path home." He extended his right arm toward the model town and the light reemerged from the outstretched glove. It leapt from his fingers, to the alca, and the toy burst into motion, zipping up one hill and down the next. It made it almost halfway along the track before coming to a rest in a small valley beside a tiny red fire hydrant.

"That's what you want us to do, today!?" asked Auri, her voice a panicked whisper, her eyes wide in shock.

"I am simply offering either of you the chance to *try* today," said Mathas, "I expect we'll be practicing this for some time before either of you succeeds."

"I can do it," said Faeron, confidently marching up to Mathas.

"Do show us," beamed Mathas genuinely as he handed the gloves off to Faeron.

Securing the straps on the gloves, Faeron crossed to the far side of the platform and climbed the steps. At the top, he readied himself. Pride, excitement, and nerves at throwing himself half-conscious off a platform all washed away as he quieted his mind. There was darkness and then light. Faeron blinked open his eyes, taking in the shimmering model city just a few yards away.

Mathas joined Auri at the edge of the mats. "As you land," he said, addressing Faeron, "capture the energy, just as you did with the ball. Pull the stress from your knees and shoulders. Still your body… let that energy escape into the gloves... into peridom. It'll fight you, but your will must be stronger. Contain it, then direct it to the toy."

"Pull, contain, direct," said Faeron, "got it."

"When you're ready then."

Faeron's half-present mind struggled to keep thoughts at bay as he reached one foot over the edge. "It's just a force diagram," he whispered to himself, picturing the scene like a chart from his physics homework. Readying his left arm, Faeron stepped off the platform.

When Faeron's feet met the mats, his knees locked and his core tensed, fighting the energy of his body, energy seeking a way out through the mats. Faeron didn't let it escape. He pulled back with the glove of take, and he felt the light, seeping from his joints, running in ropes up his torso and down his arm. It forced his hand open and slithered through his fingers, far more forcefully than the light from the ball. The gem began to shake, jerking his arm back and forth. Panic twanged through his core.

Crack

The light jumped through the left gem to the right and then burst into the air like a bright green smoke bomb. Faeron's arm bucked back, sending him stumbling into the platform. His calves smacked the wooden frame and he fell backward.

"Faeron!" gasped Mathas in concern, rushing over as fast as his legs would take him. Auri arrived only seconds later, leaping up onto the platform beside him.

"Are you alright?" she asked.

"Quinn, fetch the aid kit from my desk," called Mathys. "Bottom left drawer."

"It's fine… I'm fine…" groaned Faeron, rubbing his shoulder, "No need for that." He looked down at his right hand, resting in his lap. A glowing fissure was carved into the stone, clearly visible as it forked off the main schism. "Mathas, I'm really sorry… I think I cracked it."

"You have nothing to apologize for," said Mathas warmly. "Plenty of those lines come from Vox, myself, and even your mother. This is precisely why we started with the two-foot platform, and not the tower that Evolice built for herself."

Faeron looked up at Mathas, smiling. He imagined his mother sitting here decades ago, doing the same thing he was now. "How long did it take her?" he asked.

"Believe it or not, Evolice struggled to capture the light for some time," said Mathas. "Your affinity with the gloves is remarkable."

While Faeron blushed, Auri stomped off back to the corner.

"I'm done for the day," she announced firmly.

"Perhaps it is for the best if you all have some time to reflect," said Mathas, extending an arm to Faeron. "We can resume tomorrow night."

"Freedom!" shouted Myllie, racing for the door. "Come on Kae, let's go to the rec and practice a bit before we head home."

"Right on," said Kaelynn, and the twins ran off out of the workshop.

"Tell me, what did you learn from this?" asked Mathas, as Faeron met his grin and was hoisted upward with surprising strength.

"I didn't expect it to be so strong," said Faeron. "I panicked, and then I lost the connection."

"Then balance was struck," said Mathas, "and your shoulder paid the price. The first bruise for a new generation of kytra... you should be honored."

"Hey... you ready to get over to the Deity Lounge?" called Quinn from the corner.

"Yeah," Faeron called back, still massaging his sore shoulder. For all it hurt, he hardly cared. His heart was still racing from what he'd just accomplished. No matter how many times he heard the stories of the Hosts, how many times he told himself he'd be like them one day, nothing could have prepared him for the feeling of shaping the universe to his will. It seemed so far-fetched, an impossibility, and yet, he had just defied gravity.

"Come on!" barked Auri. "I wanna be anywhere but here." She stomped out of the workshop to the classroom, and Quinn followed right after. Through the classroom window, Faeron could see Quinn chatting away as Auri quickly collected her things.

Riding the thrill of his accomplishment, Faeron skipped after his friends. He was almost to the door when Mathas called after him.

"Faeron, I'll be needing those gloves back."

"Right!" said Faeron, who had forgotten he was still wearing them. He ran back over the table and left the gloves laying there for the old capillum. "See you tomorrow, Mathas!"

"Have a wonderful evening, Mr. Lovel."

CHAPTER EIGHT

UNYIELDING FLAME

Entering through the Court of Fantasy's colossal stone doors was like stepping into another world. Strobing lights and freshly fried smells churned about a sea of indiscernible chatter, flooding all Faeron's senses at once. Hulking white trees rose above a jungle of flashy arcade machines. Their trunks were dressed in heavy coats of shimmering sapphire moss and their canopy of luminous leaves bathed the high walls of the colosseum in their mint-turquoise glow.

The ground beneath the mossy carpet rumbled as the walls of the labyrinth downstairs shifted. Meanwhile, screaming teens flew bright pink bumper-petals about the open air. Weaving in and out of the gleaming branches, they fired lasers that slowed the other petals and used the advantage to collide headlong, sending both parties spinning in spectacular fashion.

Faeron, Auri, and Quinn stood in the arcade's front parlor, where many large groups relaxed in tree stump chairs around flat-capped mushroom tables, chatting gaily and sipping on colorful drinks. Beside the tables, a sizable reward shop exchanged tickets for all sorts of knick knacks. There were limited edition index skins and tasty treats from the Peak, but Faeron and Auri had their eye on a six-foot-tall stuffed mauturtle that had sat on display for months. If they pooled tickets, the pair were just eight-hundred shy of the thirty-two thousand they'd need to claim the plush prize for their balcony.

"Muum ears, one hundred tickets!" called a man at a white and blue striped cart near the reward counter. "Deep fried Muum ears, doughy and delicious. Get em sugared, get em spiced, get em annnyway you want them. Only one hundred tickets a plate!"

The salesman's words were hardly needed, as the warm doughy smell alone was enough to hook Faeron. As the scent drew Faeron toward the cart, he was caught by Auri's strong grasp.

"No way you're spending our turtle tickets on food when we're about to eat for free," demanded Auri, speaking for the first time since the three of them left the athenaeum.

Faeron's stomach growled loudly, but he conceded and followed Quinn and Auri down a row of arcade machines. They walked in a loose line, weaving between Coin Slope machines and Gustpuck Tables. "Looser ladders litter lockers…" yelled two dark haired teens into the microphone of a Tonguetwist Booth, shouting louder and faster as they continued to repeat the phrase, "looser ladders litter lockers… lookers lacker lickers… *Argh*!"

Faeron, Quinn, and Auri worked slowly toward the back of the arcade where the trees were most dense. Nestled beneath the hulking branches and low hanging vines was the Deity Lounge. The lounge was two stories tall, its walls painted with murals of heroes from throughout the Deity saga. There was Sir Preston the Pure, Nautilus Dawngrog, and many others Faeron remembered well from when his mother used to read the stories before bed.

The chatter cloaking the arcade was even more vibrant near the lounge. The climbing vines that often drew crowds here were now mostly unattended as people flocked together in large pods, exchanging predictions and anticipations for the match to come.

The front door of the deity lounge was a tangle of tightly woven roots, thick and barky, with no handle or knob. At the trio's approach, the roots began to move, untangling themselves and receding and reshaping into an open archway, plenty wide for Faeron and the others to pass through together.

The spacious lounge had earthy brown floors and walls, and was shrouded in a thin mist, dimly lit by azure mushroom lamps hanging from the tall ceiling. In the very center of the room was an exceptionally long deity table, spanning most of the lounge's length, though its surface was currently dark in preparation for the upcoming match. A wide lip for food and drink as well as dozens of padded stools ran all the way around the long table and all manner of people filled the seats. There were older patrons and teens alike, some chatting over drinks in groups, others enjoying a piping hot plate of spicy telcurry alone.

Smaller tables with high-sitting chairs dotted the rest of the floor in well-organized rows. Almost every seat in the house was filled, every table cluttered with food and drinks. Patrons gulped back Peak Ales and shot down Korvan Spicebubbles while glancing between their personal screens and the friendly faces surrounding them. Meanwhile, a score of sharp-dressed waiters swept gracefully to and from the kitchen, carrying large trays of steaming hot food.

"Welcome," said a man at a small podium just inside the door. He wore a black vest with an emerald button up underneath. Clean shaven and hair parted professionally, he greeted them with a warm and welcoming smile. "Do you have a reservation for a private sitting, or would you like spots at the long table?"

"Actually, I've got a room reserved," said Quinn, stepping up to the podium. "I'm Quinn Veradae, one of the finalists."

"Of course, just let me… here it is!" exclaimed the greeter, looking down at a screen behind the podium. "Room five is yours. You'll find it on the second floor. The door is coded to you, Mister Veradae, but I can add your friends as well if you like."

"Of course," said Quinn. "Auri Lem and Faeron Lovel."

The greeter raised a brow at Faeron's name but continued typing away at his screen. "Right, you're all in the system now. You can head on up whenever you're ready, just these steps here," he pointed down a short hallway behind him. "Complimentary concessions are available for your suite and can be ordered through Serris at any time. Is there anything else I can help you with today?"

"That's about it. Thanks a million," said Quinn, skipping off toward the stairs. "Come on guys!"

They followed a narrow passage to a winding staircase around what appeared to be the trunk of a narrow tree. Shimmering blue hung over the edges of the wide wooden steps and all along the coarse barky bannister.

As they climbed, Faeron realized that, in all the times he'd come here, he'd never once seen the upper floor where the VIP rooms were located. The hallway at the top of the stairs was cast in deep blue mushroom light. Tangled roots covered every inch of the wall, and the only order to their winding chaos were the six clearly formed doorways on one side. Beside each door, a glowing mushroom lamp was printed with a number.

Door number three began to shift, the roots crawling aside, as two large and clearly intoxicated men stumbled out into the hallway. Arm in arm, they toppled over into the far wall while trying to support each other. Both still donned button up shirts and straight fit dress pants, and had no doubt come straight to the lounge after work.

"Ayy!" cried one of them, a recent graduate of the academy that Faeron recognized as Dellien Durkwrite. "You're umm…" he pointed to Quinn, "you're the… the one that lost the thing… the… you're the guy.."

"Yeeaaash," said the other, his brother, Dolmen. "Quinn! He's Quinn! He loosh, to Barrow 'member!"

"Quinn!" cried Dellian, "Ayy Quinny, Quinn… Quinner Winner! I need you to…" He waved his hand wildly side to side. "I gotta, facilities… facilitaties… facaltate…"

"Right," said Quinn, stepping aside.

Faeron followed suit, as did Auri, though she eyed them annoyedly as they passed.

Once the pair had disappeared down the steps, nearly tripping on the way down, Faeron and the others continued down the tunnel of roots to door number five.

"This is it," gasped Quinn, his face painted in the sapphire lamp light, "the legendary VIP room."

At their approach, the door of roots unraveled itself, revealing a sizable room. Long draping curtains of moss hung from the ceiling, their emerald chutes tipped with tiny beads that sparkled in the sapphire light of the mushroom lamps.

Ducking through the shimmering moss, Faeron found a standard size deity table with three executive-looking chairs on each of its long ends. The seats each had their own set of displays with a nice black bezel, and as soon as Quinn entered, he ran over to the nearest chair and started tinkering on the screens. Unlike the other walls, the far end of the room was not covered in roots. Instead, it was a painted stone mural, like on the outside of the building. The painting depicted a hilbauk warrior in heavy armor that covered all but her twin beaks.

"That's Dadandum Preeh!" said Auri excitedly, rushing over to look at the mural in more detail.

"Nice tanky stall unit," added Quinn, tapping away on his screen. At a button press, the top of the table lit up with an emerald green grid.

Auri shot a cold glare over her shoulder. "You see, *that* is exactly what kills it for me, simplifying such a deep emotionally rich character into… bang pow fight kill!" She spun around and collapsed into a chair, looking back and forth across the gridded table. "This just makes no sense for Deity. I mean, in all eleven books, there's only four… maybe five big battles, if you count the Weeping Arbors. Most of the time is spent working to *avoid* combat."

"I mean, what's the armor for if not to fight?" countered Faeron. "And the big battles are the moments everyone remembers. Besides—" Suddenly, a monstrous growl rumbled in Faeron's gut.

"Wow, those rice rolls really didn't do much for you, did they?" asked Quinn.

"I guess not," said Faeron, grabbing the seat beside Quinn. "Let's get something ordered, then we can discuss Auri's hate for the game. Hey, Serris!"

"How can I help?" asked the index, popping into the air.

"Are they still serving elmafruit freeze creams?" asked Faeron, knowing the seasonal snack always sold out quickly.

"Indeed," said Serris. "Would you like me to place an order?"

"Large for me," said Faeron.

"Ooh," said Quinn, "I'll take a cocoa one."

"And you?" asked the index, zipping over to Auri.

"Nothing," said Auri, waving the ball of light away.

Once Serris was gone, Quinn pressed another button on his display and a woman's cheery voice sounded from speakers, deep within the room's root-covered walls.

"—and that'll be the toughest thing for Roethwild, won't it, Vet?"

"Indeed it will, Crystal," responded the suave tones of Vet Wheeler over the speakers. Pre-plague, he had been a Deity champion himself, but now he was the broadcaster for all major tournaments. "The nomad's a wildcard. We've already seen a number of new units from him in these past couple matches, so Roethwild won't be able to let her guard down."

"Well, we'll see if the nomad's tricks are enough to topple our four-year champion," said the first woman. "For those of you just joining us now, I'm Crystal Rayne, co-hosting live with the legendary Vet Wheeler. Tonight, the annual Cropsun Clash concludes with a first of its kind twist. Our four-year champion is facing down a nomad to defend her title. That's right. You heard me. The Nomad known as Book Peddler stands one match away from toppling the queen!

"Book Peddler," said Vet, "what a strange name for a strange contender."

"Indeed, but what isn't strange about tonight?" said Crystal. "Now, we polled the lounge, and the lounge has answered; eighty-seven percent think it'll be a Roethwild victory. What do you make of that number Vet? Does the crowd have it right?"

"I expect it'll come down to last champions on both sides, but I do see Roethwild coming out on top," boomed Vet. "If I were a gambling man I'd— Now hold on folks… I've just been informed that our contestants are readied. If you're not in your seat, I suggest you get there, because our championship match is about to begin."

As Vet spoke, the far wall of the room began to shift. The mural faded, the stone smoothened out, and the whole surface turned into a sleek window looking down on a dark room.

"Woah," said Faeron and Quinn in union, racing over to the glass.

The room below was long but narrow. The whole floor was a deity grid, its emerald lasers piercing the darkness of the chamber. At either end was a raised glass box where each of the finalists were now constructing their maps on a wide assortment of displays. In the box to the left was the familiar face of Roethwild, the best Deity player in Eredith by a long shot. For four years straight, she'd never lost a single game. Roethwild was a slender middle-aged woman with crimson streaks in her otherwise silver-grey hair. She always wore the same brown leather jacket, studded at the shoulders, and a wide assortment of rings on her fingers. Meanwhile, in the right-side box, Book Peddler wore a hooded poncho that covered all but his arms. From what Faeron could see, the nomad's muscular arms were blanketed in heavy patches of fine silver hair, and, if Faeron squinted, he could just make out a crimson tattoo on Book Peddler's shoulder.

"Book Peddler! Of course!" Faeron shouted. "Auri, it's Caidus!"

"What?" said Auri, jumping from her seat to see. Running over, Auri cupped her face to the glass and her jaw dropped. "By Glavius, you're right," she gasped, stepping back from the window. "Book Peddler is Caidus Proud!"

"Who?" asked Quinn, a lost look on his face.

"We met him at Mathas'," explained Auri, suddenly seeming to forget her mood, "he works with Mathas to bring books we print here in Eredith to the other settlements. I had no idea he played Deity as well."

As the finalists worked away at their screens, their domains began to form across the gridded floor. Caidus seemed to have a plan already in place, as his domain quickly took shape. A full row of barren flatlands appeared along his backline, taking form on both the massive grid below the window, and the smaller table in their private room. The ground was pale and cracked all over, and there wasn't a sign of life anywhere. Caidus' frontline had two more barrens, making the only notable feature in his whole domain a single patch of forested glades at the very front and center.

"Now *this* is interesting," boomed Vet.

"Five barrens?" scoffed Crystal. "I've never seen a barren played outside of teaching someone the rules."

"Barrens saw some play pre-plague," said Vet. "But there were thousands of different units then. With those we have today, I don't see any sense in it. It's just… baffling. Roethwild has a free path out of Book Peddler's domain, and if the nomad wants power from a dungeon, the only one in his whole domain is the single glade. If Roethwild robs him of it on her way out…"

"Then Book Peddler will be entirely dependent on her domain for power," concluded Crystal. "It's almost like Book Peddler wants to fight on Roethwild's side… but that makes no sense. He'll be unable to cast miracles. I think we should take this one to the lounge, get all of your opinions."

"What do you think folks?" boomed Vet. "Is the nomad making light of the game, or does Book Peddler know something about barrens that the rest of us don't? Vote now!"

"What do you say?" asked Quinn, turning to Faeron.

"No way he hasn't got a plan," said Faeron. "I mean, he made it this far… and he definitely had *something* going on upstairs. Bright dude."

"Alright, Serris," said Quinn. "Tell them two votes on Caidus having a plan."

"Three," called Auri, to Faeron's surprise.

Roethwild, meanwhile, had constructed a safe two-line approach, creating a frontline of mountains and a backline of desert. Now, the entire floor of the chamber was covered in lifelike landscapes, although Caidus' end did look quite plain.

"What in Inya is he planning?" asked Faeron, walking back his chair for a closer look on their private table.

"Maybe he's going for a timeout play," said Quinn.

"A timeout?" asked Auri, earning a look of shock from Faeron. That's twice now she'd cared about Deity.

Quinn also raised a brow. "You really want to know?" he asked.

"What?" said Auri defensively. "If Caidus is going up against some four-year champ, I want to know what's going on."

"Ooookay!" said Quinn, sounding like he'd been waiting all his life for this moment. "As I'm sure you know, in Deity, regardless of where your fighters are, the player can only cast miracles on their own domain. Since each player's troops start in the enemy's domain, you'll usually want to get your team back on your half of the map as soon as possible so you can assist them with miracles. *Sometimes* you'll want to pillage your opponent's dungeons for power first, but usually it's better to do that stuff in your own domain. Anyway, once you're home, there's not a lot of incentive to push back into enemy territory. To stop players from just sitting around forever, the map eventually begins to fall apart."

"Is that when the zones turn red?" asked Auri.

"Exactly," said Quinn. "Once both players have reached their home domain, natural disasters will start to pop up all across the map. If Caidus has a team that fights incredibly well on flat terrain, he could be betting on the disasters to force Roethwild into his barrens. Maybe Centurium as leader, or some new unit we haven't seen before."

"But then what's with the glade?" asked Faeron. "Why not just max out his chances with six barrens?"

"Hey, that's the Elemental Glade from book three," said Auri, leaning over the table for a closer look.

"Spot on," said Quinn. "There's a *super* tough dungeon there."

"The Halls of Mephinnia?" gasped Auri.

"Indeed," said Quinn. "Maybe Caidus is hoping to nab the power while he waits for timeout? Seems like Roethwild could shut that down hard if she loots it on her way home."

Suddenly, a pair of beacons appeared on the map. The twin pillars of light shone opposite each other, one in the barrens behind Caidus' glade, the other in the center of Roethwild's desert.

"The lands are laid, and the teams are in place!" cried Vet, his voice filling the room once more. "Can you feel it folks? The tension is electric!"

"Indeed it is, Vet," said Crystal. "Now, let's see what the lounge has to say about these barrens… Forty percent say the nomad is throwing the game, thirty-two percent think he's got an ace up his sleeve, and twenty-eight say he just started playing yesterday."

"A split crowd" Roared Vet. "While our finalists give orders, let's see if their team compositions can shed any light on the situation." The twin monitors facing Faeron's seat flickered, each now showing a different lineup of fighters.

"From the looks of her team, Roethwild is gunning for the Halls of Mephinnia," reported Crystal. "To those unfamiliar, that's a tier-five dungeon." On the left monitor, Roethwild's roster sported a lineup of dungeoneering-focused champions. Her leader was Capwise Strike, the legendary human archaeologist. All four of her companions were gnogland researchers, reptilians with snubby rootbeam blasters tucked beneath their lab coats.

"Now, I've certainly seen stronger teams for an all-out fight," said Vet, "but the puzzle-minded perk on those researchers is bound to have her breezing through the dungeon. Looks like Roethwild is hoping to crush Book Peddler's team with a miracle before he can get out of her mountains."

"Speaking of Book Peddler," said Crystal, "would you look at that lineup?"

On the right-side monitor was an eclectic gathering of characters.

"Grok, Treasure Sniffer," whistled Vet. "That's not a commander you see every day." The goliath leader had pale tattooed skin and a massive club. Though few could best him in a fight, his unmatched strength was balanced by his incredibly dim wits. "Maybe Book Peddler's hoping that ol' Grok's nose'll lead him back to that glade dungeon."

"Now there's a nose that knows home," quipped Crystal.

"But just as likely to find any other dungeon," added Vet. "I gotta say, Book Peddler's putting a lot of faith in those deduction skills of Grok's."

"What deduction skills of Grok's?"

"My point exactly."

The rest of Caidus' roster consisted of two diggers, man-sized rodents with massive front paws perfect for burrowing, and a pair of sea-green spirits that Faeron had never seen before. Barely bigger than Grok's mighty fists, the spirits hung in the air, shifting shapes like tiny turquoise clouds.

"Woah, check em out!" said Quinn excitedly. "Caidus has new units!"

"Diggers are a strong pick to help Grok," reported Crystal of the speakers, "but I haven't a clue what those orbs of light could be… perhaps a spirit of some kind? Ever see 'em pre-plague, Vet?"

"Spirits indeed," boomed Vet. "We had hundreds of 'em pre-plague. You see, in the books, spirits are the magic of deities made conscious… living spells, so to speak. They each have very specific effects, usually aiding a teammate in the right condition, or weakening a certain type of enemy. As for this particular pair… a strange night grows stranger, because I'm stumped! All I can tell you is what I see, their names, Isthiswee and Isthitweira"

"Isthiswee and Isthitweira?" said Auri, sitting back in her seat. "They're glade spirits, duh."

Faeron and Quinn both looked to her excitedly. Maybe her knowledge of the books could give them some idea what these new units were capable of.

"Now hold on to your seats, folks," said Vet. "Looks like both teams have their orders. This match is officially underway, and Roethwild isn't wasting a second!"

Faeron's monitors shifted again, each now following one of the two teams. On the left, he saw Roethwild's team in a dead sprint across the barrens toward the glade, while Caidus' troops began their trek across Roethwild's backline of desert.

"I wonder… since we have a private table…," said Faeron. "Hey Prophet, can you put Caidus' crew up on the table?"

"Caidus?" came a familiar voice from the table, cracked with age. "I have no entry under this name."

"Book Peddler," added Quinn.

"Consider it done," said the prophet, and the top of the table changed. No longer did they see a map of both domains. Instead, the surface of the table was one long slice of desert. Near the center was a dungeon, a swirling vortex of sands known as the Lands Below.

"Fancy," swooned Quinn.

"So, the glade spirits," said Fearon, watching Caidus' troops trek single file up and down the sand dunes. "What's their deal? I don't even remember them from the books."

"Funny you ask," said Auri, "because I've got issues with this. It makes zero sense pairing the glade spirits with the rest of his team. They're the proudest, most pretentious entities you'll find almost anywhere. No way they take orders from *Grok, Treasure Sniffer.*"

"You mean like that?" asked Quinn, pointing to where Caidus' troops were marching. The glade spirits bobbed and swirled angrily about Grok's face as he seemingly took no notice, single minded in his march toward the swirling sand whirlpool.

"That didn't take long, did it, folks?" boomed Vet over the speakers. "Look to the desert 'cause it seems those spirits are considering a change in management."

"Okay, so they got that right," said Auri, "but then why would Caidus choose this team? Glade spirits are frail outside the Elemental Glade. If Grok leads them into the Land Below, they'll die."

"Did you watch any of his other games?" asked Faeron, turning to Quinn.

"I didn't," said Quinn, eyeing the board. "Maybe it really is a fluke? What if Caidus just isn't any good at Deity? Got all this way, just on dumb luck."

"I don't see how that's possible," said Faeron. "To reach the finals… that seems—"

"Wait!" shouted Auri, a look of dawning realization painted on her face. "Prophet, go back to the full map."

The view of the desert on the tabletop shrunk as the rest of the map came into view. Auri looked back and forth, from the glade across the mountains to the desert, smiling knowingly. "I figured it out," she exclaimed.

"Figured what out?" asked Faeron.

"I know what Caidus is doing," said Auri smugly. "And… I think it's quite brilliant."

"What do you mean you know what he's doing?" asked Quinn in disbelief. "It looks to me like he's throwing a tournament match for no good reason at all."

"Well," said Auri, "that's because you're not a Deity pro like me. Come on *experts*, don't you see it?"

"Prophet, zoom back in," commanded Faeron.

The map closed back in on Caidus' troops. As Grok and the diggers waded into the swirling edges of the dungeon, the glade spirits seemingly had given up. They were now split off from the rest, making a straight line for the mountain.

"His team's split!" said Quinn in disbelief. "This couldn't be any worse for him!"

"Oh really," said Auri, grinning. "Any real player would know that's *exactly* what he wanted them to do."

"You're bluffing," said Quinn, eyes narrowed. "You're just trying to rile me up. This is nonsense, simple as that."

Just then a soft tone rang through the room.

"Excuse me," said Serris, appearing just beside the table. "Your food has arrived."

"Let 'em in," said Faeron, going to the door.

Serris disappeared and the roots moved aside, revealing a woman, dressed just like the greeter at the front desk. On her tray were two plates of freeze creams. Each plate had about twenty of the round snacks, and where Faeron's were bright and colorful, Quinn's were dark brown and drizzled in melted chocolate.

"Thanks," said Faeron, taking the plates. As the roots closed, he brought the snacks back to the table.

"So anyway," said Auri, rising out of her set across the table and coming around to the empty one beside Faeron, "got any guesses yet?" As she asked, she dropped into the chair and swiped one of the freeze creams off Faeron's plate.

"Hey, get your own," objected Faeron.

"Why? There's perfectly good ones right here," said Auri devilishly.

"I'm not falling for it," sang Quinn, though Faeron could tell from the way Quinn's eyes darted between his screens and the board that the gears in his head were turning. "Your friend isn't doing anything at all. I… I don't think there's *any* way he can win at this point."

Faeron had never seen Auri smile so wide in her life.

While they ate, Quinn didn't say a word. The boy's eyes were dead set, focused on the table where the two glade spirits were making swift progress across the desert. On several occasions, Faeron could see the outlines of ferocious borgomantises burrowing beneath the sands, but, whenever the threat was near, the glade spirits would simply drift up much higher into the sky, well out of the creature's reach.

Their paired monitors continued to follow the teams' leaders through their respective dungeons. Any time anything exciting happened, Vet and Crystal were sure to speak up and provide their take. While Roethwild's researchers were making much swifter progress than Caidus' team, the Halls of Mephinnia were also much longer than the Land Below. The Halls were a maze of dimly lit passages with oddly inscribed runes above hundreds of otherwise indistinguishable doors. Only one door held the way forward, the rest holding all manner of dangerous foes. Meanwhile, the Land Below consisted of a single long passage leading into a massive cavern, large enough to fit half of Eredith. The power trove glowed brightly on the far side of the cave, rife with vicious dinosaurs and primitive traps. Grok rushed forward, unphased by beasts and traps alike. Darts bounced off him, blades cracked upon his skin, and even the dinosaurs were nothing more than a nuisance for the goliath.

"You know," said Vet, "I admire Grok, really do. He's a simple man… he knows what he wants, and he's damn good at getting it. In a less strategic game, he might even be a good unit."

"On the other side of the spectrum," said Crystal. "It looks like those brainiacs over in the Halls have cracked the code. Faeron looked over to his screen to find Capwise Strike, confidently turning the knob of a dark doorway. The door shot open, bathing the researchers in holy light.

"Now that's a one way portal to miracle city," cheered Vet. "Only one challenge left for the Roethwild and the dungeon's power is hers."

"Chances don't look good for Grok," said Crystal. "Home doesn't seem to be in the cards anymore."

"No it does not," agreed Vet, "those spirits, however, they seem pretty hell bent on reaching their turf. Those mountains won't do much to stop our high flying friends."

"For what little good it'll do 'em," said Crystal. "Facing up against a full team of five, even against a research team, *even* on their own ground, those spirits won't stand a chance."

"Agreed," said Vet. "It'll take a real-life miracle to save Book Peddler now.

"Bold words," smiled Auri. "He's gonna be eating them soon."

"WHAT. DO. YOU. KNOW?" gasped Quinn.

"Oh, you'll see."

The glade spirits soon reached the edge of the desert and the table shifted to show a long stretch of sheer cliffs and mountainous hills. They made just as swift progress across the mountains, flying well above the valleys where deadly skorprolls hunted. Before long, the spirits were nearing the edge of Roethwild's domain. As the spirits descended the final stretch of the mountainside, the map suddenly zoomed out.

"Apologies," came the prophet's voice, "but you'll certainly want to see this."

The desert zone where Grok and the diggers were dungeoning erupted in white light. Faeron looked down to the monitor on his left where Roethwild's team was filing out of a bedazzled treasure room.

"Is this the end for Book Peddler?" boomed Vet Wheeler's signature voice over the speaker. "Roethwild's team is the first to clear their dungeon, and our champion's not planning on letting Book Peddler finish his."

On the right monitor, the cave began to shake. Huge slabs of stone were raining down from the cavern's ceiling, falling all around Grok and his diggers. The single minded commander led his team in an all-out sprint for the treasure, but at this rate it wouldn't be fast enough. A massive chunk of the ceiling came crashing down onto one of the diggers, but not before Grok threw himself on top, the huge stone breaking on his back. Faeron could tell the blow had taken its toll as the goliath struggled to stand back up. No sooner had he reached his feet, than three even larger slabs struck him. The goliath fell again, one of the diggers trapped beneath him.

"Grok, Treasure Sniffer is down!" roared Vet.

"And it looks like that last digger ain't long for this game either," added Crystal as the rest of the lost land collapsed. Faeron's right monitor was now entirely dark.

"Okay, maybe I bought it a little," said Quinn, squinting at Auri, "but I'm one-hundred percent calling your bluff now. Caidus has no strats here, and you are just trying to get me riled up. Nice try."

"Yeah..." said Faeron. "As cool as Caidus was, I'm starting to lean toward Quinn's side here."

"Wanna bet?" asked Auri.

"Nah, I'm good," said Faeron. "You clearly think you know something, and that's enough for me."

"Absolutely, I'll bet," said Quinn. "You've toyed with my mind long enough. What's your price?"

"If Caidus loses…" said Auri, thinking a moment, "I'll go to the Unity Fest with you this year. Maybe, *maybe*, I'll even let you take me on the tunnel ride."

Quinn's face instantly flushed red. "I uh— and… um," he said, trying to compose himself, "and if Caidus does win?"

"Lots of other girls in Eredith," teased Auri. "You lose your right to ask me."

"You told her?!" cried Quinn, giving Faeron a hurt glare.

"Nah, he didn't need to," said Auri. "I swear, you boys think you're so subtle."

"Well…" said the freckled boy, swallowing hard. "I suppose it's a deal then."

The glade spirits were now back in their own land, and Roethwild's troops had resurfaced from the dungeon. As the table switched to a view of the Elemental Glade, Faeron could now see the outlines of both teams through the crimson-leaved canopy. It seemed almost as though the glades spirits could sense the presence of Roethwild's researchers, as they made a straight line for the team.

"I have to admit it folks," Vet's voice returned to the room. "I saw this fight coming down to last champions, and it seems I was wrong."

"The end is here for those spirits," said Crystal, as the two teams closed in on each other, "and you've got to feel a bit bad for them. Never had a chance with a leader like Grok."

"No, they did not," concurred Vet. "These strategies might have worked against nomads, but Book Peddler was simply no match for a proper Eredithian cha— Hold on now, what's this?"

The whole of the glade was suddenly flooded with brilliant white light.

"Impossible," said Faeron, looking down to his monitors. Sure enough, the right display was no longer entirely dark. He could see the exquisite treasure coffer of the Lost Land, its top pried open by a bloodied digger, light bursting out.

"He dug through," gasped Quinn.

"A miracle in the glade!" shouted Crystal. "But will it be enough?"

"Don't get your hopes up, Book Peddler fans," said Vet. "We're seeing a tier two miracle, a wildfire by the looks of it. Maybe he'll take a unit or two with him, but this is a done match."

"And here it comes," said Auri triumphantly.

As the flames sprang up throughout the Elemental Glade, licking the leaves and crawling along the branches, the pair of glade spirits began to grow. Their sea-green bodies turned a fiery orange, and they expanded quickly until their shimmering bodies were tall as the trees.

"What in Inya am I looking at?" asked Crystal in awe.

"A win condition," said Vet, sounding just as shocked.

The flames racing through the trees pushed Roethwild's team straight into the pair of elementals, and as the first reptilian researcher breached the clearing where the colossal spirits were hovering, it was met by a beam of fire. Tendrils of flame lashed out from the elementals, wrapping around the wide-eyed researchers who struggled feebly to free themselves. In seconds, Roethwild's team was nothing but ashes.

"Unbelievable! Unimaginable! Unfathomably impossible, yet there it is!" roared Vet over the speakers. "This, folks, is the kind of Deity I live to see. For the first time in history, a nomad topples Roethwild's four-year sweep and claims the Cropsun Cup. Congratulations, Book Peddler!"

"That was a ride and a half," said Crystal. "Let's go now to the lounge and get your thoughts on this incredible turn of events."

"Holy Glavius, that was amazing," said Faeron, running over to the window.

He could see Caidus, stretching in his booth, cool as if nothing of note had just occurred. Roethwild, meanwhile, hung her head in silent defeat.

"You… you knew…" Quin said softly.

Faeron turned to see his friend, pale in the face, looking just as defeated as Roethwild.

Auri, meanwhile, seemed to be having the time of her life. "You know," she said. "I think I've been a bit hard on this game. I've got a real talent for it."

"So… about that bet," said Quinn, uneasily.

"Ah, don't fret it," said Auri. "I'll tell you what. If you show me how to put a team together, maybe I'll help you find a date. I hear Lucy Leighton is single these days."

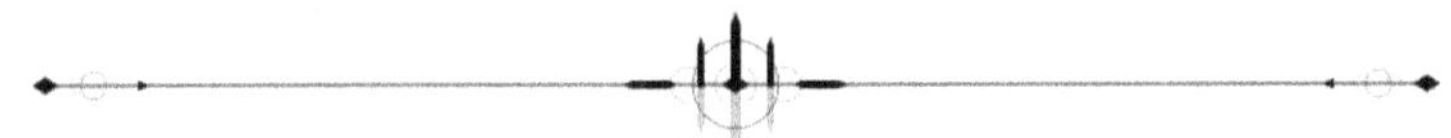

Leaving the Lounge, it was Quinn who walked in somber silence. The arcade outside had died down to a low roar, and most of the machines were switched off for the night. No bumper petals flew above, and the maze in the basement had long since closed down. They exited through massive stone doors onto a set of steps looking down on Loem park.

Where the far end of the park was bathed in golden glow from the Clearwater Cinema sign, here, the trees were washed in the crimson light of the great Forgeworks Hammer next door. Forgeworks was the sole source of repaired tech and manufactured goods in Eredith. Its glass-encased showroom, perched beside the colosseum on the edge of the park, was peaked by a great flaming hammer, rising and falling upon a massive anvil.

"You walking home, Quinn?" asked Faeron, as the three of them descended the steps onto the wide Parkside Lane.

"Yeah, trams stop running by perimeter housing this late," he said.

"We'll walk with you," offered Faeron, "at least as far as the next station."

"That's alright," said Quinn, "it's the opposite way from you."

"No point arguing," said Auri bluntly, pulling Quinn's arm. "Come on, let's get moving. I am in serious need of some slumber."

"Fine, fine," said Quinn, and Auri released her grasp.

As the three of them passed beneath the flaming hammer of Forgeworks, an odd sound from the park caught Faeron's attention. There was shouting, and voices that he could only just make out.

"Filthy cheat nomad," came a voice just beyond the trees.

"Why don't… show that face…" said the second voice. "Coward… like how you play."

Faeron turned suddenly to Auri, who returned his look of concern. There was only one person the voices could be talking about.

"Come on," said Auri sternly, veering off into the park.

"Right behind you," added Faeron.

"Wait! Guys!" said Quinn sheepishly. "What are you doing?"

"Helping a friend," said Auri.

Just beyond the trees, Faeron could make out three figures. Caidus was easy to make out in his hooded poncho, while it wasn't until Faeron got closer that he recognized the other two as the drunk Durkwrite twins from room number three in the lounge.

"Hey you!" shouted Auri, rushing toward them.

Caidus turned, his face shrouded by his hood.

"Well lookie here," said Caidus casually. "I know these ones."

"Sush… you… in the preshence of Quinn" said Derrian loudly, his black blazer thrown over one shoulder. "Quinn sh'ere, sho he'll tell you what'sh what."

"Quinn!" yelled his brother, Dolmen, "tell this… *pillow* sharft pile that he cheated. I know you saw him!" The slur for capillum fell off his tongue so naturally, Faeron was too shocked to speak.

"Excuse me," said Caidus, seemingly unphased, "it's half-pillow sharft pile, actually. At least get your insults right."

"Oh, um…" said Quinn, looking to Faeron and Auri for help.

"Come on Quinn," said Derrien. "Tell thish nomad what we do to cheaters. Tell it right to ish ugly pillow face!" As he spoke, Derrien ripped off the hood of Caidus' poncho, revealing the man's patchy fur covered face.

Caidus' eyes were human in slant but cartoonishly large. His nose and ears were as long as Mathas' though his head as a whole was smaller. Fast as a bullet, Caidus caught Darrien's arm. "Okay, that's it," growled Caidus, "patience has reached its limits."

"Help! Seriish!" cried Derrien through slurred speech, "filthy *pillow* liars' got me! Help! Sherrish, shecurty!"

"Cease hostilities," came Serris' voice, sterner than Faeron had ever heard before. Serris materialized into the air, flashing aggressively between Caidus and the twins.

"What in the world..." hissed Caidus, releasing Derrien's arm.

"Get him Serrish," screamed Dolmen. "Criminal... cheat... wants to take *our* game, just like his people took our sharftin world."

"That's right, sharft pile," yelled Darrien, backing up his brother. "We know your lot did the plague. And we aren't... never gonna let you get away with it. We're gonna -*hic*- make you pay big!"

"Try me," smiled Caidus, raising his fists.

"No, don't!" yelled Auri, jumping between the twins and Caidus. "They'll get you kicked out for good. What you do is too important."

"Hey Quinn," snapped Dolmen, "tell yer toy to move, or she might accidentally get hurt."

"Excuse me," growled Auri, "did you call me his *toy*?"

"Looksh like she can hear fine," said Darrien. "But sheems she don't lishen too good. Tell her Quinn, that pillow is hash no place here!"

"I think you two should leave," said Quinn, politely.

"Shootped as you look" spat Dolmen, sounding disgusted through his slurred speech. "Not jusht a loosher. A pillow loving traitor.."

"THAT'S ENOUGH!" roared Auri, stepping toward the twins. As she spoke, the crimson light in the park flared brighter. Faeron looked behind him to see the Forgeworks Hammer's flame leaping high above the trees, higher than he'd ever seen it burn before.

Looking to Auri, Faeron's jaw dropped as he saw fiery bronze light shimmering in her eyes. Auri's heavy breathing slowed, and suddenly the whole area was doused in darkness. A bitter cold gust swept over the park, as for the first time ever, the flame on the Forgeworks Hammer went out.

"Shorcery," gasped Dolmen. "Pillow magic!"

"Run!" screamed Darrien.

The two turned tail and stumbled hastily into the darkness of the park.

"Your eyes!" cried Faeron, squinting to see the look of shock on her face, "you just shaped, no echo crystal or anything. And your eyes... they looked like the *hosts*!"

"M... me? I did?" stammered Auri. "But I don't know how."

"Good to see you lot," said Caidus calmly. "Appreciate you stepping in, really do, but can someone tell me what in Inya just happened?"

"An excellent question," came a new voice, as Faeron could just barely make out six or seven shapes rushing toward them. "Eredithian security, please keep still. Serris, give us light!"

A dozen balls of light appeared around Faeron and the others, and he could now make out the black-vested uniform of the city's security force. They weren't a common sight in Eredith, appearing only when called, and Faeron had only encountered them a handful of times in his whole life. The leader of the pack, the only one of them not wearing a helmet, had short greying hair and a well-groomed goatee. His badge read: Sergeant Lomelle.

"We've got a report of an assault involving two citizens," said the sergeant, "and what in the blazes happened to the Forgeworks Hammer? Was that you as well?"

"There was no assault, officer," said Auri sternly. "If anything, Caidus here was being verbally assaulted by the Durkwrite twins."

"It's no biggie," said Caidus. "Drunks being drunks. These three chased them off for me."

"What about you two?" asked the sergeant, turning to Faeron and Quinn. "Can you confirm their story?"

They spent the next few minutes, each detailing the events that had just transpired, all of them leaving out the part where Auri shaped the Forgeworks fire.

"So, what about the hammer then?" asked the sergeant, as Quinn finished giving his version of events.

Auri opened her mouth to speak, but Faeron cut her off. "Completely unrelated," he reported. "Couldn't tell you what happened. One second it was burning like normal, the next we were all in the dark."

"Right…" said the officer, eyeing them suspiciously. "Well, if that's it, we'll be sending someone to escort each of you home. Nomad, you have a place to stay?"

"Room in Quilver's," said Caidus. "Mathas Grinward is putting me up."

"Gotcha," said the sergeant. "Alright then, let's move everyone."

Two officers walked with Faeron and Auri back to a corner where they ordered a tram. The moment the doors sealed and they were alone, Faeron spun to face Auri who wore a look of wild excitement.

"I can't believe you—"

"I know!"

"But how?"

"No clue. I don't even have an echo crystal!"

"That's on a whole new level," said Faeron giddily as he watched the tram near their floor of the violet tower. "You should have seen your eyes, it was just like the dancing girl. I don't even think my mom's ever done anything like it!"

"But it doesn't make any sense," said Auri, "Mathas told us that the wisest and most practiced of the Old-Scholars were the only ones who could shape without echo crystals, but I can't even shape *with* them. No crystal and no calm. It was almost… as if I reached the light through my anger somehow. Just like how I fought against the crimson last night."

"Interesting… " said Faeron. What she was saying went against everything Mathas had taught them since their very first lesson. Peace, calm, and surrender, these were the paths to peridom's light. Emotion had only ever stood in Faeron's way, but Auri really did seem to be using it to shape. "Tomorrow, we'll go to Mathas. He'll get to the bottom of it."

"Tomorrow," agreed Auri. "And hey, Faeron. Thanks for helping with my meditations. It really does mean a lot."

"Forget it," said Faeron. "We both know you'd do the same."

When Faeron and Auri finally arrived home, they both made straight for their rooms as if lassoed upon entry.

"Night," said Faeron as he swung his door closed.

"Night," Auri called as her door clicked shut.

Despite his exhaustion, Faeron simply couldn't sleep. For hours, he tossed and turned, playing back the events of his day. He dwelt on his first shaping in the workshop, the feeling he had when he stopped midair, and relived the sheer thrill of watching Caidus conquer Roethwild. Eventually, his thoughts found their way back to Auri and her impossible show in the park. He had a million questions, and any answers he did have only opened up another twenty questions of their own.

The occasional footsteps to and from the kitchen told Faeron that Auri was just as restless, her mind no doubt walking the same trails as his. Eventually, in the early hours of the morning, Faeron's mind finally found quiet. In the emptiness, the pearlescent light of peridom washed him away.

Chapter Nine

The Deadline

Jakob paced up and down the central aisle of his 3978 Pursuer as it sped down the rails of a southbound tunnel. Through the windows, he could see hundreds of other alcas, cast in the shifting glow of the red, pink, and yellow neon lights winding like technicolor waves along the tunnel walls.

Jakob yawned. He'd been up late, exploring alternate motivations for his villain, and then, early this morning, Proto had woken him abruptly. Even now, an hour and a half after leaving his home in a rush, he was still replaying in his mind the cryptic call he'd received from his agent.

"What is it?" Jakob had answered groggily from his bed.

"I need you to come in today," Maye Vennamin, his agent, had said back, coolly.

"What for," he'd asked.

"This needs to be in person," said Vennamin. "You haven't seen the new HQ at Talon Park yet, have you? Perfect chance to check it out. Be here by noon."

Jakob continued to pace as he half listened to a Quistive interview over the Pursuer's speakers.

"Now, Carlton," said Elliot Jay, the Quistive's infamous journalist, "I think what people really want to know is, why the secrecy? It's been two-and-a-half years now, and we know *nothing*." His voice was young and full of energy.

"Well, if *people* wanna pay the lawsuit I'll get for breaching NDA..." said a second voice, older and laid back. "I kid. I kid. Still couldn't tell ya."

"Can you at least give us a hint? Entertainment? Business? Heck, I'd be happy just knowing what continent you're building on."

"I promise it's somewhere on Inya," laughed Carlton. "I can tell you that much."

"Suppose I can return that space suit then," bantered Elliot. "But in seriousness, I've got a conspiracy to float past you."

"Shoot," said Carlton.

"I did a little digging," said Elliott. "It looks like your firm usually takes about six months to design. Two and a half years in... the scope of this project must be unbelievable. Whatever it is, it's going to take a shraft load of manpower to construct. So, you'll understand why I was... intrigued... when Meddow Construction Corporation suddenly became Meddow Construction Conglomerate a year back. Dozens of smaller groups absorbed in the span of a few short months, and yet none of them have any active jobs on record? Carlton... where *is* Meddow making the money to keep on buying up these no-business businesses?"

"That'd be a great question... for Mike Meddow," suggested Carlton.

"Are you denying any affiliation?" asked Elliott?

"I'm denying—"

"Sorry to interrupt," said Proto, over the speaker. "We're five minutes out. You ready to go?"

"As I'll ever be," mulled Jakob, still pacing.

His Pursuer shifted to a side track and began to rise out of the tunnel. They surfaced and then climbed further, into the skyrail network between the residential high-rises of South Wyndon. Each highrise had its own distinct look. There were wide sweeping balconies, lush hanging gardens, and sleek rooftop lounges, though a heavy layer of Lowsun snow was packed heavy atop every building in sight.

Jakob's Pursuer broke from the highrises as it sped out onto a bridge over the rushing waters of the Akai river. The murky river was spotted in shallow rapids, running from a massive lake, just visible on the eastern horizon, then disappearing around a bend of towers in the west.

It took seconds to cross the Akai into Centra, Hampson's corporate heart. Colorful advertisements flashed across gargantuan displays climbing all up and down the faces of the city-state's impossibly tall skyscrapers. There were more alcas here than anywhere else, and the tangle of rails between the towers took up over ten stories by themselves.

The only break from the sky-reaching steel and stone was an expansive snow-blanketed park walled in on all sides by towering skyscrapers. It was here that Jakob's pursuer began to slow. As he descended from the rail network toward a ground-level station near the park's grand front gate, Jakob got a perfect bird's-eye view of the snowy wonderland below. The largest and most notable feature was the four-story structure taking up almost half the park by itself.

"There it is," said Proto, "Talon Media Corporation's new multi-billion encred Headquarters."

The building had four pointed wings angled like a bird's open talon. Its walls were sleek black glass, and its roof was hidden under a thick layer of snow. The rest of the park was sprinkled with colorful shops and rides, themed after the company's many iconic stories.

Among the crowds that strolled the winding pathways below were an assortment of fictional characters. Jakob spotted legendary knights, astronauts, politicians, detectives, even aliens and fantasy creatures from novels he'd read as a boy. They looked as real as the starry eyed children rushing to meet them. Most of the magcoasters and other attractions looked shut down for the Lowsun snows, though Jakob could see a long colorful carriage chugging along in slow circles around the park as it carried guests between different themed areas.

"Coming in now," reported Proto, as the alca pulled up to the front gate. "Lucky us—got a priority spot."

The gateway's grand face was a tall crescent of glass with a wide opening cut through the center. Between the two halves, floating high above the crowds, was an enormous globe. As it slowly rotated, the continents along the surface shifted, continuously changing the globe to mimic Talon Media's many fantasy worlds. At the bottom of the glass crescents, thick stone slabs read 'Talon Park,' in bright golden letters.

"Wow, the luxury treatment," said Jakob, collecting his grey peacoat and navy scarf off a hook beside the bench, "all so they can sack me."

"Don't be so dramatic," chimed Proto as the alca came to a stop. "I'm sure Vennamin would have just done that over her call this morning."

"S'pose so," said Jakob, bracing himself for the cold of Centra. It'd been years since he experienced a snowy Lowsun. At his approach, the door of the alca slid open, and Jakob strode out into the chilly breeze of the park.

Music and merry conversation met Jakob's ears as he watched his Pursuer zip off down the rails and disappear into the skyrail network. A wide cobblestone road led from the loading zone through the arched park entry, all the way to the corporate building, with smaller pathways leading off in every direction. Thousands of guests carried large bags full of colorful toys and memorabilia as they stopped to meet their favorite fictional characters brought to life.

"How are we looking on time?" asked Jakob.

"Close, but you should be—" Proto was cut off as a golden raven appeared out of thin air in front of Jakob.

"Welcome to Talon Park!" squawked the raven, flapping his wings as he hovered at eye level. "My name is Livespark, here to introduce you to your personal guide for the day."

"My guide?" asked Jakob.

"Oh, you'll see!" chirped Livespark. "Tell me, do you have a favorite Talon Media series?"

"I feel obliged to say the Aurilius saga," answered Jakob.

"Ah, Inspector Aurilius. Smart choice," tweeted Livespark, glowing bright. The features of the crow faded and its light expanded until it began to look vaguely human in form. Details took shape again, the dark cowl and heavy coat, a reed pipe poking out of the pocket, and, of course, the inspector's signature golden watch. Aurilius' face was exactly as Jakob had described it, narrow jaw, hollowed cheeks, and young blue eyes behind an aged face.

"No way…" gasped Jakob. "There's never been a VUE adaptation… What's this model based off of? Hand crafted? Or did you generate him from my writing?"

"Now this… is unexpected," said Aurilius, taking a measure of Jakob with his eyes before grinning broadly. "Doubt I need to introduce myself to you, Jakob… a real, *meet your maker* moment."

"Your maker?" asked Jakob, intrigued. "Aren't you just Livespark dressed up like Aurilius? I'm hardly your maker."

"A simplification," said Aurilius. "Though Livespark is the vessel, you'll find me, its contents, to be more substantive than a simple illusion. I am, *truly*, the Aurilius you wrote."

"Wicked tech," said Proto, while a strong cold breeze battered Jakob's cheeks with drifting snow.

"It's cold, and we've hardly time for philosophy," stated Aurilius, looking at his golden watch. "Average pace will put us at Vennamin's office twelve minutes from now, leaving five or so for bathrooms on route… assuming you need them after your trip."

"Sure…" said Jakob. In his wonder, he'd hardly noticed the snow. He studied every detail of his creation now standing before him. The smooth voice, the attention to time, he was flawless.

"Just this way then," Aurilius led Jakob down the main road, and for a while Jakob silently observed. The many boot-prints along the wide path had reduced its snowy blanket to spotted patches of brown-grey slush, though, fortunately, there wasn't any ice. Jakob once had a nasty fall on a sleek patch on the path up to his snowy peaks apartment that had turned his backside black for weeks. Ever since then, he'd been apprehensive about long snowy walks.

Though the park was busy, traffic moved quickly along the well-organized roads. It was a short trot to the headquarters building, and as Jakob approached the entry, he was befuddled to find that there were no doors in sight. The entry was a single black-glass wall with the Talon Media logo printed in gold near the top. It appeared solid as any other pane of glass, except for the slow trickle of men and women in bulky jackets or cardigan blazers passing straight through its surface. As far as Jakob could see, the glass wasn't parting for them in any way; it was as if the glass itself were an illusion.

"A projection?" asked Jakob as they approached the glass. "Doesn't seem like it'd keep much of anything out… birds… rain… especially not the cold."

"Not a projection," answered Aurilius. "That would indeed be ineffective. This is phaseflex, cousin to formflex, if you're familiar. Should an unwanted party try to pass through, they'd find the glass quite solid, hard as steel, in fact. For those of us welcome here, however…" Aurilius stepped through the wall. "Don't worry," came his muddled voice from across the wall, "it works on *real* people, too."

"Just found a couple research docs on it," reported Proto. "Brand new tech, impressive they've already implemented it on such a scale."

"Here goes then," said Jakob, extending an arm to the glass. As his hand passed through, he felt a current of warmth, like a waterfall of hot air. "Rad," he said, stepping through fully.

On the far side of the wall was a triangular room, four stories tall with polished black-marble floors, walls, and ceiling. In the center was a thirty-foot statue of a golden raven, wings spread wide, one talon menacingly outstretched. Stark white lights ran along the seams between the walls and ceiling, and slow but steady foot traffic passed between large hallways on either side.

"This way," said Aurilius, leading Jakob to the right-side passage.

"I feel the need to ask," said Jakob, following close behind, "as Aurilus, you can turn invisible, right?" It was obvious to Jakob that Livespark could simply cut the projection, but he was interested to see how his creation reacted to this specific request.

"Can," said Aurilius, "but won't."

"Why's that?" asked Jakob.

"There's no need for it," answered Aurilius simply.

"So, it's just a practical thing, then?" asked Jakob. "What if I asked nicely?"

"I know what you're trying to do," said Aurilius. "You're curious whether or not I fear my curse's consequence in this form."

"And do you?" asked Jakob. "You clearly recognize that you're a product of livespark. You must know there's no cutting time off your life in this state."

"But what fun is that?" asked Aurilius. "The rules may not apply because, at heart, I am still Livespark... but I am as an actor, Aurilius, my role. Does the thespian laugh down the barrel of a gun because they know it fires blanks? No! To them, to the person they embody, that weapon is just as real as the curse is for me." He took a bend in the hall and paused before a pair of doors. "Bathrooms?" he asked.

"Yes, thanks," said Jakob, stepping inside.

Minutes later, Jakob stood in front of a gold gilded mirror, fixing a few stray hairs in his tired looking reflection. Shadows had settled beneath his steel-blue eyes.

"So... you done torturing that AI?" asked Proto. The lens pinned to Jakob's coat pulsed alongside the index's words.

"I suppose so," said Jakob, still struggling with a stubborn hair. "Though, the intelligence running that thing is incredible. Would certainly make my job easier if I could just consult Aurilius on what he'd do next... Shame you can't you do anything like that, huh?"

"And maybe I could... If only you'd finished your degree," countered Proto.

"Fair enough," sighed Jakob, giving up hope that the rebel strand would fall in line with the rest of his part.

He rejoined Aurilius outside the bathrooms and followed around another bend, up a flight of stairs, and down a long hallway. They stopped at a door, made of the same black marble as the walls and inlaid with a fancy gold pattern. Though there was no handle or knob, a plaque at face level read, 'Maye Vennamin.'

"She's expecting you," said Aurilius. "I'm afraid, it's here, I take my leave."

"It was fun talking to you," said Jakob. "Sorry if I was a bother."

"Not at all," chuckled Aurilius. "Your heart's in the right place, and you're bright as they come… though… I suppose you must be to write *me*." With a wink, he disappeared.

Now alone, and not knowing what else to do, Jakob knocked.

"That you, Jakob?" came a voice from the other side. "Come on in."

Without warning, the door slid aside, receding into the wall beside its thick golden frame. The modestly sized office inside was dark, even with the brilliant white strip lights outlining the ceiling and floor. There were no windows, instead, the onyx walls were littered with dozens of well-organized accolades in fancy gold frames, while a display cabinet in the corner showcased a dozen or so standing awards. Vennamin's desk was topped in black glass, clear of any clutter, with a sleek golden frame.

On either side of the desk sat a woman. Vennamin, middle aged and sporting a permanently crooked smile, waved Jakob inside. Across from her, with her back to Jakob, was a woman he didn't immediately recognize. She had short blue curls and skin black as night. At his entry, the stranger turned and smiled, her eyes glinting beneath large thick glasses. She wore a plum turtleneck sweater and, as opposed to Vennamin's heavy makeup, appeared to keep her face rather natural. Locking eyes with Jakob, her whole body tensed up.

"Oh," said Jakob, stopping in the doorway. "I didn't realize you were in the middle of something."

"No, no," said Vennamin, "This is Madeline Empire. She's here at my request to meet you."

Confused, Jakob sauntered slowly into the room. "A pleasure," he said warmly to Madeline, offering her his hand and taking the empty seat beside her.

For a moment, he thought she wasn't going to accept his gesture as she simply continued to stare. Finally composing herself, however, Madeline snapped out her hand and shook his vigorously.

"It is an…" Madeline started to say, "well… honor doesn't even begin to describe the feeling."

"Madeline has assured me that she's your biggest fan," clapped Vennamin happily. "What a wonderful start to a long and fruitful relationship."

Jakob's gaze shot suddenly to his agent, sitting back in her traditional black blazer and stark white button-up with the top three buttons undone. "Fruitful? Vennamin what--"

"I just want you to know I've read everything ten times over," said Madeline, talking over him as she raced through her words. "The fact I'd get this opportunity… It means everything to me. I'll prove it! Quiz me on anything, don't care how obscure."

"Quiz you? What opportunity?" asked Jakob, his eyes narrowed. "*Vennamin?*"

Madeline seemed suddenly to understand something Jakob didn't as she sunk back into her seat. "He doesn't know?" she gasped.

"I wanted you to be here," answered the agent, calmly, to Madeline. "Listen Jakob," she said, turning her attention to him. "Inspector Aurilius is a hit. There's real momentum behind your story, but the powers that be are concerned how much longer that energy can hold up without big news about book three."

"This couldn't happen over the phone?" sighed Jakob. "Let me guess… want me to get in front of the cameras, tell the adoring fans I'm almost done? And what's her deal?" He stuck a thumb toward Madeline. "PR expert come to save my hide?"

"No," said Vennamin, "That charade is behind us. Orders from on high are to hand off the writing of Aurilius to Madeline. She'd simply be a ghost writer, making sure the words reach the page. You'd still be directing the story, and she's the best I know at—"

"No," said Jakob firmly. "Not interested."

"Here's the thing," said Vennamin. "I care. You know I do. Your interests are important to me, but I only get so much say. There is *one* other way out, and that's if you can promise me book three, on my desk, this time next year. It doesn't need to be your magnum opus. As long as it's Aurilius, people will eat it up."

"And if it's not done by then?" asked Jakob sharply. "Inspector Aurilius isn't yours to take."

"According to your contract… the series is ours to *manage*," said Vennamin coolly. "We can't revoke your ownership, but Talon has the right to hand the writing off to Madeline. I know what it means to you, but really, Jakob, this isn't the end of the world. You'd be involved every step of the way and Madeline—"

"Hang on!" burst Madeline, leaping out of her seat. "I'm sorry, Jakob… I thought this was… I didn't realize… I don't agree to this." She looked frantically between them before her eyes steeled. "I think I'd better go," she said.

"Now hold on--" Vennamin began, but her words were lost on Madeline. The writer scowled one last time at Vennamin then strutted proudly out of the room.

"I think I'd better follow," said Jakob sternly, beginning to rise.

"Don't be dramatic," growled Vennamin. "Walking out that door doesn't take our contract away, it just robs you of your say in this decision. We both know you've nowhere else to go, neither does she. Talon *is* media. Your best bet is to work with me, the one person on your side."

Jakob looked at his agent, sickened. "How dare you pretend to care?"

Vennamin sighed and reached below her desk. Jakob heard a cabinet open and close as she retrieved two square glasses and a bottle of reddish-caramel liquid.

"Verius Nova, just over fifty years old," said Vennamin, filling both glasses up halfway. "Though not technically allowed, it can be our secret."

"Getting me drunk isn't going to help," said Jakob pointedly, as she pushed one glass over to his end of the table. He paid the drink no mind.

Shrugging, Vennamin downed her drink and poured herself a second. "I'll be straight with you," she said, leaning forward and folding her hands over her desk. "Believe it or not, I do care. I want you to have the freedom to write your book, but I also want to see you succeed. A thousand stories hit my desk every week, Jakob, and I'm telling you… Aurilius is the hottest damn thing since Deity. I've known from day one that you, Jakob Rite, were the next Annalaide Martin. It's that very reason I pulled strings to get you in print. Those old presses aren't cheap… that's real money invested, because it was important to you."

"Money invested?" scoffed Jakob. "Talon's made twice what you've spent *because* of me."

"Pocket change," said Vennamin, sipping at her second glass. "Some day, these novels could very well be the popular books in all of Irasil. In terms of profit, that'd put you just under any old Lowend morning cartoon… Tell me, do you know how exactly Talon Media Corporation came to own sixteen square blocks of the most expensive city in the world?"

"Buying up every franchise you could get your grubby paws on?" guessed Jakob.

"Wrong," said Vennamin. "That's a result, not the cause. The reason Talon became the giant it is now is because four hundred years ago, when the index room was first pitched, our founder, Charles Raven, was the only person willing to back it. 'Too much infrastructure,' everyone else whined, but Charles saw the future in visual index technology. With the backing of Talon, the first VUEs were filmed, and the rest is history. Fact is, Jakob, your print novels are… a novelty. Talon runs on VUE."

"If you want VUE so bad then do it," spat Jakob. "You've got two books to work with. I don't see why the third book is so damn important to you now."

"No producer is willing to go anywhere near a half-finished story, not when the third novel is taking you so long, especially not after what happened with the Grand Winter Saga," argued Vennamin. "Listen to me, Jakob. I know you don't want this. But look around, you think *this* is what I want?" she motioned around the windowless office. "My greatest achievements on display and none of them mean a thing. Aurilius is my ticket to a UniVUE, to an office on the east wing, to a perfect view of Koperra Tower. Every day, all day, I want to look up at those losers slaving away, and when I think of how they used me… held me back… well… Livespark won't be the only bird flying."

"Ah, there it is," said Jakob. "All this talk of helping me, and you just care about a fancier office."

"You've got it all wrong," cooed Vennamin. "If you and your stories put me in that office, Jakob… I won't forget it. Once I'm on top, I'll have the power to give you all the time in the world. Hand this thing off to Madeline… or at least work with her to get the damn thing done this year. After that, you'll never have to compromise again." She extended a hand, smooth and pale with a large diamond perched upon her ring finger.

"I'll see you in a year," said Jakob definitively, then he rose from his chair and promptly left.

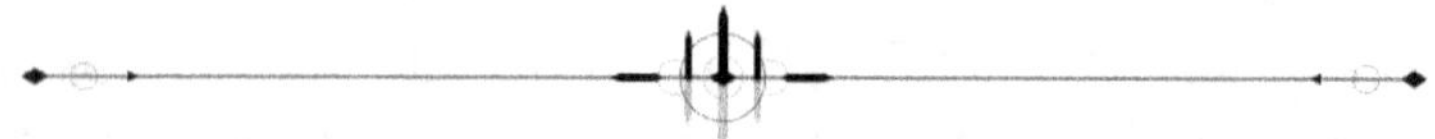

The ride home was silent. Jakob's nervous pacing was replaced with a downcast slump on the bench, and the three hour trip slogged by in a miserable blur. For all he'd expected to be in some state of panicked planning, Jakob found he couldn't seem to form a single coherent thought. Yet his mind was far from empty. Wordless emotions buzzed about his brain, stabbing at his psyche like a hive of angered wasps.

Jakob's pursuer dropped him off on the platform at the end of his block, and the whole world seemed a haze as he stumbled home. He had only just stepped in the front door when he felt it in his gut: a wrenching sensation, fueled by the frantic buzzing. All those emotions had to go somewhere, and Jakob was fairly certain he knew exactly where they were about to go. Sprinting to the bathroom, Jakob barely managed to throw open the toilet lid before lurching up his breakfast.

The wordless panic hung over Jakob the whole next week. Night after night he'd sit at his desk, staring down at an empty page, clutching his pen tight until his knuckles turned white. He wrote so many words, and yet he got nowhere. He couldn't make any sense of it. Where had the hours gone?

On the sixth day, lying in bed at noon, Jakob finally decided it was time to seek help. "Proto, can you get through to Madeline?" he asked.

"Yeah," said Proto, "one sec." A moment passed and then Proto spoke again. "She's there. Putting you through."

"Hello, Jakob?" Madeline's voice sounded nervous as it filled his room.

"Hey, Madeline," said Jakob, sitting up in bed.

"Holy…! It really is you!" said Madeline excitedly. "I'm surprised you still want to talk to me after…"

"About that," said Jakob. "Thanks for standing up for me. Bold choice, storming out of Vennamin's office like that."

"Eww, just her name gets me…" Madeline growled. "So, what's up? I can't imagine you took her offer… did you?"

"No," said Jakob. "One year. That's all I've got now…"

"I'm sorry," Madeline spoke softly.

"Anyway, didn't mean to turn this into a pity call," sighed Jakob. "I actually wanted to reach out because I had a question. Seems like you know what you're doing, when it comes to getting words on the page, you ever been in a rut before?"

There was a moment of silence.

"Jakob Rite asking me for writing advice?" he heard her speak under her breath. "Sorry," she said, louder. "This is just… wild. But yeah! Actually, there's this chick I dig, Haez, she runs a creative writing club. It's real small time… maybe it's not the most helpful to someone like… *you*. But, if you're interested, it really helps get me in that creative mode."

"Oh yeah?" said Jakob. "Sounds like just what I need. When and where?"

He heard Madeline gasp loudly. "Haez is gonna… She'll love this! Lowpae, up in North Wyndon, if you can make it there. Tenth hour."

"I'll see you there," said Jakob.

"Definitely! Yeah! Awesome chat! See you there," Madeline sounded about ready to explode with excitement as the call ended.

Despite Sylvia's constant presence throughout the week, Jakob had managed to keep her ignorant of his crisis. That is, until that Hykel evening. Sylvia had come home early from classes and was relaxing over a Quisitive docuVUE in their index room. Though Jakob was pretending to be busier than ever, he was, instead, huddled on the bathroom floor, head hung over the toilet, ready to donate another meal to the bowl. While he should have been excited for the upcoming writing club, Jakob was dreading the opportunity to flaunt his failure to a wider audience. Just as partially digested biscuits took their leave of his gut, there was a knock at the door.

"Jakob?" came Sylvia's voice. "Did you just puke?"

"Ugh," groaned Jakob, lightheaded. He frantically reached for toilet paper to wipe the tears from his eyes, then collapsed back against the bathtub, just in time for Sylvia to barge in.

"What the…" Sylvia's eyes jumped between Jakob and the remnants of his dinner, left unflushed. Her mouth curled to a grimace, though her eyes were soft and full of pity. "You're not sick, are you?"

Jakob shook his head, wiping his cheeks of tears.

"Vennamin?"

Jakob nodded.

"That shraft snake," cursed Sylvia, her strong shoulders filling the doorway. "Come on then, no use moping. There's a report on Quisitive right now that's bound to perk you up."

"I'd rather not," groaned Jakob, reaching to flush the toilet and spare both him and Sylvia the smell.

"I don't care," said Sylvia. "Not about to sit here and let you puke yourself to death. You need to think about something else for a while. This'll do just the trick. Besides, my index is bust again. I need to borrow Proto anyway."

"Ah, her true intentions revealed," mumbled Jakob, though playfully.

"Up time!" Sylvia proclaimed and marched across to where he was propped against the tub. Grabbing his arm, she hoisted him to his feet. Jakob's legs felt weak beneath him as he followed her up the wooden steps to the round index room with a couch as its only decoration.

"Proto?" she asked, holding out her hand.

"Here," said Jakob, taking the thick lens from his pocket.

"Evening, Sylvia," piped Proto cheerfully as the device flickered on.

"I've got beef with you," said Sylvia, swiping the index from Jakob's hand. "You knew what's been going on with Jakob all this time and you didn't tell me?"

"Loyal to a fault, I suppose," answered Proto. "Although… if it had gotten much worse, I'd have reached out. I assure you."

"Well, now you can make it up to me," said Sylvia, going to the center of the room. "Quisitive report, load it up."

"Of course," said Proto.

A narrow podium rose from the floor with a slot for a lens at the top. Sylvia removed her index and fixed Proto in its spot. Once Proto was secure, the podium sunk back into the floor and Sylvia and Jakob took their usual spots on the couch.

The room went dark for a moment, then the plain white chamber was replaced by a much larger room. The walls and ceiling looked like natural bark, as if they were in the hollow of a tree. There were a couple small round windows, and the floor was draped in a braided reed rug. Cubbies grew right out of the walls and were lined in colorful books and stacks of loose papers.

Just in front of the couch where Jakob and Sylvia sat was a heavy wooden desk. Two chairs had been pulled up and they were occupied by two starkly different figures. Behind the desk was an old and sickly looking capillum. Unlike the few capillum Jakob had met in his life, this man had little of his body hidden. His top, if you could call it that, was simply a few long straps that crossed his chest and disappeared over one shoulder. His fur was dark grey and patterned with streaks of black dye along his dangerously thin arms. Beside him, a young redheaded human sat with perfect posture. The man, who Jakob recognized as Elliot Jay, had abnormally large ears and a fiery eagerness in his eyes.

Taking a moment to absorb the space, Jakob knew there was only one place this could have been filmed.

"This is… Roana?" asked Jakob, bolting out of his seat and running over to a window. It was dark out, and soft moonlight filtered down from the canopy many hulking boughs above. Below, a dozen layers of heavy branches disappeared into a lightless void. He couldn't get a sense how high up he was, only that the trees must be immensely tall. All across the many towering trunks and interwoven branches, Jakob could see twinkling lights through the windows of other homes. "How'd Elliot pull this off?"

"Shh, listen," said Sylvia.

"Doctor?" asked Elliot, placing a hand softly on the capillum's shoulder. The frail looking capillum had light tremors in his arms as he stared blankly past his desk.

"Oh!" said the capillum, perking up at Elliot's touch. "I'm sorry… forgotten the question." Though his accent was strong, the capillum seemed to be at the very least conversational in Unified Standard.

"Twilights Maw," said Elliot. "In your writings, you report your team was herded to this place, by creatures you've called *felphants*. Now, I've some knowledge of Roana, but nothing I've read has ever mentioned a species of that name. Is it a slang?"

Jakob had returned to his seat, as absorbed by the exchange as he was the exotic city.

"No…" said the capillum absently. The question seemed to strike a nerve as the capillum's arms began to shake more violently. His left eye kept blinking, almost with a rhythm, and his shoulders tensed sharply from time to time. "Never … we'd never seen it before."

"A unique specimen to the Dead Coast… effect of the continued radiation from the facility perhaps?" said Elliot, scrawling furiously in a journal.

"Not the facility!" burst the capillum, appearing almost compulsive in the force of his delivery.

"Oh…?" asked Elliot. "Tell me more."

The old capillum seemed to suddenly freeze up. His eye stopped twitching, his limbs locked still as statues, and an absent gaze clouded his eyes.

"Doctor Rotier?" asked Elliot, again, touching the capillum's arm. "Does this have something to do with your expungement?"

Rotier gripped the edge of the table tight, his jaw going tight. "Mockery," he whispered. "They mock me… *you* mock me!"

"No, doctor, I swear I mean no offense," said Elliot, throwing up his hands apologetically. "In fact, I've very good reason to believe your telling of events."

Rotier looked back to Elliot, apprehensive optimism painted in his giant eyes.

"Before, you said, 'not the facility,'" said Elliot. "I'm still connecting some dots… are you suggesting there is some other power at work in the Dead Coast, something beyond the nuclear facility?"

"I shouldn't…" said Rotier, shrinking back again. "They'll never believe it…"

"Let's start with the proof then," pushed Elliott. "You are the only survivor, and to date, no footage has ever been captured within the coast, but I think I can help here. An old balloonist got us close enough to view a small stretch of land via telescope. None of our electronics worked, couldn't record a thing, but I've written what I saw there in my journal. May I share it with you?"

Roteir nodded. "The trees of the dead coast aren't like the rest of Roana, short even by the standards of home," Elliott read. "I could see for miles, to the hills where the bare ashen trees were a bit larger.

There, I saw something, lumbering in the sage fog. A shadow, the size of a home, and there was no doubt it was moving."

Fear flooded Rotier's gaze and the capillum began to shake.

"You don't like discussing them, I know," said Elliot softly, "but if you can give me finer details, something to match my account. If you confirm a detail you could only know by seeing one, you'll confirm both our claims. We've ensured the whole exchange is recorded and left no room for me to feed you the information beforehand."

For the first time in the interview, Rotier seemed calm, his ticks easing. "I… suppose it can't hurt to try," he began. "We first saw them on the fourth night. Our compasses had broken on the first day, and barren as the trees were, there was no sense to the sun above us. Direction was lost to us. There was day and night, but no logic to their order." As he spoke, Rotier was filled with a lively awareness. There was confidence in his words. "The emerald clouds were not gas, as we had expected, but spores. The felphants made them, walked among them, shrouded in them. We heard them… stomping… and then came silhouettes." Rotier's nerves suddenly shot back. His eyes widened, his breathing shallowed. "I see… I see… I see…"

"Doctor?" said Elliot, calmingly.

"I can't," said Rotier, frantically.

"It's okay," said Elliot. "Let's try something else. I've seen your sketches, the way you capture nature in meticulous exactness. Could you try drawing it, perhaps?"

Rotier nodded. Turning in his chair, he slid a paper off the shelf behind him and clutched a silver pen. Instant recognition flooded over Jakob.

"Hang on," Jakob said. "I know that pen, it's the same as mine!" He plucked the silver and gold banded pen from his pocket. "What's a Pruvian Series Q doing in Roana? Of all things to smuggle through the trade embargo… why a pen?"

"I don't know, but hush," shushed Sylvia. "I wanna see this."

Rotier flattened out the paper against his desk then, uncapping his pen, he began to draw in wide curved lines. At first he sketched the outline, rotund with a long tail, droopy ears, and fearsome tusks. Then, came finer details. Rotier added massive bulbous growths all up and down the back. As he moved to the legs, Rotier suddenly shot up in his chair, flinging the pen across the room.

"HER!" he screamed, pointing a finger across his desk.

Jakob turned to follow Rotier's point past the couch to an empty corner of the room.

In a panic, Rotier lurched back sharp into a shelf, knocking off several hardbound books. "Her!" he continued to cry at the empty corner. "You've brought her here!"

"What is…?" Jakob stood and walked over the corner, but then he saw it, a soft shimmer. It was so subtle that Jakob would never have seen it if he weren't standing so close. Like heat off a radiator, the air in the corner rippled, and, if Jakob squinted, he swore he could make out the shape of a capillum.

Suddenly, the shimmer stopped. Jakob turned to see Rotier, frozen in place. Elliot Jay, however, was still animated as he turned to face the couch directly.

"These were the last intelligible words Doctor Vukor Rotier would speak to us," said Elliot. "However, before you draw any conclusions, I'd like to present our evidence." Elliot reached into his pocket and pulled out a letter. A seal on the back pictured an emblem of a tree, its canopy shaped like the nation of Roana. "This letter has been sealed by the Council of Gau, and we've an officiator, just offscreen, to verify the integrity of its opening. Without further ado."

Elliot peeled open the letter and pulled a small handwritten note from inside. "The creatures are roughly thirty feet tall," read Elliot. "From what we can see through the masking of the clouds, their backs are lumpy and uneven, perhaps natural growths? We believe we've seen tusks, but auxiliary limbs cannot be ruled out."

Putting the letter aside, Elliot once again turned his attention to the couch. "Nature, it seems, has found a way," he said, "even in the

Dead Coast. I can only wonder what other exotic lifeforms make their home of its sage fog."

"Now, *that*..." started Sylvia.

"I know," said Jakob. "This is it! It's the perfect mystery!"

"Is that a smile I see?" asked Sylvia playfully.

"Proto, go back to the drawing," commanded Jakob, "right before Rotier jumps."

The scene rewound swiftly, Elliot facing Rotier once again. The books from the floor flew back up onto the shelf as Rotier returned to his seat.

Jakob went over to the corner where he saw the shimmering capillum. "Go ahead, play it," said Jakob. "And Sylvia, watch over here."

"For what?" asked Sylvia, wrinkling her brow.

The scene sprang suddenly back to normal motion as Rotier once again crashed from his seat and barreled backwards into the shelf behind him.

"Look," said Jakob, "you see this shimmer." Training his eyes on the ripple in the air, Jakob could make out what looked loosely like the figure of a capillum.

"What am I supposed to be looking at?" asked Sylvia as Rotier yelled, the scene paused, and Elliot began his monologue.

"Come over here if you can't see it," said Jakob. "Proto, back it up, same spot."

Sylvia grunted and rose from the couch, joining Jakob in the corner. "So, what is this about?"

"Hold on," said Jakob. "Proto, play it."

Once again, the air in the corner began to ripple. Now that Jakob saw the capillum, he couldn't unsee the figure.

"A blemish in the recording?" scoffed Sylvia. "Jakob, just now, when you described '*the perfect mystery*,' were you referring to the impossible life forms discovered by a disgraced scientist or a blemish on a docuVUE?"

"Both... and neither," said Jakob, "they're both just a piece of it."

"*It?*" asked Sylvia.

"It's just like when Proto recorded the girl," said Jakob. "Light… but from where…" His eyes snapped to one thing in the room that didn't belong.

"Proto," said Jakob, "Same spot… actually, a couple seconds more."

As the scene rewound Jakob walked over to the desk where Rotier was drawing. "Go ahead, but slow it down," he said, stepping right through the desk, putting his face at level with Rotier's hand. The pen was exactly like the silver Purvian Series Q he carried everywhere, except for one feature. On the cap of the pen was an orange gemstone, small as a pea.

"That's it… I'll bet anything…" whispered Jakob, watching as Rotier adjusted the pen, his thumb briefly passing over the gem. A moment later, the old capillum lurched back in slow motion. "I knew it!" exclaimed Jakob. "This is *my* story. I was born to solve this."

"Knew what, Jakob?" Sylvia asked, sounding a touch annoyed. "Believe me, I'm happy you're excited, just help me see what you're seeing."

"It all ties back to that day in the park," said Jakob. "I wasn't crazy, and Proto's not busted. It's *tech*. That dancing girl, her light, it's what Rotier sees, in the corner there. It triggered when he touched the cap of the pen and… a pen, mind you, that would be all but impossible to get in Roana. Whatever this light is, it must be targeted somehow. Explains why no one else in the park noticed that girl!"

"Jakob…" Sylvia started, but instead she sighed and raised a hand to her temple as if nursing a headache. "Whatever gets you writing, I guess. Proto, end VUE."

Rotier's home disappeared, and the two siblings now stood on opposite ends of the plain white room.

"You're leaving?" asked Jakob.

"You clearly have your own thing going here," said Sylvia. "I'm off to get my index repaired so that *I* can look up more about the impossible biology of the *Dead Coast*."

Jakob rolled his eyes and gave her a dismissive wave. When Sylvia was gone, and the door was shut firmly behind her, Jakob returned to the matter at hand. "Proto," he said, "how far back can we go? Was the pen on the desk when the VUE began?" It turned out, the pen had been there from the start, meaning it hadn't been gifted to Rotier by Elliot or his team, and Jakob was even more invested for it.

CHAPTER TEN

THE POWER OF PASSION

Sweat beaded down Faeron's brow as he parried a series of blows left-right-left.

"Actually," he panted, "I was *there*."

Lydia, his sparring partner, paused. Her short pink hair was tied back in a ponytail and her skin glistened with sweat. Here, her status as an art student was less apparent, as she wore the same white sparring robes as Faeron. "You saw the Forgeworks flame go out!?"

"Between us..." said Faeron, lowering his voice. "It was kytra related."

"You mean you—" Lydia cut short with a gasp, looking past Faeron. In the mirrored-wall behind her, Faeron could see the reflection of Saitum stalking toward them, a judging glare in her eyes. Marching up to Lydia, Saitum pointed across the mats to her previous sparring partner, a year-eleven girl now standing alone.

"Okay!" said Lydia, understanding instantly. With a wave to Faeron, she ran off to practice with the girl.

Saitum took Lydia's spot and raised her fists.

"Hold, you two... just a moment!" Bennehym hobbled across the mats toward Saitum and Faeron. As always, the aged scholar wore a friendly smile beneath his long braided beard. "Kel Bora..." he said, and a look of recognition swept across his daughter's face, "the waking meditation, as we call it today. Mathas tells me you have conquered the basics."

"Enough for him to let me shape," said Faeron proudly as his heart still pounded from the workout.

"Well," said Bennehym, "may I see it?"

"Of course," said Faeron, glancing over to where Lydia was trading blows with the year-eleven. When he was certain she wasn't watching, he closed his eyes. Faeron's body thirsted for oxygen but he forced himself to breathe long slow breaths. His brow cooled, his muscles numbed, and the sounds of the sparring room died away as he hunted down each thought. When Faeron's mind was silent, the light of Peridom appeared. Like a far off tram on a starless night, the distant light drew nearer, and as it approached, it shone ever brighter. It grew into a brilliant pearlescent wave and swallowed Faeron in its shimmering current. For a moment, he was carried in its streaking colors.

Open your eyes, he told himself. Blinking, Faeron returned to reality, but the mats, mirrors, benches, lockers, and every other surface of the sparring room now shimmered softly like the wave of light.

Bennehym eyed him for a moment. "I may not witness the light as the kytra do, but that look of yours I know," he said, proudly, "distant… only here in part. Your mother, Vox, Mathas, they all wore it the same." Then, without warning, he raised his cane and struck Faeron sharply on the arm.

"Ow!" cried Faeron, as the light of peridom vanished from the room. "What was that for?"

"Your connection to the light is as fragile as it is powerful," said Bennehym. "To master your craft, you must harden your psyche, learn to ignore pain and emotion alike."

"How am I supposed to not feel pain?" asked Faeron, rubbing his sore arm.

"My grandpapa told stories of the Arborals," said Bennehym, "kytra protectors of the Nylkwood and the Monastery of the Old Scholars. It was said that the Arborals would maintain Kel Bora throughout their daily routines, even whilst training in Bo Kora. By this practice, the Arborals were able to wield the light in hunts and, when need be, in battle."

"I thought the Old Scholars were a peaceful people. They had warriors?" asked Faeron. Their conversation had begun to draw curious eyes and no doubt ears.

"Peaceful and isolated a people as they were, the Old-Scholars were also well protected," said Bennehym. "Nylk's forest was a formidable defense for my ancestors, but even the Old-Spirit is not without limits. Just as Host Cresh brought the Old-Spirit Rhun to heel, Nylk was, on occasion, subject to the ploys of men. The Arborals were those kytra who learned to hear her voice and act upon her will.

"All this to say… you want me to meditate while I spar?" concluded Faeron.

"Every day," confirmed Bennehym, "now, and so long as you practice this art."

"Can't promise I'll be dodging blows, but I can try," said Faeron. Once again, he cleared his mind. When his connection to peridom was restored, he opened his eyes and turned to face Saitum. The light cast an aura about her, as if radiating through her dark skin. "Go ahead."

Saitum was lightning quick. Faeron hardly had a second to ready himself as her fist crashed into his awkward block. The strike was followed by three more in quick succession. Each hit hammered back the light, and, within seconds, Faeron's connection to peridom was gone.

"Hold on," he said, and her assault relented. "The light. I need to get it back."

Once again, Faeron performed the waking meditation as Bennehym and Saitum watched. "You know," he said, opening his eyes, "maybe I should start with someone a little easier."

"Until you can return a blow in meditation, you won't offer much experience to your classmates," said Bennehym, "Saitum will do well enough for now. She'll just have to hold back a little bit."

"Maybe more than a little bit," mumbled Faeron.

From the fiery smile on Saitum's face, Faeron doubted she'd hold back much.

By the time the bell rang, Faeron's arms were red and sore from Saitum's onslaught. In the hour he had left, he never once managed to block more than a punch or two before losing his connection. Of course, his half absent blocks didn't help.

"Faeron!" called Lydia as he exited the locker room in his academy blazer. Her pink hair fell about the shoulders of her white printed jacket. "Alright, you've got a couple minutes," she said, running over to him, "here to the elevator… what exactly happened last night at Forgeworks?"

"This stays between us," said Faeron, quietly.

She nodded, her cheeks red as they often were after a long class of sparring.

"Crazy enough," said Faeron, "it all started with a game of Deity…" As they left the classroom and made for the elevators at the end of the hall, Faeron filled her in on all the events of last night, from discovering Caidus was the nomad champion to the confrontation in front of Forgeworks.

"That's…" Lydia seemed lost for words. She stood in front of the elevator, looking awestruck at Faeron. "I never imagined either of you would have that kind of power. I don't know if I should be scared or impressed."

"Hey, I can barely catch a ball out of the air," laughed Faeron. "Besides, it was an accident. Even Auri has no clue how she did it."

"Kinda makes it scarier…" said Lydia, "though… really puts it in perspective. If that's an accident, imagine what you can do once you master your art."

Suddenly, a bright blue ball of light appeared, bobbing up and down in the empty space between them.

"Apologies for interrupting," said Serris warmly. "Faeron, you have a call from Auri Lem."

"Go ahead," said Faeron, noticing Lydia's eyes slant at Auri's name.

The index expanded until it shaped itself into a perfect image of Auri wearing a Deity-themed sweatshirt and long black pants.

"Hey," said Auri. "Come up to study room fourteen. It's about last night. I think I'm onto something."

"Be right there," said Faeron, and Auri disappeared. Turning back to Lydia, Faeron smiled, "Looks like I'll be riding up with you today… for a few floors at least."

As if on cue, the elevator doors slid open and Alannah announced, "Going up."

There were only five other students in the spacious elevator, but Faeron and Lydia huddled close in the corner, continuing their conversation in whispers. The floral scent of the dancer's perfume masked the workout they'd both just endured.

"You know, Faeron," whispered Lydia, her arm pressed to his, their hands inches apart, "someday, when you're off saving the world, I'm gonna get a kick telling people I knew you back when you were a regular ol' scruffy headed teen."

"Won't have to tell 'em anything if we're still hanging out together," suggested Faeron, a funny fluttering settling in his chest.

"Yeah," said Lydia, "I like the sound of that."

"Floor sixty-six, Lydia Ephenna," called Alannah.

"Hey, before I go…" said Lydia. "I haven't forgotten my promise. Just a few weeks left in this show and then I'll have time to visit the Athenaeum, I swear!"

"That was a promise?" whispered Faeron, his chest tight.

"Wasn't it?" teased Lydia. "Well… it is now."

"Floor sixty-six, Lydia Ephenna," called Alannah again.

"See you tomorrow," Lydia slipped from the tram, and Faeron watched her skip down the hall until the doors shut tight and the elevator once again began to rise.

Faeron got off the elevator on floor eighty, stepping into a mostly empty Rec Room. The Deity tables were vacant, though several of the study rooms around the perimeter of the open area were lit up, including number 14. Through the window, Faeron could see Auri studying a projection on a wide square table.

Striding across the quiet open space and past the deity tables, Faeron knocked on the door. Through the window, he saw Auri beckon him inside.

The back wall was a window ceiling to floor, looking out on a wide stretch of the northern wall. Far across the city was the nature reserve tower and, at its peak, the statue of Host Sombara standing among tall stalks of corn. Inside the study room, Auri was leaning over a projection of a desert keep rising out of a low square table.

"You recognize this?" asked Auri as Faeron entered the cozy study space.

"That's the keep from Prophet's Guard, right?" said Faeron, "From the Cresh challenge a couple weeks back."

"Exactly," said Auri. "Sit. Look."

Faeron sunk into a stool across the table. "Look at what, exactly?"

On the table he saw the familiar battlefield. Soldiers flooded Cresh, but the Warrior Host was undaunted. Not yielding a single step, Cresh held fast against an onslaught of arrows and blades, slamming any soldier foolish enough to come within range of her stony fists.

"She doesn't look calm, does she?" asked Auri as she watched the Warrior Host, a look of admiration in her bronze eyes.

"No," said Faeron, "it's a war, after all. I wouldn't expect her to be calm."

"But then how is she shaping?" asked Auri, looking up at Faeron directly. He could tell from her glare that this was about more than just Host Cresh.

"In class today," offered Faeron, "Bennehym told me about the Arborals—"

"Using the waking meditation in combat, I know," said Auri. "He came by my Aur Poro class earlier. This isn't that, though. Cresh is doing more than just ignoring pain and distractions. In fact, it looks like she's doing just the opposite. Watch her…"

Cresh leaped into a pack of shielded foes, bashing them a dozen feet across the sands. With each swing her golden eyes flared brilliantly.

"She's embracing her emotion," said Auri, "*shaping* with it!"

"Like you… last night," said Faeron, knowing exactly where she was going with this.

"Think about it," said Auri, "it makes perfect sense. I was in a bad mood to start, then those idiots in the park… they… they just… pushed me over the edge. There was no thought or reason to it… I didn't even see the flame burst. My mind went blank, and when I came to, everything was dark."

"It could explain how you've been fighting back the crimson," offered Faeron.

"I was thinking that, too," grinned Auri. Her eyes flicked to the window, scanning the empty rec room. "So," she said mischievously, "wanna try it?"

"Shaping?" asked Faeron.

"No dummy," scoffed Auri, "just meditating, of course. But… just in case, we should probably do it out there." She pointed to the door.

They scampered out into the vacant Rec Room and stood opposite each other in a spacious area beyond the deity tables.

"So, you just need to lose control, right?" asked Faeron.

"No… not control… just…" Auri squeezed her eyes shut and clenched her fists at her sides.

"Just what?" asked Faeron.

Auri breathed faster, her chest rising and falling rapidly as she gulped down air.

"Are you sure that's a good idea?" asked Faeron, watching her hyperventilate.

She ignored him, her breathing only growing sharper, faster. Her brow wrinkled, her lip curled menacing, and her fists clenched so tight they'd begun to shake.

"You're gonna pass out if you keep that up."

"IT HAS TO WORK!" she screamed. Auri's eyes shot open, her irises ablaze with brilliant bronze light. The wild light in her eyes was every bit as brilliant as that of the hosts or the dancing girl from Faeron's dreams. Before Faeron could find words to express his awe, the light dimmed and disappeared from her eyes. Auri teetered backward, collapsing onto a nearby canvas bench.

"You okay?" asked Faeron, stepping to her aid.

"Yeah... I think," she panted, waving him away. "We..." she took a moment to breathe, "we need to go tell Mathas."

"Absolutely," agreed Faeron.

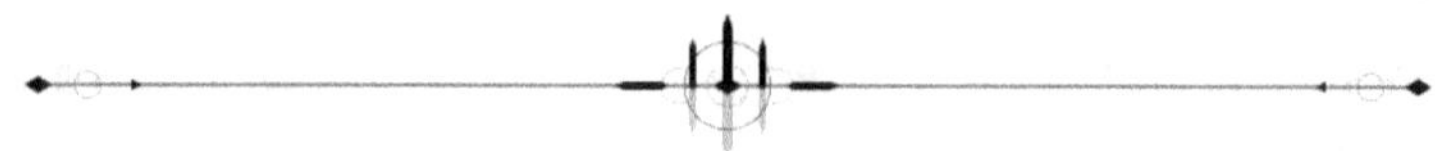

The end of day bustle meant the elevator was packed to the brink, and throngs of students littered the two blocks between the Academy Tower and Mathas' Athenaeum.

With homework and research projects on the rise, the Athenaeum steps were crowded tonight. Auri and Faeron had to fight their way up the stairs to the wooden double doors. A steady trickle of students shuffled back and forth between the halls on either side of the lobby as they perused the shelves beyond.

"Suppose Mathas is getting the workshop ready?" asked Auri softly.

"Let's see," said Faeron. He crossed the lobby to the classroom door and tugged hard. It was locked. Lightly, Faeron knocked.

When there was no reply for several minutes, Faeron knocked a second time. "Give it another minute," he said.

A soft humming sound filled the quiet space as the elevator descended from the floor above.

"Faeron, look!" said Auri.

Faeron turned to see the unmistakable hooded figure of Caidus Proud riding down the glass tube. When the elevator stopped he swept across the foyer and joined them at the door. Beneath his shadowed hood, Caidus' grin was an odd mixture of human and capillum features.

"You," he said, pointing at Auri. "You scare me... you know that?"

"Good," Auri beamed back. "You get home alright?"

"Nope, died twice on the way back," said Caidus. "Heard you knocking. Looking for Mathas?"

"Yeah," said Faeron. "We have to tell him something *very* important."

"'Bout last night?" asked Caidus.

"Yeah," said Auri. "We know why the flame—"

"Not here," interrupted Caidus. "Up in his office."

"Sure," said Faeron, and the three of them boarded the elevator.

As they rose to the second floor reading room, Caidus pulled his hood down further. The room was busier than the lobby downstairs. Students of all ages were gathered around a squat table, whispering to each other as they studied from large tomes, and a few older regulars spotted the few remaining chairs.

Caidus led Faeron and Auri down the southern corridor, the afternoon sun through the colored windows painting the half-capillum's hood like a canvas. In the small reading room at the end of the hall, a group of younger students sat in a circle, all reading the same book. Caidus led them to the familiar wooden door of Mathas' office. It was unlocked, and the three of them entered.

The scent of paint greeted Faeron as he stepped into a room with canvases of fantastic creatures and lush forest landscapes hanging all across the walls. Mathas, dressed in an apron, was washing off a brush in a small metal sink beside his easel where his most recent painting sat uncovered. The canvas featured a dead black backdrop and a creature, much like an elk, lit in the blue glow of its wide fanning antlers.

"Woah," said Auri, catching sight of the painting. "Is that real? In Roana?"

"At'll be a kelvoa," said Caidus.

"A what?" asked Faeron.

"Inhabitants of Roana's lightless forest floors," said Mathas, placing a cup of clean brushes into a glass-faced cabinet. "While predators evolved to hunt on sound, not sight, the kelvoa instead adapted their luminous antlers." He tightened the paint lids and lined the jars up orderly on the middle shelf. "From the treetop residences of Gau, they appeared like stars in the void of the forest below."

"Speaking of luminous," interjected Caidus, "can I politely ask… what in the world happened last night? Was that some kind of brain scanner tuned to the fire?"

"No, nothing like that…" said Auri, "but it's actually why we came… only…" she looked at Caidus, a bit sheepishly, "it's a private thing."

"Didn't seem very private last night," pointed out Caidus.

"Caidus would be happy to give us the room," said Mathas, looking at Caidus pointedly. "Whatever makes you feel comfortable, Miss Lem."

"Wait… Lem?" asked Caidus. "Lem like… Vox Lem!?"

"You know my dad?" asked Auri.

"Who doesn't?" asked Caidus. "He's the reason the Roane trade routes exist. Seeing as we're the only crew with an alca, he's hitched a ride with us more times than I can count. At least as far as Port Korva"

"You've *traveled* with Dad!?" said Auri, looking awed. Any nervousness she had was shed in that instant as her normal bravado returned. "Well… if he trusts you then so do I! It wasn't any kind of tech that made the fire go out… It was *emotion*."

"Emotion?" asked Caidus skeptically.

Mathas locked the cabinet and turned with a look of intrigue.

"I got fed up, like you said," Auri began, "and then I shaped. I didn't mean to… I wasn't in control then, but I've figured it out now."

"I don't understand what any of that meant," said Caidus.

"You can repeat this?" asked Mathas, ignoring Caidus' comments.

"Not the shaping, not yet" said Auri, "but I can do the waking meditation."

"It's more than that," piped Faeron. "When she does it, her eyes burst with flames like the Hosts."

"What are you on about?" asked Caidus. "I didn't see no fire eyes."

"It's not something you would have seen," said Mathas, "but it is quite the development. To make any sense of it, I'll need to see it for myself. Let's move this conversation to the workshop."

"Well, this is goodnight for me then," said Caidus. "I really should be on my way before I'm locked in. You all have fun with your magic fire eyes now." He retrieved a large backpack from behind Mathas' desk and slung it over one shoulder.

Caidus rode the elevator with the rest of them and said goodbyes in the foyer.

"Later, Caidus," said Faeron.

"Yeah, try not to die any more times on the way out," said Auri.

"I'll do my best," said Caidus, pulling up his hood. He hoisted open the broad front doors, and, with an animated wave, strode out into the evening-lit park.

When the doors shut, Mathas retrieved the key to the classroom from his pocket and led the pair straight back to the workshop.

"Serris, can you get the lights?" asked Mathas as he strode into the dark workshop. The lights flickered on and Faeron followed to find the workshop looking exactly as it had the day before.

"A quick clarification," said Mathas as he ambled toward the mats, "Faeron, you said her eyes appeared aflame, like those of the Hosts. Do you mean to say they were gold in color?"

"I wouldn't say gold, exactly…" said Faeron. "It was just like how they show in Prophet's Guard, but more bronze, like her eyes normally!"

"I'd have to see to know…," mumbled Mathas, seemingly to himself. Perking up, he said, "Auri, would you mind if I invited Bennehym and Eamon to join us by index?"

"Not at all," said Auri. "They both should know."

"Serris," said Mathas, "could you summon them please?"

"Just one moment," said Serris. Two bright blue balls of light popped into the air and began to pulse lightly as they followed alongside the kytra.

Reaching the mats, one of the two index lights began to expand until it took the form of Faeron's father.

"Evening all," grinned Eamon, standing in perfect detail beside them. "Perfect timing on your part. I just finished up for the night."

The second index light expanded as well and Bennehym took form.

"So many kytra," said Bennehym, sounding a bit taken aback as he looked between Faeron and the others. "I'm honored to be in the presence of such old souls. How may I assist you tonight?"

"We have a unique situation that might benefit from your wisdom," said Mathas. "Auri, it's your show from here."

"Alright," she said, "where to start…" Once again, Faeron and Auri gave a summary of their night, each piping in to ensure neither missed a single detail. Auri then recounted her afternoon revelation and her breakthrough with Faeron in the Rec Room. "Having done it myself…" she said, "it's so obvious now when I watch Cresh that she did the same thing… shaping with emotion, with *passion*. I can show you."

Auri stepped back on the mats and closed her eyes. Once again, her breathing quickened. Fists clenched, brow furrowed, Auri wore a look of pain.

"Miss Lem—" began Mathas.

"I'm fine," she barked between sharp breaths. Auri was clearly mumbling something under her breath, but Faeron couldn't make out any words. With a stomp, Auri's eyes shot open, her irises alight with brilliant bronze flames.

"Incredible," gasped Mathas.

The spectacle ended and Auri stumbled. This time, Faeron was prepared, and he dashed forward, catching her arm.

"You good?" he asked.

"You saw it, right?" said Auri, pulling her arm free.

Faeron grinned and nodded.

Her face lit up, though he could see tears still running down her cheeks.

"Don't gawk," she hissed. "I don't cry. You saw nothing."

"I know the color won't transmit," said Mathas, looking to Eamon. "But did you see the blur?"

"Serris, can you replay that bit, slower," said Eamon, squinting off toward the empty space beside him."

"Blur?" asked Faeron.

"When recorded by index," said Mathas, "peridom's light won't appear in color, but it will leave a mark, a slight blurring."

"I can see it now," said Eamon, eyes squinted at something on his end. "A shimmer in her eyes. Is it… like mine should have been?"

"There's no guaranteeing the accuracy of our modern portrayals," said Mathas, "but the color is not what I'd expect of the Hosts. In paintings, we've always seen a consistently vivid gold. This is darker… more of a bronze."

"Is it because she shaped with passion?" asked Faeron. "The girl from my dreams certainly *seemed* passionate in her dance, and her eyes glowed in every color imaginable."

"In a song, passed down through my family, there is a word," stated Bennehym, "*Ellueffi*. The verse goes, '*Ellueffi, eyes of wisdom, burning bright, oh elder soul.*' Until now, I had thought Ellueffi to be a name. But, given the circumstances, I wonder if it isn't something else… perhaps a state of meditation."

"We still can't rule out any possibilities surrounding Glavius and the Hosts," said Eamon. "There's no telling what to expect now that the Hoststone is gone."

"Until we have more evidence to point to the Hosts," said Mathas, "I'm inclined to believe we should explore this passion shaping."

"Really?" said Auri, who's breathing had slowed. She was beaming.

"Every text that Evolice translated tells us that serenity is the path to shaping," said Bennehym, "but we still know so very little. I agree it must be explored."

"Then it's decided," said Mathas. "We'll begin tomorrow. Auri, Faeron, I want you two to report to the Athenaeum an hour earlier from now on. As your practices grow in spectacle, I fear they will prove a distraction for your peers."

"What about Quinn?" asked Faeron. "He's older. We won't distract him."

"The twins are way worse distractions than we are," added Auri.

"Quinn looks up to you two," said Mathas. "As you two have mastered the arts in record time, Quinn has pushed himself to catch up. The more effort he puts into impressing you, the more difficulty he has in meditations. It has been a problem for some time now. Your move to shaping provides a perfect opportunity to not only give you the privacy you need but relieve Quinn from your pressure."

"But—" said Faeron.

"Listen to Mathas, Faeron," said Eamon. "I know this isn't what you want, but it's what's best for all the kytra."

"Fine," said Faeron, though he didn't want to be the one to have to tell Quinn.

Bennehym suddenly began to rub his temple, his eyes appearing glazed. "I'm sorry," he said, "I'm afraid I'm needed here at home."

"Of course," said Eamon seriously, seeming to understand something Faeron didn't.

Bennehym flashed out of existence, and Faeron shot Auri a confused look.

"What was that about?" asked Auri, voicing his thoughts.

"A private matter," said Eamon, brushing aside their question. "As for you two, would you be up for dinner back at home? I've got faux-ribs."

"Sure," said Faeron, eyeing his father suspiciously. Faeron spent quite a lot of time around Bennehym and had never seen the Bo Kora instructor do anything like that before.

"It's settled then," said Eamon, "see you two in a bit." His projection cut out.

"Auri," said Mathas.

She turned to him attentively.

"You did an exceptional thing last night," he told her, a proud smile on his face. "These are new waters you're testing, but I have full confidence that you will tread with grace."

Faeron had never seen Auri's cheeks redder as she fumbled to respond. "I... Oh— well, do you really?"

"Last evening, you shaped the light by being your entire self and standing up for another," said Mathas. "It sounds like an Old-Scholar philosophy. Maybe it is, written in some tome deep beneath their monastery. The only way we can hope to understand the process, however, is through repetition and observation. Last night, and again today, you've proven to be a pioneer, Miss Lem."

If Faeron didn't know better, he'd swear Auri was about to cry again; she looked so happy.

"Alright you two," smiled Mathas. "Let's not keep Eamon waiting."

Faeron and Auri said their goodbyes and exited the workshop through the classroom. As they reached the foyer, the large double doors opened and bright-faced Quinn strolled in.

"Hey guys, look!" he announced, swinging his backpack off his shoulder and digging around inside. "I built a body for logic in tech lab. Come on, I'll show you in the classroom."

"Erm, Quinn…" started Faeron, "because we're shaping now, Mathas wants us to do class an hour earlier."

"Did I miss it!?" asked Quinn looking panicked. "But I have tech lab up until class normally starts!"

"Not you or the twins," said Auri, "Just Faeron and I."

Quinn stared at them for a moment as if processing her words. "But…" he stuttered, "but what about… we're not going to walk home together anymore?"

Faeron didn't know what to say. As he watched genuine sadness settle deep into Quinn's brow, Faeron wasn't sure what consolation he could offer. "We can hang out more outside of class, during our off days," he said.

"As it is, we only ever hang out if we're coming from class," said Quinn glumly.

"Quinn," said Auri, sounding very serious. "There's something I need to tell you."

Faeron shot her an inquisitive side eye.

"*Alone,*" she said, this time addressing Faeron. "You head home to Host Eamon and get dinner started. I'll join you shortly."

"I see how it is," said Faeron, trying to lighten the palpable tension. "See you tomorrow, Quinn."

"Night, Faeron," said Quinn flatly.

Faeron stepped into the quiet night and had Serris call him a tram. When a nearby transpo tube flashed yellow, Faeron boarded and rode straight back to the Violet Tower.

Several minutes later, the doors opened and Faeron stepped into the most familiar part of the city. The ninety-ninth ring of the tower was cast in rays of colorful light, as the flames roared above the stained glass ceiling. Faeron had spent many nights staying up late with Auri, gazing up in awe at the glass mural above them. It depicted a boy in a temple of reds and browns, standing before a violet doorway.

The homes on this floor were all two-stories tall. They sported welcome mats and planters beneath windows, rocking chairs and standing umbrellas. None of the neighbors were out tonight. Some of them he hadn't seen since well before Cropsun began.

Faeron's childhood home, 9914, was far across the ring. Outside were two carved totems, gifts Vox had brought back from Roana. The door was unlocked, and Faeron entered into the well-lit front hallway.

The hallway had soft white carpeting and framed photographs were hung all along the walls. The first few photos were just Eamon and Evolice. They looked young, and posed in all number of exotic locations, ocean fronts, deep in a lush jungle, a rooftop in an endless city. Even in the first photographs with Faeron, when he was just a baby, his parents didn't look any older than he was now. These photos and the ones that followed were all within Eredith. The hallway opened up to a kitchen and a dining area with a more casual living area further back. Beyond the kitchen, to the right, a set of carpeted stairs led up to the second floor where the bedrooms were located.

The sounds of sizzling meat greeted Faeron's ears as he entered the tiled kitchen. His empty stomach was gripped by the decadent aroma of the cooking ribs as Eamon manned the stove.

"Long wait for the trams?" Eamon asked, setting aside a shaker of seasoning to greet his son with a hug. "And Auri… where is she?"

"She'll be along in a minute," said Faeron. "She stayed behind to break the bad news to Quinn."

"Well, dinner has still got a little bit," said Eamon, glancing down at a saucepan on the stovetop. "Come on, let's snag a seat and you can tell me about class."

They went to the living room, its floor the same soft white carpet as the hallway. On the left wall was a long white sofa and a dark wood coffee table with a set of tall and narrow ceramic vases. Across the room was a set of large comfortable chairs with a wide window between them. Outside, Faeron could see the upper ramparts of the Nylkgate and a starry sky above. He sat on the long couch, his father pulling a seat from the window over to the coffee table.

"Tell me about class," he said, nestling into the black and silver-trimmed chair.

"Physics is going great," said Faeron. "I got assigned my…" as he was speaking, a book on the coffee table caught his attention. The title read, *Quizzicle*. As far as Faeron remembered, the book had always been here, but tonight, something about the grinning face on the cover captured his attention. The man had fair freckled skin and fiery red hair. As Faeron continued to stare, his head began to spin. Faeron's vision blurred. A feeling of déjà vu washing over him. Suddenly, a vivid image filled Faeron's head, a memory from his dream. It was gone as quick as it had come, but he swore the man on the cover of this book was there.

"Faeron?" asked Eamon, and Faeron rushed back to reality.

"Sorry," said Faeron, "I just had this flashback to a dream." Faeron held up the book for his father to see. "I think he was there."

"Elliot Jay?" asked Eamon excitedly. "Quizzicle was only around a few years before the plague. Wait… this is perfect! What else do you remember? Was it a vid? Was he there, in person?"

Faeron closed his eyes, trying to reconjure the memory. Just then, he heard the front door open.

"I'm home!" called Auri from down the hall. "You two in the living room?"

"Yep, just chatting," replied Eamon.

Auri's heavy footsteps drew nearer and she emerged around the corner. From her pleasant wave Faeron guessed her conversation with Quinn couldn't have gone too poorly.

"I need to grab something from my room," she said, "I'll be back down in a second."

When she ran upstairs, Eamon turned his attention back to Faeron.

"Did you remember anything?" asked Eamon.

Faeron held up the book and studied the face. Closing his eyes, he did his best to picture the man from the cover.

"Nothing," said Faeron after some time.

"What if you meditate?" asked Eamon encouragingly. "Your mom did it whenever she wanted to help someone remember."

"I can try," said Faeron. He cleared his mind, and when the light of peridom enveloped him, he looked back down at the cover of the book, studying Elliot's face. The déjà vu hit him even harder this time, the overpowering notion he'd seen this man before. Faeron closed his eyes and saw a room unlike any he'd ever seen. The room didn't look built, but rather grown right out of a tree. The flash he saw was still, as if he were looking at a picture of his memory.

"I see him at a table," said Faeron, trying to focus on as many details as he could. "There's someone else too… a capillum I think. They're in the strangest room I've ever seen."

"Like the nook of a tree?" asked Eamon, a knowing smirk settling on his lips.

"Exactly," said Faeron.

"And this is from a recent dream?" asked Eamon.

"Last night, I think."

"Then mystery solved," declared Eamon triumphantly. "I know when Jakob lived."

"Because of him?" asked Faeron, looking at the book in disbelief.

"Because your mom and I watched that same VUE," answered Eamon, clapping in delight. "The dead coast… It was an unforgettable segment. In another life, I may well have tried to solve it myself, but that's beside the point. Newsun, just a year before the plague. I can't give an exact date, but that's the approximate *when* of your dream."

"So that proves it," said Faeron excitedly. "Mom did go after Jakob! He's out there!"

"Hold your roll," laughed Eamon, leaning back in his chair. "All we know is that Jakob *may* have lived to see the plague. We don't have any idea if he made it through."

"But if not that… then what?" asked Faeron.

The bubbling from the stove grew louder.

"A good question," said Eamon. "One I'll ponder while I get the ribs ready."

"Okay," said Faeron. As soon as his father stood up, Faeron dashed upstairs to tell Auri. He knocked on her door to no response. "Auri?" he asked, trying the knob. It was unlocked. "Auri, you good in there? Auri? I'm coming in."

Faeron pushed open the door and entered Auri's well organized room. The ceiling lamp was turned off, but purple light from the flame just above filtered through the long window on the far wall. In the low light, Faeron could make out Auri, sitting up against her headboard. Her head was buried in her knees.

"Auri," asked Faeron, coming closer. He sat at the edge of her bed and placed one hand on her knee. "You good?"

"I'm fine," she sniffled. "Just let me…" Auri wiped her eyes and exhaled deeply as she sat back. In her lap, Faeron could see a picture frame.

"It's her, isn't it?" asked Faeron. "Your missing her helps you do the meditation."

"It's both of them," sniffed Auri. She placed the picture down on the bed beside her. Tinted violet by the starlight, the picture was a family portrait from when Auri was just an infant. Vox looked brilliant as ever, strong featured and sporting a confident grin.

Auri's mother, however, looked decades older than she truly was. Myrial Lem's hair was thin and grey, her stance was slumped, and it was clear that Vox's embrace was the only thing keeping her up. While Vox's right arm was wrapped around Myrial, supporting her, his left cradled baby Auri. "I miss her, and I wish I met her, but it's these months and months without seeing Dad that I can't take. I never know if he's going to be another month or… if something went wrong… I'd never know. Would I?"

"I understand," said Faeron. He climbed across her bed, sitting just beside her. "Believe me, I understand not knowing."

"And that is why you're my best friend," said Auri, smiling at him. "I have news, by the way." She sniffed loudly. "I really should get it out now before you find out from Quinn."

Faeron raised a brow. "Well, I have news, too, but you should definitely go first."

"Don't you dare react," said Auri, "but I asked Quinn to Unity."

"You what!?" gasped Faeron, completely blindsided by her revelation.

"He was all worried we're just going to abandon him," sighed Auri. "So… I told him that even though he wasn't allowed to ask me, I was asking him. Just to prove we're still going to be friends."

"That's awfully nice of you," said Faeron.

"What can I say, I was in a generous mood," said Auri. "Now please, let's change topic. You had news, too?"

"Dad figured out when Jakob lived," said Faeron excitedly. "Last night's dream was just a year before the plague. That'd make Jakob in his fifties today."

"You really think your mother went after him?" asked Auri, knowing him all too well.

"Think about it, what else could have made her leave?"

"But it's been…" Auri began before she stopped herself. "Nevermind. You ready for dinner?"

"Starving," said Faeron, rubbing his growling stomach.

"Then come on," said Auri, rising from the bed. "I haven't had your dad's cooking in ages."

CHAPTER ELEVEN

SHAPING UP

"…And as Matron Avapaya convened the council, the Second Doctrinal Age of the Patronage began" droned Matron Muyon in class the next morning. "It would span some thousand and a half years until what event? Anyone?"

Faeron glanced at Auri, expecting her hand to shoot up. Instead, she glared blankly at the board, her mind seemingly somewhere else entirely.

"What about you, Olive?" said the Matron, calling a name at random.

A pale faced girl from Faeron's year popped suddenly to attention in her seat near the back of the room. "End of the second era…" said Olive. "Oh! With the recovery of the Archpatron's journal."

"Correct," clucked the Matron. "The writings of Glavius shed light on his relationship with the Old-Spirit Nylk. They were as mother and child. As her trees protect us now…"

"Pssst," whispered Faeron, reaching out a foot to nudge Auri. "You there?"

Auri turned, eyes narrowed. Raising a finger to her lips, she shushed him softly then turned her attention to the Matron's lesson.

Less than ten minutes passed before Faeron caught Auri staring off again. This time, her trancelike state wouldn't be broken until the familiar four-note chime signaled the end of class.

Together, Faeron and Auri rode the crowded elevator down to the cafeteria where they loaded their trays with food and searched the tables until they found Quinn, grinning from ear to ear. He was seated with a tray of crispy fish sliders at a small round table, just big enough for the three of them.

"Classes go well this morning?" asked Faeron, stepping over the bench with a bowl of steamy faux-muum stew.

"Just fine," said Quinn simply. He scarfed down one of the sliders, only to return to grinning the moment he finished chewing.

"Then why are you all smiles?" asked Faeron.

"Oh," said Quinn, glancing over at Auri, who had occupied the seat beside them, "you know… just cause." Every time his eyes met Auri, Quinn's smile brightened a little.

Auri didn't seem to mind the attention, in fact, she didn't even seem to notice. She was staring off, as if focusing on something all the way across the cafeteria.

"You alive?" asked Faeron, snapping twice beside her face.

"Yeah," she said, blinking back to the table. "Sorry, I'm just thinking about tonight."

"Excited?" asked Faeron.

"I'm ready. I know this is it…" she said, "but I'm also worried. I don't know how many times I can repeat the meditation. It takes more than just focus…"

"Is this… what you told me about last night?" asked Quinn through a mouth full of food. "With emotions and all?"

Auri nodded.

"I can't imagine how hard it must be to do it even once," said Faeron. "If you need me to do anything—"

"I don't know what you could do…" said Auri, smiling softly, "but thanks for the thought. I just need to keep myself calm today, save all that passion and energy for tonight." Suddenly, she seemed to notice her food for the first time. Her baked potatoes were topped in gooey golden cheese and the loav sprouts accompanying them glistened with butter. Wordlessly, they all dug in.

Auri carried the same focus when Faeron met her at the ape statue after classes that afternoon. Not even waiting for him to complain about his new AI Upkeep assignment, she led off at a march toward the athenaeum.

Mathas was already waiting for them in the workshop. Everything was the same as before: the bunball on the table, the platform just a couple feet off the mats, and the model alca track winding around a mountain.

"Faeron, Auri, welcome," said Mathas. He rose from a seat at the nearest table and procured the Gloves of Give and Take from the pocket of his flowing brown robe. "Ready for another run?"

"More of the same?" asked Faeron, a bit disappointed they wouldn't be trying any new artifacts.

"For the near future," said Mathas. Snatching up the ball, he limped over to them. "Think of this like your martial arts. You must master the basic motions before you can combine them into complex movements. Once you have mastered capturing and releasing energy, we will move on."

"Can I go first?" asked Auri suddenly. "This moment… it's been in my head all day. I'm ready."

"Of course," said Mathas, offering her the gloves. She eagerly snagged them and pulled them over her hands. "Faeron, would you like to drop the ball?"

"Naturally!" said Faeron. He plucked the ball from his mentor's hand and, together, he and Auri scampered over to the mats. Climbing the platform, Faeron felt his heart thumping. He felt almost as excited for Auri as she must be. Even now, without the light of peridom flowing through them, her bronze eyes were shining.

"Faeron… listen," said Auri, sounding serious, "I still can't hold my meditation for long, so don't drop the ball until I tell you."

"Sure thing," said Faeron. He stepped to the edge of the platform, holding the ball out over the mats. "Just tell me when."

Auri closed her eyes. Her nose scrunched up tight and her fists balled until her knuckles turned white. "Now!" she shouted.

Faeron dropped the ball just as Auri's eyes shot open. Deep bronze light surged from her irises like tongues of flame. Auri held out her hand, her gaze locked on the ball. Only, the ball never stopped. The fire in Auri's eyes died and the ball continued its descent, landing with a soft *thud* on the mats.

"I don't understand," she said, looking from her gloves to the ball to Mathas. "What did I do wrong? I was meditating. I focused on the ball. I've listened to all the things you've told Faeron, and I did them all! Why didn't it stop?"

"Patience and practice," said Mathas definitely. He hobbled over and placed a long hand on her shoulder. "Nobody gets it on their first try."

"Here, hand me the ball," said Faeron, reaching down. "You can go again."

Auri's second attempt was equally futile; her third as well. Each time she closed her eyes, the meditation took a little longer and lasted a little shorter. By her fourth attempt, Auri couldn't make herself mediate at all.

"I'm out," she said, her eyes blinking open. "It only works so much at once. I don't think I'll get it again tonight."

"Understanding your limits is important to growth," reasoned Mathas. "Faeron, why don't you practice for a while and give Miss Lem a break."

Stopping the ball in midair quickly became like second nature for Faeron, and, at the end of class, he was given another chance to leap from the platform. As he landed, the light rushing through his fingers proved too much to control. Faeron's arm shot up into the air, and a fresh crack appeared on the gem.

The next couple weeks at the kytra workshop went much the same; Faeron and Auri would spend the first half of the lesson trading places in the ball-catch experiment. Though she had yet to succeed, Auri gave her all in every attempt. After a few tries, Auri would need time to recover, and Faeron would leap from the platform. He could stop himself almost every time, but the sudden rush of light still proved too much to control. By the end of the second week, Auri was growing visibly tired, even outside of practice. Her eyes were shadowed and distant, and she struggled to force a single waking meditation in the hour.

"Faeron, Auri, could I speak to you before you leave?" asked Mathas one night as the two kytra finished up practice. Auri was in the worst shape yet, stumbling every so often as she walked back from the mats. "It's clear we're pushing too hard," said Mathas.

Faeron needed only to look at Auri to agree with his mentor.

"We're not—" Auri began but was cut off.

"It isn't up for debate," said Mathas. "This isn't healthy. For the rest of the semester, I want you to come in only twice a week. Lowend and Hyend nights, if that fits your schedules."

"More time for homework," said Faeron, thinking of the papers piling up back at home. He had recently been assigned his semester-long "lost law," a project that required him and a partner to attempt to piece together old laws of physics, lost when the servers went down. He and Razzy would be teaming up to tackle Eucelkin's Density Principle.

"And more time for Prophet's Guard," added Auri weakly. "Wanna go spar for a while in the Cresh challenge?"

"Tonight?" asked Faeron. "I'd topple you with a poke. Probably best if we head home."

"Probably," Auri conceded without defense.

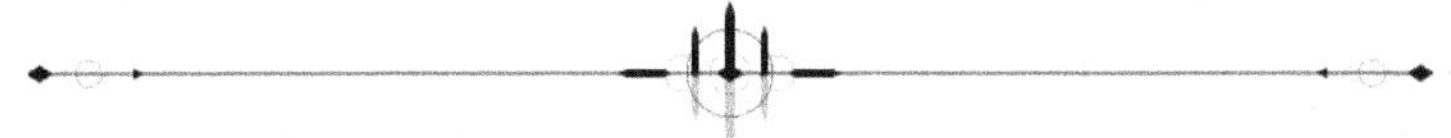

Their new schedule proved its value within just the first week as Auri was soon back to her normal self. She had yet to stop the ball, but she went into each practice with renewed drive.

Faeron continued to struggle with the light of his jump, adding several new cracks to the gem, though he was having far more success outside the workshop. In Bo-Kora, Faeron could now block and even return simple blows without breaking his connection to peridom. By the time midterms rolled around, he was even studying in his meditation.

Faeron's dreams were long, but he remembered little. The images he did have were of smoky rooms, clouded faces, and days spent hunched over a writing desk. Despite the clouded memories, Faeron woke each morning with a sense that Jakob was making swift progress on his book. He only hoped Jakob finished it before the plague, now looming on the horizon.

Exams were spread out across the week of midterms, with Faeron's last test, AI Upkeep, scheduled for Hyend afternoon. With all the extra time he had to study, Faeron felt more than prepared. Physics was a breeze and Faeron finished the exam period on a high note in a joint presentation with Razzy. She had run down a rabbit hole with their lost law resulting in a formula they believe to be close to the original. There was still plenty of testing to go, but Lieutenant P offered them praise regardless. The Global Politics and Life and Legacy exams were just memorization, tedious but straight forward. Finally, on Hyend, Faeron walked out of his AI Upkeep midterm in high spirits. The sky above was a gray haze, clouds masking the tops of the towers and walls, and a wet breeze swept through the Academy courtyard. Nothing could sour Faeron's mood. He was finally free of studying, and the only thing left between him and the weekend was another session in Mathas' workshop.

Their time in the workshop unfolded like any other night until it was nearly the end of the hour, when Mathas gave Faeron a few tries at the platform. As usual, no matter how hard Faeron clenched his hand around the slithering ropes of light, they quickly broke free and sent Faeron spinning.

"It's not a trial of bodily strength," said Mathas from the edge of the mats.

Faeron rushed around and climbed the platform, likely for the last time this hour; his impatience was beginning to affect his meditations.

"Relax your grip. *Will* the light, as you would command a limb," Mathas continued, "send it through the gem into peridom. It will fight you, but a kytra's will must be stronger. Once the light has passed through the stone, the gloves will do the work for you, holding it there until you are ready to release it."

"I think I understand," said Faeron. The whole workshop shimmered in peridom's light as he stepped off the platform. Faeron dropped two feet to the mats then pulled back with his left hand. Ropes of muted green light zipped through his body to his hand, and his arm trembled as the energy gathered there. Focusing his whole attention on the glove, Faeron imagined the gem on its back like the drain of a bathtub. He held the image in his head and the light began to form a vortex around the crystal, disappearing beneath the glassy surface. Pressure eased off his arm and the gem flared brighter.

"Excellent," said Mathas, calmly. "Hold it… look to your target."

As the last light sank into the gem, Faeron raised his right hand to the model town on the table. He focused every ounce of his attention on the toy alca and imagined it in motion. His right hand lurched upward as light poured from the gem. A streak of green flashed across the room and the alca sprang to life. Speeding up one hill then another, the alca came to rest just short of a mountain tunnel.

Unable to contain himself, Faeron grinned ear to ear and the light of peridom faded. "I did it," he said, looking down at the gloves then back to the alca. "I really did it!"

"A moment to be proud of," said Mathas. "In fact, at this halfway mark for the semester, I want to take a moment to recognize both your progress thus far."

"Both?" said Auri, sounding unconvinced.

"You've uncovered more in half a semester than we have in years of study," said Mathas, "from the concept of meditation through passion to your testing in potentials and limitations. As I've said before, this is unmarked territory."

"But…" Auri's eyes rested on the model alca.

"You will shape again soon enough," said Mathas. "And when you do, I have no doubt it shall be resplendent. This journey isn't measured by the distance of a toy on a track. You walk a new path, untread by boots. The heavy brush ahead will slow you, and at any time you can choose to turn back; the other road will always be there. Though, something tells me that's not what you want."

"No. This is me," said Auri, smiling. "A trailblazer… guess I am like Dad after all."

"More than you can know," agreed Mathas. "Now, one last—"

"Apologies for the interruption" came Serris' voice as the ball of light popped suddenly into the workshop, floating near the edge of the mats. "I have an urgent call from the Host."

"Of course, put it through," said Mathas.

"Hope I'm not interrupting," said Eamon as he materialized into the room. He wore a night-black button up and well-fitted pants with a golden belt matching the buckles on his dress shoes.

"Good evening, Eamon," said Mathas warmly. "Faeron and Auri were just finishing up."

"Brilliant," grinned Eamon. "I have Marzón Cointell in the other room. She'd like to meet our famed kytra over dinner. That dinner happens to be right now, and… you don't keep a Cointell waiting."

"Quinn and the twins should be just out front," said Mathas. "I'm sure they'd welcome dinner over class."

"Maybe not the twins," said Eamon. "The Cointells are very particular about etiquette. Quinn, of course, would be a welcome addition. Just make sure you three are on your best behavior."

"You can count on us," pledged Auri.

"I'm sure I can," said Eamon. "Now, I should see to Marzón. Meet us at the Mercy Elixer House, quick as you can."

"Wait!" said Auri. "Should we change first?"

"No time," said Eamon. "Your uniforms are fine. See you there…. And Mathas, have a wonderful weekend."

"You as well," said Mathas. "Goodluck with Miss Cointell."

Eamon disappeared and Auri marched over the tables where her academy blazer lay neatly folded next to Faeron's. "Come on," she said, tossing Faeron his blazer.

"You two enjoy the weekend," said Mathas, following them to the door. "Will you tell Quinn the same, and please, send in the twins?"

"Of course," said Faeron. He slid the gloves off his hands and passed them back to Mathas. "See you Lowend."

"Yeah! Have a good one, Mathas," smiled Auri.

In the foyer, Faeron and Auri found the twins fast asleep, slouched in their seats near the elevator. Beside them were a pair of matching bright-pink duffle bags bulging with pads and equipment. Quinn sat opposite the twins. He leaned over a small table, soldering a circuit board held up on a pair of clamps. The iron he held was linked to a small box, glowing green at the edges. At their approach, Quin waved his free hand without looking up from his work.

"The twins asleep?" asked Faeron softly.

"Think so…" said Quinn. "Myllie told me that they played three games back-to-back. Apparently a virus went around the league the last few weeks and a bunch of matches got pushed to this weekend."

"Can you wrap that up?" asked Auri quietly but firmly. "We just got invited to a diplomatic dinner with Host Eamon. You, me, and Faeron, *right now*."

Quinn tapped the iron on a sponge beside the clamps and then set the tool down. "Alright, that should do for now. What about them?" He nodded toward the twins.

"Apparently ten-year-olds don't make the best diplomats," joked Faeron. "I vote not being the one to tell them."

"Don't worry, I've got this," said Auri. "Hey girls." She spoke louder now. She knelt beside the twins and placed a hand on each of the arms. "You two taking a nap at Mathas'."

"Auri!" burst Myllie, blinking awake.

Kaelynn yawned and stretched out in her chair. "Did we miss class?" she asked, sounding somewhat hopeful.

"No, afraid not," chuckled Auri. "You two are up. Just you today."

"Just us?" asked Myllie. "What about him?" She jabbed her pointer finger toward Quinn.

"He has to go to a boring dinner with us," said Auri. "You two get to have fun with Mathas."

"Fun?" asked Myllie. "*Bunball* is fun. Mathas is old and boring."

"Maybe right now," said Auri. "But someday his advice will be very important to you. Now go on, he's waiting."

"Fine," sighed Myllie. Slinging her back over one shoulder. "Come on, Kae."

"And we should move too," added Auri.

"Works for me," said Quinn, who had just finished packing away his soldering kit.

As the twins disappeared into the classroom, Faeron, Auri, and Quinn stepped out into the cool evening. Laughter laced the chatter from the park as all number of students celebrated a much-needed break from studying. The clouds had broken and the setting sun over the wall painted the whole park gold.

"Faeron! Hey, Faeron!"

Faeron's gaze tracked the familiar voice to a pop of pink in the busy street. Lydia broke from the crowd and skipped up the athenaeum steps. Her pink hair fell freely to her shoulders, and instead of her usual white blazer, Lydia wore a pink crop top that matched her hair and a pair of high waisted black shorts.

Of all days she could show up, Faeron told himself as his heart froze in his chest.

"Had no dance tonight so… here I am," beamed Lydia. "Sorry it took so long to get out here."

"Oh," said Faeron, cold panic in his blood. "It's just—"

"Your timing couldn't have been better," Auri cut in. "Quinn and I have to be at an event, so Faeron's all yours."

"But—" Faeron began, only to be interrupted by a sharp pain as Auri stomped down hard on his foot. Glancing over, he saw Auri wearing her 'Don't be an idiot,' glare. "Actually, yeah," Faeron said, giving Auri a subtle nod of thanks. "Perfect timing."

With quick goodbyes, the two pairs parted ways. Quinn and Auri scampered down the street, while Faeron retreated back into the Athenaeum, with Lydia close behind.

"It's so pretty and… quiet," whispered Lydia, wandering the foyer. "I see why some people prefer to study here."

"Just wait until you see the windows," said Faeron. He led down the south hall and heard a gasp from Lydia behind him as he stepped into a curtain of shimmering blue light. Rays of color poured in through the stained-glass murals, and every few shelves the colors changed. Here there were shades of blue from a mural of a legendary galleon on a churning sea. Further down, the rainbow blade of a funny looking knight cast a particularly wondrous display across the book spines.

"You were right," said Lydia softly. "It really is something in the evening."

"Romantic, even?" asked Fearon hopeful.

"Oh yeah," said Lydia enthusiastically. "Give me a soft couch and the right book, somewhere we won't be disturbed…"

"I know just the spot," said Faeron. "Come on."

He led her down the hall to a round reading room with a grand spiral staircase at the rear. They climbed to the third floor, where the only difference from the rooms below was a wooden door with a plaque reading: Evolice Lovel.

"Way back before we were shaping in class or even meditating in class," said Faeron as he wandered slowly toward a wide sapphire-blue couch, running his hand along the brass banister overlooking the steps, "Quinn, Auri, and I used to come up here to do our readings."

"It's certainly peaceful up here," said Lydia. She went to the office door and examined the plaque with his mother's name. "It must be hard for you… seeing this here."

"It is," said Faeron. "In fact, Mathas asked if I wanted it taken down, but… that feels wrong. It's *her* office. She'll need it once we find her. Besides, seeing it there is a reminder of how important our work here is. Every second I waste is a moment she's out there, in danger."

Lydia turned, facing him with sad eyes. "A decade later you still fight for her… That's what I like about you, Faeron. Your drive… your ambition… they're genuine. You're doing all this because deep down you believe that you can save her. Every day I see so many gifted people waste their talent on all the wrong things; fame, riches, the high of it all. They don't realize that none of that matters anymore. The world is gone because our ancestors were self-indulgent, and now, it's time our generation asked what we can do to make things right. I… I'm ranting, aren't I?"

"No, I'm relieved I'm not hearing it from Auri for once," laughed Fearon. "I'm glad we found time for this."

"Me too," smiled Lydia sweetly. "You hang tight, make sure no one steals our spot. I'll go find a book."

"Aye aye," said Faeron, getting comfortable on the sapphire suede couch. "By the way, this floor's all reference. You may have more luck downstairs."

"Maybe," said Lydia, "but… maybe not." She skipped off down the row, and a minute or so later Faeron saw her stop sharp. "I know this book!" she called back, just loud enough for him to hear.

Lydia pulled a massive tome off the shelf and effortlessly hauled it back to the couch.

"What is it?" asked Faeron, trying to get a look at the cover.

"A Visual Encyclopedia of Irasil," said Lydia excitedly, taking a seat beside him. "My mom keeps a copy of this on our coffee table back at home. A lot of it's her work."

"Really?" asked Faeron, scooching close to see. Their arms were now touching and the scent of her perfume filled every breath. Suddenly very conscious of his hands, he folded them in his lap and looked down at the massive book.

"She's a photographer," said Lydia. "Before Eredith, she used to travel all around taking pictures for publications like this. It's funny, she said she'd never seen a physical copy of her work until she came here. It all used to be digital." She flipped through the pages, past forests and lakes, cities and sandy beaches. "Hey, I've got a question."

"What's that?" asked Faeron.

"Where would you go?" asked Lydia. "If the walls came down, the plague disappeared, and the world was suddenly as it once was… Where would you go?"

"North Ri'Kalla," said Faeron without hesitation. There was nowhere he wanted to see quite so badly as the city of his dreams. He wanted to walk the streets Jakob walked, see the storefronts of the art district for himself.

"Ooh, let's see… here!" said Lydia. She flipped to a page depicting a skyscraper made entirely of black glass with a massive golden ribbon climbing its height. Behind it, Faeron saw the familiar Ri'kallan skyline of black-glass towers and smaller white-and-gold structures. "The city of artists and aristocrats," read Lydia from the caption. "North Ri'kalla is known for its boundless extravagance and 'round the clock entertainment."

"It's not about any of that for me," Faeron interjected, feeling rather self-conscious naming a city of riches after Lydia's speech about vanity. "It has to do with… well… it's a *really* long story."

"We've got all night," said Lydia. "Go on. I want to know."

"Well, you've already heard some kytra stuff," reasoned Faeron, "so I suppose you won't think I'm completely crazy."

"I make no promises," teased Lydia. "In seriousness. My dad was the furthest thing from religious. He's an engineer, only in Eredith because he helps keep up the tech that runs our sky. After he was spared the plague in the Unity Day Miracle, Eredith became more than a home. He knew the Patronage stories had to be true, because he lived through one. So no, when it comes to you kytra, I don't think anything is crazy."

"Alright," said Faeron, his confidence breaking through his nerves. "Ten years ago I touched the Host Stone and it shattered. I remember a bright light in the stone and then… poof, nothing. When I woke up my mom was gone. Vox, Auri's dad, said I'd had a vision, but I didn't remember it at all. Since then, I've lived out that vision little by little every night in my dreams."

"Like watching a VUE?" asked Lydia.

"Sorta," said Faeron. "Except I *am* the main character. I can see and feel and think just like him. It's all so real, and it goes on for weeks at a time… well… he lives in North Ri'Kalla. So that's why."

"I don't get it," said Lydia. "If you live in North Ri'Kalla every night then why go there? Why not do something you've never done, see someplace you've never seen?"

"I only remember bits," said Fearon. "Vivid moments like the colorful displays in the winter markets. I just want to be set free, to explore in the snow, the real snow. Get all wrapped up, a coat, scarf, gloves, all of that…" He looked up into her soft blue eyes. "Maybe I'll bring a date, and we'll get drinks and exchange gifts."

"Ooh," said Lydia shifting closer. "And who would the lucky date be?"

Faeron's heart was pounding, but confidence had ahold of him. "I wouldn't mind if you came along. I distinctly remember there being dancing, so… maybe you could teach me the basics."

Lydia pursed her lips and looked off to the side as if considering it a moment. "Hmm," cooed Lydia. "I accept… only… I think we'll have to postpone. There's forecasts for plague."

"Well," said Faeron, inching even closer, "maybe until that clears up, we could do Unity Fest instead?"

"I can make that work," whispered Lydia, her face so very close to his. "Last year, I went alone. I distinctly remember there being dancing, so… maybe I can teach you the basics."

Unable to hold back any longer, Faeron moved in. Before their lips met, Lydia stopped him. Gently placing her hand on his chin.

"Not yet," she said. Instead, she kissed him on the cheek. "I want it to be special. I want to save that for the dancing."

Every day seemed longer as Faeron wished for nothing more than to fast forward to the Unity Festival. Lydia was always busy dancing. She certainly put even more time into her art then he did being a kytra. It was inspiring enough to keep him from getting too distracted. The hardest part was Bo Kora. Trying to spar in his meditation while fighting the urge to glance over at Lydia proved difficult. Any time he dared peek, she'd meet him with a smile that sent his heart fluttering, only for Saitum to land a blow that sent his head spinning. In the first couple weeks, he was bruised all over.

As Cropsun waned and Lowsun loomed, Faeron's bruises disappeared. He and Lydia studied together any chance they got, but when the Bo Kora bell rang, Faeron had to let those emotions go. No matter how he looked forward to his Unity Fest date, he knew that conquering his dreams had to come first. The longer it took him to master shaping, the longer his mother was alone. Faeron began to go entire class periods against Saitum, never taking a hit and never breaking his meditation. In the heat of their spar, he could swear he saw a shimmer in her arm any time she was about to swing. Like the light of peridom was warning him of her attacks. Their duels became legendary in the classroom as other pairs stopped dueling to watch.

In the workshop, Faeron was having equal success. Every few weeks, Mathas had to bring out taller platforms to keep up with Faeron's mastery of the light. Around six feet, the jumps became daunting. Faeron not only had to conquer the unwieldy light, but also the fear that tugged at his chest as he looked down from the platform.

Auri, meanwhile, made no progress at all, so Mathas devised a new strategy. Instead of wearing the gloves, he simply had Auri hold her meditation as long as she could. His theory was that, without shaping to distract her, Auri would be able to concentrate more wholly on her meditations, to hold them for longer. This would bring mastery, mastery would bring shaping. Auri went along with it wholly. As she would say, "If Cresh could hold it for battles, I can hold it for seconds at least."

The change in course proved effective. As homework ramped up and finals appeared on the horizon, Auri was managing to meditate for minutes at a time. Meanwhile, Faeron was leaping from a platform nearly ten feet tall. Leaping from that height, he could send the alca flying with enough force to do three full laps around the mountain.

There was only one week left in the semester, two before the unity feast, when Mathas gathered Faeron and Auri after class.

"I have something special planned for our final class of the semester," he told them, sounding quite excited about whatever it was. "On Hyend evening, I want you to meet me at the Woven Dome, same time as always."

"The bunball stadium?" asked Faeron with a furrowed brow.

"Indeed," said Mathas. "And be sure to bring a mask and padding. I trust you still have your old gear?"

"I think it should all fit still," said Faeron.

"Same" chimed Auri. "Might be worth a wash though. Neither of us have worn 'em in years."

"It's settled then."

Finals were the hardest of any year so far and Faeron was up to his neck studying all week. It was a good thing his Lost Law presentation was a hit, because the written exam was a mess of complex math that ran circles around his mind. Coming out of Global Politics, Faeron was sure his final grade had just taken a hit, though, at least Life and Legacy tests were a breeze.

Faeron and Quinn shared a mutual last exam of the week in their AI Upkeep final, and Faeron was ecstatic to learn Quinn and the twins would be joining the older kytra in their special lesson at the Woven Dome after class.

Faeron, Auri, and Quinn caught a shuttle from the Academy that dropped them right into the trophied halls of the Woven Dome. Everywhere Faeron looked he saw sports memorabilia: signed jerseys, golden cups, wooden plaques with photos of famous bunball players.

"So where is your bag?" asked Faeron as they followed a nearby tunnel with a sign reading: Field. He and Auri both had large duffel bags full of pads, a mask, and sticks. Quinn didn't seem to have anything beyond his normal backpack.

"Mathas just asked me to bring Logic," said Quinn.

"I wonder what he's up to..." said Auri, her mouth twisting to one side as she looked off in thought.

They emerged from the tunnel into a massive octagonal field, and the wall slid shut behind them. On every side of the octagon was a goal, each a different color, with matching grass spiraling into the center, making the whole field a rainbow vortex. Sparse drifts of snow fell through the open ceiling of the Woven Dome. Faeron reached out his palm, only for the shimmering flakes to disappear the moment they made contact.

"Did you know, with *real* snow," said Faeron, "people used to catch it on their tongue like this?" He leaned back his head and stuck his tongue out. "At least Jakob did. Too bad it doesn't work with the snow here."

"What in Inya are you doing?" Myllie's voice carried across the field as she ran out from another tunnel in full gear. Off-white pads with bright pink striped lights covered every inch of her. She wore a mask as well, silver with a strip of pink-lit glass covering her eyes. Kaelynn was just behind her wearing matching gear. The only difference between them was that Myllie held a single silver bunball stick, lit pink at the tip, while Kaelynn held two.

The tunnel didn't close just yet, however, as another shape emerged behind them. It looked like some sort of sack, big enough to hold one of the twins, floating several feet above the ground. It was bound by ropes of shifting green light, clearly a product of peridom. They twisted and shimmered, connecting Mathas' outstretched hands, clad in the gloves of give and take.

"Catching snow on one's tongue," said their mentor as he stepped from the tunnel, "a popular tradition before the plague." His voice sounded focused, as he continued to suspend the sack, carrying it to where Faeron and the others were waiting.

Upon closer inspection, Faeron saw Mathas was wearing some sort of backpack. The light seemed to be traveling from the backpack to his left hand, then out the right glove to the sack.

"Is that some kind of battery?" asked Faeron excitedly. He'd never considered using an alternate source of power for the gloves, but seeing Mathas now, he suspected this was how the old capillum moved the platforms in and out of the workshop.

"Indeed," said Mathas. There was a series of loud clanking noises as the capillum dropped the sack and the sage light disappeared. He then turned to show them the battery on his back. There were five rings, and each served as a track to a small ball, zipping around them in circles. "The many rings allow us to draw continuous energy, pulling from one then the next. By the time the fifth ring is reached, the first has regained its momentum."

"Rad," said Faeron. "Are we using it today?"

"No," said Mathas, reaching down toward the sack. "Not quite yet. Today, you'll be using these." He reached inside and pulled out a bunball, tossing it to Myllie. "Go on, get those pads on."

Faeron's pads were a bit tight and difficult to secure, but his helmet fit perfectly. It was silver with twin panes of glass. One swooped from the bottom left to top right, and the other mirrored it, crossing in the center of his face to form an 'X.' Faeron pulled on the mask, and the glass lit up white, the last color he and Auri had played. Auri's mask was more similar to the twins' in design, though it too glowed white. Once Faeron and Auri were geared up, Mathas walked them over the nearest goal. Its net was blue, as was the grass.

"Faeron, you were once a keeper, were you not?" asked Mathas.

"A few years back," answered Faeron.

"Good, then do just that," said Mathas, "but with these instead of sticks." He slid off the Gloves of Give and Take, handing them to Faeron. "Auri, twins, take the sack to the penalty line. When I say go, I want you to take turns shooting on Faeron."

"What about me?" asked Quinn.

"For now, just watch," said Mathas. "We'll get to you in a minute."

Auri and the twins stood about ten yards out and dumped the balls into a big heap.

"Can I go first?" asked Myllie hungrily. Faeron couldn't see it, but he knew she was grinning ear to ear behind her mask.

"Of course," said Auri. "Make sure to nail him good."

"I remind you," called Mathas, "the goal is to score in the net, not injure Mr. Lovel."

"Too late!" yelled Myllie. She scooped up a ball with her stick and sent it hurtling toward Faeron.

With barely enough time to reach, Faeron ducked out of the way. "At least let me meditate first," he protested. He closed his eyes and calmed his mind until the light of peridom flowed through him. "Okay, I'm ready now."

Auri was next up. Faeron breathed slowly and purposefully as Auri scooped up a ball and lobbed a fast shot straight toward his chest. He reached out with his left hand, stopping the ball midair. Shifting the powerful sage light into the gloves, Faeron reached out with the right and released the energy back into the ball. It zipped toward Auri, who was caught unaware. Just before the ball struck her, Kaelynn stepped in its path, catching it with both sticks.

"Mathas never said to throw it back at us," Kaelynn protested.

"Well, he never said not to," pointed out Faeron.

Kaelynn chucked the ball back at him. Again, he caught it, only this time he used the energy to chuck it out into the empty field. "Happy?" he asked.

"Alright," called Mathas, "let's try something a little more challenging. Quinn, did you load the program I asked you about?"

"Ooooohh," gasped Quinn, seemingly coming to some great realization. "Yeah, give me a second to load up something… we can start easy and then… aha!" He ran out onto the field and placed Logic a few feet behind the other kytra. "Go ahead, Logic, run the routine. Start countdown on my mark."

A dozen floating targets suddenly materialized, moving in slow patterns just above Auri and the twins' heads.

"Just like before," began Mathas as Quinn scampered back to the sideline. "Catch the ball, and use the energy to throw it. But we'll make a game of it. Let's see how many targets you can hit. Auri, Kaelynn, Myllie… get ready. On my mark, don't hold back."

With his mind still drifting in peridom, Faeron readied himself for the onslaught.

"Three… two… one… GO!"

Quick as Auri might be, Myllie was even faster. She was the first to throw a shot, and nearly scored. Faeron caught her shot just short of the goal, only for two more to fly at him. Quickly threw the first ball, smashing a target, then caught the second. He had no time to hold the balls, instantly shifting the energy between the gloves and throwing them back just in time to catch the next. By the time they're run through the whole pile, Faeron had only let a few balls in (most courtesy of Myllie), and nearly all the shots he did return hit their targets.

"Twenty-six of thirty," called Mathas from the corner. "Impressive work, Faeron." He hobbled toward them, his large dark eyes beaming with pride. "I once told you that if you mastered the flow of energy, I'd let you move on to more advanced techniques. I believe you've proved that today." Then, turning to Auri he said, "Your waking meditation has come far. From seconds to minutes, you've proven there's room to grow and that you will stop at nothing to reach that growth. Today, I'd like to offer you the chance to shape, should you wish it."

"I do!" exclaimed Auri, throwing down her stick.

"Good, because I have wondered for some time if our experiments were simply not inspiring of passion," continued Mathas.

"This experiment should prove far more intense than catching a ball. Perhaps it will bring the spark you need to shape."

"Of course," said Auri, wide eyed. "We've only ever heard of Cresh shaping in battle. And the park was… tense," She marched over to the goal. "Alright, Faeron. Hand 'em over. I think I can do this!"

Faeron passed the gloves to Auri then helped the twins gather all the scattered balls. Once the pile was full Auri's breathing quickened. Her fists clenched tight. Through the glass of her mask, he could see her eyes erupt in bronze light. "Do your worst!" she barked with confidence.

"Go ahead," called Mathas.

Myllie threw first. The ball zoomed straight into the corner, hitting the net with a swoosh. Auri growled.

"Next."

Kaelynn swept up a ball and sent it hurtling.

"STOP," shouted Auri. She reached out toward the ball, but there was no light. The ball struck her palm and Auri yelped in pain, nursing her fingers.

"Hold," called Mathas, but Auri wasn't ready to quit.

"No!" she howled. "Throw another. Faeron you're up, throw another!"

Faeron picked up Auri's stick, still resting on the ground. He looked to Mathas for permission, and when his mentor nodded, Faeron swept up a ball.

"Right at me," said Auri. "Right at my chest!"

Faeron might not be the best bunball player around, but he was confident in his aim from this distance. He threw, his aim true, as the ball stuck Auri flat in the chest. She coughed and gasped for air, her eyes burning brighter than ever.

"Again!" howled Auri.

"I think—" began Mathas.

"Again!" Auri ripped off her mask. She looked ferocious, bronze burning eyes, teeth gritted, staring them down. "Right here," she pointed to her unguarded face. "I'll stop it. I know it. Just do it!"

"That's enough of this," said Mathas, sounding sterner than Faeron had ever heard him before. "The exercise is over."

"No, it's not," shouted Auri. "I know I can do this. Faeron, please, trust me. I need you to do this."

"I…" Faeron looked into Auri's burning eyes. He couldn't deny the power, but he couldn't hurt her either. "I can't… Auri, I won't do it."

"I will!"

Myllie moved fast as lightning. She swept up a ball and threw it dead at Auri's face.

Faeron cried out, reaching with his stick for the ball, but Myllie was too quick. The ball was out of reach. He could only watch as it hurtled toward Auri. She reached out and screamed with all her might as the ball came closer and closer and—"

CRAAACK

A blinding light flooded the stadium, and the sound was like a fist to gut. Faeron couldn't breathe, his legs went weak, and he fell to his knees. Heat washed over him, like the sun beating down in highsun. Then, just as quickly, there was a chill, frigid as Talon Park in Lowsun. The sudden change sent goosebumps down Faeron's body. For a moment he couldn't think straight, but then… *Auri!*

"Auri!" cried Faeron, forcing himself to his feet. He could see better now. She was hunched over in the goal, the ball resting just beside her. Had she been hit? Faeron's chest beat as he ran to her. Mathas and Quinn were just behind. "Auri, are you all right?"

"I…" Auri looked up. Her face looked fine but for the tears leaking from her eyes. There were no bruises left by the ball. "My hands!" she managed to say, holding them up for all to see.

For a split moment, there was utter silence as everyone observed the gloves. Both gems were gone, reduced to shimmering sand at Auri's knees.

"I'm sorry," she whispered, but her words turned to sobs. "Mathas, I'm so sorry."

"Nevermind that," said Mathas urgently. "Myllie, Kaelynn, do one of you know where the aid kit is?"

"We do!" cried Myllie. "Kae, let's go!"

The twins ran off, and Mathas knelt beside Auri. "Let's get these off," he said, slowly peeling back the gloves.

Auri braced her teeth and groaned.

"Just a little more," said Mathas. "Done." The gloves fell to the floor, and Faeron could now see her hands, burnt red all over. The worst was the back, where the gems had been. The skin was already blistering.

"We've got it," yelled Myllie as the twins returned with a big white case. They set it down beside Mathas and he flipped it open.

"Some tempra gel… and gauze… we might just avoid a hospital visit." Mathas unscrewed a tube and applied the white gel inside to her hands and wrapped them in bandages.

Auri's breathing slowed, her tears dried, and all that was left was a look of shame.

"Do not let today defeat you," said Mathas softly, placing a long hand on her shoulder. "This is a lesson you will never forget, but it does not make you a failure. Not if you learn from it."

"Come on," said Faeron, reaching down to help Auri do her feet.

She didn't budge. Instead, she simply stared forward, blankly.

"Go on, all of you," said Mathas. "Auri and I will chat for a while. Have a replenishing break and a joyous Unity Festival. I'll see you in four short weeks."

One by one, they filtered out of the Stadium. Faeron was last, looking back at Auri and Mathas, speaking in quiet tones by the goal. He wished there was something he could say that would help her, but in truth he didn't have a clue. Returning to their apartment, Faeron soon found himself in bed, feeling equal parts relieved from academic responsibility and burdened by his inability to help Auri. He meditated beneath the covers until sleep took him, sailing free from his body in the currents of peridom.

CHAPTER TWELVE

AN UNPARALLELED OFFER

Faeron didn't know what Mathas said to Auri that night at the Woven Dome, but whatever it was had kept her in her room all week. The only time he saw her in the days leading up to the Unity Festival was when she made short trips out to the kitchen to cook up dinner. She looked tired and unkempt, and refused to answer his questions about her conversation with Mathas or what was occupying her time. She even turned down his offers to set up Unity decorations, something they'd done together every year they'd lived together.

Once Faeron realized Auri was adamant on remaining undisturbed, he instead split his time between Quinn and Lydia. Quinn was entirely absorbed in Deity after his tournament, going so far as to program Logic to play against him. Swiftly learning new strategies, Quinn was now beating Faeron nine times out of ten. Lydia, meanwhile, had Faeron on his toes. Some nights she'd meet him for dinner, others they'd spend in Loem Park, or the Astral Cafe, or the thirty story zoo in Sombara Tower. It was never the same thing twice. Despite the fact that Faeron had lived in Eredith all his life, being with Lydia made the city feel fresh again, like he was seeing it with a whole new set of eyes.

On the evening before the Unity Festival, a soft snow danced about the city, though Faeron wouldn't know it from a small simulation chamber in the Arches of the Ages. There, a golden afternoon sun slowly sank down a cloudless sky and an ocean breeze carried the sharp cry of circling seacrows. Dozens of children played in the sand, the same children who had played here for years. They, like the adults sunbathing and setting up picnics along the beach, were part of the simulation.

"I know it's no Prophet's Guard," said Lydia as the pair of them walked along the beach, "but sometimes I like to use these history sims to practice dancing alone, away from the studio. I only wish I could take off my shoes and feel the grains between my toes."

"Or the waves lapping at your feet," added Faeron, staring off to sea. "You know, when I look out over the waves, I could swear I've sailed before. It's like… déjà vu."

"In a dream, as Jakob?" asked Lydia.

"That's the strange bit," said Faeron. "For as long as he's lived by the ocean, I don't think I have a single memory of Jakob on a boat. Still, there's so much I don't remember…" Faeron felt his glove tighten and looked down to see Lydia holding his hand. His gaze rose to her glossy pink lips and twinkling blue eyes.

"If it's not a memory," she said, "maybe it's a premonition… or ambition. You're already shaping energy and Auri… well… she terrifies me to be honest. It's only a matter of time before you've found your mom, cured the plague, and freed us of these walls, but then what? Maybe you'll head out on the Long Sea and fight off all the monsters from the deep."

"Or, maybe I'll get the alca network back online and take you for a walk on this beach," smirked Faeron, his chest swelling with confidence.

A smile crept across her soft pink lips as her eyes gazed into his. "You know, I think I'd like that," she said, grasping his hand tighter.

He and Lydia walked the beach for the remainder of the evening, and as the sun set over the ocean, the pair exited the simulation and turned in their boots.

"My show ends a little after noon tomorrow," said Lydia, as she followed Faeron out the front door of the Arches of the Ages, "which means I should be ready by fourth hour."

"Your place, fourth hour," said Faeron, watching snow drift lazily past Lydia's pale face. "We can grab food on our way to the Athenaeum. There's a rooftop overlook with a killer view of the parade."

"And after that, the Ballroom at Bistro Elledin," said Lydia, rocking back and forth on her heels, seeming almost to burst with excitement. "I'll need to wear something extra special… though not too restrictive. You've got a dance lesson tomorrow."

"I've been looking forward to it," grinned Faeron. "Well, that… and what comes with it."

"Hmm," said Lydia, stroking her chin playfully. "I don't have a clue what you mean." She winked and then dove straight into a hug, flinging her arms around him. "Goodnight, Faeron. I'll see you tomorrow."

"I can't wait." Faeron squeezed her tight and closed his eyes. For a moment, there was only her warmth.

Faeron wore a grin all the way home. It was dark in the common area of his apartment, the only light beaming in through the long sliding glass door. Out on the balcony, silhouetted against the stars, was Auri.

She didn't seem to notice him until he slid open the door. Looking up suddenly from a book resting in her lap, Auri looked crazed. She wore a baggy t-shirt with unkempt hair and shadows beneath her eyes. It looked like she hadn't slept an hour despite having locked herself in her room for a week.

"I hope you're not planning on coming to the festival dressed like that," joked Faeron as he took his seat beside her. "Whatcha readin'?"

"I think…" Auri began, but she stopped herself, furrowing her brow as if a sudden thought struck her. "No. I don't want to tell anyone until I'm absolutely sure. All I can say is that I think I know why the gloves never worked for me."

"You afraid I'll tell someone?" asked Faeron, stung by the secrecy.

"It's not about trust," said Auri, earnestly. "I just don't have the full idea ready. This is *big*, and I want to be absolutely sure."

"I get it," said Faeron, taking his seat beside her. Knowing better than to push her further, he changed the subject, asking, "Any word when your dad's getting home?" Vox always came back for the Unity Festival, though he sometimes missed a night or two.

"Your dad got word from mine a couple nights ago," said Auri as snow tumbled about the balcony, falling heavier here than the streets below. "A sandstorm held them up for a day in East Saldun, but he's doing everything he can to get here tomorrow."

"Knowing your dad," said Faeron, "I wouldn't bet against him. What's the plan if he does show up tomorrow?"

"Don't worry," smiled Auri, "I won't abandon Quinn. We'll still join you and Lydia at the parade, just the four of us. I'm sure your dad will invite us all over after the ceremony for…"

"Chocolate brews around the fire," Faeron finished for her, practically tasting the warm confection already.

"As is tradition," yawned Auri. She folded the book in her lap and rose with a stretch. "I'm gonna go read in bed for a bit before I pass out. I'm nearly done and the quicker I fall asleep, the sooner I see Dad."

"I'm about there as well," said Faeron. They walked inside together and said goodnight before Faeron retreated to his bedroom. Wasting no time, Faeron buried himself in the covers and closed his eyes. Despite his excitement for tomorrow, or perhaps because of it, Faeron found sleep difficult. He tossed and turned, coming up with corny one-liners to woo Lydia in their first dance. Eventually the images of him and her locked in arms faded and the light of peridom took its place. The stream carried Faeron through vivid scenes of wondrous worlds to a smoky round room, cast in pink light and littered with colorful pillows. There, Jakob Rite stirred.

"Jakob… think you conked out on us… Jakob, hey Jakob!"

Jakob felt a strong grip tug on his shoulder, and he propped himself up, blinking awake. The whole room was filled with a pastel rainbow of pillows and even the floor itself was cushioned. Madeline Empire knelt before him, shadowed by the smoke swirling about the dim pink room.

"So much for staying up all night, ay Jakob?" she wafted away a plume of smoke and he could see a winning smile stretch across her face.

Jakob yawned and sat up. "Lizzy still here?" he asked, trying to remember when exactly he'd passed out.

Madeline pointed over her shoulder to a dark figure across the smoky room.

"So, this is all you?" asked Jakob, breathing in the scented haze. The whole room smelled of herbs and berries.

"One of us had to make it until morning," she fell backward and snatched some papers on the far side of the bed before springing back up to a sit. "Here," she said, then handed the stack to Jakob.

"What's this?" he asked, flipping through the papers.

"A full manuscript for that Salduni Royalty's Biographic Fantasy," said Madeline excitedly. A groan sounded from across the room as the other girl grabbed a nearby pillow and placed it over her head.

"A Biographic Fantasy?" asked Jakob.

"It's like a normal biography, except certain bits are spiced up," answered Madeline.

"And you really got through all of this last night?"

"I was in a trance," shrugged Madeline. "One second I was setting my pen to paper, the next thing I knew it was morning and here you two were, fast asleep. How late did you make it?"

Jakob looked at a smaller pile of papers, scattered beside him. "Half a chapter, I think."

"That's good!" clapped Madeline. "Means only a chapter and a half to go. You'll be shipping it off to Vennamin any day now."

"I can hope," sighed Jakob. "I've only got a couple weeks left before..."

"You can't think that way," said Madeline. "Tell you what, I'll give this draft a read as soon as I'm back from the… facilities. I just realized I haven't been all night." Madeline got to her feet and rushed through a curtain of colorful sequins.

Turning his attention to the lensed device resting beside him, Jakob whispered, "Proto, cease private mode. Any news?"

The lens flickered with blue light. "Thank goodness, I thought you'd never wake up," said Proto excitedly, "Pinstripe called. You're on."

"Pinstripe!" exclaimed Jakob, springing to his knees. "When?"

"Today."

"Today!?" In a frenzy, Jakob swept up his papers, stuffed them into a nearby leather messenger bag. "How long?"

"You'll need to leave within the hour. Sylvia is already on her way here."

"This is it, Proto," said Jakob, springing to his feet and fixing the lens to his shirt. Lizzy groaned and rolled over. "The investigation, my last chapter, Pinstripe has the answers." He rushed through the sequin curtain that Madeline had disappeared into only moments before and emerged into a cramped bookshop.

There were no windows here and the peeling egg-white ceiling was quite low. The pathways between the rows of bookshelves were hardly wide enough to walk through, and the piles of books at the foot of the cluttered stacks made the passageways even more precarious. Jakob weaved a path through the clutter, reaching a desk at the far wall. Mountains of books were heaped on top of the desk with only a small open area near an old-fashioned register, probably as old as the building he was in. Beside the desk was a shoddy wooden staircase leading upward.

The door at the top of the staircase opened and Madeline appeared. She wore a long loose sapphire dressing gown over a black tank top and grey sweatpants covered in coffee stains.

"Sneaking out?" she asked, descending the stairs slowly with a steaming mug.

"Meeting Pinstripe, if you'll believe it," boasted Jakob.

"Pinstripe!?" Madeline stopped sharp, nearly spilling her drink. "Jakob, are you sure about this? I know what it all means to you but owing a favor to a broker is a big deal."

"Don't worry. Words are my superpower," said Jakob. "I'm not going to let him walk all over me."

"If you say so," sighed Madeline, continuing down the steps. "You want me to take a look at your drafts?"

"I'll send over a copy," offered Jakob, meeting her halfway up the rickety steps. "Sylvia's already on her way."

Madeline took a deep draw of her coffee and looked out over the stacks. "Funny," she said, "all these extraordinary books, some rare as precious stones, and nobody seems to know or care that they're down here." She smiled sadly then took another sip. "Then there's you, selling your soul to a devil just to add your own story to this musty basement." She gave his arm an affectionate squeeze then continued past him down the stairs. At the bottom, she paused and turned. "Good luck, Jakob," she said. "See you here next week?"

"If my manuscript isn't on Vennamin's desk by then," grinned Jakob. "Until next time, Madeline."

Above the bookstore was a quiet coffee shop. The ceiling was much higher and strung with dozens of lights in old glass bottles. A well-tanned man with short silver hair and a tidy white apron was using the lull in business to sweep when Jakob emerged from the basement door painted with silver letters that read: Books Below.

"You look like you've seen better days," called Max, the silver-haired barista, sporting a glowing smile as he set the broom aside.

"Oh no," groaned Jakob, running a hand through his matted hair. "Sylvia is gonna beat me to a pulp."

"I'd pay to see that," said Max. He pulled out a stool from a short round table and took a seat. "So, you two goin' somewhere?"

"To see Pinstripe."

"Pinstripe!?" asked Max. "Is that what this has all come to? You know, his deals are never worth it. He preys on people who can't go anywhere else."

"I know, and chances are he's got nothing for me anyway," shrugged Jakob. "If, by some miracle, he does what I'm looking for, I'll be careful. I promise."

"I see your mind is made. Well, maybe I can still help you keep your dignity," sighed Max. "I have some spare clothes in back, just in case there's ever a spill. I think I've got something for that nest on your head as well."

"Oh," said Jakob, feeling quite self-conscious as he glanced down at his wrinkled grey tee. "Thanks Max, that's very thoughtful… but, are we even the same size?"

"Of course," scoffed Max, as if Jakob was an idiot for even asking. "And think nothing of it. I won't have you seeing an info broker looking like the Ossun Cave Creature."

He led Jakob through a door behind the bar into a wide storeroom. There were cabinets on one wall and a line of trunks at the back. Max rushed to a leather bag resting on a trunk and procured a neatly folded shirt and pants.

"This is really too much," said Jakob. "I don't want to take your stuff."

"It's really not," said Max, holding up the clothes until Jakob relented and took them. Turning back to his bag, Max began to rummage again. "I've got a mirror in here somewhere somewhere … then a comb and some spray for your hair. That is, if Lizzy hasn't 'borrowed' them again… Aha!" He set up a small standing mirror on one of the crates and placed both a comb and a metallic silver spray bottle beside it.

"Honestly Max, this is a lot," said Jakob. "Thank you for this."

"Anytime," said Max, waving him off. "You've been comin' here every week for a year now. That makes you part of the family. Just do me a favor and come out of this closet looking like a human being, alright?"

"I think I can do that," laughed Jakob then Max returned to the foyer.

Jakob took the folded clothes and did as he was instructed, fixing Proto to the breast of the slim fit navy button up. The tight grey jeans had enough stretch in them to keep his legs from feeling constricted and fell right to his ankles, as if he had pulled this from his own closet. After dressing, he approached the mirror and inspected the bottle. He gave his hair a few spritzes of whatever the bottle held and ran a comb through his locks. When Jakob looked into the mirror felt a swell of confidence brewing inside. He strode from the closet, showing off his new look.

"Like it?" asked Max.

"Love it," said Jakob.

"Of course you do," beamed Max. "Now, I think if—"

He was interrupted by the chiming of a bell above the front door.

Sylvia strode into the store, dressed in a black blazer and dress pants. Her eyes flicked between Jakob and Max suspiciously. "Are those Max's…" she began, then stopped herself. "Never mind, I don't want to know. You ready to get out of here?"

"As I'll ever be," said Jakob. "Thanks for the help, Max. I'll bring these back tomorrow."

"You better," said Max. "Now go on… and you two be careful around Pinstripe."

The bell sounded a second time as Sylvia and Jakob left the shop.

It took Jakob's eyes a moment to adjust to the blinding sunlight as a chilled wind bit at his neck. When he could see, Jakob found himself on a wide street that ran between rows of rickety looking buildings. The busy alca network formed a grid above the streets, held aloft by a series of towering pillars that cast long shadows across the slanted wooden rooftops.

There were tracks embedded into the roads as well. The middle of the street was where the majority of local traffic (mostly older-looking models in this area of Colo Flats) rode the rails unimpaired. Whenever an alca reached its destination, it would switch to the outer lanes and stop just long enough to unload its passengers before rejoining traffic and speeding off toward some distant lot.

"Proto," said Sylvia. "Mind calling the alca?"

"Already did," reported Proto. "Coming in three… two… one…"

A flash of silver emerged from traffic as Jakob's Pursuer model pulled up in front of the café. They wasted no time in boarding and the Pursuer was off. At the end of the block, they took a rising rail up to the main grid then sped south.

"You sure about this?" asked Sylvia from the bench across from him. Though her nerves didn't show by looking at her, Jakob could hear it in her voice.

"If Pinstripe's willing to hear us out, it's because he'll want some in on my book," said Jakob. "We trade favors up front, and any mention of illegal activities… we walk. I promise."

"And what if he wants to touch *my* work, my research?" asked Sylvia. "He invited *us,* not just you."

"Then you get to set the boundaries," said Jakob. "Your work, your rules."

"Fine," said Sylvia, "and we don't agree to *anything* without discussing it first."

"Deal," said Jakob.

The ride lasted only an hour and a half. The rickety buildings of Colo Flat's northern neighborhoods made way for larger mansions, just as densely packed but each taking up full blocks on their own. When the mansions ended, there were busy roads lined with shops, then a district with huge warehouses and dozens of industrial alcas. The further south they rode, the more snowy patches began to pop up on rooftops and roads. The warehouses went right up to the icy waters of Lake Akai. On clear days, like today, Jakob could see all the way across the cold grey lake to the tiny silhouettes of Centra's skyscrapers on the far shore. The rail network ran in a wide circle around the lakeshore, offering views of nearly all of Hampson's districts, each with their own distinct look; Outmarr was the only district with one and two story homes within sight of the lake, while Long Branches blocky mega-residences were draped in blankets of snowy plants. As they neared the southern-most point of Lake Akai, the imposing towers of Centra loomed tall in the east. The Purser diverted off to a sidetrack toward a cluster of snowy buildings at the lake's edge. Their destination stood out among the others. Shaped like a giant orb, some twenty floors tall and floating several stories off the ground, the incredible structure was only accessible by a wide docking ring around its central floor.

Jakob was surprised to see dozens of people standing all around the ring. Pinstripe was infamously difficult to find time with, and Jakob had always imagined a smaller, more intimate setting. The Pursuer arrived at their destination with forty minutes to spare. Jakob shivered as he stepped onto the platform, his every breath turning to mist. Heating towers were set up all around the walkway, but they couldn't stop the frigid winds from the lake.

"Mr. Rite, Miss Rite," called a voice. A bald man in a black vest and white tie walked gracefully toward them. Drawing close, he bowed. "Welcome to Pinstripe's Palace. I am Yllandro, here to guide and to serve."

"You know our names?" asked Sylvia.

"Of course," smiled Yllandro. "We receive dossiers on all our guests before their arrival. In fact, I was the very one to approve your docking."

Looking around, Jakob suddenly realized that he recognized many of the faces around him. There were movie stars, politicians, business leaders, and more. Some exchanged small talk but most kept to themselves as they waited for their fancy sports alcas to dock.

"It's a pleasure," said Jakob, stepping forward to shake Yllandro's hand. In this company, Jakob was beginning to feel a bit like a star himself.

"Likewise," said Yllandro. "If you'd just follow me, I can guide you to a nice warm waiting room where we can discuss refreshments."

Yllandro led Sylvia and Jakob to the sleek silver structure and the wall of the orb slid aside. The hallway inside was completely devoid of decorations. The walls, floor, and ceiling were all pure white, with neon blue stripes running along the corners.

Just before they reached an intersection of hallways, Yllandro stopped suddenly. "Right away," he said, seemingly to no one, then turned to face the siblings. "Pinstripe's had an early departure. Would you like to see him now?"

Jakob had all the time he needed to prepare on the ride over, so he looked over at Sylvia who simply shrugged and nodded.

"That works for us," said Jakob. No sooner had the words left his mouth than his chest grew tight. The confidence of standing among such legendary figures was still there, but he knew Pinstripe's reputation for enforcing deals. He just had to make sure to word their bargain carefully.

Yllandro led the siblings down a path on the right to a stretch of wall that looked like any other. "Just in here," said the guide, and the wall split open, making an entry to a large round room.

The round room was nearly as plain as the hallway. There were no windows, only a set of three hovering white chairs.

"Should we…?" Jakob looked to Sylvia and jerked his head toward the chairs.

"I guess," she said, marching over to take a seat.

Jakob joined her, finding that the floating chair had surprisingly good support. "Nervous?" he asked, noticing Sylvia's face slightly paler than normal.

"We don't belong here," she said, though it wasn't fear in her voice. "The whole ride over, I thought about what Pinstripe could want from us. You saw those people out there. *Legends*. A favor from any one of them could change the lives of millions."

"Do not undersell yourself, Miss Rite," the voice booming behind them was powerfully baritone but not unkind.

Jakob turned in his seat to find a figure in a white pinstripe suit towering in the doorway. His skin looked as though it were made of polished onyx, and his face was unmoving as stone. He walked forward, like a statue brought to life, and the door slid shut behind him.

"Pinstripe!" said Jakob in awe.

"You are correct in assuming I don't take audience without purpose," boomed Pinstripe, taking the last seat. His lifeless eyes made getting any kind of read on him impossible, and Jakob found it unsettling that the broker's mouth didn't move as he spoke. "Truth is, you two are no exception. In you, I see not wealth or influence, but intrigue and opportunity."

"Opportunity, how?" asked Sylvia flatly.

"Opportunity for you and me, Miss Rite," said Pinstripe, reaching into the pocket of his coat. He pulled out a small vial, looking as though it contained nothing at all. "You want to change the lives of millions? This is how it's done." He held out the vial for Sylvia to take. "Go on," he said, "have a look."

Sylvia took the glass from his hand and held it up close to her eye. "Pollen?" she asked.

"Spores," said Pinstripe. "From the dead coast."

"Impossible," said Sylvia.

"And yet, it is so," countered Pinstripe.

"Then it's worth more than I can pay," said Sylvia, handing it back.

"I don't want your debt," said Pinstripe. "I want your assurance of its thorough research. I can provide you with a lab and all the funding you ever need."

"You want me to abandon my degree and come work for you?" asked Sylvia sharply. "Not a chance."

"You can finish your education here, in my facilities," said Pinstripe, "under whatever instruction you desire. Not just from your university, but any in all of Irasil. I would not dare rob a mind like yours of a full education. Sylvia… if I may." She nodded. "Sylvia, after the Quisitive's docuVUE, some twenty thousand souls sought me out regarding the Dead Coast. You are the only soul that I've shown this sample. Do you know why?"

"Enlighten me," challenged Sylvia.

"I've read your recent publication on rapid mutations in the beasts of the Long Sea," said Pinstripe. "Your experience alone sets you apart, but it's more than that. The way you translate your deep

understanding— no, *expertise* of underlying concepts to the page...
I couldn't imagine a better champion for this cause."

"And what do you get from it all?" asked Sylvia. "Ownership over
my research?"

"Use your research to any end you wish you wish," said Pinstripe,
"and I'll apply what we learn to my own pursuits. Where those
interests cross, you have my full backing."

"I...," said Sylvia, paused a moment. "Your offer is generous," she
said, "but my answer is still no."

"I find the world is not so simple as 'yes' and 'no,'" said Pinstripe,
reaching out a hand for the vial, "but I shall accept your answer for
now, Miss Rite. Just know that there is no other path. Once you realize this, my door will be open. Now... to you, Jakob Rite, weaver
of written word," When Sylvia returned the vial to Pinstripe, he
turned his unblinking eyes to Jakob. "I am quite intrigued by the
message you left for me. You claim to have recordings, evidence
of conspiracy within the story of Doctor Vukor Rotier. Explain."

Jakob was shocked by the abruptness, but he had prepared for
this. "Near the end of the recording, there is a shimmer," he began.
"Some forums have taken to calling it The Woman in the Corner."

"I am aware," said Pinstripe. "So... do you believe in vengeful
spirits, Mr. Rite?"

"What I do or don't believe doesn't matter," said Jakob. "This
recording does. Proto, play the clip."

"Happily," said Proto. The lens on his shirt glowed blue and
an image of the park projected into the air between them. They
watched as past Jakob left the library and set off across the lawn.

"Watch the girl, there," said Jakob, pointing to the dancing figure
that had just come into view. Her body was obscured by a rippling
effect, like heat in air. It seemed to follow her every movement.

"Proto, what is this?" asked the recording of Jakob. "I've never
seen anything like it."

"Like what?" the recording of Proto chimed. "Dancing?"

"No, the light."

"Proto, pause there," said Jakob, and the recording halted. "You see that shimmering effect? It's the same as in the docuVUE. Before I passed out, I saw a light surrounding the girl. It had a powerful effect on my mind, in fact, when I woke up, I could hardly remember anything at all. I believe whatever technology she used, is housed in the pen held by Rotier."

"I'll bite," said Pinstripe. "Why the pen?"

"Just before the shimmer begins," explained Jakob, "Rotier's hand passes over a gemstone on the pen. I believe it was a switch of some kind for a device within the pen."

"And you want me to procure the pen?" asked Pinstripe, stealing Jakob's buildup.

"Exactly," said Jakob.

"Impossible," said Pinstripe. "Rotier has gone missing. The whole residence is an active crime scene."

"Missing?" exclaimed Jakob. He looked over to see his sister's eyes, wide with surprise.

"News of it hasn't even reached Irasil yet," said Pinstripe, "well, besides me. Consider that tidbit payment for that enlightening observation you brought me. But, as for your ask, it's impossible. All the favors in the world won't buy you into a Roane investigation."

Jakob sank back into his seat, letting the news wash over him. "This is all the more evidence," he said. "The message must have been a warning. It's why he reacted the way he did. I don't know if he's gone on his own, or if someone's taken him… Pinstripe, can you get me to Roana?"

Pinstripe threw back his head and a raucous laugh filled the whole chamber. "You want to visit Roana and teach the investigators to do their job?" he thundered. "Mr. Rite, a million men and women have asked me for a ticket to Roane soil, but this has to be the most entertaining of the lot."

"It's no joke," said Jakob. "A girl used this technology on me last year, and I still don't know why. If I can get to Roana—"

"That's just it though," said Pinstripe, "you can't. Of those million men and women, how many do you think ever reached Roana?"

"None," said Jakob through gritted teeth.

"There was one," said Pinstripe. "Just one in a million, he and his cause both were. You and yours are not." Pinstripe rose and offered a hand to Sylvia. "You will think on my offer, won't you?"

"My answer isn't going to change," she said, meeting his handshake.

Pinstripe then offered the same gesture to Jakob. "I do wish you luck," he said.

Wordlessly, Jakob shook the robot's cold stone hand and then Pinstripe strode from the room.

"Come on," said Sylvia, and Jakob felt her hand on his shoulder. "We'll find another way."

"We always do," Jakob responded, although he struggled to believe it.

On their way out of Pinstripe's Palace, all Jakob could think of was having to tell Vennamin he hadn't finished his story. He supposed it was his own fault, building his whole story on a real-world investigation that was always going to be a shot in the dark. As Jakob watched over the crowd of famous faces for his alca to approach, his eye was drawn to a strange light. Standing alone in the distance of the loading ring was a girl, too young to be in this company, dark skinned with darker hair that fell down her back in waves. Rainbow light glimmered in the mist of her breath, and even from here, Jakob could see the technicolor radiance of her eyes. There was no doubt in his mind, this was the girl from the park.

"Sylvia," said Jakob, tugging her sleeve. He pointed back to where he saw the girl, but she was gone. All that was left was a trail of light, leading around the bend of the loading bay. "The girl from the park. She was there. You see that light? It's her."

"What light?" asked Sylvia.

"Of course," said Jakob to himself. "It has to be me! Proto, start recording!"

"Jakob, what are you—" asked Sylvia, but, before she could finish, he ran off.

Jakob wove like a madman through famous faces, not caring how he might look. The light was fading, and he wasn't going to lose the dancing girl again. Ignoring the frigid wind, Jakob charged headlong after the trail of light. Suddenly, his body froze. Jakob couldn't move another step.

"Are you sure this is what you want?" came a girl's voice.

"Who are you?" asked Jakob. "How are you doing this?" His eyes darted around for the source of his entrapment, but he didn't see the girl anywhere. Everyone around him was perfectly still, their eyes gazing off with empty stares. Even the alcas on the rail network were moving at a snail's pace.

"Are you sure this is what you want?" she repeated. "Roana, Rotier, the Dead Coast… what do they mean to you?"

"Everything," said Jakob. No matter how he fought, his limbs wouldn't budge. "This is the same technology from Rotier's pen, isn't it?"

"You're perceptive," said the girl, finally stepping into view. Rainbow flame rushed from her eyes and surged through her hair, tumbling down her thick peacoat.

"Why me?" asked Jakob.

"Because your eyes were open and you saw what others wouldn't," said the girl. "My name is Lylliana, and if you want to know any more than that, you'll meet me, alone, at the Edgeview port in North Ri'kalla tomorrow morning. Our boat leaves at fifth hour. Bring clothes enough for a week."

"A week? Where are you taking me?" asked Jakob, but the girl walked out of view and the world sprang back to life. Frantically, he whipped his head about, searching for any sign of the girl. She was simply gone.

"Jakob!" Sylvia's voice carried from a distance.

He turned to see his sister running after him.

"What was that about," she said, huffing and puffing after him.

"It's…" Jakob started, but he didn't know how to describe what had just happened. Not that Sylvia would believe him anyway. "I have an appointment tomorrow that I can't miss."

CHAPTER THIRTEEN

LEGEND OF THE SEACARVER

The next morning, Jakob rose before the sun. Throwing a week's worth of clothes into a large backpack, Jakob fixed Proto to his airy white shirt and went up to the kitchen. He was surprised to find Sylvia awake as well, waiting for him at the table with a piping-hot mug.

"Chocolate brew?" she asked. "Just made it."

Jakob sat beside her, where a second cup was waiting. He brought it to his nose and breathed deep. "It smells amazing," he said.

"You always say that," shrugged Sylvia, her eyes moving to his backpack. "This isn't just a meeting, is it? Jakob, what are you planning?"

"I don't know," said Jakob, pausing to sip warm liquid chocolate from his mug, "but Rotier and the Dead Coast are involved. I need to do this, Sylvia… for me, for my book. Short of Pinstripe, this is the only lead I have."

"I understand… all too well," Sylvia sighed. "Just, be careful. This whole thing reeks."

"I'm used to things that reek," he grinned.

Sylvia rolled her eyes and took a long drink.

Throwing back the rest of his chocolate brew, Jakob slung his backpack over one shoulder and headed for the door.

"When will you be back?" asked Sylvia.

"A week by the sounds of it," said Jakob. "I don't know if you'll be able to reach me while I'm gone. If Vennamin calls, tell her I'm writing."

Sylvia strode across the kitchen and gave her brother a rare hug. "I will, so long as you promise to be right here, this time next week."

"I promise," Jakob squeezed her tight.

"Good," said Sylvia as they broke apart. "Otherwise, I'm calling the cops."

It was still dark when Jakob left home. A sliver of moonlight broke through the clouds, but the streets were bathed in the glow of hanging lights that zig-zagged between the shop awnings. Jakob's block of the art district was never too cold, even in the middle of Lowsun. A gentle breeze whistled through the lifeless streets. Jakob couldn't remember the last time he'd seen it so quiet.

Jakob's Pursuer was already waiting for him at the otherwise lifeless station. He stepped inside the alca and sped off toward the raised rail network. It didn't take more than fifteen minutes to reach Edgeview port, a cluster of buildings and piers around a small bay. In the distance, Jakob could see the cross-continental alca rail, carving a massive black stripe across the starry sky.

The Pursuer came to a stop in front of a plain-looking administrative building with a dozen different flags flying from its front arch. There was a small lawn and pathways leading off in either direction, bending around the corners of the building. Jakob stepped out of his alca, looking around for any sign of the girl. The building was lifeless and there wasn't a person in sight.

"Proto," said Jakob. "The girl mentioned a ship going out about this time. Any idea what port we're looking for?"

The lens on his chest flickered with light. "Odd," said Proto. "There are ships scheduled all day and night. This dock doesn't see five minutes without some sort of activity… except for right now. There's a whole hour of nothing."

"Then we're in the right place," said Jakob. "I'll bet you if we check the docks, we'll find someone that doesn't belong."

Jakob took the path around the left side of the building and wound up on a well-lit wooden boardwalk. There were hundreds of fishing vessels docked in a complex network of ports. Some were small enough to be manned by one or two crew; others were heavy-plated metal juggernauts capable of surviving run-ins with the great monsters that dwelled deep at sea. Scanning the vessels, Jakob didn't see any that looked out of place.

"Proto, go infrared," said Jakob. "Any activity."

"Not a sign of life on any vessel," said the index.

"She's got to be here somewh—"

"Hello."

Jakob nearly yelped as he spun around. The girl from Pinstripe's Palace strolled down the boardwalk, her irises blazing with rainbow light. Other than her eyes, Lylliana looked like a normal girl on the verge of adulthood. She wore a yellow floral dress that fluttered in the soft breeze and a white broad-rimmed hat. In one hand, she held a small suitcase and tucked beneath the other arm was what looked almost like a medieval knight's helmet.

"I hoped you'd come," said Lylliana, a smile on her lips, "I owe you answers, I know, but first, we need to get on that boat." Her fiery eyes shifted past him as she pointed down the row of behemoth floating fortresses to an empty dock at the end.

"A stealth vessel?" asked Jakob, excitement building in his chest. This was either a dream or he'd stumbled upon a plot so fantastical it put his stories to shame. "Where to?"

"Roana," said the girl, matter-of-factly. This one word hit Jakob list a punch to the chest.

"Impossible," said Proto, piping up at last. "No ship in the history of this dock has ever sailed there. I just checked over the logs."

"Impossible or not," said the girl, more serious now, "this is your one ticket to Roana."

Jakob considered her words a moment. "Even if your ship can get us across the sea alive," he said, "how am I supposed to walk around Roana without drawing crowds? I won't even be able to speak! Doesn't that defeat the purpose of the stealth vessel?"

"Not if you wear this." She held out the helmet for Jakob, and, in the moonlight, he could see it in detail. Steel plating shielded all but the chin and mouth with a mask covering the eyes and nose. The mask itself was inlaid with a capillum's face, bold browed and stern with massive bushy brows. Four colored stones shaped like tears were inlaid just below the holes for the eyes; they glowed, softly with pulsing light. Whoever created this had clearly put an incredible amount of time into the realism of the face imprinted upon the mask, and Jakob wondered how someone so young could have acquired such a masterwork.

Taking the helmet, Jakob held the cool steel in both hands. "What is it?"

"The mask of the Koerribot," said the girl. "Wear it and you will become him."

"Become what?" asked Jakob.

"The Koerribot," repeated Lylliana. "Capillum folklore would tell you that he is an immortal outlaw and champion of the people… but he's much more. The Koerribot is an adopted title for a long line of men and women who have fought for something greater than themselves."

"And what would that be?" asked Jakob.

"Soon…" said Lylliana. "For now, just know that whoever wears that helmet is wholly the Koerribot, from fingerprints to DNA… You'll even understand Roane."

If everything surrounding this moment hadn't been equally bizarre, Jakob would have thought it all a complex joke. Even now, he was more intrigued by her seemingly impossible technology than he was truly bought into her tale.

"However," she continued, "you *must* stay in my presence to keep up the illusion. Three days from now, the Koerribot has a secret meeting with a contact in Roana, the human counselor, Kyrillis Ma-Ikkut. That's our front to reach Rotier. The rest I will answer once we're aboard."

"For the story…" relented Jakob, pulling on the helmet.

Lylliana's eyes flared with light. "Be warned, there will be a sensation," she said. "It is perfectly normal, so try not to panic…" Rainbow fire leapt into her hair and weaved down around her torso. Jakob's gut tightened with a cramp that spread through his chest, arms, and legs. It didn't last long, nor was it overly painful.

"That wasn't terrible," said Jakob, not recognizing his own voice. He spoke deeper, with an accent he couldn't place. Suddenly, the ground seemed further away, as if Jakob were standing on a box. He looked down at his dark furry arms—

"I'm a capillum!" Jakob gasped. His hands looked like they had been stretched out and covered in dark fur that now spread across his arms and legs. Trying to get a better look at himself, Jakob made for the edge of the boardwalk. He took a step and immediately felt as though he had just hopped off a treadmill. His stride was long and effortless as he approached the moonlit waters and looked down into their surface. Sure enough, a black furred capillum with scarred lips stared back at him from behind the mask. "Im— Impossible… This must be a dream."

"Um, Jakob…" said Proto nervously, "I'm seeing it, too."

"You're more awake now than you've ever been, Jakob Rite," said the girl. "I promise, I will help you make sense of this. But, right now, we have a boat to catch."

Whatever doubt Jakob had was erased upon seeing himself as a capillum, and was now replaced with awe and a million burning questions. This was either a dream or the most important story of his life. Either way, he would see it out.

Jakob could hardly focus on walking as Lylliana skipped along the creaky boards of the pier, leading him with grace. Moonlight glinted off the still water and cast ominous shadows from the pointed bows of the massive, armored ships. In his head, Jakob tried to make sense of the morning, but there was none to be found, not in the light, nor the girl's words, nor the sensation of walking about as a capillum. He couldn't fathom how the impossible girl was going to explain all this. For now, all he could do was focus on not mucking up his role.

"Who is the Koerribot exactly?" asked Jakob, still mystified by the strange sound of his voice. "Not just the legend, but the person. What are they like: stern, outgoing? If I'm going to play the part, I should at least know more about my role."

"The last Koerribot filled every room with her energy," said Lylliana, a sad admiration in her voice. "She was bold and brilliant in everything she did, but her predecessor couldn't have been more opposite; he was distant and calculated. What I mean to say is that, for as long as you wear that helmet, the legacy of the Koerribot is yours to shape."

"Won't people be suspicious of the sudden change?" asked Jakob. The further they walked from shore the darker the pier became, but the rainbow fire streaking through Lylliana's hair was all the light they needed.

"The Koerribot has been missing for twenty years," said Lylliana. "Memories are faulty and anyone can change with time."

"I suppose," sighed Jakob, trying to wrap his head around the idea of being a legendary outlaw.

They neared the empty dock, passing the last of the giant war boats and fishing vessels. As they walked along the pier, the air started to shimmer. It began like fog over the water, but as they drew near its details took form like the focusing of a camera's lens. The ship looked almost like a speedboat, but longer, with aerodynamic curves that came to a point at the bow. The raised cabin at the rear was tinted black and a small ramp led up onto the open-air deck. There, a tall, hooded figure was waiting.

"One last thing," whispered Lylliana in Jakob's ear. "Nobody but you will be able to see me."

"Koerribot," came a young raspy voice from the figure on the pier; his accent was clearly Roane. "So, you do exist, after all. And here, I thought my mother was mad." As the capillum spoke, the strange Roane words that left his lips unscrambled themselves in Jakob's ears, becoming a message he could understand.

Jakob breathed deep and mustered every ounce of confidence. "I can't speak to her sanity," he said, "but I can assure you I'm the real thing." His words also twisted; despite speaking in his own tongue, Jakob heard Roane leave his mouth. "To whom do I have the pleasure?"

"Aeryll Takata," said the capillum, drawing close. He wore a well-fitted white tunic with black sleeves and pants. Lowering his hood, Aeryll revealed his sleek silver fur with crimson dye at the tips of his brows and in patterns down his neck. "Come, Mother is expecting us."

Jakob followed the capillum across the ramp onto an open deck with low walls.

"We're only a short way out," said Aeryll. "You can stay up on deck or go down below. It's your ship, after all." With that, the capillum entered a door near the stern where the dark windows of the cabin overlooked the ship.

Jakob and Lylliana situated themselves near the bow as the boat purred quietly to life. The docking ramp retracted and then they were off, accelerating quickly out of the bay into the open waters. Despite some small waves, their vessel cut through the waters without bumps or sway. Lylliana's hair flew wildly in the wind, the tongues of rainbow light dancing in time.

"You promised me answers once we were on board," yelled Jakob over the roar of the wind and sea. "Who are you? Why are you helping me?"

"Not yet," said the girl, "not this boat." She pointed toward a shape in the distance that Jakob had mistaken for a rock. As they approached, he could see it was, in fact, a larger ship.

The vessel was unlike any Jakob had ever seen. In some ways, it looked like a larger version of the ship they were on now, sleek and white. Only, this vessel was over thirty feet tall and shaped like a child's drawing of a cloud if an engineer had come along and smoothed out all the puffs.

"We should go below," said Lylliana. "We'll be docking soon."

They went to the door that Aeryll entered and passed into a narrow stairwell. Lylliana led Jakob down the metal steps to a room that looked straight out of a military facility. Monitors covered most of the glassy white walls and panels below them sported hundreds of tiny lights, sliders, and knobs. There was a central aisle through the equipment, and a door just beside the steps with a dozen warning signs written in Roane.

"I've never seen a ship like her," said Jakob.

"She's a prototype," said Lylliana, "the only of its kind ever made. Her name is the Seasprinter, daughter vessel to the Seacarver, which we should be docking to any moment now."

"*The* Seacarver?" Jakob gasped with recognition. Of all the ships he could be on…

"You know it?" asked Lylliana.

"Of course," said Jakob. "It's in Quisitive's Five Greatest Mysteries of History. A Roane spy vessel that disappeared on its maiden voyage. Three hundred years later, it's never been found."

"She was made to hide, and she's done her job well," said Lylliana.

"You act like you're the one who took it," scoffed Jakob, "but the Seacarver was shipnapped over three hundred years–" The whole ship gave a sudden lurch and Jakob had to steady himself on a nearby railing. He could feel them rising straight upward and, suddenly as they started, they came to a stop.

The door at the foot of the stairs swung open and another capillum stood in the entry. She was much older looking than Aeryll, with a similar style tunic in grey and crimson. Her silver hair was matted, the dye in her fur fading, but her large black eyes were full of life as they came to rest on Jakob.

"Koerribot," she smiled and bowed. "It has been too long."

"That's Temril Takata," whispered Lylliana, "captain of the Seacarver. She's the only one who knows our secret."

"Indeed, Captain Takata," said Jakob, bowing.

"And your companion, is she with you?" asked Temril.

Jakob looked to Lylliana who nodded. "She is," he said.

"Good," said Temril. "When I received your message, I had fears it might be a trap. I'm happy to find my fears unfounded. Your cabin is waiting below. I can take you there now."

The old capillum captain led Jakob and Lylliana through the door, up a half flight of polished white steps, to a wide-open lounge that looked like something out of a luxury yacht. The floor was carpeted in a wave pattern of black, white, and grey, and moonlight poured in freely through a curved observation window offering a wide view of the Seasprinter, docked to the ship's nose. Beyond it, Jakob saw nothing but dark water and stars. There were several blackwood bookshelves with glass doors keeping their contents secure and a massive telescope set up near the observation window. In the very center of the room, two white crescent couches faced each other with a round glass-topped table between them. A capillum with silver and pink fur sat hunched over the table, pouring over a book. At their approach she perked up, her excitement etched in her young features.

"You're real," she whispered softly, but in this body, Jakob could hear her clearly. "You really do exist!"

"Compose yourself, Naza," chided Temril.

"I'm sorry," said Naza, bowing, "it's only that none of us besides the captain have actually seen you. I always knew the captain believed what she said, and I trust her, but to see a legend in real life… where have you been all these years?"

"Naza, remember what I told you?" asked the captain.

"Privacy," said the girl. "Of course, I'm sorry Koerribot."

"I'm sure the Koerribot will address all our questions when he is ready," said Temril. "Until such a time, it's not our place to pester him. Now, go ahead and get the engines warmed up. Koerribot, you'll be through here."

She led Jakob through a door on the far wall into a hallway, clean and glassy white, almost like the one in Pinstripe's Palace. Along the passage were several doors with silver labels printed in Roane.

"I apologize about Naza," said Temril. "Brilliant engineer, but every word she thinks finds its way off her tongue. The rest of the crew is fast asleep. I'm sure they're just as eager to meet you."

Jakob swallowed hard, still unsure how to play his character. Now that he was on the vessel, he felt conscious of every movement and each syllable, as if the slightest misstep would dispel his ruse.

Temril marched all the way to the end of the hall where a glass elevator, just big enough for the three of them, was waiting.

Jakob boarded, making sure to leave room for Lylliana, and they descended two floors to a sizable round room. Windows wrapped all the way around the chamber, and hundreds of colorful fish filled the waters beyond. The elevator, bathrooms, and shelves were all built into a wide column that ran through the center of the room with a pair of beds on one side, separated by a dark curtain, and telescopes facing nearly every direction.

"You're safe to remove your mask here, Koerribot," said Temril as Jakob reached down and tested one of the beds for firmness. "I wish to know your face… and that of your companion."

Lylliana turned from a window near a school of bright blue fish and the light in her hair faded, leaving only the rainbow fire of her irises. Following her lead, Jakob reached up and removed the helmet. A tingling sensation ran through his arms and the helmet seemed twice as heavy as before.

"As I thought," said Temril, her eyes locked on Lylliana. "You never made it out of the Dead Coast, did you?"

"It was nearly worse," said Lylliana softly.

"Then your enemy was not so defenseless as you thought," said Temril, looking now to Jakob. "And if he's here, then I assume the last Koerribot shared your fate?"

"I thought so," said Lylliana, "But when I learned Rotier escaped, I knew she had as well. Quisitive's report all but confirmed it. She left him a message, or maybe it was for me. Either way, we need to find Rotier and that pen."

"Then we shall proceed as per your message," said Temril. "You know where to find me."

"Temril," said Lylliana as the old capillum returned to the elevator, "thank you for keeping this ship safe all these years. You've done your father proud."

The captain smiled. "Kind words, old friend," she said, and the elevator shut behind her.

Jakob rounded on Lylliana the moment the doors had closed. "Who are you?" he asked. "All this…" he looked about the spacious cabin, "your light, this helmet, the way you spoke to the captain, everything about you is impossible. Are you even human?"

"Every bit as human as you," she replied, trotting over the beds and pulling back the curtain between them. "Take a seat," she said, relaxing at the end of one bed, "I'll explain what I can."

Jakob joined Lylliana at the edge of the bed, and the engines kicked to life, sending a trail of bubbles behind them. Over the next hour Lylliana told Jakob all about the kytra. She described in detail their fantastic powers, moving objects, swaying minds, even being reborn after death. However, she warned, not all kytra use their gifts for good. By the time she was done, dawn's light had breached the waters, illuminating a world of aquatic life outside their window.

"So," said Jakob, rubbing his temples, "if I understand correctly, this technology you use, isn't technology at all? You're just a four-thousand-year-old goddess—"

"I'm no goddess," said Lylliana sternly.

"Fine," said Jakob. "A four-thousand-year-old woman with the powers of a goddess, reborn all throughout time to fight an evil so great you won't even share its name."

"You have to understand," said Lylliana. "This evil is a kytra who has made his name the very heart of his power. He doesn't just kill, he consumes the souls of others like us, then fills the husks they leave with his light and his name. Knowing that name would only make you a target."

"Then why bring me at all?" asked Jakob frustrated at her absurd and often cryptic answers. "Why show up in the park? How am I any safer now, knowing as little as I do, than if you had left me out of it?"

"I thought I'd won, that I'd finally trapped my enemy," said Lylliana, her vivid eyes staring intensely into his. "If only for a lifetime, I thought I could be free to seek out other kytra."

"And that led you to me?" asked Jakob. "But I'm just a man."

"A man who can see the light of peridom," said Lylliana, "the telltale sign of a kytra. I searched for years before I found you, but when you passed out in the park, it was clear you were too young. If my enemy did return, you would be helpless against him."

"Too young?" scoffed Jakob, staring at a girl easily a decade younger than him.

"Each life, our soul grows a little brighter," said Lylliana. "Yours is certainly bright, but, for a kytra, your soul is still quite young. In a lifetime or two, perhaps you could be a star pupil. But, with your young soul and my new mind, I doubt I could teach you to shape the light as I do."

"So, what's changed?" asked Jakob, his pride feeling attacked.

"The Quisitive Report," explained Lylliana, looking out into the endless waters. "I was part of Rotier's expedition. Together with him and the Koerribot, I ventured deep into the Dead Coast. We intended to strike a final blow on my enemy at the source of his power… but, we didn't expect felphants. The terrible creatures wielded the light as a kytra would. They were waiting for us, and we played right into their hands. I couldn't let my enemy take me, and so I was reborn."

"You died?" gasped Jakob.

"By the Koerribot's blade," nodded Lylliana. "I thought she had taken her own life and Rotier's as well, but after hearing of the doctor's escape, I suspected she must have guided him out. The figure Rotier saw in the Quisitive documentary confirmed it. Only, she shouldn't have been able to escape, not without…" Lylliana's eyes sunk down to her lap, and Jakob could see she was clearly struggling with a thought. She sighed and rose from the seat. "I'm sorry to be abrupt, but I should check in with the captain."

"No problem at all," said Jakob, whose head was absolutely spinning. This morning he'd woken up unsure of what to expect, and now, he was finding it hard to believe he wasn't still dreaming. "I think I need to write for a bit anyway, try to make some sense of this morning."

"An excellent plan," piped the girl, the fire in her eyes leaping into her hair. "I'll be back before lunch. Then, we can discuss the particulars of our meeting with the human counselor." Turning to the elevator, the girl took a step and then disappeared entirely.

"Jakob, what have you gotten yourself into?" sighed the author, collapsing back into his bed. "Hey Proto, you alive? Guess we finally get to test how you run off grid."

"Core systems check out," groaned Proto, flickering to life, "just don't ask me to call your alca. I feel like half my brain's got cut out."

"How about copying some notes?" asked Jakob, hoisting himself up and grabbing his travel bag. "If I can't find inspiration in what just happened, I won't find it anywhere."

"I think I can manage that," said Proto. "So… you believe her?"

"The girl?" asked Jakob.

"No, that fish outside the window," said Proto sarcastically. "Of course, the girl. I might be missing some libraries, but she's got more than a few screws loose if you ask me."

"But did you *see* her?" asked Jakob. "Truth or not, she's unlike anything else."

"Sure, sure," said Proto. "Just don't go getting us killed by some maniac now. Sylvia would never forgive us."

"Don't be dramatic," chided Jakob, digging through his backpack until he found his notebook and pen. "She seems perfectly kind. Now, let's see… where did I leave off? Right! Timing the guard patrols at the Simmean Compound."

Jakob wrote through the morning, ideas pouring out onto the page. The sensation of being the Koerribot was bringing new depths to the way he described Inspector Aurilius' ability to vanish. Jakob was so entranced in his work that he hardly noticed as footsteps approached.

"I brought lunch," said Lylliana sweetly, carrying a large tray. The scent of lemon and fish filled the whole room.

They ate together on the bed, and Lylliana ran through the details of their cover mission. They would be transporting a time-sensitive package from Roana all the way to the southern tip of Irasil, something only the Seacarver could manage.

"It's nothing illegal, I assure you," said Lylliana. "In fact, the seeds we're delivering could potentially save lives."

"Seeds?" asked Jakob.

"For a genetically engineered plant," said Lylliana, "designed to survive the frigid climates of the human counselor's homeland. Years of work have gone into these specimens. They're the only of their kind."

"If we're bribing counselors, at least it's in favors that'll do the world some good," shrugged Jakob, loading his fork with well-seasoned rice.

"Jakob, if you don't mind," said Lylliana as she finished off her plate. "I was hoping to spend some more time with the captain. It's been decades since I've seen her."

"That works perfectly, because I'm on a flow," said Jakob proudly. "At this rate, I'll be done with the chapter by tonight."

"Best of luck to you, then," said Lylliana, "and don't feel any pressure to address the crew today. Even the last Koerribot took her time to warm up to it." She waited a moment for Jakob to finish the rest of his food then collected the trays and skipped off toward the elevator, vanishing suddenly mid-stride.

Lylliana didn't return until dinner time. She brought trays of a hearty fish stew and fruit salad, and, once again, disappeared after they finished eating. Hours flew by and dusk fell over the waters outside as Jakob remained entranced in his writing. Just as he penned the last words of the chapter, he heard the elevator doors open.

"Jakob!" said Lylliana, rushing excitedly to the bed where he was packing away his notebook. "There's something I want to show you upstairs in the lounge. Most everyone's asleep, so it'll be just the two of us."

"As long as I don't have to talk to anyone," said Jakob nervously. He zipped up his bag and grabbed the Koerribot's Helmet off his bedside table. "Just in case," he said.

Pulling on the helmet, Jakob transformed once more into the capillum outlaw. The sensation of being three feet taller with long furry limbs was no less alien the second time around. Together, he and Lylliana rode the elevator to the Habitation Deck and followed the hallway they had come in through to the wide-open lounge. Just as Lylliana had said, the ship was quiet and there wasn't a trace of life.

Lylliana flicked off the light as they entered the lounge, the fire in her hair casting a softly shifting glow over the carpeted room. She led Jakob to the windows and looked up at the night sky. "What do you think?" she asked.

Great blue bands of stars reached like arms across the heavens. Jakob had never seen anything like it before.

"Don't get views like this in Hampson," said Jakob. "Lylliana… can I take this off?"

"'Course," she said without breaking her gaze from the heavens. "If anyone comes in, I'll just make you disappear."

"From sight or…," said Jakob.

"Yes, from sight," laughed Lylliana, shooting him a glare. Looking back up to the stars, she pointed upward.

"You see that bright one, there?" she asked.

Jakob followed her point to the edge of the starry band. There, one light was much brighter than the others.

"Imagine that's the nose," said Lylliana, tracing with her hand, "those six to the right are the body… then there's two for the Front legs… back… and tail."

"I see it," said Jakob. "It looks kind of like a cat."

"Exactly," said Lylliana. "That's Na'Zhir, the huntress. Mastoban legends say the girl could change form, between human and cat, a gift from Osaya, the spirit of stars."

"Let me guess," said Jakob. "You knew her, too?"

"No," chuckled Lylliana. "Na'Zhir is just a story, but I've always seen myself in her tale. She was the only one in her village who could hunt the monstrous beasts that called the nearby forests home. I, too, was a hunter, and I cared deeply for my people. For centuries I defended them, guided them, and after all that, it was another who would ultimately save them. My enemy wasn't always like he

is now. Once, he was the bravest and brightest kytra I'd ever met…
still, to this day, there's never been another like him. He saved us,
and when I saw my people no longer needed me, I came with him
back to his home, to Irasil. We were inseparable, like family."

"What happened?" asked Jakob.

"He heard a voice," said the girl, "and he believed it to be a
god. I don't know what it told him, only that he became paranoid.
I tried to talk him down, but one day, something changed. He
looked different, felt different, like his very soul had molded into
something new. He wielded power unlike anything I'd ever seen,
and I knew the voice was behind it. Tens of thousands lost their
lives that day, and yet, when the sun fell, I didn't mourn for them. I
mourned for my closest friend, for what he'd become." Jakob could
see tears falling from her fiery eyes. "I apologize," she said, turning
abruptly from the window. "I only wanted to show you the view,
not burden you with my failings. Perhaps we should return to the
cabin."

"Nonsense," said Jakob. Every time he looked over at her, it felt
strange seeing a girl so young and so full of stories. "If what you're
saying is true, then there's no tale ever told I'd rather hear than
yours. Let's stay and stargaze awhile."

"Alright," said Lylliana, wiping her eyes. "But let's just watch. No
more stories tonight."

"Deal."

When they finally retired to their cabin some hours later, Jakob
fell asleep nearly instantly. His dreams were full of dark figures in
misty rooms, then the mist became waves and the figures were
dragged down into darkness. As they fell, the figures burst with
rainbow flame and reached for Jakob—

Jakob woke suddenly as the ship lurched. Jumping out of bed,
Jakob looked out the window just in time to see them rise above the
waves, sunlight beating down from a partly clouded sky. Looking
up, he saw the ship's body was now hovering some thirty feet
above the ocean, sending a torrent of force down upon the water's
rippling surface.

"Welcome to the Coral Meridian," said Lylliana's voice from behind him. Jakob spun around and saw her exiting the bathroom in her loose-fitting silver pajamas, covered in little stars.

"This isn't the Long Sea…" said Jakob, suddenly realizing where he was. "We've gone East!" Thousands of tiny islands spread as far as he could see. The crystal-clear waters between them were colored by vibrant coral and countless fish. The air around them was teaming with clusters of colorful laudices, jellyfish-like creatures that floated lazily in the air. In the distance, a series of massive black towers rose from the water, forming a line all along the horizon. "Is that the EMP wall?" asked Jakob. "Even if the Seacarver can rise above the water, how are we supposed to get past that? Even aircraft can't get through."

"You can't go through, nor can you go over," said Lylliana, joining Jakob at the windows, "but nothing's stopping us from going under."

"This is a submarine?" gawked Jakob. "Makes sense, I suppose. Still, the water here's too shallow to dive. How are we supposed to go under the wall?"

"Caves," grinned Lylliana. "You'll see."

They soared over the Coral Meridian, drawing ever closer to the colossal towers. Lylliana changed and then went up to retrieve a breakfast of toast and eggs. By the time they were done eating, the EMP wall was only a mile or so out, and the Seacarver began to slow. Their cabin sank back under the water, and Jakob got a good look at the land beneath the waves. Sure enough, there was an enormous opening in the rocks just beneath them, plenty big enough for the Seacarver to pass through.

"It took us years to map these caverns out," said Lylliana proudly, stacking the trays, "and that knowledge has passed down from captain to captain for centuries. As far as I know, we're the only ones ever to travel this way."

"Oh, that's good material right there," said Jakob excitedly. "Proto, take a note! I want to revisit that idea later, see if we can't use it somewhere."

"On it," said Proto from the bedside table.

While Lylliana returned the trays, Jakob fixed Proto to his shirt and went to the window, watching as the Seacarver descended into the chasm. It was nearly pitch black, with only a little light filtering down from the surface in rays. Bioluminescent fish flashed in the darkness like colorful lightning flies on a Newsun night, though they scattered when the Seacarver's headlights came on. The cave itself was monstrous, with sizable offshoots leading out in several directions. Jakob walked around the cabin, observing the vast variety of ocean life all around them. As he was passing behind the engines, Proto suddenly piped up.

"Um, Jakob," said the index, sounding nervous. "I just toggled infrared, and there's something out there."

"We're in the ocean," said Jakob dismissively. "There's lots of somethings out there."

"No, this is something *big*," said Proto anxiously, "something really really big, and it's following us!"

"What do you—" Jakob was cut off suddenly as the urgent voice of Captain Temril filled the room.

"Uj etul u komma zo sokuk za vurokka eligmoz," she said in Roane. Without his helmet, Jakob couldn't understand a word of it.

"Jakob, Captain needs help on the bridge!"

Lylliana stormed from the elevator, holding the Koerribot's helmet in her hands.

"Wait, how do you have that helmet?" asked Jakob. "I left it on the bedside table."

"*That's* your question right now?" she asked him, marching over and handing him the helmet. "I swapped the air in my hands with the helmet on the table… in other words I teleported it. Now, put it on, quick."

Jakob placed the helmet on his head, and, once again, his body morphed into the Koerribot.

"Hold on you two," cried Proto, still pinned to Jakob's shirt, "it's building up a ton of energy. I think it's going to—"

Suddenly, the waters outside lit up like lightning in the night. The whole ship shook violently and the lights went dark. Jakob was thrown to the ground.

"Emergency power activated," said a calm feminine voice over the comms system. Small strips of red light illuminated the edges of the room, flashing toward a small service door beside the elevator.

"I thought sea monsters only lived in the Long Sea," groaned Jakob as he picked himself up. "What's it doing here?"

"Some of these caves have been left alone for centuries. Others have never been explored," said Lylliana. "There's no telling what you'll find down here. Now, we need to move… *fast!*" A new sensation filled Jakob as Lylliana's eyes flared with light. He felt as though a hole had been poked through his center and that the rest of him had been wrung inside out. Streaks of vivid color filled his vision, and, next thing he knew, Jakob was in a whole different room.

Looking around, Jakob saw he was on the ship's bridge with two large chairs for the captain and first hand, occupied by Temril and her son. They sat at stations full of displays and switches with a wide canopy that offered views above and all around them.

"How did you—" started Aeryll, spinning sharply in his chair. He glared at Jakob, looking a bit unnerved.

"Nevermind the Koerribot," said his mother. "Get ready to put all power to engines. Naza," she called, pressing a button beside her main display, "what's our time to reboot?"

"We're still cooling off," said a woman's voice over the comms. "Maybe a minute to power."

"Not to intrude," piped Proto, "but I don't think you've got a minute. It's charging up again."

Sure enough, Jakob could see a dark shape dead ahead of them. It looked like a massive squid and its many tentacles were starting to glow a faintly pulsing blue.

"Mother, she can't take another hit," said Aeryll in a panic.

"She won't," said the captain calmly. "Old friend, would you kindly lend a hand?"

"Of course," Lylliana smirked and strode to the window, placing one hand against the glass. "No monstrosity of Rhun can stand against the power of a kytra."

"A human? Who's she?" gasped Aeryll, nearly jumping in his seat. "Did she just appear out of thin air?"

"This is Lylliana," said Temril, "the power behind the Koerribot, and our family's greatest secret. Now hush and let her work."

The squid's tentacles lit up a pulsing blue as a bolt of electricity shot once more through the water. Crackling energy arced toward the ship, converging at Lylliana's outstretched palm. The rainbow flames surrounding her burned brighter than ever before, engulfing her whole body and lighting the bridge in her pearly glow.

"I'll just borrow that," said Lylliana. She danced in place, and the brilliant flames snaked around her. With grace, she bowed low, leapt, and clapped her hands together. A streak of blinding silver light shot from her body and raced toward the creature. The light engulfed the sea beast and then shot off down a nearby passage, faster than any alca. Darkness fell back over the water.

"The squid is gone," exclaimed Proto.

Jakob sighed in relief as he looked to Lylliana. She still held her pose, frozen from the moment of her clap. The light around her was dimmer than Jakob had ever seen it.

"Are you okay?" asked Jakob, approaching her.

A moment later she suddenly shook too, her eyes fluttering open. "It's far away now," she said, sounding out of breath. "It won't bother us again."

Meanwhile, Aeyll's gaze darted between them.

"What are you?" he demanded, rising from his seat.

"Show some manners," snapped his mother. "Lylliana just saved us all. She's the one who gave us this ship and a cause worth fighting for. The rest, she'll share when she sees fit."

Aeryll sank back but eyed them both mistrustingly.

"Captain, we're back online," came Naza's voice over comms. The whole bridge lit up in stark white lights, causing Jakob to squint.

"Good work, Naza," said Temril. "You too, old friend."

"It's really no problem at all," panted Lylliana. "I could use a rest, though."

"It's well earned," said the captain. "Come, Aeryll. Let's get out of here."

With the crisis averted, Lylliana and Jakob returned to their cabin via an elevator at the rear of the bridge. Lylliana made straight for her bed, collapsing on top of the covers, while Jakob dug out his notebook. Jakob began on his final chapter, a climactic race against time in a deep-sea labyrinth. Not only did he know just how he wanted this story to end, the promise of new answers on the horizon meant he'd have more than enough ammo to dive right into the next book. Lylliana rose just before dinner, but before she went off to collect food for the pair, Jakob stopped her.

"If you can turn us both invisible," he said, "do you mind if I come with?"

She grinned brightly and offered an arm. Jakob didn't feel any different as he hooked his elbow around hers, but her light weaved around him as it did for her when she danced.

The pair took the elevator to the habitation deck and Lylliana led Jakob through the first door on the left. There, they found a clean and spacious kitchen with a large table for communal dining. Three capillum sat around the table; one he recognized as Naza, while the other two were new. All of them had intricate markings in their colorful fur and wore similar hooded clothing to the captain and her son.

As they passed, the capillum ignored the pair entirely and Jakob couldn't help but feel just like Inspector Aurilius from his novels. He could hear the capillum deep in conversation, but without the mask he couldn't understand a word they were saying.

"They're discussing the Koerribot," whispered Lylliana, leading Jakob toward a door at the back of the kitchen. "It seems our story is already being exaggerated." When Lylliana was sure the capillum weren't looking, she cracked open the door and hurried Jakob inside. They entered a room full of industrial looking machines and storage. There, a pair of trays had been set on a table underneath a wide heat lamp. The smell of fried fish met Jakob's nose as he saw the bright golden fillets and crispy potatoes piled on his plate.

"This is us," said Lylliana, grabbing her tray. They took the food and swiftly retreated to the cabin.

Once they had eaten, Jakob and Lylliana spent some time simply chatting by the windows, watching the wondrous world of sea life beyond the glass. For the next day and a half, the Seacarver wound in and out of the tunnels. Every so often they would rise back up to the surface to weave between the islands only to submerge again when they neared Roane outposts or research stations. The night before they were set to arrive in Roana, the Seacarver finally reached the edge of the Coral Meridian.

"The final stretch," said Lylliana. "All that lies between us and Roana is a short stretch of open seas."

"How long until we're there?" asked Jakob. He was sitting at the edge of his bed, scribbling furiously in his notebook. The end was so close.

"We'll make port by morning," said Lylliana. "You should rest now. You'll need it for tomorrow."

"Soon," said Jakob. "Only a couple pages to go…"

Becoming invisible himself has brought a rush of inspiration that Jakob couldn't help but act on. By the end of the hour, Jakob had written his last word. It was a cliffhanger ending, but one he knew would keep his readers begging for a next entry. Vennamin would love it.

"Proto," said Jakob. "I need you to scan in these pages. Get it to Vennamin the moment you get signal. He held up the lens to his notebook, and Proto flashed a soft blue light along the pages, recording their content.

"That's it then?" asked Lylliana excitedly.

"Well, I'm sure the editor will have some notes," said Jakob. "But, yeah, that's it! I can't believe it's finally over. Just in time for me to start a new chapter tomorrow."

Lylliana chuckled and lay back in her bed with a satisfied smile. "I'm glad I chose you," she said, looking over to him.

"Me too," said Jakob, tidying up his things. "Imagine how bored I'd be right now if I'd decided not to come. I can tell you what, my readers are going to have to thank you because the old ending I was planning was nowhere near this good." He climbed into bed and got comfortable beneath the sheets.

"Do you really think there's a trap waiting for us?" he asked, pulling the covers over his shoulders.

"I don't know," said Lylliana. "Whatever we find there, I'll be with you every step of the way."

Her words calmed the many worried questions floating about his head. After seeing what she did today, he had no doubt he was safe with the girl. "Goodnight, Lylliana," he said.

"Goodnight, Jakob."

Chapter Fourteen

Unity

Faeron stirred to heavy snowfall beyond his wall of glass. Squinting, he sat up in bed and watched the sparkling drifts mask all of Eredith in a swirling curtain of white.

Images of last night's dreams swam laps through Faeron's head as he stared distantly into the snow. He saw silks and smoke, words exchanged with a shadowy information broker, and the dancing girl's impossible might aboard her wondrous vessel. Out of it all, one word reverberated through Faeron's mind: *Roana*.

Suddenly, a realization hit him. Faeron lunged for his notebook, scrawling everything he remembered from last night. His writing was sloppy as he rushed through the dense dream. When he finished, Faeron tossed the journal aside and sprinted from his room in his pajamas.

Storming into the common room, Faeron stopped dead in his tracks. The room looked nothing like how he had left it the night before. Icicles clung to the edges of the ceiling, the tables were draped in colorful cloths, and garlands with shimmering silver tips hung between the shelves of deity figurines. Auri was already up in a festive sweater and comfy looking pants. She stood on her tippy toes as she placed a golden star atop a large totem pole in the corner near the windows; the now star-topped Unity Totem was divided into eight segments, each carved from colored woods native to different nations of Ancient Irasil. Around each band were several little shutters called gifting doors, all locked tight until their nation's day of the festival.

"He finally rises," said Auri brightly as she noticed Faeron, "I know we usually do this together, but with you sleeping away the morning, I couldn't help but get a head start. Oh! Did you see all the snow outside? It's just like the tenth– "

"Auri!" Faeron interrupted urgently. "I think I know how Jakob survives the plague!"

"A Unity Day miracle," Auri grinned and gave the ceiling a thankful glance. "Go on, help me get the Unity Scene setup while you tell me about it."

"Remember when my dad sorted out that one of my dreams took place a year before the plague?" asked Faeron, meeting Auri at a small closet near her bedroom door. "Well, it was Lowsun in Jakob's world then, and it's Lowsun there again now. A year's passed… and it just so happens Jakob is on his way to Roana."

"So… you're thinking that's how he survives," Auri surmised. "The plague never touched Roana…" She looked thoughtful as she disappeared into the closet. There was a thud then the scratching of wood against floor as she reemerged dragging out a long but narrow table, about waist height. Its surface was a diorama of a historical landmark, the Humming Stones, three cracked and mossy boulders in the center of a shrubby savannah landscape.

"There's more," said Faeron, taking the far end of the table and helping Auri walk it across the room. "Jakob is with the dancing girl… Lylliana! That's her name, and she's even more incredible than I thought. She used the light to turn Jakob into a capillum. His body, voice, every bit of him changed. He could even understand Roane. It was so perfectly realistic and yet somehow effortless for her."

"It can't be a coincidence," whispered Auri as they set the table down in the corner just beside the totem. "Host Ithris passes on the Hoststone, and four years later a kytra *this* powerful appears out of nowhere?"

"From the way Mom talked about her, a secret apprentice would be just Ithris' style," offered Fearon.

"Could be… but… hmm," Auri mumbled to herself as she returned to the closet and retrieved a polished white box. Setting it down by the table, she popped off the lid and reached inside, pulling out a soldier figurine. The toy soldier was roughly half a foot tall with incredible detail in its coat of chain mail, crimson headband, and menacing scimitars. "Take these," said Auri, plucking a few more figures out of the box and handing them to Faeron. "I'll dig out the others."

Faeron took the figurines and began to pose them near the edges of the long table, facing the Humming Stones in the center. "The weirdest thing," said Faeron as he placed an Ossuni soldier, covered in furs with a pickaxe in both hands, "is that the dancing girl seemed to be on the run from something. I can't remember the exact conversation, but I do know whatever's after her is ancient and powerful. Maybe Rhun or some other Old Spirit."

"That confirms it," gasped Auri, and Faeron turned to find her with a figurine in each hand. In her left hand was the unmistakable form of Glavius, armored in gold, his eyes radiant like the sun as he held the Hostone overhead. The other figure was robed loosely in black from head to toe, his face completely hidden. Auri held it up for Faeron. "Think about it this way, there isn't a trace of the dancing girl before Jakob, we know she's a master of illusions, and she shows up out of nowhere just after Eamon became Host?" Auri spoke almost at a whisper. "Lylliana… Lyle…"

Faeron stared at the figurine, the idea seemingly absurd. "Lyle, the Deceiver? Whisking Jakob off to Roana in order to… what? Cause the plague? That's insane. Even IF Lyle is real, they're totally different people. The only thing *remotely* similar is their name, and by that logic Lydia would be Lyle too!"

"It's Lyle the *Deceiver* not Lyle the obviously evil. He's supposed to seem trustworthy," said Auri as she brought the figures of Glavius and Lyle to the table. She placed them in the very center, between the boulders, facing off against each other. "Whether Lylliana is with us or against us, I think we can both agree this explains why your mom's been gone so long. She's out there fighting something ancient, potentially alone."

"Without the Hoststone, what hope do any of us have against an Old Spirit?" asked Faeron with a pit in his stomach. "What if I've seen this vision just to learn we don't stand a chance?"

"Don't count us out yet," said Auri, gathering a few more soldiers from the box to complete the scene. Glavius and Lyle were now surrounded on all sides by fierce looking soldiers. "Like I said last night, I think– no, I know why I couldn't shape with the gloves."

"Oh?" asked Faeron as he stepped back from the table and observed their handy work. Staring at the two figures in the middle, it still seemed so unreal to him that he could someday be the one to face Lyle like Glavius did thousands of years ago.

"It's too hard to explain. I have to show you," said Auri, walking over to the sliding glass door and staring out into the heavy snow. "Tonight, when we're all gathered at the Athenaeum to watch the parade, I need you to find an excuse to slip away. We'll meet at the workshop."

"Not tonight," said Faeron definitively. "I won't ditch Lydia and Quinn."

"It'll take fifteen minutes," said Auri. "Just say Mathas needs our help with something. Besides, it *has* to be tonight."

"And why's that?" asked Faeron, folding his arms.

"Because Mathas and your Dad are going to be busy with the festival," said Auri. "Listen, there's a stone in your dad's office that I'm certain is the answer to all of this. Quinn and I are supposed to lock up after we lead the youth group carols." She pulled a golden key from her pocket and showed it to Faeron. "I'll snag the stone before I leave."

"Why not just ask for the stone any other night?" asked Faeron

"Because, Mathas won't let me shape anymore," Auri grimaced. "After the gloves… you know… he told me that we'd taken things too fast, that I needed to spend more time on my meditations."

"And what if he's right?" asked Faeron softly, joining her at the window.

"He's not," Auri demanded. "You know I shape differently. He can't teach me by the same rules he did for you, or Dad, or your mom. Please, let me prove it before I bring it to him. I'll make him say yes."

"Fine," sighed Faeron. "Fifteen minutes, a second more and I'm leaving."

"Ah, don't worry," smiled Auri. "I won't tear you away from your all important smooch."

Faeron blushed as he marched off toward the kitchen to make himself a hot mug of chocolate brew.

"Alright," said Auri. "It's about time I got ready for this thing. Quinn will be here in a couple hours."

"See you on the other side," said Faeron.

Faeron took his mug and settled down on the couch in the dimly lit index room. "Serris," he said, "let's see what's happening down at the park."

The room flickered to life; the walls and ceiling were now an open snowy sky, and the floor changed shades to the tan stone of the Loem Ampitheater stage. Just a few feet in front of Faeron, three figures flickered into existence. Joey and Jodey Kethrow, the sibling news anchors, both had sleek silver hair, despite their relatively young age. They wore matching white blazers covered in pearl sequins as they stood centerstage, interviewing Revna, the weather AI. Revna's cloudy hair was shedding a constant downfall of snow that swirled in drifts about her crystal blue dress, making wondrous patterns on the fabric.

"...Which brings us then, to the question on everyone's mind," said Joey, throwing his hands up toward the heavens. "What's with *all this SNOW?*"

"A throwback," said Revna joyously, "to the tenth anniversary, of course. Now, don't you worry yourselves. Forecast calls for clear skies, just in time for the parade."

"And there you have it," said Jodey, clapping her hands together. "Enjoy the beauty while you can folks, because it won't last long.

I want to say a special thanks to Revna for taking the time to join us today."

"It's my pleasure you two," said Revna before turning to the front of the stage where Faeron was seated, "and to all of you watching, both here in the park and at home, I wish you all a merry evening and a wonderful Unity Week!" Revna gave a bow, her hair flaring with a surge of shimmering snow before she disappeared entirely.

"In just a few short hours," said Joey, walking up and down the stage, "the sun will set, and the first night of Unity shall begin."

"All around the city," Jodey chimed in, "children will rush to their totems as the first doors open to reveal chocomallows and other sugary sweets."

"And of course," Joey said, "the Host himself will be joining us on stage for a few words about this incredible community we've all worked so hard to build."

"But before all that," Jodey announced, "we have some of the most talented acts in all of Eredith performing live from the park. First up, the incredible Erkwrite Dance Company brings us a number from their upcoming ballet, The Fall of Ossun. This is Dance of the Ghost Queen." Faeron's heart jumped at the mention of the Erkwrite Dance Company. This had to be the show Lydia was telling him about.

The amphitheater dimmed as the siblings stepped off to the side, disappearing entirely when they reached the edge of the stage. In their place, a familiar set of three boulders flickered into existence. They were massive with dozens of moss-grown cracks splitting down their sides. A soft hum filled the air. It was a low and warm note, pulsing ever so slightly, as if singing in time with the breeze. Then, came a lone cello, its slow steady song in perfect harmony with the humming stone, and a dozen figures entered from stage right. They were dressed in dark robes, their features shadowed by the dim light. Faeron tried to make out Lydia, but as soon as the figures reached the Humming Stones, they all laid down, limp and motionless, bodies flayed out and heads covered. A spotlight shone on one of them.

The lone figure began to rise, and, as they stood, a storm of ash kicked up all around them. It was like a miniature tornado, masking them for only a moment before it faded. When the ash was gone, the figure was no longer robed. Lydia now stood among the motionless figures, wearing the wondrously sewn silver and navy blue bodysuit of the Ghost Queen. She began to dance.

The Ghost Queen's dance was desperate, an act of mourning as she observed the dead soldiers around her. Stopping at one of her fallen comrades, Lydia reached down and placed her hand on his chest. A storm of ash surrounded the dancer as he rose, his robes replaced by sparkling chainmail. The soldier collected himself and followed after the Ghost Queen as she repeated the motion for each of his companions.

As the warriors came to life, they formed two rows around the Ghost Queen. They held their swords high, in reverence to their queen, but the blades melted in their hands, becoming smokey tendrils of ash. The tendrils snaked around the panicked soldiers' arms, forming chains that tugged them toward the edges of the stage. Kicking and pulling, lashing and ultimately stumbling backward, the soldiers stood no chance against the ashen chains.

The Ghost Queen rushed to the nearest soldier and took his hands, dancing him back toward the center of the stage. So long as they held hands, the chains seemed powerless against the soldier, but the moment she released her grip, the soldier was snared once more. Faeron couldn't help but imagine it was him dancing with Lydia, though he wondered how he'd possibly keep up. Her every motion was fluid, each step a graceful bound in perfect form. The Queen danced ferociously from soldier to soldier, spending only a few seconds with each, leaping desperately toward center stage. Ultimately, her efforts were doomed as the music picked up speed and the chains pulled faster. One by one, the soldiers were dragged offstage. They vanished into a shimmering cloud of ash accompanied by a wailing cry from the orchestral strings.

Alone on the stage once more, the Ghost Queen fell to her knees and dropped her head. Ash surrounded her, but she didn't fight her fate. The queen vanished as the light faded and the music slowed to only the hum of the boulders. The dance was over.

After the dancers returned for a bow, Joey and Jodey took back the stage.

"Serris," said Faeron over the excited chatter of the siblings, "can you connect me with Lydia?"

"I'm sorry," said Serris, popping into the air beside him, "Lydia is still on private. Can I leave a message?"

"No, that's fine," said Faeron, settling back into the couch. "I'll tell her in person soon enough."

Faeron continued to watch different acts take the stage playing music or performing comedy skits. After some time, he slipped into daydream, imagining his dance tonight with Lydia, until a sudden knock at the door jostled him awake.

Faeron leapt up from his seat and rushed out of the index room to the front door of his apartment. There, he found Quinn in a fitted black suit and bronze tie, his fiery hair neatly combed. Logic, fastened to a harness with four metallic legs, sat on Quinn's shoulder and waved.

"I like the tie," said Faeron, holding the door open for his friend.

"Thanks, said Quinn, entering. "It's to match Auri's hair."

"Speaking of…" said Faeron. "I think Auri's still getting ready. We can hang out in the index room until she's done if you want."

"Hold on, I'm just finishing up!" called Auri loudly from her room. "I'll be out in just a second."

A few moments later, she emerged looking like a wholly different person. Her long elegant black dress and dark makeup made the bronze of her irises pop, and her hair was done up, with her shimmering bronze ends securing the rest of her sleek black locks in a fancy bun.

"You going to make that face the whole night?" asked Auri as Quinn stood gawking.

"Sorry," said Quinn. "Are you… uh… ready then?"

"It is just about that time," said Auri. "Faeron, I'd recommend changing soon, unless you plan to pick up Lydia in your pajamas."

"Har har," said Fearon. "I've got a couple hours still, but I will start soon. See you two tonight?"

"Tonight!" said Quinn.

Two hours after they left, Faeron was nearly done getting dressed. He was showered, shaven, and dressed in a new black suit his father had gotten him for his birthday. Staring into the bathroom mirror, Faeron imagined his reflection was Jakob.

"Hey buddy, if you have a hidden talent for dancing, now would be a great time to share," Faeron said to his reflection. His nerves wouldn't stop buzzing now that there was no Auri or index to distract him from the enormity of tonight; his first dance, his first kiss, and, of course... *Roana*. "Alright, Serris," said Faeron, swallowing his nerves. A ball of light popped into the air beside him. "Go ahead and call a tram, Homewood. I think I'm ready for this."

"Tram inbound to elevator T-3," said Serris. "ETA two minutes."

Faeron exited his tram from a cyan transpo tube in the frost-tipped grasses of Homewood Lawn, where pastel-colored townhomes strung with festive lights lined the foot of the colossal northern wall. Sombara Nature Reserve, one of the city's six great towers, loomed over the heavily-forested western end of the lawn, with moss, vines, and flowers climbing up and down the skyscraper's tan windowless face. On the very top of the hundred story tower was the animated statue of Host Sombara, a woman in a long airy skirt and woven top. She stood hunched over slightly, picking stone berries from a large bush and placing them into a basket slung about her other arm.

The still-heavy snowfall did little to damper the moods in the bustling lawn; playing children left trails of footprints in the frosted grass as carolers went from house to house along the wall, singing hymns. A large round skating rink had been set up in front of the nearby Hearth and Heart bakery, a burnt-rose brick building shaped like a giant paw which had the whole lawn smelling of freshly baked dough. It seemed as though half the town was out this afternoon, as everywhere Faeron looked he saw families spending time together, sharing giant doughy orn claws from the bakery or gathered around the Creation Center, further east, to watch the ice sculptors work.

Faeron approached a yellow slice of townhouse just across the lawn from the Heart and Hearth bakery. A small pergola had been constructed over the cement pathway to the front door and strung up with luminous silver strings that formed a sort of gate. At Faeron's approach, the silver strands turned a welcoming green and the strings undid themselves, sliding back around the wooden base to let him pass. Faeron climbed five short steps to a scarlet door with tall panes of glass on either side and the number 27 printed in golden numerals just above a peephole. Swallowing hard, Faeron knocked.

The moment Faeron's knuckle rapped wood, the sound of a chime rang throughout the house. Quick footsteps followed, and several seconds later a pair of young faces peeked through the windows on either side of the door. The wide-eyed boy on the left was three or four; he was still in his onesie pajamas and his short blonde hair was a mess. In the other window was a girl Faeron assumed to be the slightly older sister. A foot taller than the boy, the girl had electric blue locks down to her shoulders and a steely suspicious glare. Faeron knew he definitely had the right house as both children looked like miniature versions of Lydia.

The sound of muffled shouts leaked through the door and both children scampered off further into the house. At last, the door opened, and Faeron could hardly breathe. Lydia stood in the doorway wearing a plunging backless pink dress. Her vibrant hair was down in waves and her matching pink makeup made the blue of her eyes pop more than ever. As the flowery scent of her perfume filled the porch, Faeron's heart had his brain in shackles and he could only stare.

"Sorry about the munchkins," Lydia said, slamming the door shut behind her. "Dad and mom are both working so Cole is supposed to be watching the little devils, but somehow he's *still* in bed."

"I'd never… I mean… I hadn't ever met your siblings," said Faeron, still struggling to find his words. "The kids are adorable. And you… you're stunning."

"Aww, you clean up nice yourself," said Lydia with a big grin as she grabbed the knot of his sleek black tie and pulled it snug. At her touch, streaks of pink erupted across his tie, perfectly matching her dress. "Look at Mister Exclusive," said Lydia, pulling on his tie to get a better look. "That's a Forgeworks Intellitie… those aren't even out yet."

"I didn't even realize," balked Faeron. "It was a birthday present."

"I'll bet that makes this their new suit as well," she fawned. Running her hand down his lapel, she snagged his arm and skipped down the steps. "So, tell me about our secret perch for the parade. I never knew the athenaeum had an outdoor–"

Lydia stopped sharp at the luminous string gateway halfway up the path. Instead of turning green and moving aside, as the strings had for Faeron, they instead turned bright red at the pair's approach, refusing to budge.

"Dad thinks he's so funny," sighed Lydia, breaking arms with Faeron to walk around the gate. "He loves Unity traditions, especially Liar's Traps."

"Like we used to make in Arts and Crafts?" asked Faeron, joining her on the far side of the gate.

"Exactly, fun little traps to keep Lyle out," said Lydia, looking back at the gateway. "Only dad's gotta put his engineering twist on everything, hence the giant gate. It'll let anyone through, but of course dad's rigged it up so sometimes it stops me or Cole. All so he can get a laugh."

"It must be fun having that tradition though," said Faeron, finally finding some semblance of confidence as they set out across the busy lawn. The snowfall was starting to lighten while the narrow sidewalks winding through the grass were beginning to bustle. Everywhere, people were rushing to find spots for the big parade. "Dad loves that kind of thing, but he's always busy keeping the festival running," said Faeron. "When I was young I'd mostly just tag along with him while he worked, but as Auri and I got older, he let us do our own thing."

"So you really don't have any Unity traditions?" asked Lydia curiously.

"Putting up decorations," offered Faeron.

"That's like… the baseline for celebrating Unity," scoffed Lydia. "This simply can't stand. Come with me!"

"Where are we going?" asked Faeron as she skipped across the lawn, leading him toward Sombara Tower.

"To start a new tradition!" Lydia moved like a current of air, her stride more graceful in heels than his in simple dress shoes. As they passed into the woods at the base of Sombara, Faeron couldn't help but find himself staring rather than watching where he was going.

"Look out there," said Lydia, giving his arm a tug.

Faeron stumbled aside, narrowly avoiding a thin branch hanging low over the path.

"A little distracted, are we?" teased Lydia.

"No… I," bumbled Faeron.

"Relax," grinned Lydia, squeezing his hand and running her thumb gently along his knuckles. "I'm flattered."

The base of Sombara Tower was a lattice of several wide roads cutting through a heavy forest. The boughs above were so dense that Faeron could hardly see the colossal wall and tower through the leaves. Lydia wove through the crowds and Faeron did his best to keep up, connected to her by the tips of their fingers. Following the westernmost road, Lydia led Faeron to a clearing that smelled like a medley of dishes, seared meats and cheeses, toasted breads and undertones of garlic, pies, fish, curries, and noodles, all at once. Picnic tables were scattered about the grass and balls of colored light, much like Serris, floated lazily between the tables, casting the whole area in blue and silver. At the edges of the woods around the clearing were several small shacks with lines of hungry Eredithians leading up to their order windows. The pop-up restaurants housed mostly nomad chefs and rotated regularly throughout the year.

"You ever had a silly shake before?" asked Lydia, pulling Faeron into a short line on the close side of the clearing.

"Don't think so," shrugged Faeron, eager to see where this was headed.

"I'm not surprised," said Lydia. "It's a spice drink– *Big* in the Peak, but we only ever get it here around Unity. My whole family's obsessed."

When they reached the front of the line, a kindly looking old man with a thin grey ponytail and tasseled leather vest waved them up to the window.

"Two mystery shakes please," said Lydia.

"Mystery shakes?" asked Faeron.

"You'll see in just a sec," whispered Lydia eagerly.

The old man disappeared into the shack and emerged a minute later with a pair of frozen drinks in neon pink and green cups complete with matching twisty straws.

"Go on," urged Lydia with a giant grin.

"Is it gross or something?" asked Faeron, eyeing the shake suspiciously.

"Don't be so scared, just take a sip."

Faeron pulled hard on the straw and he was met with the pleasant taste of frozen cinnamon and other spices he couldn't place. Apart from the quality, which Faeron couldn't contest, he had no idea what made the shake so special.

"What was that mystery bit about anyway?" asked Faeron, his voice suddenly high-pitched and shrill as a rodent.

Lydia burst out laughing. "I think you've answered your own question."

"It changed my voice!?" squeaked Faeron.

"I don't think you're hitting those octaves normally," giggled Lydia. "Okay, okay, my turn." She took a long sip of her drink, paused a moment, and then said, "So, how do I sound?" Her voice was deep as a whale and coarse as sandpaper. This time it was Faeron's turn to break composure, losing himself to a fit of high-pitch laughing.

"Oh my Glavius," snorted Faeron, his voice still wondrously high. "It's like what I imagine an orn would sound like if it could talk."

"That's right," roared Lydia. "I'm a big bad orn, so gimme all your fish!" She lunged at Faeron, throwing her arms around him. She giggled as she held him, then rested her head on his shoulder. "Thank you, for indulging me," she rumbled in his ear.

"I should be the one thanking you," piped Faeron as Lydia released him. "To our new tradition." He held up his glass and she met him in a toast.

"Now that we've marked the occasion," said Lydia, her voice already returning to its normal melodies, "we should probably start moving. It's not getting any less busy out here."

"We can sip these on the way," said Faeron, "and if anyone holds us up, you can just roar at them."

"I basically have a kytra power," gasped Lydia excitedly.

As Lydia took his hand once more and met his gaze with genuine joy, Faeron felt the heat rush from his palm straight to his cheeks. They drank and walked, having fun with their silly voices as they followed the slow flow of the crowd through Loem Park. The snow was barely even noticeable by the time the pair approached the towering stained glass windows of the Athenaeum. All up and down the street, city workers in bright gold polo uniforms were clearing a path through the crowds and setting up long lines of ropes for parade-watchers to stand behind.

"Hey down there!"

Faeron followed the voice upward to see Auri leaning over the parapets of the Athenaeum's central spire. A second later, Quinn peaked over as well, waving down at Faeron and Lydia.

"I'll be down in just a second to let you in," called Auri. "Come on, Quinn."

"I didn't realize you could go on the Athenaeum's roof!" said Lydia, turning to Faeron. "The view must be magical."

"You can see all four towers and most of the parades," said Faeron excitedly as they climbed up the steps to the massive wooden front doors. It was a minute before Faeron heard a soft *clunk* and the entry swung open. Quinn and Auri stood in the opening, the only souls in the dark Athenaeum.

"Quickly," said Auri, motioning them inside. "We don't want people thinking this place is open."

Glancing back over his shoulder, Faeron could already see heads turning in the crowd, watching him and the others with interest. Lydia whisked inside and Faeron followed. As Auri shut and locked the door, a profound silence overtook the lobby. The only light in the room was shed by Logic on Quinn's shoulder, casting long and shifting shadows along the walls.

"This way," said Auri softly, leading them toward the glass elevator and pressing the soft blue panel. "You all do anything on the way here?"

"A new tradition," grinned Faeron, holding up his colorful cup. "What about you two?"

"The kids were actually really talented," chimed Quinn as the elevator door opened and they all boarded. "I never thought helping out with Unity carols could be so fun."

"Third floor," said Auri and the elevator started to rise. "We just got here a few minutes ago, ourselves. Brought some of the extra donuts from youth group if either of you are hungry."

"What about your dad?" asked Faeron. "Any word?"

Auri shook her head disappointedly.

The elevator door opened and they shuffled out onto a dark carpeted ring overlooking the lightless second-floor reading room. Auri led the pack with Serris just over her shoulder, illuminating the way. Faeron ran his hand along the banister, watching for the familiar break in the bookstacks. At last, they came to a gap in the otherwise unbroken wall of shelves. Barely visible in the regress was a skinny wooden door, tall and arched at the top.

Auri withdrew a small bronze key from a pocket in her pitch-black dress and fiddled with the lock. Pulling open the door, she revealed a narrow stairwell winding up and around the spire. Golden evening light and muffled music poured in through slit windows in the grey stone walls. Quinn was first up the rickety wooden steps with Lydia close behind.

"Faeron, hold up," whispered Auri, grabbing Faeron's arm as he made to follow Lydia. She paused a moment, glancing up the steps to be sure the others were out of earshot. "Things didn't go as planned."

"You don't have the stone?" asked Faeron.

"The display had a different lock," she murmured. "I didn't have time to dig around. Do you know where he'd keep the key?"

"I think there's another set of keys in his desk," said Faeron, thinking back on the many days he'd spent in his father's office, "but you can't just run off and abandon Quinn."

"Not me, us," said Auri. "We'll be in and out in five minutes."

"No way," protested Faeron.

"Listen, we don't even have to *take* the stone," pleaded Auri. "I just want to hold it, just for a minute. Then we can come right back."

"Auri…"

"Faeron please. Just wait for my signal, when your dad starts his speech. I'll say Mathas needs us downstairs. Then, we can leave from the loading bay. If anything, it'll be quicker than my last plan."

Before Faeron could object, Quinn's voice echoed down the stairs. "Hey guys, get up here," he called. "The Parade's starting!"

Faeron and Auri scampered up the steps, their rushed footfall in time with the beating of drums sounding through the windows. They climbed a full spiral around the spire and reached a trapdoor to the roof where Quinn and Lydia were already munching on donuts. There wasn't much room to maneuver, only a narrow walkway circling around the faded blue-shingle spire, but the chest-high parapets ensured they were all plenty secure. The clouds had cleared and the sun, setting below the walls, painted the sky a sherbert of pink and orange. A slight breeze brushed Faeron's skin as he closed the trapdoor and took in his surroundings.

Roped off pathways split the crowds from the park to the great towers, and spotlights from the cinema next door surfed the ocean of faces below. Where he stood, Faeron could see all six towers, the black glass Roethram Academy, the overgrown Sombara Nature Reserve, Cresh Capitol's shimmering golden sandfalls, the Twinfire Towers topped in crimson and violet flame, and the spotlessly white Ibanu Hospital. The statues atop them stood at attention, all looking to Glavius atop the Twinfire Tower Bridge.

The statue of Glavius held up his hands, bringing the crimson and violet flames in each palm together. As he cupped his hands, the flames formed a solid sandstone orb, glowing gold in the last evening light. Watching the spectacle, Faeron and the others finagled themselves until the two couples stood side by side, with the overly large box of donuts propped open on the ledge between them. Lydia rest her head on Faeron's shoulder.

"Hosts from all throughout the ages," came Eamon's voice booming from the statue of Glavius. "Who do you bring to this union?"

"I lead the sand children of Saldun and the mountain guides of Ossun," boomed Host Cresh from the capitol building on the far end of the city. Her massive stone hands shed sand and rock.

"Then they are as one" said Glavius. No sooner had he spoken than a massive golden cloud of sand kicked up all around the statue of Host Cresh, and the whole city rumbled. The sand enveloped her entirely, and when it faded, she was gone. Seconds later, the same golden sandstorm erupted at the foot of Cresh tower. The statue of the host now stood in the cleared street.

"I lead the beast hunters of Mastoba and the seaswords of Voh," spoke Host Sombara next, bowing quaintly with her basket.

"Then they are as one," Glavius said once more, and Sombara too was transported from the rooftop to the forested streets in a whirl of golden sand that shook the city.

"I lead the scholars of Eredith and philosophers of Akai," said Host Roethram atop the nearby academy, his voice old and cracked. Clad in scholarly dress robes, the statue held one palm out balancing three floating orbs of different materials.

"Then they are as one."

A violent vortex of sand came for Roethram as it did the other Hosts.

"I lead the healers of Copaquette and the soothsayers of Kalla," Host Ibanu was the last to speak. He leaned on his large but humble staff, knotted around the hoststone at the top.

"Then they are as one."

With all four statues now on the street, Glavius spoke again. "We come together as eight nations, celebrating our differences."

"So we might be as one," chanted the Hosts in unison, and they began to march.

"Faeron look!" said Lydia, tugging his arm and pointing toward the academy.

Just as Host Roethram began to move, a line of giant horns on heavy carts wheeled around the street corner behind the statue. They thrummed a powerful series of slow reverberating notes that filled the whole street. They were followed by a formation of hefty wheeled drums and then a crowd of figures dressed in all black with featureless white masks.

"Knowledge bearers!" Quinn squealed excitedly, pointing down at the figures. "I submitted an abstract on Logic's new intelligence chip. Wonder if someone's reading it down there right now."

The knowledge bearers moved erratically, lunging from person to person, handing out small papers as they went. Usually containing a factoid, poem, or similar work, Faeron's favorite slip he'd ever received was several years ago and simply stated: "Plenty of cheese ensures a happy life."

"Hey, you can see Sombara's parade now," said Lydia, looking north. The statue of Sombara led a band of great puppet monsters out of the forest. Each monster was held up by a dozen or more performers as they writhed and roared through the streets.

The parades wrapped around the block, doing a wide circle back toward their towers. As they came around the final bend, Auri leapt into sudden motion.

"Excuse me, restroom," she called, squeezing past Lydia. As she shuffled around Faeron, Auri whispered softly, "Be ready, when I get back," then she clambered back down the trapdoor to the Athenaeum.

The statues now stood vigil at the foot of their towers and a golden sand embraced them once more, returning the Hosts to their high perch. A moment of quiet settled over the city, then a spotlight shone on Loem Amphitheater. A lone figure took the stage, not much bigger than a bug from where they were standing. Huge displays on either side of the amphitheater flickered to life and footage from the stage projected across the city's great wall. Everywhere Faeron looked, he could see his father's winning grin and bright golden eyes.

"I have always been fond of history," said Eamon, his voice echoing through the city, "so you will excuse me if I take the opportunity to tell a story. Four thousand years ago, Glavius Adaeus stood on the precipice of peace. Seven nations had signed a pact, and Ossun, the last nation remaining, was a close ally. In that moment, when all seemed won, Lyle made his first strike."

A loud "boo" resonated from the crowd.

"Indeed," laughed Eamon. "In his cunning, Lyle saw an opportunity to take everything Glavius had fought so hard for: peace, unity, a future for humanity. Glavius was outnumbered, ten thousand to one, by soldiers ready to reignite the flames of war. It was only through miracle, that Glavius gained the power to turn Lyle's armies to ash, and left for us the power of the Hosts.

"Twenty years ago," continued Eamon. "I was granted my own miracle. This was no great power like the other Hosts, but a vision. Our great city was prescribed by Glavius but built by human hands. These walls, this miracle, belongs to each and every person here tonight.

The crowd erupted in cheers. As Eamon began to speak again, Faeron heard a squeak. The trapdoor opened and Auri's head poked out.

"Hey Faeron," she called up, "Mathas needs us for something. It'll only take a minute."

"I can go!" volunteered Quinn.

"That's generous," said Auri, "but Mathas said it has to be Faeron."

Quinn looked puzzled but didn't argue as Faeron glanced at Lydia, trying to get a read.

"Go on," she said. "I'm sure it's important."

"Thanks," Faeron squeezed her hand softly and then let go. "Be back in a minute."

He followed Auri back downstairs. As soon as the trapdoor was shut, both broke out in a sprint down the steps. They reached the dark third floor landing and Auri asked Serris for a light. Rushing to the elevator, they rode down to the storage bay.

"Serris," said Auri in the mostly empty room, "get us a tram to the midnight chapel."

"On the way," confirmed the ball of light.

"Hold on!" cried Faeron. "I still haven't agreed to this."

"You're here, aren't you?" asked Auri.

"Like I really had a choice," said Faeron. "If I argued with you, I'd have blown everything."

"So what, are you just–" Auri stopped suddenly, looking behind Faeron.

"What," he asked, spinning around. He didn't see anything out of the ordinary.

"The elevator went back up," said Auri, sounding worried. "It shouldn't have done that unless…"

Sure enough, several moments later the elevator re-appeared, with Quinn and Lydia on board.

"So, what's this really?" asked Quinn, marching from the elevator.

"Like I said," Auri insisted, "Mathas needs us."

"Like he needed you to snoop around Eamon's office after youth group?" asked Quinn. "Or how he needed you to sneak a conversation with Faeron on our way up to the spire? Or maybe how he needed you to run off to the restroom and reappear minutes later conveniently needing Faeron's help? What are the chances Mathas is even here?"

"Low to none," said Lydia coolly.

"Go on, Faeron, tell them," said Auri, but Faeron didn't speak.

Faeron didn't need to meet Lydia's cold glare to know he'd messed up. If he wanted any chance of salvaging this date, honesty was his best option.

"You're really no help," balked Auri. "Fine, you want to know the truth? We're sneaking into Eamon's office."

"What?" gasped Quinn.

"Well, if you don't want to get in trouble," said Auri, "you don't have to come."

"No way!" demanded Quinn. "You don't get to ask me to Unity and then ditch me for an adventure with Faeron. That's not how this works. Where you go, I go."

"Well said," doubled Lydia.

Auri growled with frustration as the tram doors opened. "Fine," she conceded begrudgingly. "Everyone on, but you have to promise, no distractions."

"Oh, I'm sure you won't even notice I'm there," said Lydia shortly.

The tram ride was silent. They sped through the underground, up the walls, and climbed the dome to the very peak of the city. Here, the tram doors opened to a wide hallway, carpeted in crimson and gold, with dozens of doors for trams.

Faeron peaked his head out first, scanning the area. Great crystal chandeliers with dozens of flickering candles lit the long empty entrance hall. "Coast is clear," he whispered, and everyone left the tram.

"Alright, Serris," said Auri, "put us all on private."

"Are you sure this is a good idea?" whispered Quinn as they began walking toward the great golden door at the end of the hall. "I know Faeron's his son and all, but this still feels very, *very* illegal."

"Having second thoughts?" teased Auri.

"Considering what we're about to do," said Lydia, "I'd be concerned if he didn't."

They approached the giant golden double doors engraved with the likeness of two Hosts. In the center was a massive eye with arched handles forming a great golden iris. Auri pulled open the doors just enough to see inside.

"I don't see anyone," she whispered, "but act natural."

They slipped into an expansive cathedral with no ceiling, the lightless abyss above their heads darker than any night's sky. The floor and pews were black marble, and pearly white columns reached up toward the void where they crumbled into spiraling trails of floating debris. The onyx walls found no ceiling, instead, their decorative golden tops made the space look more like a courtyard than an enclosed room. At the far end of the central aisle, was a marble altar and a grand mural that filled the rear wall. It depicted two grand flames, violet and crimson, snaking around each other in a circle.

As Auri and Quinn led the charge down the aisle, Faeron hung back.

"Hey," he whispered to Lydia. "I'm really sorry about what happened. I wasn't... well..." He stumbled through his words, wishing he could tell her it wasn't his idea without it sounding like an excuse.

"It's fine," Lydia insisted, not meeting his look. "Really I get it. Kytra business."

"No I–," Faeron began, but as they reached a break in the pews about halfway down the aisle, Auri and Quinn stopped and waved them over. On either wall was another set of golden doors, leading to a hallway full of prayer rooms, gathering spaces, and, of course, his father's office.

"Quinn's had a pretty good idea," Auri told them.

"We should keep eyes out here," explained Quinn, taking Logic off his shoulder and placing him on a nearby pew. He reached underneath Logic's harness and pulled out a small glass coin. "Logic, can you signal me if anyone comes through here?"

Logic pulsed green.

"We shouldn't be long," said Auri, "but it'll give us one less thing to worry about."

They took the doors on the left to an incredible passage. The floors were sleek white and luminous, and lines of light ran along the corners where the walls met the floor. Much like the ceiling of the chapel, these walls were unworldly, their clear glassy surface covered in watery ripples. Behind the transparent wall, was an endless sea of black, broken only by the many doors lining either side of the passage. The hallway curved around to the right where Eamon's office was at the rear of the building. With large golden double doors carved in the likeness of Glavius, it was impossible to miss.

Auri procured the key and led them inside. Eamon's office was long and spacious, with a wide window at the rear. Through the glass was a flurry of snow, painted by the Crimson and Violet flames of the Twinfire Towers. Their glow cast shifting hues across the dozens of maps on the walls and the long purple carpet draped across the polished tile floor. The only other lights in the room were pinpoints of color, shining in the many display cabinets along the shadowed walls. Hanging masks, hand drawn maps, and historical weapons covered every inch of the walls, and standing candles flickered to life as Faeron and the others entered.

"The key's in here," said Faeron, walking quickly to the large wooden desk resting just in front of the window. He slid open the bottom right drawer, as he'd seen his father do a hundred times, but was surprised by what he found. The drawer contained not only the key, but several dozen fragments of black crystal, the remnants of the Host Stone.

Careful not to touch the crystals, given his last interaction with the Host Stone, Faeron snagged the key and ran over to Auri. "Show's yours," he said.

Auri rushed to a nearby cabinet and unlocked the latch on the glass. Sitting on a shelf at waist-level was a crude orange gemstone, about the size of a plum. The light inside it was brighter than most other echo crystals and pulsed irregularly.

"What is it?" asked Faeron, joining her at the cabinet.

"I've never seen an echo crystal do that before," said Quinn, peeking over her shoulder.

"What do you mean '*do that*'?" Lydia scrunched up her face in confusion as they all gathered around the stone. "It looks like any other crystal to me."

"Only a kytra can see the light of the crystals," answered Auri, plucking the stone from its display, "but this is no ordinary echo crystal. Have you noticed that every other echo crystal, both the ones in Eamon's collections and in stories, are all shades of blue, green, or purple? There's only one exception I could find, an orange crystal wielded by a Host."

"That's impossible," argued Faeron. "Hosts can only use the Hoststone."

"For most, yes," grinned Auri, as if she'd waited weeks for this moment, "but there's one exception; Host Nokruvokani wielded a second relic, a purging stone which could clean any water, known for its unique orange hue. Seeing this stone now, I think I know what made Nokruvokani's relic different from all the others. Look how it glows, like pulsing… energetic…"

"Passionate," Faeron finished for her.

"Exactly," said Auri, staring deep into the pulsing crystal. "When I first discovered passion shaping by watching Host Cresh in the VUEs, I couldn't understand why I still failed to use the gloves. Then, I had this thought: what if the light of peridom is more like a spectrum, and we kytra are attuned to different parts of it?"

"And if we can be attuned to different parts of the spectrum," added Quinn, "why wouldn't the gems be the same way?"

"This gem could be proof of it," Auri's excitement was impossible to hide. "To our knowledge, nobody has ever been able to shape with this stone, not even Evolice. Passion shaping might just be the key. Now, you'd better step back, we don't know what this is going to do."

Everyone made a wide triangle around Auri, watching eagerly as she shut her eyes. Auri's breathing sped up, her fists clenched, and her brow furrowed. Her chest began to rise and fall rapidly and Auri's eyes shot open, burning with fierce bronze light.

"This has to work," shouted Auri, holding out the stone. Sure enough, fierce bronze light erupted from the crystal. The room grew bright as all around the flames roared above their candles. Heat rushed over Faeron as Quinn and Lydia looked on in awe. "I'm doing it!" yelled Auri. "I–"

Craaack

The sound split the air as the office went dark, every candle extinguishing all at once. A moment later a wave of cold washed over Faeron.

"Auri! Are you okay?" burst Quinn, rushing forward.

"I'm fine," she panted. "Honestly, I'm great!"

In the low light, Faeron saw Auri hold up the stone. The glow in the heart of the crystal made it plain to see that the damage was minimal, a small splinter on one face.

"This'll prove to Mathas–" Auri began, but she was cut off by a sudden beeping.

Quinn held up the coin in his hand, now blinking red. "Someone's in the chapel," he said frantically. "It could be nothing but…"

"I'll check it out," offered Lydia. "I'm no help here anyway."

"I can go as well," added Faeron. "If it's Dad, we'll buy you some time to lock up the gem and get out."

Faeron handed Auri the desk key and then followed Lydia back toward the door. As they stepped out into the hall, Faeron paused a moment.

"Hey, Lydia," he said. "I want to apologize again, for earlier–"

"Listen," Lydia interrupted and took his hand. "Back at the athenaeum, I could tell you weren't comfortable leaving. Auri's your best friend, and she asked you a big favor. I get that, and I respect you for having the courage to help her out, even tonight. Now, had you snuck off with any other girl, you'd be in a lot more trouble right now."

"You're really not mad?" asked Faeron meekly.

"Mad? No," said Lydia. "I just wish—"

"AURI!"

Quinn's horrified shriek sounded through the door, causing both Faeron and Lydia to jump. They didn't waste a second, rushing back into Eamon's office. Quinn was behind Eamon's desk, huddled over something, and Auri was nowhere in sight.

"Auri, wake up! Please, say something!" Quinn was choked up shouting.

Faeron sprinted over, finding Auri lying limp behind his father's desk.

"What happened?" blurted Faeron, rushing to her side. In one hand she still held the key while the other was wrapped around a shard of the Host Stone. Her eyes were wide open and filled with fiery bronze light as she stared blankly at the ceiling.

"I don't know," whimpered Quinn. "She was just putting the key back when she stood up all still. I heard her mumble something, *roam* or maybe *home*. Her face was pale, and it was like she was looking past me. Then, she just fell."

"Serris, take us off private," ordered Faeron desperately. "We need help, NOW!"

"Auri's father is in the chapel now, meditating," reported Serris as the ball of light popped into the air beside Faeron. "Shall I interrupt him?"

"Vox is home!?" gasped Faeron. He knew the chapel was always the first stop for Auri's father when he got back from his trips.

"That must be who set off Logic," said Quinn.

"Yes, interrupt him!" cried Fearon. "Tell him it's Auri. Tell him she's in trouble!"

The minutes that followed felt like an eternity as Faeron and the others waited for help to arrive. Heavy footsteps in the hall outside finally broke the silence. The doors to the office burst open, revealing the massive frame of Vox Lem.

Vox's normally neat dark hair was longer than normal and his beard was shaggy. His blue-grey eyes scanned the room, resting on Faeron and the others. "What happened here?" roared the diplomat, and Faeron and Quinn explained everything.

"Just like ten years ago," whispered Vox, "only, we don't have Evolice. Damn it all."

"Vox, I'm so sorry," said Faeron. "I didn't think–"

"No time for that now," said Vox, determination in his voice as he effortlessly hoisted Auri into his arms. "We need to get her to a hospital."

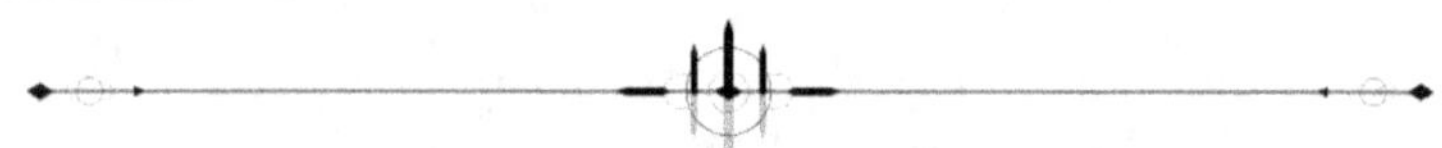

Faeron didn't know how long he and the others had been sitting in the spotless white waiting room, hours at least. The whole room smelled like sanitary wipes and, through the tall windows, Faeron could see the crowds in the park start to disperse. Every so often, the doctor came around just to tell them nothing had changed. Auri was stable, despite her coma. In fact, medically there seemed to be nothing wrong with her at all.

Eventually, the elevator doors slid open and Eamon stepped out.

"Dad!" exclaimed Faeron, shooting up from his seat.

"Thank goodness you're alright," said Eamon as he marched across the room and threw his arms around Faeron. In that moment, Faeron forgot all about Lydia and Quinn. He buried his face in his father's shoulder and tears ran trails down his cheeks.

"I'm sorry, Dad," he wept. "I'm so sorry."

"I know," soothed Eamon. "It's alright. She'll be alright."

When they broke contact, Eamon turned to Lydia and Quinn. "Come on," he said, "let's get you all home."

"No!" demanded Quinn. "I'm staying here. I won't leave until Auri wakes up."

"It could be hours or days," warned Eamon, Faeron could tell from the fire in Quinn's eyes that he wasn't going to back down. "Alright," Eamon sighed, "just be sure to check in with your parents."

From the hospital, Eamon and Faeron dropped off Lydia at her home. Faeron hugged Lydia goodnight and she gave him a kiss on the cheek.

"I know it's not what you were hoping for," she whispered in his ear, "but there's a whole week to celebrate. Sleep well tonight, Faeron. I'm sure Auri will be okay tomorrow."

When the door shut behind Lydia, Faeron and Eamon began the trek back to the Twinfire Towers. There was hardly a word between them as they walked. That night, Faeron slept at home in his childhood bed. As he lay in the satin covers, Faeron couldn't help but cry again. He wept for Auri, for his inability to help her, and, more selfishly, for his date gone awry. The one beacon of light in the darkness was a single word still living at the back of Faeron's mind... *Roana.* Whatever else, his dreams tonight were sure to bring answers.

CHAPTER FIFTEEN

THE LAST DREAM

Steam from the shower fogged the bathroom mirror as Jakob dressed, pulling on a set of ash grey garments Lylliana had left beside his bed that morning. What she had described as a traditional capillum tunic looked more like loose monk's robes on Jakob as the tattered ends of the fabric brushed the tiled floor. Beneath the loose outer cloth was a flexible material that fit Jakob well and was the only thing keeping the tunic from slipping right over his shoulders.

As Jakob fumbled to figure out what he was supposed to do with a long strap hanging just above his waist, he felt the ship shift and slow. Jakob steadied himself against the counter then went out into the cabin, the strap still hanging limp in one hand.

Lylliana sat at the edge of her bed in the same black sundress she'd worn that day in the park. Her dark wavy hair tumbled freely down her back as she stared out the wall of glass surrounding their room. The shallow sea beyond was a tropical menagerie of colorful fish and fields of vibrant reefs stretching out into the distant depths. As Jakob approached, Lylliana turned and chuckled.

"What's so funny?" asked Jakob.

"Your tunic is backward," laughed Lylliana. "Here, let me help you. Pull your arms in real quick."

He did as she asked, then she grabbed the sleeves and rotated his tunic.

"Now that we're on the right way, you can put your arms back through and this can go…" Lylliana pulled the strap under his left arm, up around his right shoulder, and looped it to the left side of his waist. "Perfect!"

Meanwhile, the ship had come to a complete stop near a series of jutting rocks overgrown with coral.

"Is this it?" gulped Jakob, excitement gripping his chest.

"We'll moor here and take the Seasprinter to shore," said Lylliana, going to the bedside table where the silver helmet rest. "Are you ready to find your answers, Koerribot?"

"You'd think after everything I've seen, the shock would have worn off," said Jakob, "but it's still so surreal. How many humans have set foot on Roane soil in the last millennia? A handful at most."

"And you're as deserving as any of them," said Lylliana, pressing the helmet into Jakob's hands. "Soon, we'll know the truth of Rotier's fate."

After pinning Proto to his chest, Jakob once again donned the Koerribot's helmet and rainbow light flared from Lylliana's eyes, raging through her dark curled locks. Jakob's limbs stretched and extended until his tunic fit perfectly and a thick layer of charcoal fur covered every inch of his skin.

Lylliana eyed him up and down. "The Koerribot looks good on you," she said, then made for the elevator.

They rode up to a long white hallway with half a dozen capillum rushing between the crew quarters, bathroom, and kitchen. It was no doubt a changing of the shift. They stopped suddenly as Jakob stepped from the elevator, all eyes on him.

"So he is real," he heard one of them whisper, their strange Roane words untangling themselves in Jakob's ear.

"Koerribot!" called a nearby capillum, wide and muscular with an airy vest over his black fur striped with navy dye. "I'd be lying if half o' me didn't think you a myth. But here you are, real as the Seacarver itself."

"After all these years," an older-looking capillum, silver haired and thin, crowed from a nearby doorway, "why now, Koerribot? Why return for this job?"

"Enough!"

Temril Takata's commanding voice silenced her crew as she marched from the opposite end of the hall. "The Koerribot has joined us, it's true. To many of you, the Koerribot may seem as a celebrity, but you will do well to remember that his authority on this vessel is absolute. I trust you will treat him with the respect of his position."

"Aye, Captain," called the crew, returning to their bustle.

"Forgive them," Temril said, approaching Jakob and Lylliana. "Aeryll has the Seasprinter prepped for launch. It'll be just the four of us, whenever you're ready."

"Lead the way," said Jakob.

Jakob had forgotten just how fast the Seasprinter could skim the open waters as fierce winds whipped his robes and salted spray from the sea spattered his face. The droplets felt strange in his fur, as Jakob still marveled at his new body. He'd never been able to grow a beard, let alone a blanket of hair from head to toe. He leaned against the sleek white rail of the Seasprinter's bow, observing the detail in his long lanky hands.

"Koerribot, look," said Lylliana, pointing dead ahead.

At the edge of cloudy grey sky was a cluster of dark silhouettes jutting above the horizon.

"Skyscrapers?" asked Jakob.

"No, not buildings," said Lylliana. "Trees."

Jakob stared in awe. He'd always heard Roane forests were so tall that entire cities were built in their boughs, but he'd never imagined the treeline would be visible from this distance.

"Proto," said Jakob, "can you record this? I want to remember every detail when I'm writing later."

"Brought to sea, stripped of the grid's power, and reduced to a simple camera," groaned Proto from Jakob's robes. "Becoming a capillum has made you cruel."

"Oh what a hard life you–"

Jakob was cut off by a sudden high note ringing from the back of the boat.

"What's that?" asked Jakob.

"Our beckons," said Lylliana, her hair a wild tangle of technicolor flames, thrown about in the wind. "We should join the captain downstairs."

Between the sway of the sea and his unfamiliar legs, Jakob was clinging to the railing with each step as he followed Lylliana to the door at the back of the boat. Entering the stairwell, Jakob and Lylliana descended into the narrow hallway lined with all manner of buttons, switches, monitors, and capillum devices Jakob had never seen before. Temril stood before a wide screen, swiping between photo-realistic models of ships on the display. Settling on what looked like a long rusted freight ship, she leaned in toward a microphone extending from the steel-topped desk.

"Initiating physical camouflage," the captain said.

A humming sound filled the chamber and the ground beneath Jakob's feet began to vibrate. It lasted only a minute before the sound died and there was just the sway of the sea.

"Physical camouflage deployed," came Aeryll's voice from the monitor.

Stepping back from the controls, Temril turned to Jakob and Lylliana.

"We'll be docking soon," said the captain. "Aeryll and I will handle the business with the Counselor. How long will you need at land?"

"It's an hour's ride to the dome," Lylliana said as she joined Temril at the screens. "From there, well… it depends on what we find. I'll signal you as soon as we're on our way to the pickup point."

"We'll hold the Seasprinter in the fishing lanes," said Temril, "but the generators can only maintain the disguise so long. Be safe but swift."

Taking a seat to steady his wobbly legs, Jakob watched on a small screen as a yellow blip approached what he assumed to be land. Sure enough, he felt the ship losing speed.

"I'm heading up to help Aeryll dock," said Temril. "You're free to join me on deck. Kipotke Bay is no bustling Gau port, but it's still quite the sight."

"We'd be delighted," said Lylliana happily, skipping after the captain.

Jakob followed the pair back upstairs, until Temril paused sharply at the door.

"You're best off hiding yourselves from here on in," said the captain. "There'll be a close eye on us, no doubt."

"Wise as ever," said Lylliana. The fire in her eyes and hair flared brighter, and suddenly, Temril was staring right past them.

"Very good," said the capillum, opening the door and leading them out onto the deck.

Jakob was surprised to see the ship looked nothing like it had just minutes before. Gone was the sleek white floor and rails, with old rusted metal taking their place. The deck was wider, and even the observation window overlooking the steps had changed shapes. Jakob could only assume this was the physical camouflage the captain had referenced.

Just off the bow, massive trees, triple the size of Centra's skyscrapers, dominated the cloudy horizon, their enormous canopies hanging far over the crystal green waters of the bay. There were several other boats further out on the idyllic sea, but most were strange-looking fishing vessels, long and angular with giant sails.

"A signal!" chimed Proto suddenly. "Jakob, there's a network here."

"One you can connect to?" asked Jakob excitedly. He wondered what troves of data the capillum had stored in their networks.

"Yeah it's–"

"Better if you don't," called Lylliana over the crashing seaspray. "An unidentified human device connecting to the Roane network would trigger a million alarms."

"Covert, smart," sighed Proto. "Guess I'll just keep on with half a brain."

Their ship passed into the shadow of the trees and closed in on a lone pier jutting from a black-sand beach. Two figures stood waiting about halfway down the walkway, one, clearly capillum, towering above their human companion. The capillum had darkened ends to her silvery-white fur and a regal purple tunic covered in dozens of golden jeweled brooches. Beside her, the human looked almost like a child in comparison. Not only was he several feet shorter than the capillum, but his face was young, clearly closer to Lylliana in age than Jakob. He had dark skin and long dreadlocks with a floral pattern shaved into one side. From his silver robes, tailored specifically for a human, Jakob knew this could only be the human counselor to Roana.

Close to shore, all manner of strange and colorful birds swooped through the air, their mesmerizing songs a chorus over the crashing waves. What Jakob first thought to be lily pads, leapt into the air, revealing frog like bodies that bloated to float on the breeze. As the Seasprinter pulled up alongside the dock, Temril secured the boat and lowered the ramp.

"Where'd you find this one then?" called the capillum over the dying engine of the Seasprinter. "Looks like you dragged her right off the seafloor."

"Empoleo's private collection, if you'll believe it," said Temril, strutting down the deck with open arms.

Jakob looked to Lylliana for direction, but she raised a hand, giving him pause.

"Oh ho, don't let the counselor hear such slander," laughed the capillum, meeting Temril in a hearty embrace.

Several moments later, Aeryll emerged from the stairwell and joined his mother on the dock.

"Counselor VuLukau," said Temril, "I'd like to introduce my son, Aeryll."

"A spitting image," said the Counselor as she and Aeryll exchanged a mutual bow.

"If I may," the human Counselor spoke up hesitantly. "I can't help but wonder if this…" he motioned toward the rusted transport, "is the safest option."

VuLukau chuckled. "Counselor Ma-Ikkut, you have much to learn about appearances."

As the four figures walked down the dock toward land, Lylliana waved Jakob on. They followed from a distance, despite the fact that nobody there could see them. When Temril and the others took a left toward a sleek metallic shack down the beach, Lylliana and Jakob made straight for the massive fence at the edge of the forest. The bars of the fence were thick, with abundant flowers and vines growing through the cracks. Set into the metal was a large gate.

"Assuming the counselor held up his end of the bargain…" Lylliana said, pulling open the door.

Jakob had to push through a lush curtain of branches as they pushed into the forest's dense underbrush. There were no clear paths on the far side of the fence and hardly enough room to stand in the dense foliage. The smell of fruit and flowers overpowered the wet and heavy air as wide leaved trees blocked out nearly every inch of the sky. What little light leaked through the branches and slits in the fence quickly faded into the black depths of the forest. Jakob could hardly see twenty feet into the darkness.

"How are we supposed to get anywhere in here?" asked Jakob, turning to Lylliana, her fiery light a fantastic contrast to the shadowed forest around them.

Facing the darkest part of the woods, Lylliana raised her hand and a brilliant blue glow shone from her fingertips. The light pulsed, as if in code. Several seconds later, there was a response in the darkness. Something, deep in the woods, was pulsing back at them in similar patterns.

"Our rides are here," said Lylliana, lowering her hand.

The creatures approached without a sound. In fact, Jakob didn't realize they were there until the pair of hulking silhouettes were only a few feet away. Their massive antlers suddenly lighting up the foliage in an incredible display of bioluminescence. In their glow, Jakob saw two enormous elk-like creatures with white diamond markings down their snouts. He had never witnessed anything like them.

"They're always so majestic to see with a fresh set of eyes," said Lylliana, pulling Jakob closer. Feeling his hesitation, she turned and said, "Don't worry. Kelvoa are regal animals, smarter than most people you'll meet. In fact, they can even see the light of peridom."

Still somewhat apprehensive, Jakob moved cautiously through the underbrush, trying his best not to startle the creatures. At their approach, the kelvoa bowed down on one knee and lowered their massive heads.

"Go ahead, climb aboard," said Lylliana, effortlessly swinging herself onto the back of one of the kelvoa. The creature rose to its grand full stature, and Lylliana now towered above Jakob, even in his capillum body.

"It'll hold me like this, right?" asked Jakob, running a hand along the remaining kelvoa's maned neck. Its fur was thicker than any elk or deer but soft to the touch. "I'd imagine I'm much heavier than a human."

"Of course," giggled Lylliana. "Though, it's a good thing they only understand visual language. Kelvoa are proud beasts, after all."

"I didn't mean—"

"I'm just toying with you," Lylliana smiled. "Now, hop on. We're in a hurry, remember?"

Jakob awkwardly swung one unfamiliar leg over the creature's back and hoisted himself into a sitting position. As alien as his limbs were to him, Jakob could tell they were made for climbing. The capillum had evolved in the trees of this wondrous continent, after all.

As the kelvoa rose, Jakob clung tight around its neck to keep his balance. Once again, Lylliana let out a pulse of light from her hands, and the creatures seemed to understand. They began at a quick trot before breaking out into a gallop. Despite their enormous size and incredible speed, the kelvoa's muffled footfall was impossibly silent.

Jakob found his capillum eyes to be exceptionally adapted to the lightless forest, as the dim glow of the kelvoa's antlers were enough to let him see dozens of feet in any direction. The heavy brush soon gave way as the forests became open and seemingly devoid of life, though Jakob couldn't shake the feeling something was lurking just beyond the edges of his sight. Birdsongs faded to the far upper branches, and even the chirping of bugs was gone.

"Hey, Lylliana–" Jakob began, but she raised a hand to her lips. Suddenly, Jakob heard her voice in his head.

The predators of this land hunt on sound alone. Silence is our ally here.

Understood, thought Jakob.

They rode for nearly an hour, a comfortable experience, despite the lack of a saddle. Occasionally Jakob would see twinkling specks of light above them, no doubt the fabled tree cities of the capillum. Though he knew Rotier lived in one such city, Jakob couldn't fathom how they were supposed to climb up from all the way down here. Perhaps there was an elevator where they were going.

To Jakob's surprise, they didn't stop at any great tree or elevator, but a pearly stone dome built right into the forest floor. The kelvoa returned to one knee, as they had before, and Jakob and Lylliana dismounted.

As the creatures trotted back into the lightless forest, Lylliana's voice echoed in Jakob's mind.

It should be around here somewhere… she said, her arm barely illuminated by the flames burning from her eyes as she ran one hand along the dome. *Can your AI give us some light?*

"Proto," whispered Jakob as loud as he dared, "illuminate that stone for us."

"One pocket sun, coming–" Proto began loudly, but Jakob clasped his speakers, shushing urgently.

"Quietly!"

Light flooded the forest, and Jakob was blinded. His eyes took a moment to adjust, then Jakob finally got a good look at the world around him. The mossy floor was carpeted in thousands of mushrooms while clusters of spindly leafless plants rose like twisted purple street poles from the soil. There was only a single tree in sight, but its size exceeded even the wildest rumors; Proto's light couldn't even capture its full width at the base. Up and down its seemingly endless trunk were hundreds of enormous pale-skinned creatures. They were clearly agitated, crawling over each other as they bared their fangs and spread their wide fleshy wings threateningly.

Those are akrul, Lylliana's voice was in Jakob's head. *Much nastier cousin of bats. Completely blind so long as we don't make another sound… Just keep still… A bit longer now… here it is!*

Vines of green energy leapt from her hand and shaped themselves into the outline of a door. As the entryway slid open, a grating sound filled the silent forest. It seemed the disturbance was the last evidence that the akrul needed to pinpoint Jakob and Lylliana. With a chorus of hellish shrieks, they leapt from the trees, swarming the sky.

"In here, hurry!" cried Lylliana, grabbing Jakob by the arm as the creatures began to dive. She pulled him sharply through the passage and slammed the door behind them. Outside, they could hear a dozen claws scratching violently at the stone.

"Can they get in?" gasped Jakob, realizing he hadn't breathed in half a minute.

"We're safe."

As Jakob caught his breath, he took in his surroundings. In the very center of the hollow dome was an emerald crystal, set upon a stone pedestal. The floor was smooth, almost impossibly so, though the walls weren't so plain. Carvings wound in rings around the room, strange symbols that Jakob didn't recognize.

"Hey Proto, what does this say?" asked Jakob, examining a series of symbols.

"Nothing in my standard bank on this language," confessed the Ai. "But, from the looks of it, our friend here seems to know."

"Coordinates," Lylliana answered as she held a ball of light in her hand, using it to study a segment of the inscription. "This is an Atomic Dome, the best way for kytra like us to travel incognito."

"Normal transportation would leave a trace," Jakob supposed. "How does it work?"

"You remember in our cabin, when I moved your helmet to my hands?" Lylliana dissipated the light in her palm and approached the stone in the center of the room. "Same idea, bigger scale."

Lylliana ran her hand over the crystal, causing it to flash dark green. Jakob was expecting some dramatic change, but the only noticeable difference was the return of silence. The scraping of claws was gone.

"Welcome," said Lylliana, "to Old Vaerorr Hallow." She went to the section of wall they'd come in through, and, at her touch, the door reappeared. With a grating sound, the entry slid open of its own accord.

They exited the dome to the grey-bark floor of a cavernous tree-hollow. Darkness settled in the top of the cavern, making it impossible to get a true scope of the space, but a monstrous opening splitting the far wall revealed it was no less than a dozen stories tall. Through the gaping hole, Jakob could see a network of hulking branches and the zipping tail-lights of flying trams. The smell of sap hung heavy on the still air and a constant pecking noise rang out all around them. Straining his eyes, Jakob could make out thousands of shifting shapes clinging to the shadowed walls like living wallpaper.

"Those aren't akrul, I hope," said Jakob, and Proto's light flicked up to the wall. At this distance, Jakob couldn't make out the wall in any detail, just masses of grey crawlers on the bark.

"From my scans they look like some kind of worm," said Proto, " but not any species I've ever indexed, at least not that I can remember."

"Drill worms, eating the dead tree," said Lylliana, "Atomic Chambers are built where nobody would bother to look. In this case, the half-rotten corpse of the great-tree Vaerorr."

There were no stairways or other doors out of the hollow, and the only object in sight was a silver telescope on a stand, like something Jakob would expect to find at a nature park but far more ornate. A series of tickers displayed numbers along the side of the telescope and a small green gemstone twinkled on top. Lylliana motioned Jakob over to the telescope as she peered through.

"Let's see, there's Katorr," said Lylliana as she pointed the lens to a distant tree. "Too high… No… Ah, Alythau branch, just east from there and… got it! Hurry, take hold." She reached out toward Jakob.

Jakob did as he was told. No sooner had his fingers wrapped around her palm then he felt his whole body wring through his center. The world became a blur, and, next thing he knew, Jakob was standing on a branch, wide as a city road and flat on top.

It was at least half mile of empty branch-road from where Jakob stood to the tremendous trunk of a much healthier looking great tree. Clusters of bulbous bark structures grew from either side of the road, and hundreds of similarly colossal branches criss-crossed overhead. Plenty of light filtered down through openings in the canopy far above, where dozens of alca-like transports sailed freely through the wide open spaces between the branches.

Despite the many home-like pods on the street, and the abundance of life beyond, there wasn't a person in sight.

"Is the whole branch closed off for the investigation?" he asked as he walked to the bark railing that ran along the edge of the road. Peering over the edge, he saw a labyrinth of branches disappearing into the lightless depths below. It was impossible to tell just how high up they really were.

"Crime in Roana is taken very seriously," said Lylliana, "and Rotier is an ex-counselor. We shouldn't have any interruptions."

Lylliana began down the branch toward the trunk and Jakob followed. As he walked, Jakob continued to study every inch of the forest.

"You're getting all this, right Proto?" he asked.

"Oh, you wanted me to film?" asked Proto. "Just kidding, of course I'm getting this."

Beyond the tips of the longest limbs was a huge expanse of darkness. Where other branches might once have filled the space, there was now only the barren corpse of the great-tree Vaerorr.

Its top a rotten and jagged stump, and a short way down its ashen bark was the hollow they'd been in only moments before. It was incredible the miles of distance they had traveled in an instant.

"Rotier's home," said Lylliana, stopping at a natural walkway splitting off to a round bark building. The single-story pod-shaped building had a few round windows in the front, but there wasn't a single light on inside. "This is it, Koerribot."

"Do we just… go in?" whispered Jakob.

"Stay behind," said Lylliana. She paused as she grasped the old wooden handle, turning back to Jakob, a seriousness settled into her young brow. "And be careful what you touch. There's no telling who else has been here."

Deja vu flooded over Jakob as he stepped into Rotier's foyer. The braided reed rug, portly windows, and cubbies grown right from the bark walls, it was exactly as he'd seen a thousand times in the Quisitive docuVUE.

"No sign of her," whispered Lylliana, pacing across the rug to the shelves.

"The last Koerribot?" asked Jakob.

Lylliana nodded and began poking through the shelves. "She was an actress, a master of illusions. I've never seen someone take to the helm like she did."

"And the pen is one of her illusions then," reasoned Jakob. He went to the sturdy desk where Elliot Jay had interviewed Rotier. Though there was nothing on top of the desk, several drawers lined the far side. They were unevenly carved with small brass handles.

One by one, Jakob pulled open the drawers, finding them already cleaned out. Jakob guessed the investigators must have taken anything of interest from the home, though he hoped they'd missed the imported pen. Just as Jakob finished checking the last drawer, he noticed another handle dead center, just beneath the lip of the desk.

Sliding open the wide but narrow compartment, Jakob found a stack of papers and several writing utensils. The top sheet was a sketch, drawn with a shaky hand; the creature it depicted looked like an elephant with large sacky growths all up and down its back. Jakob was so fascinated by the strangeness of it, that it took him a moment to notice the silver pen resting against the edge of the drawer.

Jakob's heart leapt. From the signature silver base and black-stone grip to the fine gold cursive Q at the bottom, there was no doubt in his mind this was a Purvian; his pen back on the ship was exactly the same. Just as he'd seen in the docuVUE, Rotier's pen had a modification, an orange gemstone fixed to the very end of the cap. It was flawlessly cut and Jakob could swear a faint light came from deep inside the stone.

"Hey Proto," said Jakob quietly. "The gem on the end of this pen, is it glowing for you?"

"Glowing how?" asked Proto, and Jakob was certain.

"Found it!" He called out to Lylliana. "And it's got a gemstone just like my helmet."

"Excellent, Koerribot" she said, prancing over to the desk. "Let me see it."

Jakob handed Lylliana the pen.

"Please, be good news," whispered Lylliana, barely audible as she ran her thumb over the stone. "I need you to be alright."

The light inside the stone shone brighter than before and its radiance began to spill from the gem in thick plumes of golden smoke. The incredible gas poured down over Lylliana's legs and swirled about her ankles. Expecting what he saw in his dream, Jakob was surprised when the smoke didn't spread further. It simply stuck to Lylliana. He was about to ask if perhaps she hadn't used it right when the gemstone flared even brighter.

Suddenly, the gas burst into golden fire. Shock spread across Lylliana's face as she collapsed to her knees and shrieked in pain. The flaming gas contracted into rope-like threads that bound tight to Lylliana, trapping her on the floor.

"What do I do?" cried Jakob as he rushed around the table, reaching for the pen.

"STOP!" Lylliana's screamed and her voice flooded Jakob's mind. His body was no longer his to move, his limbs disobeying his will. Jakob came to a screeching halt in front of Lylliana. She too had stopped, her body and the fiery chains holding her completely frozen in time.

Run— aagh! Jakob, you need to run! Her voice was pained and desperate in Jakob's mind. *Don't touch me, you can't help, just run!*

I won't leave you, Jakob protested.

There's no time to argue, I can't protect us both, her thoughts were strained, the words fading in and out. *The helmet will hold long enough, even without me. Find an airstation and get to Kokota Island. Wait at the southmost beach for pickup. Go, now!*

Time snapped suddenly back into place as Lylliana writhed on the floor. Jakob hesitated, watching the burning chains spread up her neck.

"GO!" her command reverberated through Jakob's thoughts, drowning his protests and forcing his feet to move. He sprinted from the home and cut up the street. The world was a blur as he raced toward the trunk, no idea where he was headed.

Jakob neared a massive arching doorway, built right into the bark of the trunk, and the entryway slid open automatically. Rushing headlong into a massive and bustling chamber, Jakob tripped straight through a line of police rope blocking off the door he'd just come through. He fell face first down a couple short steps, drawing the attention of a dozen passing capillum.

As Jakob got back to his feet, he noticed that the capillum here were dressed much differently than those on the Seacarver. Many wore flowing robes and the patterns painted in their fur were much subtler. Fortunately for Jakob, the chamber seemed to be a thorough way so nobody stayed to gawk too long. They moved in groups, chatting as they flitted between the dozens of passages around the edges of the room. Each doorway had a color coded sign with symbols Jakob couldn't read.

"Proto, forget secrecy," whispered Jakob so the other capillum wouldn't hear him speaking unified, "we need to get out of here. You still see that network?"

"Of course," Proto said, "should I connect?"

"Do it, find us the nearest station!"

"Connecting now…" Proto paused a moment, and when he spoke again, Roane words left his speakers, unscrambling themselves in Jakob's ears. "Oh, wow," he said, "Jakob, this is incredible. I've never processed anything like it."

"Gawk later," insisted Jakob, looking around nervously. "We gotta get out of here." He had no idea what Lylliana's enemy looked like, but was sure they'd recognize the Koerribot in an instant.

"I found blueprints for the tree!" called Proto. "There's a station close by. Third passage on the left, yellow sign."

Jakob tore across the crowded room and up the passage, bumping his unfamiliar shoulders as Proto guided him.

"Left at the fork! Then right, here!"

The hallways reminded Jakob of a colossal anthill, with organic and uneven walls that turned, rose, and split off seemingly at random. Softly glowing petal lamps hanging from the wall looked grown rather than made, and the floor was carpeted in well-trodden moss. After a couple turns and a steep climb, Jakob finally came to another set of double doors. They slid open to reveal a much wider branch with dozens of transports parked along both sides. The station was alive with people boarding on and off transports or waiting under naturally grown awnings.

"Proto," said Jakob, joining the crowds on the branch, "Any public transportation to Kokota Island?"

"Doesn't look like it," said the AI. "Most of these are private."

"We'll find someone," said Jakob.

"That's about a two hour flight south from here, and we don't have a single Teterra… that's their currency."

"I'll convince someone," insisted Jakob. "I have to. Besides, I'm good at stories."

"If it's our only option," sighed Proto. "Looks like there's two private transports already headed that direction… Blue one, twelfth on the right and silver just a bit further on the left.."

"Good work," said Jakob as he walked briskly along the branch. "Download whatever you need and disconnect from the network. We don't want to risk anyone following us, especially if we're asking a stranger for help."

Proto let out a low groan. "There goes my mind again. I'll grab some local dialects and maps first, just in case."

Jakob moved quickly through the crowds of the station, doing his best to look hurried but not aggressive. There were fewer branches in this area, and all around the open air, transports formed neat traffic lanes that spiraled to other parts of the tree and rose above the canopy.

Jakob was nearly at the first transport, a sleek sky-blue craft that looked just big enough to hold two, when it suddenly took off. As Jakob watched it speed off, the pressure of his situation weighed down on him. If he couldn't reach the second shuttle in time, things were going to get a lot harder.

Doubling down, Jakob took off toward the second transport. It was a boxy ship, easily twice the size of the first. A lone figure, tall even by capillum standards, was loading cloth bags into a hatch near the back of the craft. Seeing his opportunity, Jakob rushed in.

"Excuse me," he called, drenching his voice in desperation. "You, sir, excuse me!"

"I don't want any," called the man, not bothering to turn from his task.

"Sir, please," continued Jakob. "I know this is a long shot, but are you by chance heading south, Kokota Island region?"

The man paused and turned slowly. Every inch of fur from his arms to his face were painted in intricate black patterns. His cold stare screamed mistrust as he took in Jakob.

"Who are you?" The capillum's low growl was as menacing as his glare.

"I'm sorry, I know it was a longshot… I just," Jakob paused, he needed a story quickly. Whatever he came up with, it had to explain both his need for distant travel and lack of any money. "My daughter! It's my daughter."

The man's expression lightened a touch. "Go on."

"She… she's run off," said Jakob, finding his stride. "Waited until I'd gone off on business and withdrew every Teterra I owned. Now I can't even afford a tram back and– ever since her mother passed–"

"Listen," said the man, placing one large hand on Jakob's shoulder. "I want to help but… I've got a daughter of my own." He pointed to the open tram door. Inside, a capillum infant was strapped tight into a seat.

Jakob knew better than to push. After all, there was a chance he was being followed even now. He couldn't drag a baby into it. "I understand," he said. "I'll find another way."

"And here," said the man, reaching into his pocket. He pulled out several stone coins, offering them. "It's all I've got after groceries."

Jakob thanked the capillum profusely before he boarded his transport and flew off.

"Well, now what?" asked Proto.

"You know how much this is worth?" Jakob held the coins up to the lens.

"Not enough for a ride to Kokota–"

"Excuse me," a crackly voice sounded behind them.

Jakob turned and saw an older capillum woman, hunched over a cane with dark glasses and a sweet smile that was missing several teeth.

"I couldn't help but overhear," she said. "I have nowhere to be. Could I please offer you a ride?"

"Really?" asked Jakob, grinning at his luck.

"I've lost children," said the woman feebly. "Nobody should have that pain, not even the worry."

"I won't forget it."

"Then we've no time to lose." The woman ushered Jakob to the next transport down, a long black vehicle with an open ramp near the front.

Jakob followed the woman on board. There were two seats on either end of the spacious craft with windows running the walls between them. Like alcas, these transports appeared to have no pilot.

"Go on, make yourself comfortable," said the woman as she settled into a leather seat. On the divider beside her was a black sphere, smooth as glass. Taking a seat opposite the woman, Jakob couldn't help but keep glancing back at the orb. He could swear there was a soft gold light coming from inside.

Before Jakob could say anything, the ship lurched to life. He watched out the window as they pulled away from the branch and soared toward the traffic lanes.

"I must say," the woman's voice pulled Jakob's attention back from the view. "It's been so very long since I last set my eyes upon that mask. It has become unfamiliar to me."

An ice cold grip took hold of Jakob's heart as he scrambled to respond.

"That's right, Koerribot," she grinned cheekily. "I know what you are. After all, I wore that mask once."

The frost in Jakob's chest melted as fast as it came. "You're the last Koerribot!" he blurted.

"I was." The woman ran one bony hand over the orb beside her and a storm of golden sand flooded the cabin, swirling about the old woman. It spiraled like a tornado for just a moment before it faded, and a new woman now sat across from Jakob. Gone was the cane and toothless smile. This woman was younger, dressed in white and gold robes and entirely furless despite her capillum features. Where her glasses once covered her eyes, the brilliant golden flames of her irises now shone freely. "What I am, is Ithris, Host of Glavius," her voice was powerful, projected with pride.

"Host of–" Jakob began, but he stopped himself. "That doesn't matter now. Lylliana is in danger. The enemy has her trapped in Rotier's home!"

"The enemy? That's rich," laughed Ithris. "Lylliana will be fine. Her chains will buy us the time we need, and I assure you, the pain is well deserved."

"But, why?" gasped Jakob, the ricochet of emotions had his mind in scrambles.

"I'll show you," cooed Ithris. "Look out the window. Tell me, what do you see."

"That's easy," scoffed Jakob. "It's just tree–" His voice caught in his lungs as the world outside had changed. Gone were the lush trees and branch cities of Roana. In its place were miles of scorching gravel with flickering embers rising to meet their transport. There were no trees, no life, nothing but stone and fire. The sky above was just as menacing; lightning cackled in a violent cyclone that spread to the edges of the horizon.

"This isn't real," Jakob sputtered, remembering what Lylliana had told him; Ithris was a master of illusions.

"What you see is Labrum," crowed Ithris. "Glavius Adaeus found this place in his travels, a universe parallel to our own. In this world there were no kytra, no lights to guide humanity. Destruction and selfishness brought ruin, not just to a city or even a world, but the whole universe."

"Labrum… Glavius… this is Eredithian Mythology you're talking about."

"It is the truth," Ithris countered. "For millennia, Glavius has worked through the Hosts to prevent this fate, but always Lyle… your *Lylliana*… has stood in the way."

"Why?" asked Jakob, turning from the window. "If this is what you want to prevent, why would she fight you?"

"Because she is of Labrum," said Ithris simply. "Her kind seek power through deceit. You cannot imagine how much of your life she has influenced, cities overstuffed, technology solving every need; she's built a world where kytra cannot shine."

"No!" Jakob stumbled back into his seat. "Her last words before the chains were, 'I need you to be alright.' She cares: about the world and about you."

"Lyle the Deceiver says and does many things to earn trust," said Ithris, "I'm not asking you to fight her, but you can end this war. Here and now, you can ensure our world never meets this fate."

"Me? How?"

"In a moment, we will come to a stop," said Ithris, she took the orb and crossed the cabin, sitting beside Jakob. "I will show you, if you'll allow me. You have my word, I won't harm you."

"And what if you're the one lying?" asked Jakob. "You tricked Lylliana with the pen and fooled me into joining you here now. Why should I trust you?"

"Because I've been nothing but honest with you." She set her orb on the table between them. From this close, Jakob could see the golden light inside the sphere pulsing and flaring up in fiery tongues. "I revealed my true self freely, showed you why I fight. In all this time I have not harmed you nor asked you who hides behind the Koerribot's mask. Surely, I've earned some benefit of the doubt."

"If I go," surrendered Jakob, knowing he had little other option, "this isn't a commitment to help. I'll hear you out. That's all I can promise."

"As you wish." Ithris ran her hand over the orb and the violent world outside disappeared, replaced with darkness. It took Jakob's eyes a moment to adjust, and when they did, he saw a familiar silver telescope.

"Old Verror Hollow!"

"I see you're familiar with Atomic Translation," said Ithris, pressing a panel on the door beside her. As the ramp lowered, she rose from her seat. "Hurry now, into the dome."

Jakob had to sprint to keep up with Ithris as she crossed the bark floor of the hollow to a shadowed section of the wall. Placing her hand against the wood, Ithris produced a stream of golden flames that formed into the outline of the door.

The entry grated open and Ithris rushed inside.

Catching up, Jakob paused in the doorway. "Before I go in there, you promise to return me here when we're done?"

"I swear it," said Ithris.

Jakob swallowed his nerves and entered.

"You've made the right choice, Koerribot," said Ithris, flicking her fingers. The door slammed shut behind them.

"Proto, light on." The chamber flooded with light.

Ithris walked to the stone on the central pedestal and waved Jakob over. "Come, Koerribot. I have coordinates here, if you'd do the honor."

"The honor?" Jakob stood dumbfounded a moment until he pieced together what she was asking. "Oh no," he chuckled. "I'm not like you and Lylliana. I can't use that."

"Apologies. Silly of me to assume," said Ithris. She took the emerald crystal off the pedestal and set her orb in its place. "We'll have to settle for the next best thing. Come, place your hands on the Hoststone."

Jakob did as he was told, placing his long capillum hands on the orb. It was smooth and warm to the touch. Suddenly bright golden flames leapt from the orb and climbed Jakobs fingers. The tongues of fire were warm but not hot as they spread up Jakob's fur-coated arms then engulfed the rest of him. In moments, the golden flames were all that Jakob could see, their brilliant warmth making it impossible to breathe. Jakob panicked and tried to pull his hands back from the orb, only he couldn't feel hands. Jakob couldn't feel anything but heat. Just as suddenly the spectacle began, it ended.

A cool darkness returned as Jakob now stood in a notably different dome. There were several dim lights in the cement floor and a clear door outlined against the uninteresting metal walls. The pedestal was gone, as was Ithris and her stone.

Not only had the room changed, but Jakob had as well. Looking down he noticed *his* arms, not the Koerribot's. Where fur had covered every inch of him only moments ago, Jakob was now fully human, though skin was absolutely radiant. It was almost as if his body was made of the golden fire that had swallowed him.

"Hello?" called Jakob. "Ithris? Anyone?"

I'm here, Ithris sounded in his head. *I've projected you but stayed behind to protect our bodies.*

"Then I'm still the Koerribot?" asked Jakob.

Here, yes. And worry not. I cannot see your face there. I can only speak.

"Where am I?" asked Jakob.

Nearly to our destination. It's late here so there shouldn't be any workers about, but even if there are, they won't be able to see you.

Jakob cautiously went to the door and grabbed the plain-looking handle, giving it a half turn. The door swung out to a dingy supply closet. As he exited, Jakob saw the door was well hidden from the far side, posing as a stack of empty shelves. Shutting the door behind him, Jakob couldn't see any obvious switch or trigger in the shelves to re-open the passage. Whoever hid this clearly didn't want it found.

"Keep going?" he asked.

Out of the closet, then straight down the passage. You're looking for an engraved set of doors.

Jakob left the closet, careful not to be too loud with the door, and entered a long hallway with a luminous white floor. There were a dozen or so other doors in the passage and the walls and ceiling were covered in tarps reading: Meddow Construction.

Jakob hurried, wanting nothing more than to return to his body and find Lylliana. Even the strangest expectations he'd had when boarding the Seacarver were nothing to what his adventure had become. He wondered how the world could go on as it did without anyone knowing beings like Ithris and Lylliana existed.

Lost in thought, Jakob nearly didn't notice as soft light crept through a jarred door just ahead. Urgent voices trickled from the crevice, and Jakob stopped sharp.

"I'm not alone," Jakob whispered, easing up to the crack.

There were two voices, a man and a woman, both young sounding.

"Shirt, shirt, shirt, shirt, shirt… Eamon!"

"Here… what's wrong."

"I heard a door. Someone's close, I can *feel* them."

Koerribot, you need to move. Ithris' voice was urgent in his head. *That girl can see you, and if she does, everything is ruined. You need to—*

"Hello?" the door swung open and a man strutted out. He looked like a mostly normal human, a bit disheveled with his shirt unbuttoned and dark hair a mess, but his wondrous golden eyes were just like Ithris'. He looked straight past Jakob, down the hall, then turned and looked the other way.

"Hello? Anyone there?" he called loudly. He perked an ear, seemingly listening, then shook his head and went back into the room, closing the door behind him.

"Not a sign of life," his muffled voice sounded on the far side. "I'm tellin' ya, just gotta *relax*. We're the only two in this whole city."

Jakob sighed relief as he continued down the hall. The last thing he wanted to do now was to make Ithris angry. At last, he reached a wondrous set of golden double doors, engraved with the visage of a man. The carvings were clearly Eredithian in design.

In there, hurry.

Jakob pushed open the doors and entered a spacious office with a wide window at the far end. A blizzard raged across the night sky, while, inside, the office was mostly barren. The only furniture in the room was a desk near the window. There, a glassy black sphere was set upon a golden stand. It looked just like Ithris' orb.

"Another Hoststone?" whispered Jakob, approaching the desk. "That's what you called it, right?"

Mine, yes, but this is a different soulstone. It houses an ancient and powerful consciousness, one who has seen a universe die. They alone can spare us our fate. And you, Koerribot, can free them.

Jakob stared down into the glassy black surface of the orb. Deep inside, a faint light glowed. He reached out his hand, but paused.

"I don't know," he said. "This could have huge implications. I don't have a clue what I'm freeing."

Have I offered you any reason to doubt me?

"No, but neither has Lylliana." Jakob's mind raced. He'd said it was his decision, and he knew what he needed to do. "I want to talk to her… Lylliana. If you're telling the truth, then I'm sure she'll listen."

There's no time, Ithris hissed sharply in his thoughts. *We may never have this opportunity again, Koerribot. If Lylliana learns of this stone, she'll do everything in her power to ensure the soul inside is never freed.*

"I can't make this decision without giving Lylliana her chance to speak."

You've known her all of a few days. I was once her closest friend. You can not possibly know the treachery she is capable of.

"Then… I can't help you," Jakob pulled back his hand. "I want you to take me back."

I can't do that. Not until you touch the stone.

"You promised."

Do not speak to me of promises and honor, whatever patience was left in Ithris' voice had now faded, *not when you turn your back on every soul in this world.*

"I've told you my decision, and my decision is final!" said Jakob, regretting ever setting foot in the dome. "Now take me back, unless you want me to march back down the hall and find that girl who can see me. I wonder what she'd think of all this?"

You dare? Ithris growled.

Jakob's body suddenly burst with golden flame once again. For a moment, he thought she'd finally decided to smite him, but the flames died as quickly as they rose and Jakob was back in the dome with Ithris. He looked down, confirming his arms and hands were once again covered in fur.

"Come on then, Koerribot," said Ithris shortly. Waving her hand, the door to the dome flew open.

Ithris marched to the entry, grabbing Jakob gruffly by the robes as she went. Her grip was much stronger than it looked as she dragged Jakob from the dome. Back out in the hollow, constant pecking sounds rang out all around them.

"If you won't aid me in defending our world," she hissed, "then you can at least help me stop Lyle from destroying it."

"I won't–"

"Kneel!" Her word reverberated through Jakob's skull, sending him to his knees. He couldn't move an inch.

"I needed you to act willingly before," crowed Ithris, "but your cooperation is–"

Ithris' voice suddenly cut out. The pecking was gone. Outside the hollow, the streaking trails of lights from trams had frozen in place.

Sorry I'm late.

The calm soothing tone of Lylliana's voice in Jakob's head was one of the most wonderful sounds he'd ever heard.

I've freed you of her command, said Lylliana. *As soon as you get a chance, run to the shuttle. Don't stop. Don't try to help. Get as far from here as you can. I will find you.*

But–

This is not your fight, Jakob. What you can do is help me know that you will be safe. Promise me you'll run.

I promise.

"Meaningless now!" Ithris suddenly continued her rant as time unfroze and the sound of the drillworms resumed. Jakob wiggled his fingers, and sure enough he was in control again. Now, he just needed to keep up the act. "All you're good for is drawing out–"

"Your old friend?" Lylliana's words rang about the chamber. "Ithris, after everything you and I faced, the horrors we witnessed. How could you become Host?"

"Because your ideals are a lie," spat Ithris. "He showed me that. You build a world where kytra cannot thrive, for what purpose? To protect them from the Host? How can you protect what never exists? All you've done is doomed us all to burn like Labrum."

"What could you possibly know of Labrum?" Lylliana boomed. "I lived it, survived it. Even Glavius couldn't save that depraved place."

"But he can prevent it," countered Ithris passionately, pacing in circles as she studied every dark corner of the hollow. "Without the guidance of kytra, humanity will burn Inya to ash."

"Without the guidance of the kytra, or without the guidance of Glavius?"

Ithris growled and spun on Jakob. "I told you, there is no sense reasoning with her." Reaching her free hand into her robes, Ithris pulled out a long black dagger. Swirling lines of silver ran up and down the onyx blade and the butt of the hilt was fashioned like a silver mask, the same as the one on Jakob's helmet.

"I've driven this through your heart once," she yelled, holding the dagger high. "Show yourself, so I can do it again. Unless… you'd rather I introduced the Koerribot to his blade?" She flicked her hand to Jakob's neck.

A bolt of silver cracked through the dark hollow, slamming Ithris dead in the chest. The Host didn't have a second to react as she was sent reeling, dropping the dagger to the floor.

Jakob dove for the blade, and as he rose to run, he saw Lylliana.

Tongues of rainbow fire surged from her furious eyes and licked every inch of her skin. She stepped past him. "To the transport, *now*!" she commanded.

Lylliana leapt into a streak of silver light, crossing the distance to Ithris in a moment. The Host was still getting back to her feet when Lylliana's lightning fast strike met her… or would have. On impact, Ithris vanished in a cloud of sand and Lylliana stumbled.

A flash of gold erupted behind Lylliana. It was a different woman that reappeared. She wore the same white and gold robe as Ithris, but was shorter. Her long strawberry hair flowed freely and her tanned human arms were dotted in freckles. She held the Hoststone overhead and it flashed brilliant gold. Where the light shone upon the ground, hand-like branches sprouted from the bark and began reaching for Lylliana.

Lylliana quickly found her footing and spun into a leaping kick. Silver flames leapt from her strike, splitting the branches in half.

"Jakob," cried Proto. "I think now would be a very good time to run."

More living branches began to sprout from the ground. While most clambered toward Lylliana, a few stray growths began crawling after Jakob.

"I think you might be right," gulped Jakob, turning heel and sprinting for the shuttle. "Proto, your time to shine. Reconnect to the network. See if you can't figure out how to get that transport started."

As Jakob ran, flashes of gold and silver lit up the hollow. He looked back to see colorful flames roaring all around the incredible women. The fire spread up the wall and across the floor where half a dozen hand-shaped branches were chasing after Jakob.

Pushing his alien legs to the limit, Jakob made a mad dash for the door of the shuttle. He was nearly through when the first of the growths leapt from the floor, aimed square at Jakob. Instinctively, he swung the dagger and connected. The sentient branch fell in two pieces and Jakob slammed the door, just in time for the others to collide with the metal.

Jakob caught his breath, peering through the long window. The other growths had seemingly lost interest, crawling back toward the heavy smoke and fire that now enveloped huge swathes of the hollow. Through the smoke, all Jakob could see of Ithris and Lylliana was a pair of brilliant lights, silver and gold, crashing against each other in a deadly dance.

"What's our status?" Jakob heaved.

"I'm working," called the AI. "Not easy breaking security systems you've never seen in a language you've just learned."

Outside, blazing debris began falling from the ceiling, slowly at first, then faster and faster, like fiery teardrops. Wondering what it could be, Jakob had the sudden sickening realization that the pecking sounds had stopped.

"I think I'm starting to get the hang of this!" called Proto, "I'm past the–"

Crash

Something slammed into the side of the transport, its impact throwing the vehicle several feet and sending Jakob reeling. Glass flew everywhere and Jakob was in a daze as he got to his feet.

"Proto," Jakob groaned, steadying himself, "we still good to fly?"

"Systems green and I'm nearly through," reported Proto, "but… look!"

Finally, Jakob saw what it was that had hit them. Lylliana lay limp against the broken window, blood and bruises covering her skin.

"We gotta get her in here!" said Jakob in a panic. He leapt toward the door, when a second force shook the transport. Protruding from the ceiling was what looked like a hummingbird's beak, only three feet long and pale gray.

"The drill worms are falling," shouted Proto. "We *need* to go."

"Koerribot, get out," Lylliana groaned weakly through the broken window, picking herself up. "You have to make it home, to your sister. Forget me and my war. Take your story and go."

"I can save you, too!" Jakob pressed the panel beside the door, but nothing happened. He reached for a lever at the bottom, what looked like an emergency handle, but it didn't budge either. "Proto, how do I open this damned door?"

"It's jammed," said Proto. "You'd need– well, more time now!"

"What do you–" Jakob began, then he saw the figure stepping calmly from the golden flames. She was a human, tall as a capillum and wide as a tram. Her white and golden robes looked ready to burst at the seams from her incredible muscles, and her monstrous hands erupted with flame. Fixed to a pauldron on one shoulder, the Hoststone radiated light.

"Lylliana, get in, you can climb through the window," begged Jakob. "We don't have any more time."

"I can't," she coughed up blood, struggling to stand. "I will… buy you time. You go–"

"Did you really think such a young body could stand against the might of the Hosts?" The enormous woman's voice boomed all around the hollow as she stomped toward the transport. "You have acted in haste, Lyle."

"How have you become these Hosts?" Lylliana's rainbow flames returned, though weaker than Jakob had ever seen them. "What madness have you conjured, Ithris?"

"You haven't the faintest idea what we've become," growled the Host. She marched straight up to Lylliana, grabbing her skull in a single burning hand. "The Hosts have evolved."

Lylliana beat back with all her might, silver flame surging from each blow. It crashed off the woman like waves against the shore, but she paid it no mind.

"The Dead Coast taught me that this war cannot continue," the Host dragged Lylliana away from the tram and then slammed her to the ground so hard the sound echoed. Raising her fist, she slammed down with a second thunderous blow. The whole tree groaned from the force and Lylliana's light was gone. "There will be no more death, no more rebirths, no more chances to doom us all. Our dance is done, my old friend."

"I don't…," gasped Lylliana.

"Shush now," The woman crouched and grabbed Lylliana by the hair. Pulling her up so their eyes were level."There's one more face, I'd like you see," she cooed, "before it all ends."

The Host burst into a vortex of shimmering golden sand. Swirling for a moment, the sand took a new shape. This time, a man stood over Lylliana. He was bald with a handsome beard and dark skin. Of all the hosts, he wore his robes most regally. There was a pride to his stance as he rest a hand on Lylliana's forehead.

"G– Glavius," she coughed.

"It has been millenia," he said, "but our story, *your* story, ends today. I cannot let you stop what's to come."

"I'll–"

"Nothing," said Glavius. "You'll do nothing. You can do nothing, for I have struck a new accord."

As he spoke, every golden flame in the room flared. They roared even more violently then burned a terrible crimson, shining through even the densest smoke.

Lylliana's eyes were terrified, watering.

"Jakob, we're good to fly," called Proto. "I'm getting us out of here."

"No!" yelled Jakob. "I have to stop this!"

"You can't!" begged Proto.

"Goodbye, old friend," cried Glavius. Blood red flames erupted from his palm and snaked like veins down Lylliana's face. Her shrieks of pain were unlike any sound Jakob had ever heard.

Unthinking, Jakob charged. He leapt through the window, cutting his knee and hand on the broken glass. The pain was nothing. Proto's objections were nothing. Jakob was dead focused on Lylliana, his blade drawn. Diving at Glavius, Jakob plunged his blade into flesh.

"FOOL!" Glavius erupted into a cloud of sand, rushing all around Jakob. When it took form again, Ithris was already swinging. She struck Jakob with impossible force. He felt his insides shatter as he was flung back and slid across the bark.

"Jakob! Jakob get up!"

The voice was distant and faded, echoing in Jakob's ears. He blinked and realized where he was. Every inch of Jakob hurt, but adrenaline pushed him. Jakob rose to his knees, shocked to find himself steadied on human arms. Glancing around in a panic, Jakob saw larger chunks falling from the ceiling and countless drillworm beaks sticking like spears from the floor. The tree groaned again as Jakob caught sight of Koerribot's helmet. It had been flung far across the hollow. Then, his eyes rest on something glinting just past the helm.

"Proto!" Jakob yelled, feeling the torn cloth at his chest He pushed himself to his feet and sprinted toward the small mechanical lens.

Stop, Ithris' command dominated Jakob's mind and his aching limbs froze. *Now turn.*

Cracking noises sounded all around Jakob as his body forced him to obey. Groaning again, the tree shook and a massive schism broke across the hollow. It split the floor from the entry, just missing the transport, and running well up the far wall.

"I was wrong about you," hissed Ithris as she calmly approached, ignoring the destruction around her. "You are more than bait. Your soul shall serve a glorious purpose."

"No!" Lylliana screamed. Her flames were back, surging strong as ever. She stood with newfound strength, dark scars cutting like forked lightning across her face and blood trickling down to her chin.

"An impressive display," said Ithris, "but you cannot compete with what I have become."

"Maybe not," spat Lylliana. "But I swear this: Ithris is the last soul you will ever take."

Lylliana sprinted headlong, meeting Ithris in a blinding flash of silver light. Suddenly, they were both gone.

"Hello?" called Jakob, looking all about him, but he was alone.

A roaring groan from the tree shifted the whole hollow and forced Jakob back into the emergency at hand. The tram was now his only way out.

"Proto, I'm coming!" yelled Jakob, racing across the hollow.

The tree shook again, sending Jakob to his knees and he could only watch as a wide chasm opened up right beneath Proto.

"Jakob!" screamed the device as it plummeted into the dark.

"Proto, no!" screamed Jakob. He lunged toward the crack, reaching at nothing. "Proto! Shine your light if you can–"

With a last deafening cry, the tree gave out entirely. The ground beneath Jakob crumbled and the ceiling collapsed. Jakob found himself in free fall.

Time slowed as Jakob plummeted. His arms flailed, searching for any escape, but there was only loose bark and debris. Realizing what this meant, Jakob closed his eyes and surrendered. He let his thoughts wander to Proto, his sister, his parents, even Vennamin waiting on his next book. He'd let them all down. And yet, knowing what he did of Lyllliana and the kytra, Jakob didn't know if he'd take any of it back. It brought a sense of calm, and in that serenity was a light.

A pearly white river cut across the darkness of Jakob's mind, and, reaching out, he could feel its tug. Jakob was pulled deep into the current as his body struck wood and broke beneath the crushing weight of the great tree Vaerorr.

Interlude: Peridom

Faeron was flung bodiless through the current of peridom. Pearlescent light shimmered all around him as wondrous colors streaked through the milky white stream. In their brilliance, Faeron saw alien and impossible worlds, a field of electrified mushrooms, a labyrinthian city where the streets and walls twisted together, an endless moat where dark lurking shapes peeked their heads above the water.

Pulled along faster than ever before, Faeron rushed through the current. His thoughts were a blur, Jakob's last moments replaying over and over again. Even though he didn't have lungs to breathe, Faeron felt as though he was going to suffocate. Jakob was gone. The dream was over. What would happen when he slept now?

Faeron wanted to scream, to fight, to return to Jakob, but he was nothing. He could do nothing. Just then, the light of the stream began to dim. For a moment, Faeron thought he might be waking up, but he was suddenly somewhere else. Still shapeless, Faeron floated down a dim hallway. The floor glowed with unbroken violet light and the walls and ceiling were rippling films of darkness, similar to the midnight chapel. He felt a pull tugging him somewhere, but he couldn't see where.

On either side of the hallway were countless doors. They all looked exactly alike, carved from stone and engraved with the image of two flames circling each other. Again, Faeron couldn't help but note the similarities to the midnight chapel. Could this place have inspired it? Pulled by some other will, Faeron let himself stop fighting. Whatever this was, it could be important to where his mother went. He needed to focus on keeping up the dream. Too much fighting and he'd wake up.

Finally, the tunnel ended at a single pair of golden double doors, the same two flames engraved on the door. They opened at his approach and Faeron was pulled into an incredible temple. The space was wide open, with six doors around the outside and another mural of two flames on the domed ceiling. Here, they were colored, crimson and violet, circling each other endlessly. But nothing compared to what was in the center of the temple.

A lone obelisk of pearlescent light rose to the domed ceiling. Its walls were alive with rippling light and a terrible crimson chasm tore its side open, like a vein pulsing with energy. Faeron had seen that light, only moments before through Jakob's eyes.

Faeron was terrified he'd be pulled straight into the crimson light. After all, he had just seen the destruction it was capable of. He was pulled closer and closer, and as panic set in, the temple began to fade. Knowing that fighting would only force him to wake up, Faeron calmed himself. He approached the obelisk and began a slow orbit, spinning circles around the structure.

Rather than be consumed by the crimson chasm, Faeron sank slowly into the pearlescent surface of the Obelisk. It felt familiar as images of landscapes streaked through the light around him, just like the colors in peridom's current. Only, these places were familiar, sights he'd seen in books or lived as Jakob. This was his world.

As Faeron sank deeper into the obelisk, the temple beyond was shrouded in shifting clouds of violet. Faeron could feel his connection to that place fading, and he was ready to wake up, until he saw a door open.

One of the six doors on the outer wall of the temple creaked open and a figure stepped out, shrouded in violet mists. She was dressed in capillum robes, but was clearly human with shoulder-length chocolate curls and a mask that Faeron knew well.

Emotion flooded Faeron and it took all his focus not to wake up on the spot.

Evolice Lovel removed her mask, revealing a soft face and brilliant sky-blue eyes. "Faeron!" she shouted and rushed to the obelisk.

He hadn't heard the voice in a decade, but it was like a drug to him.

"Faeron, it's really you!" His mother's joyous call was soothing to the core.

Faeron wanted nothing but to claw his way out of the obelisk, to tell her to come home, to throw his arms around his mother and never let go. Only, Faeron had no body or will of his own. If Faeron had a heart, he knew it would be pounding as a waterfall of emotions crashed down on him. He tried to call out to his mother, but no words came. Even now, the temple was fading.

"Don't try to speak," Evolice shushed, placing her hand against the obelisk. She was so close, Faeron swore he could feel her warmth. "We've precious little time," her words faded in and out with the pulsing current of light. "I'm safe but… can't tell you… I am." every second her words were slipping away further and further. The more Faeron strained to hear, the faster the temple faded.

"Tell no one… dream ended… Es… Auri," Evolice's soft face blurred as violet smoke closed around her. "If Eamon finds out… Ithris… in danger…"

Faeron calmed his mind as the whole temple faded into darkness. He knew he had only seconds now, but he needed to hold on as long as he could.

"Use… –brary key… go North… Jakob's home… Faeron? …fading, Faeron! I love you… my son…"

The temple was gone. His mother was gone. There was only darkness and the warmth of Faeron's sheets.

Faeron blinked awake, everything he'd just seen heavy on his mind. Outside his window, lazy drifts of snow sparkled in the moonlight. It wasn't morning yet, but Faeron could see nomads down the park, setting up their tents.

A feeling of free fall clutched Faeron's gut. He'd never been afraid of heights, but looking at the city below, all he could see was Jakob plummeting. He could feel his stomach rise into his chest, and the body shattering moment the great-tree crushed Jakob. Suddenly, Faeron wretched forward and lost the remnants of his dinner all over the sheets.

Groaning, Faeron pushed himself out of bed, and stumbled across the hall into the bathroom. Washing his face and spritzing the foul taste from his mouth, Faeron gazed absently into the mirror. If he let his eyes unfocus, he could almost see Jakob looking back at him.

Faeron sank to his knees and the emotions finally won out. Running through the dream over and over in his head, Faeron sobbed. He was unable to make any sense of what he'd seen.

Jakob was in Eredith, he'd *seen* Eamon. Yet somehow Ithris was still around. That made no sense. Ithris faded when Eamon became Host. Then again, she was a master of illusions. But, if Ithris was still Host… what would that make–

"Faeron, that you?" Eamon's voice called through the door. There was a soft knock. "You alright, bud?"

Faeron panicked, his mothers warning still in his mind. He couldn't tell anyone, except Auri, at least if he'd heard right. He certainly wasn't going to take any chances. Maybe Evolice knew Auri was the only one who could keep his secret. Eamon, however, would start a war over this, and Faeron didn't even know what his father was. Certainly, he couldn't be the host.

"Faeron? You doing okay? I'm coming in."

The door creaked open, revealing Eamon in his navy pajamas. His radiant gold eyes rested on Faeron, as a soft and caring look crossed his brow.

"Hey," said Eamon, going to his knees. "You're ghostly pale. Is this about Auri?"

"No," stuttered Faeron, instinctively, "it's mom–." More than anything, Faeron wanted to tell his father that Evolice was alive, but revealing that would unravel the whole truth. "I miss her, that's all."

"Me too," confessed Eamon, sitting on the floor beside him. Taking Faeron in his arms, Eamon pulled his son to his chest. "I know this week is hard, but I promise you, Evolice would be proud of the kytra you've become."

Faeron hated lying as his father held him close. He might not know what exactly Eamon was, but he was certain of his father's love. There wasn't an ounce of Ithris in him. Still, he couldn't say a word. Not yet. For now, the only person he could tell the full truth lay unconscious in a hospital bed across the city.

"Come on," said Eamon, pulling Faeron to his feet. "Let's get you cleaned up."

Obelisk: Violet Stars Part 2 coming soon!

Follow the journey at **Obelisk.ink**

www.ingramcontent.com/pod-product-compliance
Lightning Source LLC
Chambersburg PA
CBHW071234300726
48975CB00002B/411